Born in Sydney in 1932, the darkest year of the Great Depression, Marion von Adlerstein sailed to London in 1957 and worked there as a copywriter for seven years before returning to Australia and joining J Walter Thompson as a group head. Nine months of her term at JWT were spent at the agency's headquarters in New York. She returned to Australia to marry Hans von Adlerstein, a German-born baron, and they moved to Melbourne to work together at USP Needham, where Marion ultimately became a creative director and board member. Her first magazine article, published in *Vogue Australia* in 1975, led to a contract with the magazine spanning more than twenty years. Her work for *Vogue* took her on countless journeys overseas and enabled her to base herself in Venice for more than a year. Marion is the author of *The Passionate Shopper* and *The Penguin Book of Etiquette*. *The Freudian Slip* is her first novel.

GW00692289

Inside cover photo of Marion von Adlerstein at The London Press Exchange, where she was a copywriter for five years.

MARION VON ADLERSTEIN

The Freudian Slip

hachette
AUSTRALIA

'Oh, What A Beautiful Mornin'' by Richard Rodgers and Oscar Hammerstein II.
Copyright © 1943 by Richard Rodgers and Oscar Hammerstein II.
Copyright Renewed. International Copyright Secured. All Rights Reserved.
Used by Permission of Williamson Music, A Division of Rodgers & Hammerstein: An Imagem Company

hachette
AUSTRALIA

Published in Australia and New Zealand in 2011
by Hachette Australia
(an imprint of Hachette Australia Pty Limited)
Level 17, 207 Kent Street, Sydney NSW 2000
www.hachette.com.au

Copyright © Marion von Adlerstein 2011

National Library of Australia
Cataloguing-in-Publication data:

Von Adlerstein, Marion

The Freudian Slip/Marion Von Adlerstein

978 0 7336 2896 2 (pbk.)

A823.4

Cover design by Christabella Designs
Cover photograph courtesy of Corbis
Text design by Bookhouse
Typeset in 11.5/17 pt Sabon Pro by Bookhouse
Printed and bound in Australia by Griffin Press, Adelaide, an Accredited ISO AS/NZS 14001:2004 Environmental Management System printer

MIX
Paper from
responsible sources
FSC® C009448

The paper this book is printed on is certified against the Forest Stewardship Council® Standards. Griffin Press holds FSC chain of custody certification SGS-COC-005088. FSC promotes environmentally responsible, socially beneficial and economically viable management of the world's forests.

For April and Robin Huxley
who were there with me

Chapter 1

Guy K Garland leaned across the table that served as his desk and fingered the pointy coloured pencils in a white Casa Pupo pot. After a moment's deliberation, as though choosing a pocket handkerchief to match his silk tie, he singled out the dark blue pencil. He placed it on his diary, open at Monday, 10 September 1962, then shook a cigarette from a soft pack of Kents and stuck the filter end in his mouth. As he lifted the telephone receiver he dug into the fob pocket of his waistcoat for his lighter and said, 'Mavis, love. Give us a line.'

'Yes, Mr Garland,' murmured the voice in his left ear. There was a click, then the sound of an open line. He placed the rubber-tipped end of the pencil into the wheel on the telephone face and began to dial.

He drew deeply on his cigarette, exhaled a wobbly smoke ring and let the casters on his Danish Modern chair swing him gently back and forth. Through the window a facsimile of the Eiffel

Tower, sitting on top of the AWA Building in York Street, shone optimistically against the clear blue sky. To him it symbolised the tendency of Australians to be influenced by overseas designs rather than summon up the courage to originate. A hangover from colonial days, he supposed. The creative department of this very advertising agency was a case in point. Freddie Hackett was forever sticking ads from Doyle Dane Bernbach in New York or Leo Burnett in Chicago on his corkboard and urging his writers to study them.

'Cowper.' The voice sounded more like a command than a response. At least this client answered his own direct line instead of hiding behind a secretarial barricade.

As though activating a light switch, Guy turned on a smile in the hope that it would be reflected in his voice. 'Russ! Guy here. You free for lunch?'

'What, today?' Although he was merely the marketing manager of Crop-O-Corn Foods—or maybe because of it—Russ had adopted the aggressive characteristics of those above his station.

'We need to discuss the direction for next year. Beppi's, I thought.' There was no response from Russ so, after a few seconds and because he subscribed to the belief that the best work is done over a good lunch, Guy went on, 'I know it's early in the week but I'd like us to agree on a few basics before we involve anyone else. When we brief the team, we need to set them off in the right direction.' Guy was smart enough to use the collective 'we' in order to engage his client in shared responsibility for whatever creative outcome the agency might present.

'Yes, well I was just looking at my schedule.' Russ pronounced it 'skedule' because he liked to remind people that he'd once spent three months in Crop-O-Corn Foods's Chicago headquarters. 'Okay. One o'clock?'

'You're on.' Guy replaced the receiver and yelled, 'Stella!' Although he was barely five foot six and about as weighty as George Moore, who'd ridden Prince Aly Khan's horses to honour and glory in France a few times in the recent past, Guy longed to be thought macho, like Marlon Brando in *A Streetcar Named Desire*. In fact, he sometimes wondered if the deciding factor in his hiring Stella Janice Bolt two months before had been her name.

Stella's beehive appeared around the open door. 'Do I need my notebook?' At least she wasn't as slatternly as Kim Hunter in the movie but he did wish she'd get rid of that beehive hairdo, a hangover from the fifties. It didn't suit her narrow face, or the agency's image. Only a man with a bee in his bonnet could find it attractive, thought Guy, pleased with what he considered a witticism. But all he said was, 'Book a table for two at Beppi's. I'm taking Russ Cowpat to lunch.' His smirk was Stella's cue to giggle at his crude joke and say indulgently, 'You are naughty, Mr Garland.'

In a businesslike tone she then asked, 'One o'clock and a cab to get there?' As she turned to leave he glanced appreciatively at her round bottom; if she weren't so flat-chested she'd have a good figure. She was quick on the uptake, though. What she lacked in sophistication she made up for in willingness. Guy recognised the effort she was putting in to succeed in the job but there was no mistaking her origins. While her mother had moved a notch up the social scale when she inherited a bungalow in a suburb on the Cronulla line, Stella had Western Suburbs stamped all over her. It was there in the cheap material of her chartreuse princess-line dress—sewn on a Singer by her mother from a Butterick pattern, no doubt—to her nasally voice that cawed like the crows on the hobby farm of his parents-in-law at

Windsor. She had good ankles, though, and they were set off to advantage by a pair of black winklepickers with stiletto heels.

'You got it, Stella.'

Back at her desk, Stella made the telephone calls, wondering what it would be like to lunch at Beppi's, the Italian restaurant she understood was filled with advertising executives charging their lunches to the job numbers of print ads and television commercials. She knew this because it was her task to process Guy's expenses, which usually amounted to the price of a new frock from Mark Foys Piazza Store.

When the hands on her watch told her it was eleven, Stella clickety-clacked along to the staff kitchen to prepare Guy Garland's morning tea.

Desi, a producer from the television department, was already there talking to Assunta, the tea lady. To Stella, Desi seemed sort of elongated, as though someone had grabbed her head and feet and stretched her, like a piece of Wrigley's Juicy Fruit chewing gum. She towered over Assunta, bending down to converse with her in a language that was double-dutch to Stella, whose only brush with a foreign tongue had been at St George Girls High, Kogarah. 'Frère Jacques' was about all she retained from two years of French lessons.

Assunta finished loading paper cups on to a trolley already burdened with two large metal urns, bottles of milk, a jar of white sugar, a stack of wooden stirrers and two packets of Arnott's Assorted Biscuits before she pushed off.

'Ciao, Assunta,' said Desi, as she poured boiling water over Nescafé powder. She paused to smile at Stella and hand her the tea jar before reaching into the cupboard above the sink for a packet of Iced VoVos. Stella couldn't help noticing the enormous hunk of glass on the third finger of Desi's left hand.

'I love your rhinestone ring,' she said with genuine admiration. 'I've never seen one that flashes like that.'

The size of the rock on her finger was an embarrassment to Desi but Tom would be hurt and bewildered if she left it in the safe at home when she went to work.

At that moment, while Desi tried to decide what to reply, Kelvin the skinny kid from despatch came in to raid the biscuit cupboard.

'It's a diamond, boofhead,' he snorted.

Desi blushed and smacked his hand as it delved into the Iced VoVo packet. He managed to take two anyway and went off, whistling, leaving Stella speechless with mortification. Since neither girl knew what to say next they fussed with spoons and jugs and trays and paper napkins for about the length of a fifteen-second radio commercial.

Finally, 'How was your weekend?' broke the silence. Desi pronounced her vowels as beautifully as a news reader on 2BL, although it sounded to Stella as though she still had her adenoids and they were swollen.

The moment the words were out of her mouth Desi could have bitten her tongue. She was not interested in probing into Stella's private life, only anxious to divert attention from her own. She now realised she'd offered an open invitation for Stella to reciprocate.

Since she'd started working at Bofinger, Adams, Rawson and Keane (aka BARK) more than a year ago, Desirée Whittleford had come to the conclusion that when most people found out about her background and where she lived, they were either intimidated or resentful. It was certainly not a good idea to dwell on the attractions of her fiancé, a young man destined for an outstanding career as an architect—or so her parents said.

Safer to keep all that to herself. She didn't want to be thought different from the people she worked with. She was determined to fit into the team, one reason why she was pleased that they shortened her name to Desi.

'Um . . .' Stella was momentarily at a loss for words, not so much cowed by the accent, but discomfited because she had to find a way to make something interesting of a Saturday morning spent paying off her mother's lay-by on a kidney-shaped coffee table at Bebarfalds, the afternoon washing and setting her hair in rollers and pushing her cuticles with an orange stick, and the evening at the pictures with Dolores, who lived two doors away on Wyralla Road, Miranda.

'I saw *West Side Story* on Saturday night,' she said at last. 'I'm rapt. Mum's buying me the LP for Christmas.'

'Yes, it is an exciting musical.' Desi remembered being in the audience at the premiere of the stage version in London in 1958 but she was too well-mannered to mention it because it would seem like showing off.

Her fear that there might be a question about her own weekend turned out to be groundless; Stella had not been schooled in the social niceties of the Eastern Suburbs of Sydney so she didn't recognise the cue. She just busied herself with warming the teapot, re-boiling the water, trying to put her blunder out of her mind and thinking of something that might impress Desi. How could she have known that Desi was already more than impressed, she was touchingly grateful?

'I'm going to Palings at lunchtime to buy the new Shirley Bassey single,' Stella said at last.

'You're a fan?'

'Oh yes,' said Stella, then her voice faltered when she realised she might have said the wrong thing. 'You're not?'

'I prefer Elvis. Have you heard "Only Fools Rush In"?'

'Oh yeah, I like him too,' squawked Stella.

'I'd come with you, but we're all going to lunch at Diethnes,' intoned Desi of the perfect vowels. 'It's Freddie Hackett's birthday.'

Stella knew that Freddie was the creative director and that the 'all' Desi referred to would be the writers, art directors and television producers. Judging by past performances, half of them would return tipsy after five o'clock and stumble into the boardroom with Freddie to raid the fridge for more drinks. As for the other half, they'd probably go to the Journalists' Club and not turn up at the office until the next day.

Desi was watching her. 'I don't suppose Guy would let you come.' There was an unspoken law in advertising agencies that secretaries did not fraternise with the 'creatives'. Male art directors in particular posed a dangerous threat to discipline. There was that incident when Noreen from accounts got back from lunch legless and was found snoring under her desk when her boss, the company secretary, needed some urgent typing done. There were more unsavoury episodes than that one, but they were kept quiet, at least officially. Just whispered about in the washroom.

Stella didn't allow herself to be tempted by the suggestion of lunch at the Greeks even though she knew Guy would be late back from Beppi's and he'd never know where she'd been at lunchtime. Except that someone might let it slip, deliberately or not, and she didn't want to lose his trust and risk her job. This secretary knew her place. At least for now.

'I'd better not,' she said. 'Anyway, I want that Shirley Bassey.'

The afternoon dragged. The whole place was silent except for Lavinia Olszanski, the casting director. As everybody in the agency knew, she'd been on the stage and seemed to think she was still there, projecting her voice to the back row of the gods at Her Majesty's. She claimed to have been one of the Tivoli Lovelies, but Stella found it difficult to imagine that a face as craggy and a backside as bountiful could ever have been described as lovely. Her legs were long, though, so perhaps she'd done some high kicks in her day, but that must have been a long time ago.

Lavinia's office was at the other end of the floor from Guy Garland's, but Stella could hear her holding forth on the telephone about composites and over-exposure and same old faces. 'Not her again, for godsake.' The voice rose dramatically. 'She looks like a pommie housewife. I want a reffo, New Australian, or whatever you call us now, an exotic . . . Lollobrigida type but older, like her mother. You know, it's for spaghetti, hon, not porridge.'

Stella was updating Guy's Rolodex when her own telephone rang. She was so grateful for the distraction she picked up the receiver before there was time for a second ring.

'Mr Garland's office.'

'Is he there?'

'May I ask who is calling?' Stella hadn't meant to parody Desi but that's how it came out, plummy but squeaky at the same time: *My ay ahsk whoise coiling.*

'Eh? It's Tim Broughton from Slazenger. I'm the product manager for balls.'

'Mr Garland is not here at the moment. He's in conference with a client. I don't know when he'll be back.'

'Well, it's urgent. Can you transfer me to Freddie Hackett?'

'He's in a client meeting, too,' said Stella. The lie came easily. 'Can I be of assistance?'

'We need a script for a thirty-second spot to go live on 2UE this afternoon.'

'Can it wait until tomorrow?'

'No!' He was agitated. 'Rod Laver has just won the Grand Slam in America—with our balls! Is there a copywriter there?'

Stella didn't even hesitate before replying, 'You're speaking to one.'

Chapter 2

English had not been Stella's best subject at school but she had often earned reasonably good marks for her compositions because of their fanciful imagery, if not for their construction. 'Stella is very imaginative,' went the comment on one of her teacher's reports from primary school, 'but she needs to pay more attention to spelling and grammar.'

Rather than give herself a headache trying to sort out the mystery of gerunds and split infinitives, Stella had learned to get by on the work of others. By the age of ten she had taught herself to read simple words upside down, a skill that stood her in good stead throughout her life. Any feelings of guilt at being a cheat were buried beneath a belief that something was owed to her, although she couldn't have said precisely what it was.

Her parents were still living together in Granville at the time. Most afternoons when Stella came home from school through the back door, first wiping her feet on the wire mat, then letting the screen door bang behind her, her mother would be sitting at the green Formica table in the breakfast nook shelling peas or stringing beans as she listened to the wireless. About the only time the Bolt brick bungalow was free of the airwaves was when everyone had gone to bed. Although the only program Stella paid attention to was *The Search For The Golden Boomerang*, she couldn't help absorbing the full range of her mother's favourites, in particular *Doctor Mac* ('Hullo. Hullo? Aye, it's me, Doctor Mac') and *When A Girl Marries* ('Dedicated to those who are in love and to all those who can . . . remember').

On a typical afternoon, without turning down the volume or looking at her daughter, Hazel would ask: 'Did you wipe your feet?' It was such a predictable question, Stella found it irritating. What was she supposed to say? She *always* wiped her feet.

Old bat, she would say to herself.

'Go and wash your hands. I've made pikelets.' Hazel was not large, but she moved heavily, as though dragging a dead weight strapped to her waist. Her faded cardigans were almost worn through at the elbows and her hair often looked as though it hadn't seen a comb since before breakfast. No wonder Dad makes himself scarce, thought Stella, as she turned on the tap in the bathroom and picked up the cake of Palmolive soap. Her feelings for her mother—her shabby appearance and her attitude of defeat—were ambivalent and confusing; shame, anger, pity, resentment and love were all tangled up together, like strands of wool in a messy knitting basket.

After Stella had eaten three pikelets with golden syrup and drunk a glass of milk, she would take her school bag across the street to the Drummonds. The daughter, Jean, had grown up with an instinct for the correct use of language and she was the best speller in the class. All Stella had to do, when she and Jean did their homework together at a mouldy marble table in the fernery, was take a peek-a-boo over her friend's shoulder for a lead in what to write down in her own exercise book. If Jean or her mother noticed her sneaking a look, they didn't say so. Stella was small for her age, had a lot of charm and an impishness that made people forgive her for not being perfect. They let her get away with almost anything, so she came to expect it. They felt sorry for her because her father was a no-hoper and her mother seemed to have dropped her bundle.

When Stella was fourteen, she bought a bunch of Dorothy Perkins roses with her pocket money and made a special card for her mother's fortieth birthday. By then, her father had done a bunk and they were living at Miranda. On the front of the card she pasted a print of Picasso's portrait of a mother and child from his rose period. Inside the card, in her best handwriting, was a piece of poetry that brought compliments from relations and neighbours—and tears to her mother's eyes—except for Mrs Riley, next door, who noted that the words were oddly old-fashioned and said so to her husband.

Stella's poem read:

> *Today's your natal day,*
> *Sweet flowers I bring;*
> *Mother, accept, I pray,*
> *My offering.*
>
> *And may you happy live,*
> *And long us bless;*
> *Receiving as you give*
> *Great happiness.*

Opposite these words, Stella added:

> To Dearest Mother on her 40th Birthday.
> From your Loving Daughter, Stella.

That the poem was written in 1842 by Christina Rossetti when she was eleven years of age was a piece of information Stella chose not to reveal. She'd copied it from a book in the school library. Since nobody in her family was much of a scholar, her borrowing remained undetected. They were left with the impression that Stella was gifted with rare creative ability.

So it was that when Tim Broughton from Slazenger rang the agency that afternoon, when everyone in the creative department was full of moussaka and retsina at Diethnes, Stella had the confidence and the chutzpah to write her first radio commercial.

By the time Guy returned to the office after four o'clock, Stella had read a draft of her script to Tim over the telephone, he'd cleared it after two minor adjustments—replacing 'terrific' with 'super' and including 'all Australians' in the congratulations—and Stella had dictated it to a production assistant at 2UE. It was due to go to air just before the six o'clock news.

'Any dramas?' Guy took off his jacket, put it over the back of his chair and lit a cigarette.

'Almost. But I fixed it.' Stella's small dark eyes had a sparkle in them that Guy hadn't noticed before. Bright and shiny, like jet beads.

'Fixed what?' He sat back and yawned. She thought how well he held his booze.

'The radio spot for Slazenger.' She was quivering with excitement, wound up like a tight little spring.

'What radio spot?'

'Rod Laver just won the Grand Slam in America. Tim Broughton needed a script. So I wrote it.' The look on her face was a mixture of triumph, apology, pride and guilt.

Guy sat up. 'Where was Freddie?'

'They all went to lunch for his birthday.'

'You'd better show me the script. Then sit down and give me a blow by blow.'

At about five o'clock they heard the lift doors opening, some muffled giggling, 'Ssshhh!' then the sound of footsteps, which were light, as though on tiptoes. Freddie's over-excited voice was hushed but unmistakable; his words tumbled out, as though fighting each other for precedence. 'I'll see what's doing in my office and meet you in the boardroom.'

'Freddie, have you got a minute?' Guy was on his feet. Stella stood up to leave, but he motioned for her to sit down again. 'No, you stay.' She began to feel uncomfortable, fearing a clash between the two men, especially since they'd both been drinking. Stella would do almost anything to avoid a confrontation; there'd been too many at home.

It amazed her that nothing of the kind took place. Guy was generous in explaining what had happened, as though he and Freddie had been saved by Stella's heroic deed.

Freddie surveyed her with the benevolent gaze of one who has imbibed enough to become sentimental; there was something about her shy smile and her nervous manner that reminded him of himself when he first came to the big smoke as a vulnerable kid from a poultry farm at Tamworth. He gave her a flamboyant kiss on both cheeks and said, 'Darling, you've been hiding your light under a bushel! Come and have a drink in the boardroom and we can listen in to your masterpiece when it comes on.'

She looked at Guy and, when he nodded his approval, she smiled and stood up. 'I'd better ring Mum and say I'll be late home.'

'You do that but don't sneak out on us, will you, darling? Let's go, Guy. I'm thirsty.'

By now the switchboard was closed and Mavis had plugged a direct line into Stella's extension. She dialled her home number wondering when—if ever—she had felt so elated.

'Mum? It's me!'

'What's wrong?' Hazel regarded a ringing telephone with dread. Calls were rare and they usually meant trouble.

'I've been asked to work overtime, so I'll be late home.'

'Well, don't be too late.'

'No, no. Only an hour or so.'

'I'll leave your tea in the oven.'

Stella had been in the boardroom only twice before, to take dictation from Guy at a client meeting and to help tidy up afterwards, but it had a totally different atmosphere this time. It was noisy with talk, hazy with smoke and there was an occasional burst of laughter. The long polished-metal table was smudged with fingerprints and scattered with a few spent butts from full ashtrays. There were rings of moisture where chilled glasses had been. Bottles were lined up in a reckless way on the black lacquered bench that ran the length of one wall. Somebody had forgotten to put tops back on the Beefeater and the Johnnie Walker.

'Stella, darling, what can I do you for?' Freddie pointed to the bottles. 'I know,' he went on before she had time to say anything, 'champagne!' He opened the fridge door and grasped something with gold foil capping its bulbous cork.

'Great Western is not champagne,' said a gravelly voice behind Stella. It sounded like a weary version of the foreign actor she'd seen not long ago in *Let's Make Love*, with Marilyn Monroe. She turned around to look but what she saw was no Yves Montand. Slight and sallow-faced, with dark eyes and full lips, Jacques Boucher was attractive in an ugly way.

'Ah, Jack,' said Freddie, easing the cork from the bottle. 'Call yourself an art director? You're a pedant.'

'I am *not* a peasant.' Jacques sniffed in a semblance of disgust as the cork popped out of the bottle. 'Champagne comes from Champagne, not from some backyard vineyard in the Antipodes.'

'You frogs, you're all the same. Up yourselves.' Freddie used slang to indicate, in case there was any doubt, that he was one of the blokes. For the same reason, he pretended to be interested in football. And he was. Not for the game, but for the balletic footwork of the soccer players and the muscular thighs and body contact of the big boys who played rugby and footy.

He filled a glass and handed it to Stella. 'How about you, Jack?'

'*Mais oui*, since you ask and I am courteous.' He turned to Stella. 'And my name is Jacques, despite what you hear from the creative director.'

'Oh,' said Stella as she realised they were having fun and not spoiling for a fight. 'I'm Stella.'

'*Salut*, Stella!' Jacques raised his glass, so she did the same with hers. 'Stella,' he repeated, when he'd taken a mouthful. '*Une étoile.*'

'What?' She looked startled.

'Stella means a star. In French, *une étoile*.' He spun out the word, as though weaving a stairway to the moon. Stella thought she had never heard such a beautiful word. Ay-twahl. She determined to commit it to memory.

'Now can we have a bit of shush here?' called Freddie. He gave his glass a few taps with his signet ring to make it tinkle like a bell. Most faces turned to look at him, the others were so engrossed in conversation they took no notice and kept on talking. 'Hey, Bea. Control your group!' The hubbub calmed down. All eyes were now on Freddie. He basked in moments like this, could have warmed himself in the glow of their attention forever. He pulled his stomach in and seemed to grow even taller than his rangy five foot eleven.

'As you can now hear, Guy has switched on 2UE because in a minute or two we'll be listening to a spot that would not be going to air if it weren't for Stella Bolt, Guy's secretary here.' He paused. There was dead silence. Everybody looked at Stella, who didn't know what to do so she stared at the floor.

'While you lot were fighting over dolmades and spanakopita and guzzling the rotgut,' Freddie went on, 'Slazenger needed a script. So what did Stella do?' He looked from one blank face to another, then fixed on a junior copywriter. 'What did she do, Gary?'

'I suppose she wrote one.' Gary fiddled with his spectacles and shuffled from one foot to the other. 'Big deal.'

'Yes, you're right,' said Freddie. 'It was a very big deal, so let's show Stella how much we appreciate it.' He raised his glass and said, 'Stella, you're a star!' A few voices echoed the toast without much enthusiasm, except for Jacques, who bowed to her in an exaggerated way and said, 'To *l'étoile*.'

Before Stella had a chance to savour Jacques's tribute, Guy said 'I think it's on now' and turned up the volume. From the twin speakers in the room came a few notes of 'Waltzing Matilda', followed by these words, read slickly by the station announcer:

Slazenger joins all Australians in congratulating Rod Laver on his super Grand Slam. What a winner! Has he got balls? Slazenger makes 'em, Rod makes 'em win. We're proud of you, Rod Laver!

The last strains of 'Waltzing Matilda' were accompanied by canned applause.

When Guy turned down the volume the first words anyone heard came from Kelvin, the despatch boy, who'd sneaked in and now stood at the back of the room. 'I wouldn't mind giving her a grand slam!' There was a burst of laughter. Stella pretended not to have heard, turning to smile at Jacques as he topped up her glass.

'What did he say?' asked someone.

'He wants to get into her pants,' said someone else.

'Whose?'

'Guy's seck-a-tree's.'

Freddie glared at Kelvin, who looked the other way and starting fixing himself a vodka martini.

'Take it from me,' Freddie said, bending down to whisper in Guy's ear, 'that kid'll find himself in real trouble one day.' His speech was beginning to slur and he was swaying, like bamboo in a variable breeze.

'Or he'll be managing director,' said Guy, who was having difficulty keeping the room in focus.

Freddie hooted. 'You're kidding.'

Stella checked her watch and disappeared to put on her fawn edge-to-edge duster coat, proud that its tent shape with no fastening was so up-to-date. With her handbag on her forearm she returned to the boardroom and found Guy and Freddie together. She laid a gloved hand on the arm of each of them and said quietly, 'I want to thank you both for what you've done for me. I'll be grateful to you, always.' As she turned to go, she said, 'Nigh', nigh',' like a good little girl at bedtime.

A few tears followed. Not in Stella's eyes, but in Freddie's and Guy's.

Chapter 3

Bea O'Connor's leaf-green coat flapped behind her as she sprinted down the hill to Cremorne Point Wharf on Tuesday morning just in time to catch the 8.45 ferry. Neither her speed nor the damp wind blowing from the south had much impact on her long black hair, which was brushed up and away from her face, tucked into a pageboy and sprayed to armour. Her eyebrows were as thick and sculpted as Elizabeth Taylor's, but there the resemblance ended. Bea's eyes were moon-shaped and dominant, set a bit too far apart so that she looked perpetually startled. Her cheekbones were wide and prominent but beneath them her face fell away to a little pointy chin. Although her mouth was small her lips were full and when she smiled—which happened often—she revealed the rewards of preventive dental care, in two rows of perfect teeth. She was engaging, with a warm personality that succeeded in putting people at ease and encouraging confidences. Her colleagues had nicknamed her Possum. They meant it affectionately because she was respected and popular, so she tried not to be irritated by what she felt was a patronising put-down.

She usually tried to get a seat outdoors on the port side as the ferry ploughed and shuddered and shook its way to Circular Quay because the most interesting sight these days was the massive construction going on at Bennelong Point, where the old neo-Gothic tram depot used to be; it was supposed to give birth to an opera house, if enough lottery money could be raised and the authorities ever stopped wrangling over the feasibility of the design. But the southerly had brought a sprinkling of rain this morning, so she took a seat inside where the air was smoky and the windows were fogged up, and thought about the script for Lustrée shampoo that needed to be re-worked before an internal review later this morning.

As she flipped through her copy of *The Australian Women's Weekly*, Bea's attention was arrested by photographs of Tania Verstak, Miss Australia of the year before, who'd just been crowned Miss International 1962 at Long Beach, California. At twenty-one she was truly beautiful and perfectly proportioned. As everyone knew, her measurements were 35-inch bust, 23-inch waist, 35-inch hips, she stood five feet five and a half inches tall, and weighed 120 pounds. And her hair was naturally dark, voluminous and shiny. A kind of electric jolt hit the inside of the top of Bea's head, making her almost jump out of her seat with excitement. Lustrée! Bea skimmed the words in the magazine: 'Chinese-born Russian refugee . . . Australian citizen, poised and charming but modest too . . . devoted to her adopted country . . . tireless fundraiser for the Cerebral Palsy Leagues of Australia.' Here was a major talent. But would she agree to do it?

Bea closed the magazine and let her mind grapple with ways to persuade someone as principled and admired as Tania Verstak to endorse a shampoo. The only real possibility for success would be to suggest that her fee be donated to the Spastic Centres. Unfortunately, the correct procedure for approaching talent meant involving Lavinia Olszanski, the casting director, who was about as tactful as a rhinoceros.

On her walk up Pitt Street to the office, she considered her strategy. Freddie would be hopeless; he'd overdo the flattery. Desi, with her Whittleford family background, had the right stature and subtlety for this sort of challenge. Maybe the chairman could be roped in too; he would give the proposal weight and indicate the seriousness of the enterprise.

Her brainwave elated her, so on reaching Martin Place she stopped for a bunch of shasta daisies from Rosie, hoping not to be serenaded by the flamboyant redhead in gumboots. She was in luck; Rosie was not in the mood to warble. Rain does squelch the spirits, thought Bea, as she paid and made her way past the GPO as its clock struck 9.30. She picked up her pace and was in her office five minutes later, arranging the daisies in a copper pot on the windowsill.

'From an unknown admirer?' Desi was at the door looking at the daisies with her beautiful pale blue eyes as she tucked a strand of fair hair behind her right ear. Bea didn't have to see the label to know that Desi's teal blue suit had been custom made by Germaine Rocher; it was incongruous to see a couture outfit on someone walking around an office on a Tuesday morning sorting though an armload of documents. Desi slid one across Bea's desk.

'No such luck, Desi.' They both smiled. Among friends an exchange of looks is sometimes more eloquent than a whole lot of words. Bea didn't bring her private life to work but, after one too many glasses of Pimm's in the Hotel Australia last Melbourne Cup Day, she and Desi had confided in each other. Since then there'd been an unspoken bond between them because each had honoured the other's trust. Bea knew that her friend had doubts about marrying Tom Boyd, despite family pressure. That confession had prompted Bea to talk about her marriage to Aidan O'Connor in London and why it had ended so disastrously.

'What's this?' Bea picked up the stapled papers in front of her.

'Call sheet for the shoot tomorrow.'

'Oh, yes. The baby food commercials. Tricky to bring off. How many babies do we have?' She flipped through the three pages.

'Three definites and two on standby, just in case.'

'Child welfare permission?'

'All cleared.'

'Client coming?'

Desi made her face longer than usual. 'I'm afraid so. Marketing manager and product manager.'

'In that case,' said Bea, thoughtfully, 'why don't I bring Freddie? He can get them out of the way by taking them to lunch.'

'Good thinking, ma'am.' Desi feigned martial obedience to a superior officer by tipping her forehead with the stiffened fingers of her right hand.

Bea scanned the first page again. 'Rod Webb's studio. I'll see you there.'

'Nothing will happen before ten, so don't hurry. We'll just be setting up. Have you met Werner?'

'No, I don't think so. Is he the one who directed the Penny Layne commercial?'

'He is. As you've seen, he's good with talent and that includes dogs and babies. They're fascinated by his pipe.'

'And his continental accent, no doubt.'

'It's almost undetectable now. He sounds more American.' She cocked an eyebrow. 'Although he's never lost the European charm.'

Before Bea had a chance to broach the subject of Tania Verstak, Freddie Hackett was in the doorway. 'You sheilas talking about me again?' He was in shirtsleeves of blue and white stripes with a white collar and French cuffs, quite the dandy with a red-and-white spotted tie and Georg Jensen stainless-steel cufflinks. The snappy outfit didn't help his face much, though. It was an unhealthy shade of ash.

'Not bloody likely,' said Bea.

'Tooddle-oo,' said Desi as she closed the door behind her.

Freddie flopped down elegantly on the sofa, crossed his long legs, helped himself to a cigarette from a silver box on the coffee table and reached for the lighter. His head seemed to be full of fog this morning and he was flat out just coping so he didn't want to tax his brain unnecessarily.

'What did you think of Stella's radio spot yesterday?' He looked at a poster on her corkboard showing Sean Connery looking sexy and wondered how he could persuade her to let him have it. The smoke drifting into his eyes made him squint. He stubbed out the cigarette and stood up.

'Full marks for initiative, if not for inspiration.' Bea's expression was noncommittal as she busied herself at the in-basket on her desk.

'Reckon she'd make a copywriter?'

'She's keen enough, so she's halfway there.' Bea scratched the base of her skull delicately with a forefinger. Her skin there was protesting at all the products she'd inflicted on her hair to bring it under control. She hadn't been paying much attention to what Freddie was saying until she realised the implication of his questions. She looked sideways at him. 'I hope you're not thinking of foisting her on me?'

'I thought you could do with some help.' He was jiggling coins in the side pocket of his trousers as he gazed through the window at the street below. His stomach growled, reminding him that he'd eaten nothing the night before. People were going in and out of David Jones in George Street and he thought about the chocolate walnut cake in the food department. Better than Underberg for a hangover. Not so good for the Chesty Bond physique, though. He was worried about getting a paunch.

'A trainee is no help, Freddie, as you know. They make too many demands. I don't have time to be a teacher. What sort of experience has she had?'

'Well, she's written a radio commercial.' He knew he was being cute, so he pulled a funny face, came over and put an arm around her shoulders. The peppermint on his breath failed to mask a stale smell that reminded her of words from a folk song called 'The Little Brown Jug': 'And when I die, don't bury me at all, just pickle my bones in alcohol.' It could be Freddie's epitaph.

'You're the most outstanding creative talent in this agency and you know it. Don't be mean! Share it around. You could be the makings of this little girl.'

'I've got scripts to write before a meeting at twelve. Let me think about it.'

'Well, don't take too long. Otherwise I might offer her to Dan.'

'Pigs might fly,' said Bea. Dan Barnes's creative group had the blokey accounts: Emperor Motor Oil, Studley Series 21 Sedans and Convertibles, Go-Go Tyres, that sort of thing. The only women anywhere near that group were typists with 34-22-34 statistics. Stella was too flat-chested to qualify.

* * *

When Bea arrived in her office at 9.30 on the following Monday morning, she was startled to find Stella Bolt sitting in the guest chair at her desk. ('Bolt-upright' is how she thought about the stance afterwards.)

'My goodness,' said Bea, peeling off her black kid gloves and putting them in her pocket before taking off her black-and-white houndstooth check jacket and hanging it in the cupboard. 'Haven't we shown you where your desk is?'

'Oh, I am sorry,' said Stella, leaping to her feet and looking distressed. 'I just wanted to report to you straightaway. Did I do something wrong?' She knew perfectly well which desk had been allocated to her, but she was determined that her presence be noticed straightaway; waiting in Bea's office also gave her a chance to sneak a look at any papers that might be on her desk.

'Of course not.' Bea managed a big smile. 'Now, let me think what I can give you to do.'

'I'll do anything,' said Stella. 'Could I make you some coffee?'

Bea needed to stall for time while she tried to invent some task that Stella might be capable of doing on her own. 'Well, just this once then. I don't expect my people to wait on me.'

'I don't mind, really. I'm used to doing it for Guy. How do you like it?'

By midday, Bea had begun to revise her opinion about the new recruit. Stella had volunteered to do the filing, the most tedious task in any office and one most people tried to avoid. She took Bea's messy out-tray and applied herself with dedication, asking for guidance only when it was absolutely necessary. For instance, should scripts be filed according to client or the name of the particular product? Was it really necessary to have a file marked 'Miscellaneous', which only encouraged sloppy filing, instead of making separate files for the various items in there?

Meanwhile, Bea tapped away at her manual Underwood re-drafting the strategy for Lustrée shampoo for the umpteenth time.

'Damn,' she blurted out, banging on the m key. Stella turned from making a new file for Personal Shopping to see Bea fiddling with the typewriter ribbon. 'This wretched thing is stuck. Yech!' She looked with disgust at her inky fingers.

'Let me do it,' volunteered Stella.

'It really needs a new ribbon.' Bea waved her hands about as if she thought she could shake the ink loose. To Stella, her delicate fingers looked as though they'd be better at gesturing with a cigarette holder than dealing with grubby mechanical activity.

'I'll get one from the stock room. Black and red, or just black?'

Twenty-five minutes later, Bea had made telephone calls to postpone the meeting until late afternoon, her typewriter had a new ribbon and Stella had cleaned the keys with a nob of putty and a stiff little brush. She knew to pay special attention to a, o, e, c, d, q and u, which were gluttons for collecting ink residue. As Stella worked she couldn't help glancing at the words Bea had typed under the heading 'Lustrée Conditioning Shampoo, Revised Product Strategy 1963/64'. Sub-headings to the various paragraphs were 'The Product', 'Unique Selling Proposition', 'Positioning' and 'Image'.

'Excuse me, Bea,' Stella said. 'What is a product strategy?'

Clearly Stella was going to be a keen pupil. Bea was pleased. 'It's a plan that sets out exactly how a product is to be presented to a target audience. When we, the creative team, come up with ideas, they must conform to the strategy before they are considered viable.' Stella's brow wrinkled a bit, so Bea went on.

'You see, it's not enough just to have a bright idea, out of the blue, without it fitting into an overall plan. Everything must be consistent with the product: its packaging, its promise and the aura around it. They combine to make it attractive enough for people to choose it over competitive brands.'

By then it was lunchtime. Bea put on her jacket. 'I'm going to Cahill's. Won't be long. You going out?'

'No, I brought my lunch. I'll just wash my hands.'

The office was empty when Stella crossed the art department to return to her desk. On the way, she passed a stack of magazines beside Jacques's light box, so she took one off the top. Its title, *Ladies' Home Journal*, was unfamiliar to her. The glamorous quality of its printing and the weight of its glossy paper told her it was American.

She opened the bottom drawer of her desk and took out an apple and the brown paper bag that held a cheese-and-salad sandwich she'd made at home that morning. Beetroot had stained the soft white bread and the sliced tomato had made it soggy, but Stella was too absorbed by the glamour of the publication to notice, although she was careful not to let any bits of food stray on to the pages.

The ads were so clever and bright she wanted to buy everything they promoted: Aunt Jemima's Pancakes, a Maytag washing machine, Betty Crocker's instant cake mix, Mr Clean foaming cleanser, and cans of corn and peas from the Jolly Green Giant. But most engrossing of all was a page showing a commanding woman in a swish office dressed for business, except that she'd forgotten her shirt. The headline read, 'I dreamed I was a tycoon in my Maidenform Bra.' Stella studied the page for several minutes and read every word of the copy. This was the fulfilment of her own particular fantasy. Although of course she would never dream of going without her blouse in public.

At ten to two Stella returned the magazine on the way to the ladies' room to freshen up and re-apply her lipstick. As she approached the washbasin beside the window she noticed something sparkling at the side of it. It was Desi's ring. She let out a little gasp. It seemed shocking that something so precious had been abandoned, like a child left on a doorstep. Her hand reached out to it tentatively, as if to pat a living creature. She slipped the ring on to the third finger of her left hand but it was too small to pass over the knuckle so she transferred it to her little finger. She lifted her hand and held it away from herself, imagining how someone else would envy her wearing it. It looked white-hot from a fire that seemed to start inside and escape through its facets.

Suddenly, Stella remembered the earrings her friend Dolores wore at her birthday party at Miranda, how they'd dangled and flashed as she'd leaned over the cake to blow out sixteen candles. The stones were diamantes and Stella thought they were beautiful; on her own sixteenth birthday, all she got from her mother was a childish trinket, a silver angel for her charm bracelet. In the whirling and twirling of square-dancing afterwards, Dolores lost one of the earrings and it was never found. At least, that's what everybody thought, with the exception of one person. When Stella saw it wedged between the leaves of a potted succulent on the patio, she turned her back to it and reached behind her to pick it up while nobody was looking. She took it home and buried it in the rubbish. When she heard the garbos banging bins around early on the next collection day, she got up and pressed her nose to the window, excited to imagine the earring being crushed to bits at that moment in the back of the truck. Dolores cried for days. Stella felt no remorse. During the following week, when she went through the motions of helping Dolores look for the earring, the only emotion she felt was boredom.

Now, in the washroom at BARK, Stella ached to own the ring on her little finger, but she knew she'd never get away with it. Footsteps approached. She wrapped the ring in a tissue from an open box on the shelf under the mirror and put it in her pocket.

Bea was back at her typewriter when Stella returned to her office. 'Excuse me, Bea,' she said. 'Look what I found in the washroom.' She opened her hand and parted the tissue.

'Ah,' laughed Bea, reaching for the telephone. 'A Freudian slip, if ever I saw one!' Stella stood staring at her in puzzlement as Bea picked up the receiver and dialled. 'Desi,' she said. 'Have you looked at the third finger of your left hand lately?'

She paused, listening and nodding. 'Stella found it in the washroom. She's on her way to you now.'

Later in the afternoon, Stella plucked up the courage to ask Bea what she had meant by that whatsitsname slip.

'The Freudian slip? Oh,' said Bea, wondering how to explain it simply. 'Well, Sigmund Freud was an Austrian, known as the father of psychoanalysis. He believed that our subconscious often makes us say or do things that reveal the truth that our conscious mind denies. A Freudian slip applies to one of those instances.' She stopped, not wishing to imply that Desi was doubtful about the wisdom of her engagement. 'I was only joking when I said it about Desi forgetting her ring.'

To steer the subject further away from Desi, she said, 'I've often thought what a fabulous name it would be for a line of lingerie!' She laughed, expecting a response to her cleverness but none was forthcoming. It made no sense to Stella, who went back to dusting Bea's books and arranging them in alphabetical order, according to author.

At one point, when Bea paused to consider whether she should mention Tania Verstak in the strategy, then decided to keep that idea up her sleeve until she knew there was a good chance of bringing it off, she noticed Stella peering into a copy of *The Hidden Persuaders* by Vance Packard. In profile, she looked like a little bird of prey fixing a glittering eye on its quarry.

'That is worth reading, Stella.'

Stella hurriedly closed the book and wiped it.

'It's about the psychological techniques advertisers use to manipulate consumers into buying their products. Borrow it, if you like.'

'Could I?'

'Of course.'

'Oh, that is so generous. I'll take good care of it.'

'I'm sure you will.' Bea ripped her draft out of the typewriter. As she put two sheets of carbon paper between three fresh sheets of copy paper and wound them into the typewriter she decided that Stella was ready for her next step as a copywriter. She would take her to the meeting next Monday when Guy Garland would brief her group on the re-positioning of an old-established breakfast cereal from Crop-O-Corn Foods.

Chapter 4

At dusk on Saturday evening, the time when currawongs in bushland at the back of the house called to each other in their mournful way, Hazel opened the screen door to the patio and poked her head out.

'If you took your nose out of that book you could set the table,' she said. She'd made an effort to look attractive by putting on the nylon frock, sprinkled all over with printed strawberries, that she usually kept for best. She wore a white lace-trimmed slip underneath and an apron on top to protect her dress. That meant the new boyfriend her mother had met at the RSL must be coming over for tea, Stella concluded, as she shut the book. Still, she asked, 'Who's coming?' The swinging love seat creaked as she got up.

'Just Roy,' called Hazel, as she turned and went back to the kitchen, patting her hair. During the week she'd permed it herself into tight little yellowish curls and there was no sign of darkness at the roots. Her self-respect was coming back. Funny what a man could do for you, thought Stella.

'Should I use the best cutlery?'

'If you like.' Hazel decided it was better if the choice was her daughter's, not her own. She had mixed feelings about tonight, excitement muddled up with dread. I don't know why I'm so het up, she said to herself. In a way, she looked forward to cooking for Roy for the first time, but she didn't want to frighten him off by appearing too keen. Her stomach felt a bit funny, not exactly nauseous, but filled with butterflies.

The canteen of cutlery was opened only on special occasions and when its contents needed polishing. As she took the pieces from their cream satin bed, Stella thought the pattern a bit too fancy for her taste but the weight of the silver-plated knives felt important to her. Like the cut-crystal salad bowl with matching servers, the tiered silver cake stand and six etched wineglasses with gold rims and red stems, the canteen of cutlery belonged to a special category of goods made for practical purposes that were instead revered decorative objects in her mother's eyes.

Sometimes Stella peered through the glass doors of the walnut-veneer display cabinet in the lounge room at the figurine of a shepherdess with a crook, an arrangement of shells set in plaster of Paris, a polished moneybox made from a coconut, a pair of Spanish castanets with a picture of a bullfighter on one and a Flamenco dancer on the other, and a pottery biscuit barrel shaped like a vine-wreathed English cottage. She had been told many times where each of them had come from but she still wondered why her mother treated them as treasures.

Hazel lifted the lid off an aluminium saucepan on the stove and poked the corned beef with a fork. It would take another half-hour. The white sauce just needed to be re-heated and the parsley chopped. She had put the scrubbed potatoes on to boil and was cutting up cabbage when the doorbell rang.

Stella's first thought when she opened the door was, What does she see in him? His pink scalp was visible through thinning fair hair slicked down with Brylcreem. There was a scar on his right cheek and his nose was flattened—punched in, surmised Stella, or maybe kicked out of shape in some football scrum. The skin on his forehead and nose was peeling from sunburn. He wore a dark striped suit that could have done with a press and a checked sports shirt that was out of place with it. In one hand he held a bottle of Sparkling Rhinegold and, in the other, a six-pack of Vic Bitter.

'Hello, I'm Stella,' she said.

'G'day, Stella.' He smiled, revealing amalgam fillings in two teeth in his upper jaw.

'Is that you, Roy?'

Who else does she think it is, thought Stella, squirming at the attempt at girlishness in her mother's voice. The apron had been whipped off before Hazel came into the hallway to smile at him awkwardly. She'd applied lipstick in a shade of violent cerise that made her narrow lips resemble a wound.

'You look nice,' he said.

'Oh, this old thing?' protested Hazel, to Stella's astonishment. 'Come and sit down. You hungry? Tea won't be long.' She ushered him into the lounge room.

'I had a bit of a win at the pokies last night,' he said by way of explanation as he handed her the bottle of wine. For a moment she seemed not to know what to do with it. Then she looked at the label and said, 'I'll get some glasses.'

'I'll do it if you show me where they are.' He shrugged off

his jacket and slung it over the arm of the sofa. 'Take it easy and enjoy yourself.'

'Oh, I've got things to do in the kitchen.'

'That's what daughters are for, aren't they?' He flashed the amalgam in Stella's direction.

She suddenly felt that she didn't belong there. Their cooing at each other made her feel embarrassed, like some kind of peeping Tom. 'I'll do it, Mum. You sit down and talk to Roy.'

Hazel perched primly on one of two donkey-brown leatherette chairs belonging to the lounge suite while Roy opened the bottle, took a wineglass from the display case, filled it to the brim and placed it on the coffee table beside a bowl of crisps. Then he sat down on the sofa with his legs wide apart, said 'Bottoms up!' and took a swig from a bottle of beer. Stella was grateful to get away from them. Any minute, she thought, he'll kick his shoes off and turn on the television.

At the table, Roy droned on about the demands of being a brickie's labourer, the impossible expectations of the clients and the incompetence of his bosses. Hazel gave him her full attention and did her best to seem fascinated. He cited disasters that could have been averted had anybody listened to him. 'This bloke says to me start stackin' 'em here, but I says nah, that's hopeless . . .'

Stella's thoughts drifted to the chapter entitled 'Class and Caste in the Salesroom' in the book she'd spent most of the day reading. Clearly, Roy belonged to 'labourers and unassimilated foreign groups', the lowest class of all. Where did she and Hazel fit on a scale that went up from there through lower middle, upper middle and lower upper to upper, the last group comprising 'old-line aristocrats'? The best she could aim for was lower upper, 'the new rich'. Rich. That'd be nice. Old or new, it was much the same to her.

'. . . sure enough, the whole lot started to shift before we even got to the end of Narellan Road.' He paused to chew. 'You certainly know your way around a stove, Hazel, that's cracker corn beef.'

'There's plenty more where it came from.' Hazel beamed.

Her eyes are so soppy, thought Stella, she looks like Bambi.

'I don't mind if I do.' He held out his plate. Hazel took it into the kitchen.

'Well,' he said, acknowledging Stella's presence, after sucking his teeth and picking at a piece of parsley stuck between the front two. 'What's a pretty girl like you doing at home on Sat'dy night?'

'Study,' said Stella. There was no point in telling him she was above mixing with the local talent. Dave, always under a car in his grimy mechanic's overalls, with only two words in his vocabulary: cripes and dunno. Bob with BO and pimples who worked at the abattoir at Homebush and sometimes turned up on a Saturday afternoon to see if she wanted to go to the pictures; no matter how many times she said no, he never got the message. Frankie with his mouth hanging open and a sniffling habit due to his breathing problem; he'd been in trouble with the police but he was reformed now, or so people said.

'What sort of study?'

'Advertising. I'm a trainee copywriter at the agency where I work.' She couldn't help the pride in her voice.

'Copywriter, eh? Does that mean you copy what other people write?' He laughed.

Her face reddened. 'No. It means I think up the words for ads and commercials.' She had the feeling he was sneering at her.

'Why do they call it copy then?'

She hesitated, never having thought about its origin. 'I suppose it's because the words will be copied for publication.' Her voice sounded squeaky and too defensive to be convincing.

Hazel returned with Roy's second helping and as he ate he turned his attention to politics. 'It's the Reds we oughta be worried about, stirring up the Yella peril in Vietnam.' He wiped a smidgeon of white sauce from his mouth with the side of his hand. Stella wanted to point out the folded paper serviette sitting untouched beside his plate but she held her tongue. 'Send in the troops, I reckon. Menzies'll do it, no two ways about it. Stop the domino effect before it starts.'

'My cousin's son is in the army,' offered Hazel. 'Do you think he'll be sent over there?'

'No question,' said Roy, who had become the authority on all things. 'There'll be conscription too, no two ways about it.' As far as he was concerned there was only ever one way about anything.

After Stella cleared away the dinner plates, Hazel produced a lemon meringue pie. It was her speciality. The silver cake slicer from the canteen of cutlery was put in service. 'Well,' said Roy. 'You've excelled yourself tonight, Haze.' Stella thought the pastry was a bit doughy underneath but Hazel glowed from the praise and the effects of the wine. She only ever drank to be 'sociable' and then it was usually a shandy. She'd been put off the grog by Ted, Stella's father, who'd done enough imbibing in their eleven years together to last the two of them for life.

When he'd finished a second slice of the fluffy pie, Roy pushed his chair back from the table and belched. 'Excuse me, ladies, but in Turkey that's a sign of satisfaction after a meal. So consider yourselves in Turkey.'

'I'll try.' Hazel, accustomed to male crudeness and resigned to it, gave him her taut little smile. Stella found it difficult to disguise her disgust. What next, a fart? With that, he farted.

'Would you like to go for a drive?' he asked Hazel quickly, as if to cover the effects of his backfiring.

'I'll do the washing up,' volunteered Stella, seizing her chance to get rid of him. 'Go on, Mum. It'll do you good to go out.'

Outside in the street, his Holden ute revved up and moved off. Stella put the leftover corned beef into a plastic bowl and let it cool before she covered it and put it into the old Crosley Shelvador; although it had seen better days, Hazel still liked to boast that it was American, the first brand of refrigerator to put shelves in the door. Stella washed, rinsed and dried the glasses carefully and put them back into the display case in the lounge room.

As she took each plate from the suds in the sink and ran the dish mop over it, she looked ahead between the spotted voile curtains at her reflection in the kitchen window. The darkness outside had turned it into a mirror. Did she look like her mother? According to tribal wisdom, a young man was advised to observe the mother before proposing marriage to her daughter to see what he'd be in for, long term. Stella couldn't detect any similarity, except for a rather pointy nose and a short upper lip. She was determined that she would never, ever, allow herself to go the way of her mother.

When the sink was wiped down and the lump of steel wool put back in a jar of liquid soap in the cupboard underneath it, she shook the damp linen tea towels—one with a kookaburra printed on it and the other with waratahs—and took them outside to dry. The sky was dark and the air was heavy. Clouds blanketed the moon and stars. A rustling sound made her look up to see the bulbous eyes of a possum staring down at her from the branch of a ghost gum.

What was Bea doing at that precise moment? Stella tried to imagine how someone who'd worked in London for five years and now lived in Cremorne would spend Saturday night. She sat down on the old swing under the peppercorn tree and closed her eyes. Maybe Bea was in a seat at the Phillip Theatre laughing and applauding the antics onstage. More likely, though, she'd be at something more serious, like *A Man For All Seasons* at the Palace in Pitt Street. In any case, she would have a gentleman friend beside her, someone of distinction, a doctor or a bank manager, well dressed and well heeled. He'd take her to supper afterwards. Stella imagined Bea wearing an orchid corsage and smoking through a black cigarette holder.

As for Desi, she would probably be in evening dress with her fiancé at the most glamorous place Stella had ever heard of, Romano's, in the basement of the Prudential Building in Martin Place. She had no idea what it was like inside, but she imagined it would be similar in decor to the Prince Edward Theatre nearby, all marble and deep carpets and a fountain. She'd been there with her parents to see *Singin' In The Rain* when she was ten. The lights were dim in the theatre, they sat in the dress circle and Dad had bought Fantales from the lolly boy. Noreen Hennessy, rising up in a circular motion at the Wurlitzer organ, had left a lasting impression, especially when she played 'I Love You Truly' and Hazel fumbled in her purse for a hankie.

Romano's, that's where I will be when I become a member of the lower upper class, thought Stella, as she pegged the tea towels to the line. Then she turned the handle of the Hills hoist and watched them rise and swing around gaily. One star showed itself above the washing line and she saw it as an omen—*une étoile*. It lifted her spirits and she returned to the house with purpose.

She picked up *The Hidden Persuaders* from the love seat where it had been left, took it into her bedroom, turned back the chenille bedspread and placed the book beside her pillow. It would be useful in helping her plan her strategy.

Chapter 5

Through binoculars Desirée recognised her father's streamlined blue and white cruiser slicing through Vaucluse Bay on its way home to the jetty at the bottom of their garden. Tom was standing aft, his dark hair writhing like Medusa's in the wind, an expression of boyish pleasure on his face. At six foot two, he was three inches taller than she, one of the few people she didn't have to stoop to talk to. He was an uncomplicated man, good husband material, steady and loyal. Maybe that's the problem, she thought, he's not complicated enough for me. She could see her life with him as a stretch of road that went straight to the horizon. No twists and turns, just a few small ups and downs. No surprises. No shocks, either. As straightforward as the Nullarbor Plain, and just about as exciting.

The easterly breeze that had been balmy all afternoon had turned bitter, causing her to retreat to her dressing room for a cashmere cardigan. Just as well she hadn't yet asked May to bundle up her winter clothes for the drycleaner. You could never be certain of consistently warm weather until November.

To get to the chest of drawers where her jumpers were stored, she had to fight her way through the jungle of debutante finery from her coming-out in London six years before. The full skirts of billowing tulle, rustling taffeta and Vilene-lined satin in their cloth shrouds stuck out assertively, trying to waylay her, dragging her back, every time she was in a hurry. Gladly she'd have given them away or auctioned them for charity, but her mother was adamant that one day she would treasure them. Desirée sighed. If only she could pull on a T-shirt and a pair of jeans like James Dean wore in *Rebel Without A Cause*. She chuckled to herself at the absurdity of the idea.

She went downstairs to join her mother in welcoming the mariners, as though they'd been at sea for a month instead of tootling around the harbour for the day. It was a ritual they all enjoyed, the women and dogs paying tribute to those who braved the sea. Dotty and Spot, Springer Spaniels, rushed ahead, scampering along the pier, barking and panting and shouldering each other aside in competition for the first pat. While Bo and Desirée watched as Blyth moored the boat and battened it down for the night, May performed the role for which she was retained, setting out a tray of drinks and canapes on the terrace.

Tom had his arm around Desirée as they walked up the path towards the house. 'I wish you'd been with us. There was a shark scare at Balmoral, a sudden mass exodus from the water, a lot of signalling and shouting.'

'Oh fun. I don't think I missed much.'

'You missed the seagulls chasing a fishing boat at Balls Head Bay. You missed the tugs hauling a mighty ship out to sea.' He blew into her hair. 'And you missed me, I hope.'

'I saw the liner from my bedroom.' What she didn't mention was that the sight of it gliding resplendently towards the heads made her stop what she was doing and experience a great longing to be one of its passengers, heading for Naples or San Francisco. She smiled at him. He was a good man. I am lucky to have this man, she said to herself. If I keep on repeating it I will come to mean it. 'I didn't allow myself the indulgence of missing you because I knew you'd be back.' She kissed him on the cheek.

'Look at the lovebirds,' said Blyth, with a glass of scotch in his hand. 'Can't wait for the wedding, can they?' He'd made himself comfortable among cream canvas cushions on a wooden bench under a pergola hung with wisteria. Spot sat gazing up at him. Dotty was asleep with her head on one of his espadrilles.

'You're the one who can't wait,' said Bo. 'Why are you in such a hurry to give away your daughter?' She looked at her husband teasingly. If you disregarded the reddened cheeks and purplish nose under his suntan, the result of a brandy too many at the club, and her tendency to hold her nose in the air and look down on everyone, the outcome not of snobbery but of sinus trouble, they were quite a good-looking pair. Although they were both thicker in the middle than they once had been, they were tall enough to remain reasonably statuesque. At least, they thought so. Right from the beginning of their courtship, they'd been a perfect match. Everyone said so. Blyth and Bo had everything: a privileged life, three healthy and clever children, one of the best pieces of real estate in the Eastern Suburbs, status in the community and style to match their money. For these blessings they experienced not gratitude but a sense of entitlement.

'While I am loath to use a cliché, I have to say I am not losing a daughter but gaining another son.' He took a gulp of his single malt. 'And precisely when might that be, do you think, Dizzy?'

The name Desirée had given herself in childhood was such an amusing misnomer, it stuck.

'It's not settled yet,' Desirée said hurriedly. 'Maybe March.'

'Maybe sooner,' said Tom.

'Maybe you chaps should think about changing for dinner,' said Bo. She steered the conversation in a different direction knowing Desirée needed more time, that she was not as convinced as she should be that Tom was the right one. For some time Bo had been looking for an appropriate moment to raise the subject with her daughter but it hadn't presented itself and she didn't want to blunder in and lose her trust. She decided to wait and hope that Tom would be as patient.

Blyth was just as keen to have a heart-to-heart talk with Desirée but his purpose was different. After Tom left to walk home to Olola Avenue to shower, change and get behind the wheel of his 1953 MG TF, the dogs suddenly sprang to life and followed Bo into the kitchen for their dinner. Blyth poured Noilly Prat over ice cubes in a cocktail glass and added a twist of lemon peel for Desirée, then helped himself to another Scotch.

'How's the job?' He knew she loved working in the relatively new medium of television but he secretly hoped that she would tire of it, that the novelty would wear off and she'd do what was expected of a young woman of her class: make a good marriage, be a full-time housewife, provide support for her husband and raise a family, just as her mother had.

'It's wonderful. I can't believe my good luck in being a producer. I never know what to expect. Every day is a challenge.'

'You know,' he said carefully, rubbing his chin like a man in a Gillette commercial, 'when you marry Tom you're going to have to give up work and devote yourself to helping him in his career.'

She looked away, across the water to the darkening bushland on the other side of the harbour. At sunset the wind had dropped and the air had become humid. The fingers of her left hand touched her mouth lightly, as though to stop inappropriate words from escaping. Then she put her drink down, hugged herself a little and looked at her father. 'I don't see it that way.'

'Oh?' The jovial weekend sailor had turned into the professional barrister. 'How *do* you see it?'

'I see my work as a career, not just a job.' She tucked a lock of hair behind her ear in a characteristic gesture. He thought how elegant she looked—and how irritating she was.

'What about your duty as a wife?'

The idea of spending her life playing bridge and being on fundraising committees with a lot of twittering self-important do-gooders filled her with panic. 'I believe in an equal partnership, not one where one person is subservient to the other.'

'Being a dutiful wife doesn't mean subservience. It means being female, doing what women do best, supporting, comforting the male.'

Desirée picked up her glass, took a big gulp of vermouth and said, 'Bollocks!'

Blyth looked as though he'd been punched in the chest. 'There's no need to be vulgar.'

'Apparently yes, there is. You don't seem to understand. Men have been unfair to women for too long, holding us back, using us, infantilising us. It's got to stop.'

'Where do you get these ideas?' He was genuinely shocked. 'If that's what your *career* is teaching you, you'd be well advised to choose another one.'

Neither of his sons would have dared to give Blyth the steely look Desirée now turned on him. 'I know you were only trying to help when you asked Sir Frank to offer me a job on *Women's Weekly*. But an etiquette column? Me? Answering ladylike questions on where to place the butter knife and how to address a duchess? That's not me, Daddy.'

'Any of your friends would have leapt at an offer like that. But, no, you had to be contrary and go your own way.'

'I'm proud that I got the job at BARK. They didn't employ me because of my family connections. They gave me a chance because I'd been to film school in London. Very few people here have that kind of experience. I was promoted because I'm good at what I do. You ought to be thrilled that I'm the only female television producer in a Sydney agency.'

'It's not a role for a woman. Has it occurred to you that you're keeping some breadwinner out of a job?'

There was silence for a few moments. 'You play dirty, Daddy.'

Blyth turned his head away as though he hadn't heard.

She sighed and stood up. 'You know I love and respect you, but your ideas about women are out of date.' She bent down and kissed him on the forehead where his hair had begun to recede. 'Please don't give me any more advice. I'm old enough to take responsibility for my own mistakes.' She gave him an apologetic little smile and patted his shoulder before she left to go upstairs.

As she changed into tapered black pants and a red satin tunic top with bouffant sleeves, she thought about their conversation and the decisions she was going to have to make. Being at odds with her father made her uncomfortable, but she couldn't help feeling that she was in a trap and the door was slowly closing.

She wasn't looking forward to the party at Palm Beach this evening wth Tom. Without willing them, the words of an old

Cole Porter song came into her mind, all about the wrong time and the wrong face.

Downstairs, the terrace lights came on. 'You're still down here?' said Bo, as Blyth blinked in the sudden glare. 'We're due at the club in half an hour.' She tried to keep the irritation out of her voice at being forced into the role of nagging wife.

'Of course, Bridey,' he said, amicably, getting to his feet. He'd given her the pet name on their honeymoon and he still used it when they were alone.

Three melodious toots announced the arrival of Tom's car. Spot and Dotty scrambled to their feet and ran barking towards the front door. A few seconds later Tom was there, handsome in black tie, just as Desirée came down the stairs with the gliding motion that came naturally to her. Blyth and Bo followed them and stood on the front steps, each restraining a squirming dog by its collar. As the cream MG crunched the gravel on its way out, the front gates opened automatically. When the car sped off and the gates closed again, the dogs were released to chase each other down the drive then gambol in mock combat on the lawn.

'They're made for each other,' said Blyth, and he didn't mean the dogs.

'I hope so,' was all the optimism Bo could manage.

'You have doubts?'

'I don't know. Dizzy doesn't behave like someone in love.'

They went back inside. Blyth still felt diminished by his daughter's forthright words. He was used to obedience, in the courts and at home. He received it from his sons—Peter at Oxford and Nicholas, right now on a school excursion to the Blue Mountains—but his daughter was out of his control, an unknown quantity with a will of her own. She looked like an angel but sometimes behaved, not exactly like a devil, more like a tiger.

'Bridey, I need to talk to you about our daughter.'

'What, now? We're late already.'

'The club can wait. We need a united front to ensure that Dizzy makes the right decision about her future. She's what, twenty-four now? Not a lot of time to waste. There aren't too many young men like Tom around, and he's not going to wait forever.' He put his arm around her shoulders. 'I need your woman's intuition in how to deal with it.'

'Oh darling,' Bo said. She thought carefully about what to say next and, more importantly, how to say it. A believer in the wifely dictum 'More flies are caught with honey than with vinegar', she decided to turn it into a joke. 'If you think I'm going to plot against my daughter, you'd better think again.' She gave him a mischievous grin and rumpled his salty hair. 'Hurry up in the shower. We're leaving in fifteen minutes.'

Chapter 6

If Bea had known what Stella imagined she'd be doing on this Saturday night, she'd have whooped at the absurdity of it. Glamorous evenings with a dashing suitor were not unknown to her but they were long ago and far away. Most of her salary now went on paying off the mortgage. There wasn't much left for clothes and cosmetics aimed at turning her into a siren. Besides, she wasn't ready for it. Maybe she never would be.

She plonked her thick paintbrush into a tin of turps, straightened up and rubbed her back, the way heavily pregnant women do. When she realised the similarity she felt the familiar mixture of relief and regret that her marriage hadn't produced children. At thirty-two, she wasn't exactly over the hill but there weren't too many child-bearing years left for her. Before she could even think of starting a family, she'd need the stability of marriage to the right man and an appropriate nest for them to share. There was about as much chance of that happening as there was of landing a man on the moon.

The feature wall was starting to look good in its new burnt-orange incarnation but she was too tired to acknowledge it. Once the woodwork was painted glossy white, it would make a big difference. Then she could hang the Marimekko curtains and cover the polished floorboards with a shag-pile carpet to match the stone colour of the other walls.

It was almost nine o'clock, her hands were a mess, her overalls were spattered with orange paint and she hadn't eaten since lunchtime. She put the kettle on and fossicked in the fridge for eggs and cheese to toss together into an omelet. The physical work of the afternoon and evening had succeeded in taking her mind off herself and her preoccupation with the deviousness of her ex husband. Now that she had begun to relax she began to feel again and it wasn't pleasant.

Some masochistic compulsion, or maybe just self-pity, made her take her cup of tea into the living room, even though it smelled strongly of paint, and search through her collection of LPs. With the windows open and the lights turned out she sat back in her prized avant-garde Verner Panton wire cone chair to listen to the soundtrack of *Irma La Douce*, the big musical hit of London's West End in 1958. At a party in Keith Michell's dressing room afterwards, she had met Aidan O'Connor.

Her date for that evening had been Edwin, an account executive who worked with her at Justin, Ainsworth & Pitt. She often covered for him. Some day, homosexuality would be decriminalised but so far it was still illegal, so a trustworthy woman could have a lively social life as a queer's girl in London. Bea was in her best finery, a cocktail dress in dark blue *peau de soie* with a scoop neck and a full skirt. Her pointy-toed shoes had been dyed to match it.

Edwin had connections with someone in the wardrobe at the Saville where *Irma La Douce* was playing so that's how they came to be invited backstage. In the hubbub of people trying to get a drink and calling each other 'dahling' they were separated, and before Bea could rejoin him, she was hemmed in against a rack full of fancy clothes. The fronds of a feather boa teased the back of her neck. She flicked her hand at it as though brushing away flies with an Aussie salute.

'And who might this be?' asked the stranger beside her as he lifted the pesky boa and tossed it over the rack. They stood much closer to each other than is usual when people meet for the first time because the room was far too small for the crowd. It was so noisy Bea could barely hear her own reply. He leaned down and inclined his head so that his ear was close to her mouth as he said, 'I didn't catch it. Did you say Betty?'

'It's Bea,' she shouted. 'My name is Bea Terry!'

'Ah, Beatrice. That is a beautiful, classical name. The heroine of Dante's *Divine Comedy*. Also a saint.'

'Oh, I don't think I'm either of those. Especially not the saint.'

'For that I am glad.'

She assumed he was queer. Almost everybody else seemed to be. He asked where she was from. She took the question as social banter, a way of filling in the silence, rather than a quest for an answer or a genuine interest in her. She answered accordingly.

'I'm a digger. Can't you tell?'

He was quick to match her tone. 'I'm bog Irish meself, so what would I know?'

When she laughed, he continued, 'You're a long way from home.' He then assumed an exaggeratedly Irish accent: 'Ye mither must be missin' ye.'

'I doubt that,' she smiled. 'Are you an actor?'

'Sometimes.'

'Between engagements?' She widened her eyes and gave him one of the mock-naive looks that she did so well.

'You might say so. As a matter of fact, I'm also a bit of a wordsmith.'

'A writer?'

'More a poet, perhaps.' He looked away, as though his mind were on uplifting thoughts. 'But I fear poetry is dead.'

'You think so?'

'Nobody wants to publish poetry, because nobody wants to read it.'

'I don't know about that. I love Shelley and Byron and Keats . . .'

'Yes, but they're dead, you see.' His attention returned to earth and he looked at her. 'Let us speak of the living. How long are you here for?'

'This is my fourth month. I'm a copywriter at JAP. It's an advertising agency.'

'One who is paid to write! Ah, you must be very clever, Beatrice. I am impressed.'

People were beginning to leave. As the crowd thinned out she saw Edwin waving at her.

'Your husband?'

'No, no. A colleague from the office.' She excused herself and went over to join him. They were due for supper at The Ivy. As they left the room she noticed that Aidan was still watching her.

The next morning he rang her at the office. It wasn't long before they'd become a couple. He wasn't queer at all.

Of course she'd heard about the stereotypical Irishman with his blarney but she hadn't expected to be so enthralled, so totally consumed by him. The way he moved with a shuffling, apologetic gait. The skinny frame, the pale skin, the black floppy hair, the dark blue eyes that turned him into a romantic figure. A helpless Heathcliff played by a method actor like Montgomery Clift or James Dean. She had to strain to hear the soft brogue that came out of his mouth. She took his half smile to mean that he was shy.

As she sat in the dark, listening to Elizabeth Seal sing plaintively about the streets being cold and hard, Bea hit on what she considered an awful truth: it's not the strong you have to be afraid of, it's the weak. They're the ones who do the greatest damage because they have no courage and they have to lie to cover it up.

The smell of paint made her feel sick so she got up and went to the open window for some fresh air. She heard a clanging noise as somebody put the lid on the garbage tin next door. Dishes were being washed up in the flat below. The sounds faded and the night was silent. Compared to London, Sydney closed down at such an early hour, it was as though the people who busied themselves in the streets during the day abandoned the place at night, leaving it to supernatural beings. House lights started going out at around nine o'clock and rarely did one wink out of the blackness after eleven.

Tonight, the only sign of life she could see, through the tops of trees and ugly telegraph poles with wires strung between them, were the lights of a ferry on its way to Manly. In the darkness it looked somehow brave, like a loner whistling to keep the evil spirits away. Bea sat down again. She realised she was wallowing in misery but she didn't care. By now the tea was cold but she drank it anyway. She leaned back in the chair and put her feet on the tea chest that served as a makeshift coffee table.

Six months after they had met they were married in the registry office at Islington. He moved into her flat in Russell Square and they accommodated themselves compatibly, or so she thought at the time. He had a wonderful way with words but he didn't seem capable of holding a job for long. He did some sub-editing on the *Evening Standard* and picked up part-time work as a reader for a publisher of reference books. He took a job as a guide on tours of Soho and theatre land but after three weeks the novelty had worn off. He lacked motivation, or application, or staying power, or the willingness to compromise, or whatever else it takes to attain self-reliance.

Most of all he resented knuckling down to authority, so he told Bea he'd be better off working for himself and she agreed. Doing what, though? When he said he had an idea for a play she bought him an Olivetti portable and two reams of foolscap and encouraged him to write by saying she'd be happy to keep him until he produced the masterpiece that would make him the new John Osborne.

Although he wasn't an alcoholic, he spent more time in the pub than he did at the typewriter. There was no end to the schemes he devised for making money, as he told them at the Salisbury in St Martin's Lane, where he spent most afternoons waiting for Bea to finish work.

'What the theatre in London needs, in my not uninformed view,' he was fond of saying over a pint, 'is a serious magazine for the intelligent theatregoer. Not just a guide to what's on, but something with depth and erudition. Informed opinions. Interviews with artists of the calibre of Harold Pinter, Laurence Olivier, Charles Laughton. I'm acquainted with them myself, so it would not be hard.'

Another big idea was to put together tours to theatres around the world. 'Jean-Louis Barrault, you know, the great mime, does not perform abroad. You have to go to Paris. That would be the drawcard for a tour of French theatre that would include the Comédie-Française, l'Odéon and so forth.' He improvised as he went along and his ambition became more grandiose. 'We would cover the bars and restaurants of the Rive Gauche and meet the intellectuals who frequent them. Sartre and de Beauvoir at Les Deux Magots and Café de Flore . . .'

Then he'd leave a minute or two for the information to sink in, and to listen to comments, if anyone cared to air them which mostly they didn't, before continuing. 'Now, you may say that we have fine musical theatre here in London and I fully acknowledge that. But you'd have to agree with me that there's no sound in the world like the sound of a musical on Broadway.'

The only obstacle between Aidan and the realisation of his schemes was money. They all entailed capital upfront and he didn't have any. But Bea did. When her parents died within three months of each other in 1954 she had inherited an equal share in the family home at Roseville with her sister. After it was sold, the money gave her a modest but comforting nest egg.

In Bea's eyes, Aidan's charm never faded and she was too smitten at the time to see through it. She just paid the rent, paid for food, paid for clothes, paid for tickets to the theatre, paid for the drinks at interval. For a woman, she was earning above average, but they were living way beyond her means, an easy trap to fall into in London, where there was so much to see and do. Their needs and wants started eating into her inheritance.

The first scheme she funded was his trip to Hong Kong to buy wholesale five hundred gross of an item he said had as great a future as velcro and the hula hoop.

'Queen Elizabeth herself employs this device,' he said, drawing to his side a powerful and unlikely ally. 'Could there be a greater spokeswoman for any item a lady might wish to own?' The item turned out to be a handbag hook, a piece of curved metal a lady attached to a restaurant table to hang her purse on, to keep it off the floor. Whether or not the monarch used one was never verified.

Was it because Aidan lacked the persistence to get retail distribution in the UK? Or was that the year when a clutch was the bag every woman wanted and there was no way she could dangle a clutch on a hook? Or was it that times were changing and giving women a sense of freedom to identify with someone racier than Her Majesty? Jean Shrimpton would never have gone in for a handbag holder, Bea realised, only far too late. Whatever the reason, the O'Connors' boxroom at Russell Square became the graveyard for around seventy thousand unsold handbag holders.

As she sat in the dark, recalling the farcical nature of that enterprise, a chuckle started in her throat and spread to somewhere under her rib cage. For the first time, she began to see the humour of it. That's a healthy sign, she thought, maybe some day soon I'll be able to regale Freddie and everybody else at the office with the divine comedy of life with Aidan. She laughed so much that tears ran down her cheeks but by that time her mood had turned and they were not tears of happiness. She was howling like a neglected dog chained up on a summer night in Spain.

She took a handkerchief out of the pocket of her overalls, blew her nose and thought about Aidan's next idea. Dwelling on this one was worse than picking the scab off a sore. He decided to become a photographer, 'like Irving Penn,' he'd said, having recently admired the American master's portrait of Pablo Picasso.

His plan was to specialise in portraits of theatre people. Money was needed not only for cameras but for studio space equipped with lights and a processing room. This was the source of their first serious argument.

It was a Wednesday evening. Bea had been to the Bank of New South Wales in Berkeley Square to pick up her latest monthly bank statement. Her account was not in the red but it showed yet another steady decline, just like the others of the past several months. Her assets were being drained, like blood from a dying soldier's wounds. On the hall table when she arrived home were envelopes she knew contained bills for electricity and the telephone.

Aidan was in the kitchen taking a small parcel wrapped in butcher's paper from a Harrods shopping bag. 'Dutch milk-fed veal,' he said, parting the paper to present pale pink escalopes on the upturned palm of his hand. 'Nothing but the finest for milady.'

She turned away and busied herself unloading her own supplies from a Sainsbury's bag and putting them away: a bottle of milk, a dozen eggs, back bacon rashers and half a dozen Cox's Orange Pippins.

Aidan's bag of treasures seemed bottomless. Out came a packet of butter. She noticed that it was from Normandy and wondered silently what was wrong with butter from England or New Zealand, which was half the price. The next extravagances he must have felt they couldn't exist without were from Fortnum & Mason: a pretty caddy of Earl Grey tea and a jar of rhubarb and ginger preserve. Half a week's pay gone in an afternoon. Fortunately, it wasn't truffle season.

Bea didn't want to remember the insults they'd flung at each other that evening but his pitiful demand, 'Why are you so determined to limit my creativity?' stuck in her mind. When he left the flat he banged the door behind him and didn't come back until the next morning. She gave him the money for the camera but she drew the line at the rest of it and that riled him. From then on, their relationship began to disintegrate.

The record finished with a click but Bea continued to sit in the darkened room haunted by the vision of herself as a dupe. How could she have been so naive? She'd misread him completely. He was weak. Sly. Manipulative. Dishonest. He didn't give a damn about her. She'd been forced to face the truth when he moved out to live with a flamboyant elderly actress, who'd played second lead in many drawing-room dramas and sometimes still took character roles in comedies produced at Pinewood.

Bea eased herself out of the chair, dragged her feet into the bathroom, brushed her teeth, decided she was too tired to have a shower, shuffled into the bedroom and fell into bed.

Chapter 7

Walking along the corridor to the boardroom at ten o'clock on Monday morning Stella kept herself a few steps behind Bea, not so much out of respect for her leader, as to study her appearance without being obvious about it. Bea's hair was as black and polished as her patent leather pumps. The seams of her nylon stockings drew two perfect parallel lines down her calves. Her buttercup silk dress, with its white cowl, three-quarter sleeves and narrow skirt just covering her knees, fitted her like a glove. She looked so important Stella was aware of the unsuitability of her own outfit: a gypsy blouse with a drawstring neckline tucked into a floral poly-cotton skirt; on her feet she wore a pair of white Jane Debster toe-peepers. She felt like a hayseed in the corporate world, as out of place as if she'd been Elly May from *The Beverly Hillbillies*.

Guy Garland was already at the head of the table, trying to fit a carousel of slides into a projector while his new secretary,

Myra, recruited from the typing pool, set a writing pad and an HB pencil on the table in front of each chair. Boxes of various breakfast cereals were lined up on the side bench.

'Good morning, Guy,' said Bea with professional cheerfulness as she seated herself at the table.

'Good morning, Guy,' echoed Stella, thrilled that she'd dared to address him as an equal, yet a little fearful at what his reaction might be.

'Morning, ladies,' he replied without taking his eyes off the task that occupied him. A blunt-cornered square of white light appeared on the wall opposite the projector. After a couple of raspy clicks, an upside-down picture of a cornfield filled the screen. 'Damn technology,' he blurted out. 'Give me a flip chart any day.'

'Thank you, Myra,' said Bea as a jug of water and a tray of tumblers were placed beside the cigarette box in the centre of the table. Before Stella took her place on Bea's right, she reached for the jug and filled a glass for her boss and one for herself. She took no notice of Myra, who was trying to catch her eye. As a copywriter, she felt that she was now above the level of secretaries and typists.

Further greetings were exchanged upon the arrival of Humphrey, a media planner, and again with Jacques Boucher, who turned up with a sketchbook and sat down opposite Bea. He opened the cigarette box, offered it to Bea then helped himself. As Bea fitted the cigarette into her tortoiseshell holder, Jacques stood up and leaned over the table to light it. This little ritual left Stella feeling even more unsophisticated. She had never been attracted to smoking—the image of a bumper hanging off the lip of her shickered father and the foul smell of his breath had been an effective deterrent. Until her arrival at BARK, she had never associated refinement and elegance with smoking in real life, only in films.

Guy's battle with the projector seemed to have been won because the screen was now filled with the words 'Crop-O-Corn Foods, Re-positioning of Cornicles Breakfast Cereal 1963/64'. He looked at his watch. It was 10.15. He turned to Bea. 'Are we waiting for anyone?'

'Just Gary,' she said, as the young copywriter slid into the room.

'Sorry,' said Gary. He sat down beside Jacques without looking at either him or Bea and adjusted the glasses on his sunburnt nose. 'Bus was late.'

'Again? That is a very wayward bus.' Jacques lifted a sceptical eyebrow, causing Stella to notice how unnaturally black it was, like his hair.

'Yeah,' said Gary. 'The bridge was up at the Spit.'

'Was the surf also up at Curl Curl?' If he hadn't known Jacques, Gary might have thought the enquiry innocent.

'How would I know?' His hair wasn't wet but bits of it were stuck together as though he'd forgotten to run a comb through it.

Guy cleared his throat. 'Now, are we all settled?' He paused for dramatic effect, looking at each of them in turn. Then in his I-am-in-charge-here voice, he declared, 'I want you to pay attention because, at this point in time, we have a very important assignment.' His eyes narrowed, so that fine lines fanned out from them like spiders' legs on his tanned skin. He was by nature relentlessly cheerful, like a jolly games instructor on the ocean liner that had taken Bea to England, except when he felt the need to take command. Then he became self-conscious and pompous.

Today he also seemed distracted. It crossed Bea's mind that the agency's relationship with this client might be a bit shaky.

Although, maybe Guy was just feeling the effects of a weekend of familial demands and finding it difficult to adjust to work. It took a certain kind of personality, a lack of shame or real conviction, to take on an account-service role, she thought, because you were the go-between, trying to please the client on one side and the creative people on the other. Inevitably, they were almost always in disagreement, the writers and art directors trying to push something original and risky, the client sticking to formulas that had succeeded in the past. Guy had to shift his allegiance constantly, manipulating one and then the other. She looked at him with a mixture of pity and distaste and felt grateful that she wasn't in his shoes.

Guy picked up a packet of Cornicles from the group on the bench and held it up. 'I don't need to tell you much about this product because it's already as familiar to you as Aeroplane Jelly and Vegemite. Even to *you*, Jacques, you've been here fifteen years.' He cleared his throat again. 'It's an old staple. Been around for yonks. That's its strength. And also its weakness. It's tired. Its consumers are growing old. And the young are not interested in it.'

At this point he manned the rackety projector and clicked through a series of slides that covered the history of the brand, a tedious travelogue from the cornfields of Iowa to Chicago where the ingenuity of a patented process allowed corn to be extruded into cute little cones that found their way into the breakfast bowls of the whole English-speaking world. The show concluded with a series of histograms plotting a gradual decline in market share as competitive brands, such as several Kellogg's and Sanitarium products, continued to gain.

The only person keenly interested in the journey was Stella, who had never been over this ground before, and to whom it was a novelty and an adventure. She was excited not so much by the thought of devising a successful advertising campaign, but of being the copywriter who would become heroic by coming up with the winning idea.

Jacques was doodling in his sketchbook. One cartoon showed a hand pulling the string on Stella's gypsy blouse. The next showed the blouse having fallen down to reveal two bare ballooning breasts with cherries for nipples.

'Our task,' said Guy, switching off the projector and lighting a cigarette, 'is to come up with a whole new personality for the brand, including a new design for the package, that will appeal to a younger audience and still not alienate its current users.' He picked up the product and placed it on the table in front of Jacques.

'Young people are interested in health food,' offered Gary, picking a loose piece of skin off his nose. 'Why don't they make it wholegrain?'

Guy exhaled a cloud of smoke aimed at Gary. Slowly, as though to a child, he said, 'The client has asked us to sell the product, not to re-invent it.' He drew on the cigarette again, was overcome by a fit of coughing and dug into the pocket of his trousers for a handkerchief. 'Besides,' he managed to wheeze, 'the health food craze is a fad. It'll never catch on.'

'A new package can make a big difference,' said the diplomatic and determinedly optimistic Bea. 'And it gives us a chance to slap that magic word "New!" on the front.'

'Precisely,' agreed Guy.

'But didn't you just say the recipe would be the same?' Stella was confused, otherwise she might not have risked appearing ignorant.

'Yes,' Guy and Bea said in unison. Then Bea shut her mouth as Guy continued, 'But the design of the packet will be new.'

'But won't it make people think that the contents are new?'

Only Gary was bold enough to explain, 'Yeah, *that's the idea.*' He grinned at her. He had one of those faces that looks more sinister when it smiles than when it doesn't.

'But it's not new, is it? The actual product I mean,' persisted Stella.

'The package will be new,' said Bea.

'But you don't eat the package.' As soon as she'd said it Stella realised she'd made a mistake. The others were silent.

Bea was beginning to sound cross. 'No, but a more up-to-date package can change perceptions of what is inside, make the contents seem better.'

Stella realised she had a lot to learn about the advertising business and decided to ask Bea if she could borrow a few more of her books.

Jacques had turned the page of his sketchbook. He picked up the box in front of him and studied it on all sides. 'I'll work up something. Maybe simplify the elements.' He started to sketch. 'Now, what would Saul Bass do?' he mused.

'Who?' The name rang a bell with Guy but he couldn't remember why.

'The American movie designer. He does great posters. Dynamic and simple.' Jacques started talking to himself as he sketched. 'Maybe I could play with the cone shape.'

'That would stand out at point-of-sale,' said Bea.

'I guess we have to keep the logo?' Jacques knew the answer but hoped he might be wrong.

'You are dead right.' Guy stubbed out his cigarette.

'Same colour scheme?'

While Guy thought about the question, Bea made a characteristically practical suggestion. 'Why don't we do some alternatives, Jacques? Any new package will have to be tested in group discussion, anyway. Won't it, Guy?' He nodded and she continued, 'I'd like to see us design something we really believe in.' She turned to look hopefully at the gauche faces of her two writers. 'In the meantime, why don't we have a brainstorm and see what we can come up with?'

Walking back to her office with a box of Cornicles, Bea felt uneasy. Stella had raised a subject creative people tended not to think about when they devised campaigns: ethics. She also felt ashamed of herself for uttering the words, 'something we really believe in'. She was glad that neither Gary nor Stella, who were trailing along behind her, seemed to find it ludicrous that she had elevated the look of a packet of cereal to the level of a deity.

In Stella's mind the redesign of the box of cereal took her in a quite different direction from the one Bea was following. Stella's train of thought was set off not only by what she had witnessed in the meeting but by the way it connected with what she'd read in *The Hidden Persuaders*.

She now understood that most people judged the quality of a product by its packaging. Bea had just confirmed the fact. They were convinced that anything that was in a good package was superior to the contents of an unattractive, cheap or unsuitable package even when those contents were exactly the same. So, reasoned Stella, the power of appearance should not be underestimated, whether it was of something as inanimate as a box of cereal or as alive as Bea O'Connor. Or Stella Bolt.

Clever and talented though Bea was, thought Stella as she pulled a chair towards Bea's desk and sat down, a large part of her authority came from the way she looked: commanding, capable and immaculate.

'Now, team,' said Bea in a light-hearted way. 'Does anyone have any bright ideas?' Her fingers worked open the pack of cereal and shook some of the contents into the empty ashtray on her desk. 'Instant inspiration, Gary?'

He picked up one of the little golden cones and balanced it on the tip of his forefinger. He twirled it and scrutinised it. 'Looks like a coolie's hat. Me tink it's a Chink,' he said cheekily. 'We could have all these little animated Chinamen wearing Cornicles on their heads.' He put the little fingers of both his hands at the outer corners of his eyes and pulled the lids so they became slits. 'Chew chin chow! That's our slogan.'

Bea laughed. 'You're a comedian, Gary. Very funny.' She turned to Stella. 'What about our newest recruit?'

Stella felt her face redden. Her mind had been elsewhere. 'Oh, um . . . There's something I don't understand.'

'What's that?'

'How can a commercial appeal to everyone? I mean, if your mother likes it, you probably won't. I mean, you know.'

'Yes, I know what you mean.' Bea was pleased with Stella's curiosity, so she welcomed the chance to explain things to her; it was also a way of clarifying her own thinking. 'The answer is that there'll be more than one commercial to express the idea. One directed at the mums' market and run on daytime television, and a different version targeted specifically at teenagers and shown on programs such as *Bandstand*, early on Saturday evenings. We'll probably also need one for kids with a special offer, a competition with an attractive prize, or a gift inside the pack, that kind of thing.'

'I see,' said Stella. It sounded like a lot of work.

'In any case,' said Bea, 'we all need to collect our thoughts. It's not an easy project. We need a slogan, something memorable to stick in the mind and associate with the brand.' She sat back in her chair. 'You know, we could do worse than a catchy jingle. Anyway, I don't want to inhibit you. Why don't we all give it some thought and get together again on Thursday morning?'

As she got up to leave, Stella realised that another important dimension to the status of Bea was how she sounded. She was articulate and confident in her speech, which came out in proper sentences. Her voice was well modulated, her Australian accent softened by her years in London. Everything about her projected quality. Bea had a first-class brand image.

On the way back to her desk, Stella stopped to look at the magazines on Jacques's bookshelves. He was peering through a magnifying glass at transparencies on his light box. She smiled sweetly at him and put her hand on a copy of *McCall's*. 'Could I borrow some of these?'

'For you, Étoile, anything,' he said, without appearing to have noticed her. 'Bring them back, though, won't you?'

'Of course. *Merci*, Jacques.' Stella was learning fast. She helped herself to as many copies of *Vogue, Harper's Bazaar, Glamor, Good Housekeeping* and English *Woman's Weekly* as she could carry.

As she sat at her desk flipping through page after page of photographs of classical beauties glamorously outfitted in the latest fashion, with eye veils, ropes of pearls, long gloves, wasp-waisted dresses, elegant pointy shoes and sleek cigarette holders, she paused to look down at her rumpled skirt and toe-peepers. Stella pondered her own brand image. Her packaging did not reflect either the way she felt or the ambitions she had for herself. Except for her hands. Well-groomed nails, meticulously painted, had been an obsession ever since she was in her teens and began to be repelled by the damage housework had inflicted on her mother's hands.

It was there, pretending to think up ideas for Cornicles but instead studying fashion photographs of Anouk Aimée, Jean Shrimpton and nameless goddesses with sucked-in cheeks and haughty demeanours, that she decided it was time to repackage and re-position herself, to turn herself into the star she felt was her destiny.

Chapter 8

The room was in semi-darkness when Desi entered and closed the door gently behind her. Coming in from the brightly lit reception area, she took a few moments to make out the two figures sitting in the seats facing the screen.

'Afternoon, Miss Whittleford,' uttered a voice behind the projector.

'Hello, Darryl,' smiled Desi and waved a kiss at him. She'd been fond of him ever since she heard him sing 'Nobody Loves a Fairy When She's Forty,' at the Christmas party last year. 'It's Desi, remember?'

'Only when the boss isn't around,' he quipped, in an exaggerated stage whisper.

Rod got up from his seat. Werner Dresner stood up, too, to move along so she could sit between them. She slid down in her seat to try to make herself less conspicuously tall. The men on either side of her now were both shorter than she was by at least an inch and that made her feel like an Amazon.

'How do they look?' she wanted to know from Werner when she'd settled into her place and found her spectacles; she was short-sighted so she needed them to pull the screen into focus.

'The rushes?'

'What else?' She lifted her chin and brushed a lock of hair away from her face to tuck it behind her right ear. She was unaware of this nervous habit but others couldn't help noticing it.

'Terrible.' It was his little joke; Werner's humour was founded on pessimism. They must be really good, she thought. She turned to look at Rod. He was smiling. Ah, thought Desi, what a happy sight. The shoot had gone well but you never knew what had been captured by the camera until you saw the footage.

'Ready when you are, Darryl,' called Werner over his shoulder. The lights went out and the projector began to whir.

Take after take, identified by a clapperboard, showed various babies performing a number of actions: gazing benignly at the model playing their mother, looking angelic, looking diabolical, squirming in discomfort, sticking fingers in their mouths and noses, being spoonfed, swallowing, dribbling, burping, vomiting, laughing, rubbing their eyes, clapping their hands, bawling until they turned red with rage, sleeping contentedly. There were close-ups of a woman's hand spooning pap-like food from a small can of Bonny Baby Food, and shots of a stack of unopened cans of it on a kitchen shelf.

Over drinks in Rod's office afterwards, Desi felt as delighted as though she'd directed and shot the footage herself. It was better than good, it was exceptional and there was enough of it for three different commercials. Their shared achievement had produced a camaraderie between producer, director and cameraman of a kind Desi had never experienced in her other relationships, in business or among friends. They had common ground. They were even of one mind about which takes for Darryl to use in editing the finished commercials and which to discard. Over her second glass of wine Desi had a bright idea.

'You know, Werner, some of those out-takes are so funny, with everything going wrong, we could make an amusing film for the client to show at trade presentations.'

It was rare for Werner to laugh but when he did it was a deep and infectious chuckle. 'We could call it Bonny Baby Bloopers.'

'Yes! Brilliant. I'll bring Bea over when you've done the first cut. She'll love writing an irreverent script.'

It crossed Desi's mind that Bea and Werner might find each other attractive, if they had the chance to meet again in the right relaxed circumstances. On the set the week before, he'd been so preoccupied there was no opportunity for them to exchange more than a few words of greeting and Bea left before they broke for lunch. Her friend deserved to meet an interesting, talented and successful man, thought Desi.

Was he eligible, though? She hoped so. At forty—or whatever age he was—a man of his worldliness was certainly old enough to have been married, perhaps more than once. Whether or not he was attached now was too delicate a question to be asked directly, certainly not by her, but her instincts told her he was available. He looked a bit unkempt to be married. Married men wore shirts lovingly starched and ironed by proud women at home. Werner's regular garb was baggy trousers and a black turtleneck jumper that needed a brush. His hair could have done with a cut. He was the brooding type. Desi's father would have called him bohemian.

'One for the road?' said Rod.

Desi looked at her watch. She was startled to find it was nearly eight o'clock. She gathered up her things hastily, muttering, 'I should have been home an hour ago.' Tom would be there already. She'd forgotten that his parents had also been invited. Dinner was about to be put on the table. Her mother would be worried. Her father would be displeased. None of them would understand. 'Why didn't you ring?' they'd want to know. Why hadn't she? With alarm, Desi realised it was because she'd forgotten them, as though they didn't exist.

'I'll give you a lift,' offered Werner. 'Where do you live?'

'I don't want to take you out of your way.'

'You live in Katoomba?'

Desi smiled to let him know she got the joke. 'Vaucluse.'

'A small detour for me.'

His car was a navy blue Ford Falcon with a dent in the left front mudguard. Inside, it smelled of leather and tobacco. The back seat doubled as a shelf on which a briefcase, cans of film, files, newspapers, books, cartons and slithery drycleaner bags of clothing had been slung carelessly. The windscreen was speckled and smudged with dust. She felt comfortable, as though she'd slipped off her shoes. She sank into the seat and wound down her window. The evening air was sweet with the scent of jasmine trailing over a neighbouring fence in Gosbell Street.

It wasn't until they turned into New South Head Road at Rushcutters Bay that she asked, 'Where do you live, Werner?'

'Just back there.' He indicated the direction with a tilt of his head.

'Then I *am* taking you out of your way.'

'I enjoy this drive. Sydney is a beautiful city and this is the best part of it.' He was a good driver. His hands on the wheel were well formed and capable.

'How long have you lived here?'

'In Ithaca Road?'

'In Australia.'

He didn't answer for a while. They were negotiating the bends between Double Bay and Rose Bay. 'A few years,' he finally said.

She knew enough to drop the subject. For the rest of the ride they dwelt on industry gossip.

When they stopped at her address, he got out quickly and walked to the other side of the car to open the door for her. She took her handbag and briefcase and thanked him as she stepped out. Behind a stone wall about five feet high a flagstone path bordered by shrubs and a well-kept lawn led to the kind of heavy-looking brick house he associated with northern Europe. It was substantial and defiantly British. At the end of a gravel drive at the side of the house was a garage big enough to house four vehicles.

Werner waited until Desi closed the gate behind her and started trudging up the path to face the family before he started the car and drove off.

Bea sat at her desk regretting her decision not to go with Desi to look at the rushes of the Bonny Baby Food commercials. She'd made virtually no progress with ideas for Cornicles or names for a new spray-on furniture polish to be test-marketed against Mr Sheen. The telephone hadn't stopped ringing, as though deliberately timed to disrupt her concentration.

Worse than that, but just as Bea had feared, Lavinia Olszanski had presented her with half a dozen reasons why Tania Verstak would not agree to endorse Lustrée shampoo.

All Bea could say, as she stood in the doorway of Lavinia's office with her arms folded, was 'What do we have to lose by approaching her? At least, let's give it a try. Just feel her out. Ring her agent.'

'I will not make a fool of myself by speaking to her agent,' Lavinia decreed. She shifted her bulk and settled it more firmly into her swivel chair.

'Why ever not?'

Lavinia pursed her lips. 'It would be no use. I would make myself look like an idiot. Tania Verstak will not agree. She is above commercials.'

'How do you know that? She might welcome a generous donation to the charity she works so hard for.'

'I do not believe in wasting my time on a lost cause.' Lavinia had decided to play at being snooty. In her mind she was Lady Bracknell. To Bea, who was not about to be intimidated, she was a parody, the perfect subject for Jacques to caricature.

'Then I will,' said Bea. 'Who is her agent?'

'It is not your job.' Lavinia turned her head and looked out of the window at a brick wall. She fiddled with a book of matches.

'Then I'll make it my job,' Bea retaliated. She was furious with herself for not trusting her own judgment—she should have bypassed Lavinia in the first place. She turned, marched back to her office, closed the door and dialled Freddie. He was in a client meeting, or so his secretary said. Since it was nearly five o'clock, Bea surmised he'd be at the Journalists' Club.

She decided to call it a day, take the ferry and let the north-easterly breeze clear her head on the way home. As she packed up her things, another worry surfaced in her defeated state of mind. Why was Lavinia being so obstructive? Did she know something that Bea didn't? Finding an idea for Lustrée that pleased the client was proving to be a problem that would not go away. As she walked down George Street towards the Quay the thought occurred to her that Freddie might have gone behind her back to throw the challenge at another group. He wasn't to be trusted. But then, who was?

Chapter 9

O ne of Stella's most useful attributes was her memory. As she stood in McDowell's dress materials department at lunchtime on Tuesday, turning the pages of a large book with drawings of outfits that could be sewn at home, she came upon one that was almost identical to what Jean Shrimpton wore in a photograph by David Bailey that she'd seen that morning in *Vogue*. It looked like a dress but it was in two pieces: a collarless curved tunic top that reached the hips, over a slightly flared skirt that just covered the knees. Very snappy for the office, she thought. Impressive at a client meeting, when the time came for her to be invited to one.

She bought the pattern and started fingering a bolt of shocking-pink Moygashel linen when she saw Desi. What was she doing in the dressmakers' department of a middle-of-the-road department store? She didn't make her own clothes. Even Stella could tell by looking at her that they came from Paris or maybe local couturières like Beryl Jents or Germaine Rocher. She was wearing the cream silk high-waisted dress with a blouson bodice that Stella was convinced she'd seen photographed by William Klein in *Vogue*. She must be going to a cocktail party after work.

As Stella approached her, the mystery grew deeper because the shop assistant attending to her was measuring several yards of red-and-white checked gingham cloth while Desi looked on. For what? Stella was intrigued. The statuesque Desi was not a cutesy Heidi-of-the-Alps type.

Stella advanced slowly until she stood immediately behind her, her eyes about level with Desi's shoulder blades. She craned her neck to say, 'Hello, Desi.'

Desi gave a start, like a frightened filly. She turned and the alarmed look on her face changed to a smile as she realised the greeting came from Stella. She liked the girl. There was something vulnerable and touching about her.

'Aren't we in a glamorous business?' said Desi, mockingly. 'When the creative director needs a prop for a spaghetti commercial, who's the lucky patsy who's sent out to find it?'

'The producer!' said Stella, eagerly participating in the game. They both loved what they did. Bitching about their glamorous jobs was an act of joyous collusion. It also knocked down social barriers, even the big one put up by the disparity in their accents.

'Have you had lunch?' Desi took the package and the receipt. 'I wouldn't mind a Welsh rarebit at the Vienna Coffee Lounge. It's on the way back. Freddie can jolly well wait for his tablecloth.'

Downstairs among wood panelling and the trappings of old Vienna, Stella seized her chance to enlist a faultless arbiter of elegance to help in her makeover, cunningly hiding her opportunism behind the mask of vulnerability. Desi approved of the pattern she had bought and suggested that gabardine would be a more appropriate material for it than Moygashel, which crushed easily and tended to hang limply.

'In navy,' she said decisively, stirring the whipped cream on top of her cup of coffee.

Stella thought for a few moments. 'Wouldn't that be a bit like a school uniform?' She extracted a tiny bit of toast and runny cheese with her knife and fork and paused before putting it into her mouth as delicately as possible. She was making a big effort to be ladylike. Desi had an invisible way of eating. Almost sleight of hand. You didn't notice her doing it but suddenly her plate was empty.

'Navy blue is very chic and understated.' Desi's voice carried such authority, her vowels were so rounded, her tone so sonorous, Stella had to believe everything she said. 'And practical because you can vary it with accessories. Very striking with a white shirt. And striped ones. A rollneck jumper when the weather is cooler.'

'I understand,' said Stella, because she was beginning to see the difference between flashiness and refinement. And that reminded her of another thing she'd noticed about Jean Shrimpton in the photograph: her hair. It fell naturally to just above her shoulders and was tucked under in a loose pageboy. It looked classy. Like Desi's.

Stella didn't finish the rest of her dish because Desi was calculating the bill in readiness to leave. The moment was not to be missed. Stella leaned across the table and said, 'Can you recommend a good hairdresser? I'm sick of this beehive.'

On Thursday morning in Bea's office, Gary overcompensated for his nervousness by standing up and raising his voice, like a racing commentator. 'There's this contestant,' he said without looking at his notes. 'And Bob Dyer says you've answered all the questions correctly and made it to the top. Then there's a kind of drum roll and he says, which will it be, the money or the box? And the bloke says, how much money? And Dyer says five hundred quid, or something. And there's a pause and the tension mounts and the audience is shouting take the money and he says, no I'll have the box. And what's the box? You've guessed it. And the slogan is . . . da-daaah! . . . Pick a box of Cornicles.' He sat down.

Bea and Stella both looked at him wordlessly. Bea straightened some papers on the desk in front of her, looked away to formulate her reply and consider how to frame it. 'Yes, well there's some merit to that idea, Gary. It is a popular show and it would give prominence to the pack.' Gary grinned and thumped his chest, not quite as zealously as Tarzan.

'But there are two major problems that I can see.' She looked at him and watched him gradually diminish as she went on. 'The first is its narrow appeal. I can't see how it could persuade teenagers to buy Cornicles. Bob Dyer has an older demographic for an audience, his appeal is to their parents.' Gary pushed his spectacles up his nose and sank further into his chair. 'And the second problem is that *Pick a Box* is a top-rating program on the Seven Network—I don't think the other channels would touch a commercial that's based on it.' Bea did not allow herself to feel remorse. It was clear that Gary had given the problem very little thought. He was capable of much better work than he'd tried to pass off here. That irritated her. She was in a brutal mood.

It was Stella's turn. Her eyes sparkled. She felt encouraged by Gary's failure and confident of the validity of her own suggestions. 'Well, I think that most Australians love sport, no matter what age they are.' No question about that. She twinkled her eyes at Bea, who smiled back, encouragingly, so she continued. 'So we could have these champion sportsmen, like Rod Laver and Murray Rose and people like that. And the slogan would be "Cornicles, Breakfast of Champions".'

Bea's smile faded.

'Where did you get that idea, Stella?'

'I made it up.' Stella's eyes glittered, challengingly. She felt confident in making the claim because she'd never seen Bea looking at an overseas magazine; only the local ones seemed to interest her. 'But I've got another one,' she hurried on, 'if you don't think that one's right.' She transposed the two sheets of paper on her lap. This time her voice faltered slightly as she said, 'We could just have a really simple presentation, a bowl of cereal, with a spoon stuck in it and the pack behind it, on television and on posters everywhere. And the line says "Go to Work on Cornicles".'

Although Stella didn't notice, there was a look of derision on Gary's face.

'Well,' said Bea. 'I think it's back to the drawing board. We seem to need more time. Why don't you give it a bit more thought, Gary, maybe talk to Jacques. He's got some really interesting ideas for the pack that might spark something. It sometimes helps to work with an art director.' When Gary got up to leave, Stella also made a move.

'Wait a minute, Stella,' said Bea. 'We need to talk.'

Stella sat down again and looked at her toe-peepers. There was a nasty scuff-mark on the left side of the right shoe. How did that get there? Bea got up and closed the door. When she'd resumed her seat behind the desk, she said, 'Stella, do you know what the word plagiarism means?'

If Stella knew, she wasn't saying. She screwed up her face in the semblance of a smile. 'Something to do with the plague, I suppose.' It was an insolent reply and Bea was not in a tolerant mood.

'You are a wordsmith, are you not?'

'I'm trying to be.' Stella's voice had become whiny and defensive. Her right eye gave an involuntary twitch.

'Get the Oxford dictionary, please, Stella. It's on the shelf over there, next to that Marshall McLuhan book.' Stella retrieved the book and offered it to Bea.

'No, you hold on to it. Look up the word plagiarism.' Bea knew she was behaving like the worst kind of schoolmarm but this was a lesson she wanted Stella never to forget.

Stella turned the pages, chunks at a time, to find the Ps, then a few at a time until she ran her finger down the column that contained words starting with 'pla'.

'Got it?' asked Bea.

'Yes.'

'Read it.'

Stella fiddled with her lower lip and began to read silently.

'Aloud,' commanded Bea.

'Plagiarism, 1621. The action or practice of plagiarising.' She looked up at Bea hoping for mercy and finding none.

'Is that all?'

'No.'

'Go on, then.'

Stella took a deep breath. 'The taking and using as one's own of the thoughts, writings or inventions of another. A purloined idea . . .'

'That'll do,' said Bea. 'Close the book and put it back.'

When Stella was seated again, Bea said in as reasonable a tone as she could manage, 'I should also have asked you to look up the word "gullible" because that's what you must think I am. "Breakfast of Champions" has been the slogan for Wheaties in America since before you were born. "Go to Work on an Egg" is an award-winning campaign from Mather & Crowther in London for the Egg Marketing Board.'

Stella squirmed and tried not to show the fear and resentment she was feeling. 'I didn't know . . .'

'Don't lie to me, Stella.'

'I mean I didn't know that we couldn't use them.'

Bea felt that her message might be driven home more force-fully if she lowered her voice and tried to keep emotion out of it. 'Plagiarism is not only unethical it might be illegal, in these circumstances. The agency and the client could be sued if they ran a campaign copying the slogan of somebody else's brand. Apart from that, it would also backfire on the product, if enough people recognised its association with a competitor.'

Little sobs started to emanate from Stella, as she looked down at her hands, placed demurely in her lap.

Maybe I've been too tough, thought Bea, beginning to feel a small measure of guilt. The child was only twenty. Clearly, nobody had pointed out these things to her before. She'd probably had little or no guidance in principled conduct from her parents. Bea reached for her handbag in the bottom drawer of her desk and passed a dainty linen handkerchief to Stella.

'Never mind,' said Bea. 'You'll know next time. It's not a major tragedy.'

Stella blew her nose. 'Yes it is,' she gulped. 'I've broken a fingernail.'

Chapter 10

When she saw the pack designs Jacques had developed Bea started to feel excited and optimistic. The one he referred to as his 'Saul Bass version' made brilliant use of a conical theme, echoing the golden shape of the cereal itself, with the sun rising behind it. It would be a clear winner on the supermarket shelf and with a young demographic.

However, it was a different story at the second run-through of campaign ideas from her writers. At the end of their spiels Bea knew that nothing viable was likely to be wrung from either of them.

Gary's idea was for corny jokes to be put in the pack, like the messages in fortune cookies, to entertain people at breakfast. It was a smart gimmick that could be the basis of a promotion, but it was not strong or persuasive enough to sustain a whole campaign.

As for Stella, she seemed flummoxed. Hers was not so much an idea as a distilled re-enactment of Guy's presentation, starting with the cornfields of Iowa and the patented process that gave rise to Cornicles. Boring. Bea didn't say that, though. All she asked was 'What is the promise, Stella? The consumer benefit?'

When they shuffled out—Gary huffily, Stella looking like a child released from school—Bea closed the door and opened the middle drawer of her desk. There, carefully laid out in a folder marked 'Crop-O-Corn' were three scripts she'd developed at the weekend. Inspiration often came to her at home, where she was a consumer like everybody else and her thoughts were not constrained by the dictates of clients and account directors. If a good idea occurred to her there she wrote it down and kept it among others in a manila folder in her desk in the sitting room.

Bea didn't believe in competing with her writers when she gave them assignments. She felt it was fairer for them to have a chance to come up with fresh ideas before she applied herself to the task. At least, that is what she told herself. In truth she experienced a measure of self-satisfaction in holding back while others groped for solutions that came easily to her. It was a way of testing herself, of verifying her ability. Bea knew she was good. She defined herself by her work.

It was clear now, given the poor performances of Gary and Stella, that she'd have to rely on her own resources. She had not felt very inspired, but the work she'd done was adequate. It wouldn't win any awards but it might sell Cornicles and that's all that really mattered.

She picked up the telephone and dialled Freddie. 'Got a minute? I'd like to run something by you.'

'I am literally running out the door.'

'An idea for Cornicles I want to present to Guy. It'll only take a minute.'

'I'm ten minutes late for a casting session.'

'Casting what?' Lustrée crossed Bea's mind.

'Hunks for Studley Convertibles, darling. The client's waiting.'

'I want to move this along, Freddie.'

'Bea, I'm sure it's brilliant. I trust you. Go ahead. Fill me in later.'

Guy sat on Bea's sofa with a glass of the dry Cinzano she'd taken out of her fridge and listened to her explain her idea.

'It's hard to believe, isn't it, Guy, that it's almost twenty years since *Oklahoma!* opened on Broadway?'

'As long ago as that? A great musical never dies.'

'Precisely. We've based this idea on one of its most popular songs.' Bea always used the collective 'we' when she talked about her own ideas, as though they'd come out of a collaboration when, more often than not and certainly in this case, she'd given birth to them without any assistance. 'It would probably cost a lot of money to secure the rights to use the song but, hell, this is an international client with a big budget and a lot at stake. Am I right?'

Guy nodded. 'Could be.' He sipped the drink. 'Let's have it.'

Bea handed him a copy of the main script to read as she went through it, acting out the parts, singing to the best of her ability—she was no Julie Andrews—and finishing by flourishing the packet of Cornicles.

The script went like this:

> The scene: a typical family kitchen. The table is set for breakfast. An empty bowl is in front of each person.

Video	Audio
Wholesome forty-year-old dad at the table sings to camera	*Oh, what a beautiful mornin'!*
Cut to pretty blonde sixteen-year-old girl with shiny hair and perfect teeth.	
She sings to camera	*Oh, what a beautiful day!*
Cut to seven-year-old boy with freckles and a turned-up nose.	
He sings to camera	*I got a beautiful feelin'*
Cut to smiling mother. As she brings an open packet of Cornicles to the table she sings to her family about the Cornicles coming their way.	
Cut to close-up of Cornicles being poured into a bowl.	**Male voice-over:** *There's a whole field o' corn in golden crisp Cornicles.*
Milk is added. Then a sprinkling of sugar and three slices of banana.	
Quick succession of Dad, girl and boy eating Cornicles with obvious relish.	*Cornicles are rich in Vitamins A, B and E, plus essential minerals*
Cut to Dad giving Mum a grateful kiss. He has a hat and briefcase in his hands.	*to keep your family top o' the morning*

Video	Audio
Cut to girl in mortar-board and gown holding diploma.	*—and top of the class,*
Cut to boy with eager face and hand up in class.	*no matter what age they are.*
Cut to close-up of Cornicles pack on breakfast table with bowl of cereal in front of it.	*Cornicles.* **Chorus voice-over:** *Oh, what a beautiful day!*

Guy put down his glass. The expression on his face was noncommittal. 'What about the youth market?'

Bea was ready. 'We've written a rock 'n' roll version targeted at 18- to 24-year-olds for *Bandstand*, and so on. Could work well on radio, too.' She refilled Guy's glass and proceeded to present script number two, which required her to imitate, as best she could, the voice of Johnny O'Keefe and the movements of a cool teenager.

The script she handed to Guy read like this:

The scene: Dawn in the city.

Video	Audio
Boy and girl (Montgomery Clift and Jean Shrimpton types) exit a below-ground nightclub. They are dressed as beatniks: black pants, tight for her; leather jackets. She has short hair, a beret and dark eye make-up. His arm is around her shoulders. They move in time to the beat of the music.	**Voice sounding like JO'K sings:** *Oh, what a beautiful mornin'!*

Video	Audio
She yawns. He kisses her on the mouth.	*Oh, what a beautiful day!*
Cut to shot of them from behind moving in sync with the beat along a cobbled street toward the sunrise.	*I got a beautiful feelin'*

Dissolve to close-up bowl of Cornicles as milk and sugar are added and a voice sings of the Cornicles heading their way.

Video	Audio
Zoom out to show boy and girl, beret and jackets off, seated on bar stools in a kitchen, sharing a bowl of Cornicles.	**Male voice-over:** *Time for bed? You're kidding. Cornicles give you the energy to get up and go—no matter how late you were last night.*
Boy and girl, wearing beret and jackets again, roar off on a Vespa.	*Cornicles.*
Superimpose Cornicles pack.	**Reprise of singing:** *Oh, what a beautiful day!*

Without waiting for Guy's reaction, Bea delivered the third script in a straightforward manner without acting the parts, since it was self-explanatory, only fifteen seconds long and aimed at children watching television from 4 pm to 6 pm midweek and on Saturday mornings.

The script went like this:

The scene: a typical family kitchen.

Video	Audio
Boy aged ten and girl aged eight at breakfast table eating Cornicles enthusiastically.	**Children's chorus sings:** *Oh, what a beautiful mornin'!*
Pan to close-up of Cornicles pack on the table.	**Male voice-over:** *Hey, kids! Fill in the coupon*
Pack spins so that the back fills the screen.	*on the back of the Cornicles pack,*
Cut to series of stills of Disney fairy castle, Mickey Mouse, Donald Duck and other characters.	*and you could win a trip to Disneyland!*
Close-up of front of Cornicles pack.	**Reprise of chorus:** *Oh, what a beautiful day!*

Guy made a steeple out of his hands, pursed his lips and gazed into space, somewhere between Bea's left ear and her bookshelves. Although she was irritated by the performance, it didn't worry her. She was used to his posturing, his studied way of assuming what he thought was control. She had an urge to suggest that he adopt the meditative stance of Rodin's sculpture, *The Thinker*. But she resisted and instead gave him her wide-eyed look of innocence at the same time noting that he seemed to have put on weight, under the chin and around his middle; the client lunches were beginning to show. Finally, he said, 'I like it. Client-wise, it could be a winner—as long as we can get the rights to that music. That is the 64,000-dollar question.'

'The television department can handle that. In the meantime, I'll get Jacques to do storyboards.'

'We can't present anything to the client before we know for sure.'

'Of course.' Bea felt so relieved she refilled his glass. 'One more thing,' she continued. 'Wait till you see the packs.' She grinned at him, then hurried out of the room and returned two minutes later with Jacques, who carried three dummy cereal boxes, each with a different design on the front.

'They are only roughs,' said Jacques as he marshalled them, one behind the other, on the coffee table in front of Guy. 'If you like them, I will take them to finished art.' Jacques was a persuasive presenter because his voice, though gravelly, whispered rather than proclaimed, and he seemed to be impartial. He proceeded to explain the thinking behind each one. 'They represent an evolution, starting with this one, which is not much different from the current pack in its use of colour and traditional elements. But we have replaced the old-fashioned serif type with Helvetica, a streamlined new type from Switzerland.'

He slid the first box sideways so that the second one was revealed. 'Then we move to a more modern setting, the pottery breakfast bowl, the stainless-steel spoon, the straw tablemat— things that younger people favour. Very informal and very chic.'

'And here,' he whipped away the second box and tapped the top of the third one, 'we have become radical. There is no breakfast bowl, just a dominant golden cone, with the rising sun behind it. As you look closely at the cone you see it is made up of lots of smaller ones, like a window into the pack to see the contents.'

'And across the bottom,' said Bea, 'we add the line, "Oh, What A Beautiful Morning!"'

Guy seemed to have forgotten his need to appear bossy. He was positively enthusiastic. 'Well done, team,' he said. 'They're terrific.'

'Good,' said Bea. 'You can buy us lunch.'

When Guy had left to get his jacket and tell Myra to book a table at Beppi's, Bea gave a whoop of joy, hugged Jacques and called Desi. 'We need to talk business over lunch. Are you free?'

'I'm supposed to do a costing on this spaghetti commercial for Freddie.'

'This is more important, Desi. Guy's taking us to Beppi's.'

'I'll be downstairs in five minutes.'

Chapter 11

Looking back in later years, Bea often wondered how they ever got any work done at BARK. They didn't have long, boozy lunches every day—at least, she didn't—but no-shows at the office after lunch were not rare. When Guy had paid the bill at Beppi's late that afternoon, they all went back to Jacques's flat at the Cross for cognac and talk that seemed important at the time but was barely recalled, or recalled with embarrassment, the next day.

The afternoon had started productively. Over a shared entrée of deep-fried whitebait and a bottle of Frascati, Desi was charged with the responsibility of obtaining permission to use the song from *Oklahoma!* How she was to do that, she was not sure, but her first thought was to seek advice from Werner Dresner, who she knew had worked in Hollywood.

'Ring him,' said Guy, who'd grown more affable with each sip of wine. 'Get him over here.'

'I'm not sure that's a good idea,' said Desi, looking at Bea for assurance.

'Why not?' Guy was well away already. He'd had a head start with the Cinzano in Bea's office. 'Let's fast track it. We've got an anxious client and he's a big spender we can't afford to disappoint.'

'It can't hurt to ask him,' said Bea. She looked at Guy who was signalling Aldo for another bottle of Frascati and she burst out laughing. 'Nobody can say this is not a serious business lunch.' After her small triumph of the morning she felt happy and therefore a bit reckless.

'I suppose so.' Desi got up and asked Norma at the front desk if she could use the telephone. She knew Rod Webb's studio number by heart. As she waited for Werner to be summoned to the telephone, her eyes settled on Bea, enjoying herself with Guy and Jacques and drawing smoke through her long cigarette holder. In the painterly light, filtered through the fake grapevines adorning the windows, Bea looked soft and pretty. Desi thought how fortunate it would be if Werner could join them and meet Bea in a relaxed mood without the corporate guard she cultivated.

'You are inviting me to lunch?' Werner's voice could not conceal his pleasure but he tempered it with a joke. 'Miss Whittleford, this is so sudden.'

'Don't blame me, I'm merely the messenger. Our host is Guy Garland and we want to talk serious business.'

'In that case, this is a command performance. How can I refuse?'

Stella was at the glass counter in Olmi's milk bar staring mindlessly at the woman on the other side of it piling curried egg on a slice of meagrely buttered brown bread when Gary turned up beside her.

'Boo!' he said. 'What's on your mind?'

'What?'

'Salt and pepper?' said the woman.

'Yes, thanks. And the lettuce.'

'If you're dreaming up ideas for Cornicles, forget it,' said Gary.

'What do you mean?'

A few shreds of iceberg lettuce landed on top of the mixture before the whole thing was flattened with a slice of bread and a heavy hand. The sandwich was cut in half diagonally, semi-wrapped in a slip of greaseproof paper and eased into a brown paper bag. Stella's coins clanged on the glass as the woman twisted the ends of the bag to close it. She handed it across the counter.

'Next?'

'I'll have a ham and mustard and a cheese and tomato. On white bread,' said Gary.

'What do you mean, "forget it?"' Stella held her sandwich horizontally on the upturned palm of her hand to keep it intact.

'She's done it already.' He looked sideways at Stella, then at the ingredients going into his sandwich.

'Who?'

'The busy Bea.' He gave a disdainful laugh. 'Possum.'

'What has she done?'

Gary took his bag of sandwiches and paid. He opened the door for Stella. 'She's written the Cornicles campaign and sold it to Guy.'

Stella was so stunned she said nothing until they got to the corner of King Street. 'How do you know, anyway?'

'Connections,' he said slyly.

That meant he'd been chatting up Myra, Guy's new secretary. Stella began to feel angry, not only with Bea but with Gary for knowing so much more than she did. She had to lash out at somebody. 'What was all the fuss about, then? Why did she bother asking us to waste our time on something and then knock back our ideas?'

'Power,' said Gary. 'It goes to their head.' He was tactful enough not to remind Stella that her ideas were not her ideas at all. 'You want to eat outside?'

They found an empty bench in Wynyard Park. 'They're at Beppi's, talking about it,' said Gary, as they sat down to eat.

'Who?'

'Guy and Bea. And Desi, I suppose.'

Stella looked at her sandwich and frowned as she thought of Beppi's. She had been made a copywriter but she might as well still be a secretary. Nothing had changed, except that she felt demeaned. And she could now afford to buy a sandwich instead of having to make one at home. She did not regard that as progress.

'There's Kelvin,' said Gary, screwing up his empty sandwich bag and dumping it under the bench. Stella looked across the lawn at the despatch boy with his mouth open over the spurt of water from the bubbler. When he'd turned off the tap and wiped his mouth, he saw them and came over.

'How youse going?' he said.

'We're okay,' said Gary. 'What's new?'

Kelvin stood in front of them shifting his weight from one leg to the other. He looked malnourished. Maybe that's what makes him so eager, thought Stella, he's hungry for something. She had never seen him wearing a tie before. He'd loosened it and undone the top button of his shirt, as though he found it uncomfortable, despite the collar being too big for his skinny neck. She wondered if the shirt belonged to someone else, his father or an older brother.

He was appraising her, too, using the rating system he'd picked up by listening in the pub and the urinal, places absent of women. Without saying so he reckoned he'd give Stella eight out of ten for her legs, five out of ten for her face and three out of ten for her body. Her chest was as flat as his own.

'Meet the new account exec,' he said, cocky and grinning.

'Who, you?' said Gary, as though a cockroach had announced itself as the new managing director.

'Yeah.'

'Bully for you,' said Stella without a trace of enthusiasm.

'Who'd you bribe to get that?' asked Gary, in a friendly way.

'Talent, mate. Natural leadership ability.'

'What accounts did they give you?'

'I'm a trainee. A floater. It means I'll gain experience by working wherever I am required.' The words sounded too formal to be his own; he must be echoing corporate-speak, thought Gary.

'Good luck to you.'

'Thanks,' said Kelvin. He trotted off towards Barrack Street.

'Bet he's spending his lunch money on a lottery ticket,' said Gary, watching him disappear in the crowd. As an afterthought, he said, 'Want to share one in the Opera House lottery? They're only five quid.'

'All right,' said Stella.

'If we win the hundred thousand, we can tell Bea O'Connor to stick her Cornicles up her jumper.'

At that moment, much kerfuffle was going on at Beppi's as Werner arrived and Aldo and Beppi himself extended a table for four into one for five. Another basket of bread and grissini was brought to the table, along with a large plate of antipasto. Orders were taken for the main courses.

Because half the advertising executives in Sydney seemed to use Beppi's as their company canteen, Guy lowered his voice in the conspiratorial manner of a Cold War spy to explain to Werner the mission he was expected to accomplish. Werner said he couldn't guarantee a positive outcome but he certainly knew how to go about it.

'So, Werner, where are you from?' Guy was not worldly enough to know that foreigners hate the question. Bea and Desi exchanged looks. Jacques rolled his eyes and shifted in his chair.

'Elizabeth Bay,' said Werner, as a fillet steak was put in front of him. Bea lowered her head to conceal her grin and avoid Desi's eyes.

'I mean, originally.' Guy was not sensitive.

'I was born in Germany. We moved to Los Angeles when I was thirteen.'

'How's the veal, Guy? My chicken livers are superb,' said Bea.

'What brought you here?' He was relentless.

'I was invited,' said Werner, 'by your lovely colleague.'

Everybody laughed. Even Guy. 'Sorry mate,' he said. 'I didn't mean to interrogate you.'

Jacques looked at Bea and whispered, 'He got it.'

'At last,' she murmured.

At six o'clock, Stella's train was rattling along the rails between Como and Jannali, Gary was running with his board into the surf at Curl Curl and Kelvin was still at the office, as usual at that time of day.

The former despatch boy had cottoned on early to the fact that the most important decisions at the agency were made by a chosen few after everyone else had gone home. Not in the boardroom but in the chairman's suite and the managing director's office. Kelvin made it his business to be seen in the vicinity regularly because, apart from impressing his superiors with his devotion to duty by working late, he was sometimes privy to useful information.

For instance, once when he was the only minion around, the chairman's secretary had asked him to take shredded files to the basement for disposal. Some of the papers hadn't been shredded properly and he saw a confidential memo from the managing director naming a certain employee as 'incompetent' and 'a bad reflection on the company'. That's how Kelvin knew the bloke was about to be sacked. He didn't tell him, though. But whenever he passed his office, he looked in with interest, hoping to witness the moment of his doom.

Another time, when the door to the managing director's office was not quite closed, he overheard the MD dressing down the head of account service. He said, 'I know I instructed you guys to drink vodka martinis instead of gin at lunchtime but I'm reversing that decision. I'd prefer the clients to think you're drunk rather than stupid.'

His most treasured find was scrounged from Jacques Boucher's waste basket. Kelvin tacked it on the wall of his bedroom at home in Kingsgrove where he could see it when his head was on the pillow: the cartoons of Stella, with and without the gypsy blouse. The likeness was unmistakable, except that he'd exaggerated the size of her knockers. Jacques must be screwing her, Kelvin concluded.

* * *

Up at the Cross, Jacques was doing no such thing. He was sitting on the floor with Desi, happy to be able to speak in his native tongue. They were discussing existentialism and French new-wave films. Out of the corner of her eye, Desi could see Werner and Bea seated comfortably together at one end of a very long sofa that curved around two walls; his arm rested on the back of it behind her as she listened intently to what he was saying. The story of his life? Sweet nothings? Whatever he was telling her was clearly riveting. At the other end of the sofa, Guy had gone to sleep with his mouth open. Desi decided it was time to leave.

As soon as she stood up, turning herself into a tower, the others roused themselves too. Guy remained in his state of blissful oblivion.

'We can't leave him here like this,' said Bea. She went over to him, shook his shoulder and said, 'Time to go, Guy.'

He stirred, lifted his head and stared at her. 'What day is it?' He looked around and realised where he was. 'Shit!' he said. 'Excuse my French.' He staggered to his feet and started looking helplessly for his jacket. Jacques brought it from the coatstand in the hall and helped him into it. Werner offered to drive the women home. Tipsy though she was, Bea had the presence of mind to suggest that she and Desi take taxis. 'Guy seems to be the one who needs a lift home,' she said.

'Where do you live?' Werner asked him.

'Pymble.'

'That's miles out of your way, Werner,' said Desi. 'It's Katoomba! We'll put him in a cab.'

'At least let me drive *you* home,' Werner said to her.

'Next time. It's been a long day.'

Chapter 12

When Desirée woke on Saturday morning, a shaft of sunlight through a slit in the curtains hit the ring on her bedside table making it sparkle like fireworks on bonfire night. That sweet girl at the office had thought the stone was crystal. The longer Desirée stared at it, the more showy it looked to her, the sort of device a vulgar woman would use to draw attention to herself. She decided not to wear it to work any more. Tom need not know. If he did find out, she thought, as she lay back against the pillows and gazed at the rotating ceiling fan, she would say that she was worried about security, that covetous eyes had been cast at the ring and she didn't fancy the thought of being attacked and robbed in the street.

As she lingered there, delaying the moment when she had to face the obligations of the day, she wondered if Werner had made a date with Bea. And if so, when and where. They were so interested in each other, sitting there on Jacques's sofa on Thursday, that some action must have come of it.

Desirée had a moment of envy, not because she was attracted to Werner, but because she wanted dearly to feel passionate love for a man. She'd read about it in great literature, seen it in films, from *Wuthering Heights* to *Hiroshima Mon Amour*, and she believed herself capable of it. But that was not what she had with Tom. Although they'd made love, they'd never gone All The Way. Technically, she was still a virgin, and it hadn't been difficult for her to stay that way.

Unlike Bea, who cherished her weekends for the chance to shop, work on her flat and relax, Desirée found hers dull and dutiful. Especially this one. She couldn't wait for the independence that Monday morning represented.

She was due to join her three cousins and two of their friends for a fitting of wedding finery at Madame du Val's salon in Castlereagh Street at eleven. Fortunately, the nuptials-to-be were not hers. She was simply a member of the wedding party of her cousin, Fern, known in the family as Fee. Since, even in ballet slippers, Desirée stood a head above the others, including bride and groom, she would be required to be the last of the five bridesmaids—the other four in pairs—to walk down the aisle, as a kind of mobile sentinel bringing up the rear.

What bothered her most about the event was not the fuss and excitement—it was infectious and she was fond of Fee—but the unspoken expectation in everybody's minds that she would be next. Lamb to the slaughter, was how she had begun to think of it. As she got up and slipped on her robe, she looked again at the ring and wished she could summon the courage to give it back.

* * *

At that moment, Stella left the train at St James Station. Ten minutes before her appointed time of 9.30, she was in the scented rosiness of Digby Darling's hairdressing salon in Elizabeth Street. She'd been too excited to have breakfast, so the moment she sank into a squishy pink leather sofa opposite the receptionist, her stomach started to protest in a way that sounded as though she'd swallowed a litter of kittens and they were mewing to get out.

She pulled in her stomach in an attempt to silence it and picked up a copy of *Modern Beauty Shop* magazine. She stared at the pages of hairstyles without registering anything. Her mind was too aware of her own anxieties. Although she'd saved enough money, and her mother had given her a little extra, just in case, Desi had told her that she should tip ten per cent of the total bill. How did she know what the total would be until she saw the bill? How much of the ten per cent should go to the girl who did the shampooing? How much for the cutter and stylist? How to do it without awkwardness? 'Just pass it over in a handshake, or slip it into the pocket of their uniform,' Desi had advised. Easier said than done, thought Stella.

There was another variable that added to her woes. If Digby Darling himself chose to cut and style her hair, she should not tip him anything, advised Desi. 'You don't tip the owner, only the staff.' The trouble was, she didn't know what he looked like. She imagined he was the one with iron-grey hair who was snipping around the edges of a wet head—he was older than the rest—until someone called him Mario and she lost her nerve again.

By the time she'd been swathed in pink, ushered to a chair and told to lean back so that her head hung backwards over a sink and her throat was bared for anyone who might care to take a stab at it, she regretted ever having asked Desi for advice. The procedure was so undignified. When at last she sat before a mirror, all artifice was gone. Her defences were down. She looked like a drowned rat.

A slender man with a head of luxuriant chestnut hair, a toothbrush moustache and mottled skin hovered behind her. He studied her reflection wordlessly with his head on one side. Then he tilted his head the other way. Then he stepped to the side of her and surveyed her profile, his left hand cupping his chin while his right hand supported his left elbow. Then he lifted a lock of her hair and fingered it. Under his intense scrutiny, Stella felt desperately self-conscious and wondered in panic how she could reach the purse at her feet for a handkerchief to pat away a drop of water running down the side of her face.

'Pageboy, yes. Quite short,' he said. He picked up his pointy scissors and clicked them in mid-air several times. 'You have good hair, but you have abused it.' He began cutting. Her hair fell to the floor in lengths of several inches. 'Broken ends due to back combing,' he went on. 'It will take more than one visit to effect a full repair.' Guilt was added to the rest of Stella's painful emotions.

When she was shorn to his satisfaction, he summoned an assistant and told her what needed to be done, using his hands to describe the shape he had in mind. 'Yes, Mr Darling,' she said and set about stretching individual locks of Stella's hair around rollers. The knowledge that her hair had been cut by the master flattered Stella, but while it solved one tipping problem, it introduced another: how much should she tip the girl with the rollers? It was a difficulty that occupied her for the length of time she sat under the helmet that served as a dryer carefully turning the shiny pages of an intimidating French fashion magazine titled *L'Officiel*.

By the time the whole ordeal was over and Mr Darling held a mirror to the back of her head so that she could see its reflection in front of her, Stella was in no state of mind to judge how her hair looked but she gave him a sickly smile and nodded. Then he drifted away to attend to another client, leaving the boy who'd been sweeping up the hair from the floor to help Stella out of her pink robe and whisk a brush lightly across her face. Did she have to tip him too?

In the end she solved the problem when she paid the bill. Although inexperienced, she was not stupid. She calculated ten per cent, gave it to the receptionist, asked her to distribute it to the appropriate people, and fled.

On her knees in the hall, washing the black-and-white rubber floor tiles with a bucket of hot water, a cake of Sunlight soap and several cloths, Bea wondered if she was by nature a masochist. This kind of punishing physical work was far more satisfying to her than her job at the agency. At least she could see results and it truly was all her own work. Nobody else had a say or a hand in it. All at once the thought made her sad. The downside of her solo achievements was that there was nobody to share them with.

Something had happened to her, over the past year or so. Her sex appeal had diminished. Instead of being regarded as a target for romance, or even just a dalliance, she seemed to have become a kind of mother confessor. All Werner Dresner could talk about on Thursday was Desi and her talent. Bea tried not to be resentful but it was hardly flattering to sit beside an attractive man whose only topic of conversation was another woman. She decided to ring her sister and suggest they go to a matinee at the Orpheum.

'Stand up straight!' commanded Madame du Val. Desirée did as she was told. Madame reached for the spectacles that hung around her neck and put them on to her nose. Bet she takes a lorgnette to the theatre, thought Desirée, as nimble fingers began to stick pins into the back of her peach silk dupion dress to make figure-forming darts. Then she was helped on to the table, so that the hemline could be measured to make it even. She feared that her head might touch the ceiling. It didn't, but she was eye-level with the Bohemia crystal chandelier. She concentrated on its filigreed branches, fanciful floral arrangements and clusters of teardrops in an effort not to feel giddy. All she could think was, What am I doing here?

Hazel was at the sewing machine when she heard Stella's high heels clattering up the front steps, then her voice calling, 'I'm home!'

'I'm in the sunroom,' Hazel yelled back. 'Give us a squiz at your hairdo!' She was biting a piece of thread when Stella presented herself, so she removed it and said, 'Show us the back.' Stella turned around so that her hair swung out in a natural way and bounced back into place.

'You happy with it?' asked Hazel carefully.

'Yeah, I think so. What do you think?'

'It's very nice.' Hazel felt disappointed but she tried not to show it. She'd expected striking results from that expensive city hairdresser instead of something so . . . plain. But she smiled, held up a length of green-and-mauve floral cretonne and said, 'New bedroom curtains.' She put her half-done work aside and stood up. 'You must be famished, darl. I'll get us some lunch.'

In the kitchen, Hazel made mayonnaise from salt, vinegar and mustard added to half a tin of sweetened condensed milk, while Stella put slices of Devon sausage, tomato, cucumber, beetroot and chunks of iceberg lettuce on two plates. Hazel cut two thick slices off half a loaf of white bread and put one on the side of each plate. She placed a tub of margarine on the table.

The two women sat at the kitchen table in silence for a few mouthfuls before Hazel put down her knife and fork and said, 'There's something I want to talk to you about, love.'

She hates my hairdo, thought Stella.

'Roy wants to move in.' The look on Hazel's face was both sheepish and pleading.

'What, here?' Stella was taken aback. She wasn't really surprised but she'd hoped that somehow he'd disappear. Buzz off, like her father.

'Yes, here,' Hazel laughed. 'Where'd you think?'

'You mean you're getting married?'

Hazel looked at Stella helplessly. 'I'm already married, Stella, you know that.'

'Yes, but you could divorce him.'

'If I knew where he was.' She picked up her knife and fork and used them to detach the inedible strip around a slice of Devon and put it on the side of her plate. 'Anyway, he's married too.'

'Roy's married?'

'She was no good. He kicked her out. He caught her on the couch with his brother. Middle of the afternoon . . .'

Hazel started to go into a lot of detail about Roy's ex wife, the brazen hussy who'd done him wrong, and the unspeakable brother who'd cuckolded him while they thought he was at work. But they hadn't banked on the weather turning bad, had they? He got home early. Stella knew her mother was trying to elicit sympathy for him but she didn't want to hear. She mistrusted Roy, couldn't bring herself to believe anything he said. He was just a blatherskite.

'You'd be his de facto,' she cut in, silencing her mother. The only place Stella had seen the term was in *Truth*, the Sunday tabloid that traded in scandal. Like many other people at the time, she associated an unmarried couple living together with low life and squalor.

'That's nobody else's business,' said Hazel with indignation that was a cover for her guilt. 'Anyway, who's to know we're not married?'

'Everyone. They'd talk about you behind your back.'

Hazel started to sniffle and fumble for her hankie. She blew her nose. 'One day you'll understand. A woman needs a man around. Roy's got a regular job and he's a decent man. I'd be a fool to let him go.'

'Then I'm the one who'll have to go.' Stella stood up and took her empty plate to the sink. She'd been handed a perfect excuse to do exactly what she wanted.

'Don't be like that, Stella.' Hazel got up too and put her arms around her daughter. 'We've stood by each other all this time. You should be happy for me.'

'I am,' said Stella, returning her mother's embrace and beginning to shed crocodile tears. 'But it's so embarrassing to have a mother who's living in sin.'

Chapter 13

'Guy tells me you had a win last week,' said Freddie. Schedules permitting, Bea joined him in his office about once a week for an informal rundown of work and gossip. This Monday morning happened to be convenient for both of them.

'Let's hope so. Cross fingers we can get the rights to the music.' As Bea sat on the sofa facing the corkboard behind his desk she noticed a new Marlboro Man poster pinned there. Freddie had a friend at Leo Burnett in Chicago who shared his tastes. As though paying his respects to the poster, Freddie flipped open the Marlboro pack on the coffee table and offered it to her before taking a cigarette for himself. It occurred to her that all he needed was a ten-gallon hat, and maybe two weeks of drying out at a clinic, to look like the cowboy of his dreams.

'I want to talk to you about Lustrée,' Bea said, as she fitted the cigarette into her Monday-to-Friday holder, the one in tortoiseshell. She kept the ebony and ivory ones for after dark.

Freddie made an elegant stop sign with his hand. 'That's just what I wanted to talk to you about. Client has changed his mind.'

'Again?'

'Instead of pushing the shampoo, he wants us to do a campaign for the new hair colour.'

'What, and do nothing to promote the shampoo?'

'It's now well established. They can do special offers and gondola ends at point-of-sale. That's all it needs to keep its market share.'

So much for Tania Verstak. Bea knew she'd have to file that idea in the waste basket, often the depository of the best ideas in advertising, in her experience. Tania Verstak's beautiful hair had never been touched by artificial colouring. Besides, Bea would not dream of approaching a lady of her integrity and stature to endorse a hair dye.

'Maybe Stella can come up with some ideas,' said Freddie. 'Did you see her new hairdo this morning? Quite classy.' He sounded genuinely impressed, as he ran a hand through his own well-kept mane. 'I knew you'd be a good influence on her. How's she doing, by the way, with the work, I mean?'

Bea was tempted to tell him that Stella's contribution to the creative process had been zilch so far and that she had worries about her values. But she knew that would be unkind and possibly unfair, so she made do with, 'It's a bit too soon to say.'

On the way back to her office, Bea took notice of Stella's new hairstyle and complimented her. If she got rid of those shoes and wore something plain instead of afloat with flowers she could turn heads. With Gary now happily writing a humorous script for the Bonny Baby Bloopers trade film, she asked Stella to step into her office and gave her a brief on the new campaign for Lustrée.

Late on Tuesday morning Stella knocked on Bea's door.

'I've got two ideas,' she said, tucking her hair behind an ear in a gesture reminiscent of Desi. She sat down and opened the small notebook she had lately begun carrying with her everywhere. She cleared her throat, and gave a little cough. 'Pardon me,' she said, touching her mouth delicately with her immaculate fingertips. 'The first idea is designed to overcome any worry the consumer might have about her hair looking dyed.'

'Good,' said Bea, hopefully.

'The headline goes, "Surely She Doesn't Do It? Ask her Hairdresser."'

It was so obviously borrowed from Shirley Polykoff's smash-hit campaign, 'Does she or doesn't she? Hair colour so natural, only her hairdresser knows for sure' for Clairol, that it left Bea momentarily speechless. Clearly, her lesson on the pitfalls of plagiarism had not been understood.

Because she was at a loss about what to say, Bea just murmured, 'Go on,' so Stella offered her next headline: 'This one positions the product in the luxury category. "Any woman who pays 4/6d for a hair dye ought to have her head examined."'

It was another rip-off. Bea had been in London when Mavis Chamberlain won an award for her brilliant headline, 'Any woman who pays 11/6d for a pair of stockings ought to have her legs examined.' She tried to remain calm.

'Stella,' Bea said at last. 'Do you remember our conversation about plagiarism?'

Stella screwed up her face in a frantic, mirthless smile. 'Yes, but these words are not the same as those other ads.'

'Not identical, no. But so heavily influenced it's glaringly apparent. Anyone in advertising would recognise the origins immediately.'

'But we're not advertising to them. We're advertising to ordinary people. They wouldn't recognise them.'

Bea was exasperated. 'That is not the point.'

'What *is* the point?' Stella's right eyelid began to twitch.

'We ourselves would know those ideas were borrowed. And the whole industry would know. We'd lose our integrity and everyone else's respect.'

The look on Stella's face had turned sullen. Bea knew she'd have to guide her through the process of trying to think creatively or she'd never get anything useful out of her.

'Get your bag, Stella. We're going out to lunch.'

The look on Stella's face turned to childish delight. 'Beppi's?'

Bea laughed at the audacity of it. 'Not quite so special. I was thinking of the Hellenic Club.' She resisted adding, 'We'll keep Beppi's until you come up with something original.'

A dish of lamb with okra and two glasses of retsina were successful in relaxing the tension between them. Back in the office they started brainstorming, once Stella had been persuaded to put other advertising campaigns out of her mind and grapple with the question of how to draw attention to the brand so that women might be persuaded to try it.

After a few false starts that read more like a strategic plan than a persuasive expression of it, Bea said, 'What about playing round with "it's to dye for"? You know, d-y-e instead of d-i-e.'

'You mean Lustrée is to d-y-e for?'

'Something like that. Maybe, "Hair by Lustrée? It's to dye for."' She scribbled the lines on the notepad in front of her, studied them, then shook her head and sighed. 'Dye is a problem.'

'Dye is a problem?' echoed Stella.

'Negative connotations. Dyeing implies something crude and obvious.' She grinned guiltily and whispered, 'Like Jacques!' They both giggled and Bea continued, serious again. 'Bottle blondes. Peroxide. Women who colour their hair don't want anybody to think they're dyeing it.'

'But they are.'

'Of course they are, but it's not in the interests of our product to dwell on reality. We're selling a dream. It's the same when we write strategies. We don't talk of problems. We talk of challenges. Euphemisms are our business.'

They sat in glum silence for a few minutes. Bea lit a cigarette. 'What they want is their natural colour back again. Their youth, I suppose.' The thought made her feel morose.

'Back to nature?' offered Stella.

'That sounds like a vegetarian in a nudist colony. I was thinking of something else. What about, "The colour nature intended."'

'Sounds okay.'

'We show a woman looking worried about a few grey hairs, and copy goes, "What's the difference between the age you are and the age you want to be?" and we show the same woman smiling, looking much younger, with gorgeous thick glossy hair and no sign of grey in it. And the tagline is, "Lustrée, the colour nature intended." Why don't we see what the art department can do with that? Let's ask Jacques to get in a few composites and do a mock-up.'

'Composites?'

'Composite photographs. Models have them, several photographs of themselves printed together on one sheet to show how they look on camera in different moods and roles. Then he can do a mock-up ad to show Freddie.'

Jacques was summoned. Of the three layouts he roughed out that afternoon, the one Bea decided to take to Freddie showed before-and-after head shots of a woman: first looking grey-haired and dowdy, and her transformation into a glamorous brunette with incredibly thick and glossy locks without a grey hair in sight.

The three of them trooped into Freddie's office the next morning to present the idea. When he said he loved it, Bea generously shared the credit with Stella, as well as Jacques, although Stella's only real contribution was a few words of body copy that had to be revised by Bea before they could be presented.

On the train home that evening, Stella felt that she had made progress at last, given that Bea had treated her like an equal instead of a junior by inviting her to lunch and paying the bill. Stella also convinced herself that she was satisfied with the work she had done. In fact, in her mind the importance of her creative effort grew with every stop from Sydenham to Miranda, so that when she got off the train she had done the whole thing single-handedly.

As she walked home from the station her thoughts turned to Roy, who was due to move in on the following Saturday to live in sin thereafter with her mother. She had to find a flat of her own, if she could afford it. Otherwise, one she could share with a girl her own age.

With Roy's impending arrival had come an unexpected and beneficial side effect for Stella: Hazel was so consumed with guilt, she'd applied herself tirelessly to turning the navy blue gabardine Stella had bought at McDowell's into an outfit similar to the one worn by Jean Shrimpton in the *Vogue* photograph. Such extraordinary care had been taken in the cutting, tacking, stitching, pressing and finishing of it that it could almost have come from Desi's couturière. With her next pay, Stella planned to settle her lay-by on a pair of navy-and-white pumps at Farmers. Head to toe, she would be a new woman, risen at least one class—more likely two, she thought—on the social scale. All she needed was an address to match.

Chapter 14

Word that Stella Bolt was looking for a flat went around the agency without prompting any response except for a snide one from Kelvin. He sauntered up to her desk one afternoon to whisper that a lady named Tilly Devine had a spare room in her house at Palmer Street, Woolloomooloo.

'Ha, ha, very funny,' countered Stella, who knew about the notorious brothel-keeper because for decades *Truth* had chronicled her every altercation with the police. She looked at him with contempt. His eyes were so guarded, she couldn't tell what colour they were. 'You'll keep,' she said haughtily before turning to her typewriter and the list of names she'd been thinking up for a new spray-on furniture polish to compete with Mr Sheen. All she had so far were Mrs Glow, Mr Polish, ShineO and WaxEasy.

Towards the end of the week, Bea had some good news. A couple she'd been friendly with in London were moving into a rundown terrace house in Underwood Street, Paddington. To help with the mortgage they needed a tenant for a small self-contained flat downstairs at the back.

'Paddington?' queried Stella. 'Isn't it a bit . . . you know . . .' Stella desperately wanted to be able to tell people she lived in Double Bay or Bellevue Hill.

'Seedy, you mean?'

'Well, yeah.'

'It's changing. Artists and writers are moving in. It's starting to become quite smart, in a European way. These people are in the theatre. They're interesting. You'd be quite safe with them.'

When Stella told Hazel, she was in the laundry dumping wet clothes from the Hoovermatic into a plastic basket ready to be taken out to the Hills hoist. Her mother paused, horrified. 'Paddington?' she screeched. 'It's a slum! Why in the world would you want to live there?'

'You don't understand. Paddington is very smart now. It's avant-garde.' Stella had been impressed when she heard Jacques use the term in relation to design.

'I don't care if it's Avon calling,' said Hazel, oblivious of her own wit. 'I won't have my daughter living in a slum.'

That fixed it. Stella had been in doubt, but the ferocity of Hazel's reaction made her determined to take the flat. Defying her mother was a way of inflicting further punishment on her. 'Look who's talking,' said Stella, loftily. 'If you're prepared to live in adultery, who are you to tell me I can't live in Paddington?'

* * *

At the first chords from the organ in St Mark's Darling Point, the congregation rose from pews adorned with November lilies and satin bows, and turned to watch a flower girl and pageboy scatter rose petals on the carpet in front of the bride, on the arm of her father, as she started her measured walk up the aisle to the altar. Everybody agreed that Fern looked radiant in white Duchesse satin. And wasn't it a charming idea to have each of the bridesmaids in a different pastel shade?

The reception for a hundred and sixty took place under a marquee in the garden of the bride's home at Wolseley Road, Point Piper. To add to the magic, the night was clear, the moon was almost full and the bottles of Veuve Clicquot never stopped popping. Dancing with Tom on a temporary floor built over the swimming pool and under a spell that persuaded her that he was her destiny, Desirée agreed to set the date of their wedding. 'April,' she whispered in his ear. 'In that case,' Tom said, running his hand up and down her back, 'let's go to Paris for our honeymoon.'

As the festivities drew to a close, Desirée caught the bride's bouquet. It would have been odd if she hadn't; the reach that made her a formidable tennis player gave her an advantage over the other bridesmaids. As she held it up in jubilation she saw, by the mixture of triumph and tenderness on her father's face, that Tom must have told him. She'd pleased him at last.

Later, when it was all over, she and Tom went skinny-dipping in the pool at his place after his parents had gone to bed. In the cabana afterwards, they went All The Way. When he started to withdraw just before they climaxed Desirée tightened her grip on him. 'It's okay,' she said. 'I'm on the pill.'

* * *

'He doesn't have to,' protested Stella. 'I can get there on my own.'

'It was his idea. He wants to help,' Hazel insisted. She hovered around Stella trying to make herself useful and getting in the way as she watched her pack the last of her things in the suitcase. Stella felt like swatting her, like she would a mozzie. A tidy little pile of panties and four linen handkerchiefs with an S embroidered on them were on top as the lid closed and the locks clicked into place. 'Anyway, I want to see what you're getting yourself into.'

Stella was in turmoil about Roy moving her and her belongings into her new flat in Underwood Street on Saturday afternoon. The upside was that she could take everything together—her six LPs, ten books, Marilyn Monroe and James Dean posters, Martin Boyd wall plate, Chianti-bottle lamp with a raffia shade—instead of making trips by public transport over several days. The downside was that she hated the idea of the arty couple who owned the house meeting anyone—even her mother—from the life she was trying to shrug off. Her landlord and landlady were from another demographic (a term she'd learnt at the agency). That was clear from the vehicle they drove. Them with their red Fiat Topolino. Him with his old fawn ute. Worlds apart.

In the end she gave in, hoping the two diverse groups would not collide at the front door. She was in luck. They must have gone out. Stella led Hazel and Roy—all of them bearing her chattels—down the narrow hallway to the back of the house.

When she opened the door to her bed-sitter, it was so dark she had to pull the cord that turned on the overhead light.

Hazel lowered the carton she was carrying on to the bare floorboards and looked around. She noted the divan, the trestle table, the three mismatched chairs and a wardrobe that she could tell had been made of plywood by some ham-fisted amateur carpenter. Fortunately, she did not see the two mice sniffing nervously around the stove in the kitchen; they'd disappeared behind it by the time she did an inspection.

'I should've brought the Handy Andy,' was all she said when she looked at the shabby bathroom, and made a note to buy Stella a pink shag-pile toilet-seat cover and matching mat as a housewarming present.

'Well,' said Roy in the main room. 'You've got a nice little set-up here, girlie.'

'I think so,' she said, although she thought the place looked a bit forlorn considering the dazzling sunshine outside. She was grateful for Roy's positive words even if the reason he said them was because he didn't want her changing her mind and going back to Miranda to spoil the cosy little arrangement he'd made with her mother.

He opened the back door and surveyed the cement courtyard. A round-topped metal table with chipped green paint and two rusted chairs huddled in a corner. 'Southerly aspect,' he said. 'You won't get much sun in here. Nice old loquat tree there but you'll be lucky if it bears fruit without the sun. You'll have to watch that morning glory.'

All of a sudden he'd become an expert in botany and it irritated Stella. 'Thanks for your help,' she said, hoping he'd take the hint and start making tracks. Her mother was opening and closing drawers and cupboard doors in the kitchen. 'You'll need an egg-timer and a vegetable-peeler,' called Hazel. Then she let out a piercing scream.

'What's up?' Roy rushed into the kitchen.

'Cockroach!' she screeched. 'There!'

'Where?'

'It went under there.'

'Don't worry about it, Mum.' The kitchen was too small for three people to fit into without a squeeze, so Stella chose to stand in the doorway. She was almost as sickened as her mother by the idea of crawling insects in the kitchen but she didn't want to show it.

'Come on, Haze,' said Roy. 'It won't hurt you. A bit of DDT'll fix it.' He looked in the cupboard under the sink. 'Nothing useful in there. You better get something when the shops open on Monday.'

'It's getting late, Mum,' said Stella.

'Yes.' Hazel looked at her marcasite watch. 'It's going on four. I suppose we'd better be getting along.'

Stella saw them off at the front gate. 'Don't leave any food out, will you?' Hazel instructed. 'They're filthy things.'

'Yes, Mum.'

'And give me a tingle and let me know when you're coming over for tea.'

'I will, Mum.'

They hugged for a few moments. Roy insisted on giving her a kiss, so she presented her cheek like a good little girl. With relief, she waved as the ute coughed into action and started rattling up the road. She took a Kleenex from her sleeve and wiped her cheek. Then she went inside and skipped merrily down the hall.

'Where's your ring?' was the first question Bea asked when she met Desi in the washroom on Monday. 'You haven't . . . ?'

'Broken it off?' laughed Desi, pulling at the roll of huckaback hanging from a container on the wall and wiping her hands on it. 'No.' She turned to study Bea, who was patting the colour on her lips with a tissue and applying another glossy layer of Revlon Poison Apple. 'Quite the opposite. I've just left it in safekeeping at home.'

Bea finished the paint job, checked her teeth in the mirror and put the lipstick back in her make-up pouch. She noticed for the first time that Desi had a self-conscious grin on her face and her eyes were clear and unusually bright. 'You've named the date.'

'April.'

'You're sure about him?'

'Absolutely.'

Bea reached up to put her arms around her friend so Desi had to stoop to receive the embrace. 'I'm so happy for you! What happened?'

At the sound of flushing in one of the cubicles, Desi said, 'Let's have a drink after work and I'll tell all.'

'Can't wait,' said Bea.

At the production meeting for Taranto Spaghetti later in the morning, Freddie was quick to notice. 'What's with the naked finger, darling? You haven't lost it, have you?'

'Not the ring, no,' said Desi, her face impassive.

'Your handsome fiancé?'

'Not him, either.'

'Drat,' joked Freddie. Then he turned to Lavinia and the work in hand. 'Have we found an eye-tie presenter yet?'

'Perhaps she wants to be seen to be available,' said Jacques when Stella, returning magazines to his shelves, told him that Desi wasn't wearing her engagement ring.

Stella pondered his words. 'You mean she wants other men to think she's unattached?'

Jacques was lining up a photograph with a T square. 'Why not? She is a woman of the world.'

'But she's engaged.'

'Is she?' He sliced a quarter of an inch off the print cleanly with a stanley knife. 'Still?'

Imagine giving back a ring like that, thought Stella, returning to her desk. Not in a million years. No woman would turn down a man as rich and handsome as her fiancé was supposed to be. He must have thrown her over.

At the screening of the first rough-cut Bonny Baby Food commercials at Rod Webb's studio that afternoon, not a word was said about the absence of the ring from Desi's finger.

'Desi's fiancé's broken off the engagement,' Kelvin confided to Miss Leonie Braithwaite, the chairman's secretary, at the end of the day. 'She had to give the knuckleduster back.'

'What made you change your mind?' The sugary rim of Bea's brandy crusta glass left a sweet taste on her lips.

Desi twirled the cucumber rind in her tumbler of Pimm's and ice cubes rattled against the glass. 'I know it must seem sudden to you but . . .' She took a sip and put the glass back on its coaster. The Hotel Australia's palm-court orchestra was playing 'Smoke Gets In Your Eyes'. 'I suppose I was swept up in the excitement of it. Fee's wedding, I mean. It was magical.

Like a dream come true. And I felt comforted by all that love and goodwill. I wondered afterwards why I've been struggling against the inevitable.'

Bea dearly wanted to be convinced but she couldn't help feeling that Desi was deluding herself. Her change of heart had happened too hastily. Bea was familiar with the feelings that follow a fulfilling sexual encounter; you were left replete and at peace. But that blissful state of grace was fleeting. You couldn't build a life together on that alone.

'Are you in love with him?' Bea knew it was not her place to probe but she couldn't help it. She didn't want Desi to make a mistake.

'In love?' The question seemed to have surprised her. 'Well . . . I love Tom. I don't know that there's much difference.'

'Oh, yes,' said Bea. 'There is. A big difference.'

Chapter 15

A fortnight after she moved into her flat, Stella wore her new gabardine suit with the navy-and-white pumps to the office for the first time. As she left the lift and walked past the typing pool and through the art department, eyes flicked up from typewriters and drawing boards. She heard a wolf whistle but pretended she hadn't. By the time she reached her desk she believed she knew how thrilled Suzy Parker must feel every time she saw her picture on the cover of *Life* or *Vogue*.

Her snappy new appearance was not only a tribute to Friday, it was a calculated effort to make an impact at a meeting of all creative, television and account-service staff in the boardroom to view a reel of current US commercials sent by the agency's affiliate in New York. At such times, chairs were lined up in rows facing a screen and the boardroom became an improvised theatre.

As Stella entered through the door to the right of the screen just before 4.30 that afternoon, Jacques waved at her from the back row. At the same time, Guy in the second row beckoned her to the seat beside him. She hesitated, loving the opportunity to spend a few moments being conspicuous, in full view of three dozen pairs of eyes, as she smiled to acknowledge the greetings. Then she took a seat beside Freddie in the front row.

They watched the inevitable brilliance from Doyle Dane Bernbach for Volkswagen followed by a lot of sunny-faced WASP types rhapsodising over Pepsi, Coca-Cola, Canada Dry, Chevrolet, Kodak, Schlitz, Pontiac and Lucky Strike. The newly re-packaged Stella felt quite up to the standard of the images projected on the screen.

When it was over, Freddie stood up to make a speech. He said he was sure they all joined him in thanking Spender Fisk Morgenstern, their associate agency in the States, for the opportunity to view the commercials. He said that, purpose-wise, the show was not to invite comparison but to stimulate everyone's creative juices. He pointed out two cases where a mnemonic device had been used in connection with a product name. That, and the rest of what he said, meant little to Stella whose attention was taken by a snatch of muttered dialogue from a writer from Dan Barnes's group who was sitting behind her: 'Verbal diarrhea, that's always been this dude's problem . . .'

After Freddie, Guy felt compelled to endear himself to the writers and art directors by adding his own few words. 'Creative-wise,' he said, 'though we're not the biggest, we can compete with the best of them. At this point in time, I just want to encourage you to feel comfortable about running your ideas up the flagpole in my office—or in Freddie's—any day to see if anyone salutes them.'

A few pairs of hands flapped together, Stella's among them, to express appreciation of their words. There was a general stirring, as most people got to their feet and hung around pretending to discuss what they had seen. In truth, they were waiting for the bar to open.

'It's not that we don't have great ideas,' Dan Barnes, a middy of Reschs Pilsener in his fist, said to Bea. 'It's that we don't have clients with the brains to recognise them. Or the guts to go with them.' He was a straight-talker, chunkily built like the Land Rovers he used to sell, his overall colouring speckled and rusty-looking. He looked secondhand.

'Couldn't agree more,' said Bea. 'We've just presented an integrated campaign to Crop-O-Corn and they're watering it down already.'

'How come?'

'Oh,' she said, regretting having raised the subject. She was still smarting from the morning's presentation, and revisiting it was the last thing she wanted. 'They went for the middle-of-the-road pack design instead of the brilliant one. And they thought the TV commercial for the youth market was immoral.'

'Hey!' Dan was impressed. 'Who wrote it, you?' His look was lascivious. She was divorced, after all. Damaged goods.

'It was a group effort.'

'Yeah, well, just what I was saying. No-hopers. Specially the product managers with their marketing books. We had a victory on Tuesday, though . . .'

Bea didn't like the way he was looking at her. Nor did she want to hear him crow about his triumph, but she was caught in her own trap, so she took as big a mouthful of wine as was thought appropriate for a woman and turned her face towards him, hoping that her attempt to show interest seemed genuine without being taken the wrong way.

She hadn't bargained on being given a long-winded history lesson on car tyres. By the time he got to the racing slick she was a desperate woman. Out of the corner of her eye she noticed Gary slouching near the refrigerator with Kelvin.

'Boys!' she called, and waved in their direction. 'Come and listen to this. You'll be fascinated by what Dan has to say.' As they dawdled over, she turned to Dan. 'I'm sorry to interrupt, but you're so knowledgeable and they have so much to learn.'

A few minutes later, she was able to extricate herself without his seeming to notice. By then he had the two juniors mesmerised as he took them on an imaginary Formula One race at Brands Hatch with Jack Brabham.

'Could I borrow the reel for a day, do you think?' Desi asked Freddie. 'I'd like to show it to the boys at Rod Webb.'

'Sure,' he said. He made a point of staring at her left hand and pretending to be surprised. 'I see you got your ring back.'

'Tom's picking me up after work. He is not happy if he sees my finger unadorned.'

'I'm not surprised. You got the guys a bit excited.'

She laughed. 'You're pulling my leg, Freddie.'

He smiled and moved away to spread his charm around. As he was about to pass Stella, in a huddle with Jacques, he stopped when he heard her say, 'What a shame.' Jacques had a gloomy look on his face.

'Cheer up, Jack,' said Freddie, patting the Frenchman's shoulder and making him even more irritable. 'We had a win with the middle pack. We can use the music, as long as they've got the squillions to pay for it. And they liked the overall television campaign. That youth-market spot will work just as well on radio as it would on television, without offending anybody.'

'Yes,' said Jacques glumly. 'A compromise all round.'

'That's the name of the game,' said Freddie. He turned to Stella and looked her up and down. 'Well, you are a sight for sore eyes. All dressed up for Friday night on the town?'

It crossed her mind to pretend to be going somewhere exciting, but she lost her nerve when she couldn't make up the details quickly enough. She looked down, flicked a non-existent speck off her skirt, then tucked a lock of hair behind her ear and said, 'Not really. I need an early night.'

'Nonsense. Why don't we show her off, Jack? Let me take you both to dinner at Attilio's.' He looked around the room for Bea but she was gone.

Stella had never been the life of the party before that evening. As they descended to the softly lit cellar she more than shone, she positively scintillated in the candlelight. The head waiter made a fuss and referred to her as 'la bella signorina' and the other waiters stopped what they were doing to watch. Her stylish appearance, the luxury of being taken to a sophisticated restaurant by two attractive men (even though one was what Roy would have called a 'poofter') was exciting enough. But added to it was the secret pleasure of knowing that Bea and Jacques were downcast. She'd never heard the word Schadenfreude but she certainly knew how it felt.

Little by little, Jacques began to find her high spirits infectious. After the oysters (mornay for her, au naturel for him, kilpatrick for Freddie) he asked her to dance and they took a turn around the little polished floor. 'Your song, Étoile,' he crooned in her ear and she realised the band was playing 'Stardust'. His proximity, together with the wine she'd been sipping, was intoxicating until his right hand slid just a bit too far down her back for decency, so she pulled away and they sat down again.

Whether Jacques was offended by her prudish reaction or suddenly bored with the company was anybody's guess, but he became sullen again. As soon as he'd consumed his veal parmigiana—Freddie was yet to finish his steak valdostana and Stella was only halfway through her Hawaiian ham—he said he had to leave because he was expecting a telephone call from his mother in Paris.

After his exaggeratedly polite thanks and apologies, they watched him disappear up the stairs to the street. 'That's the lamest excuse I've ever heard,' said Freddie, picking up his knife and fork again. 'What did you say to him on the dance floor?'

'Nothing,' said Stella. 'I didn't say a thing.' Surely Freddie must have seen him feeling her bottom?

Alone with her, Freddie felt slightly alarmed. Did she expect him to make a pass at her, like Jacques had done on the dance floor? Freddie was unaware that his homosexuality was apparent to most people, including someone as unworldly as Stella. Although his face was quite rugged-looking, there was something about the pitch of his voice, his fluid hand movements and the loose-hipped way he walked that did not conform to the standard image of masculinity. He told himself to relax. Being her boss was a useful cover because it would be inappropriate for a man in his position to take advantage of her.

What he did have was an obligation to amuse her, or at least capture her interest, so he reverted to the tried-and-true technique of asking her about herself and giving her his full attention. First of all, he ordered crêpes suzette, guaranteed to surprise her when the dessert was flambéed beside their table.

When the novelty of the blaze had passed, he asked, 'How are you finding things at the office, Stella?'

'Oh, I love being a copywriter,' she said, slicing the pancake with her fork. 'It's so challenging, and everyone is so interesting.'

'How are you getting along with Bea?'

'She's wonderful. So clever and creative. I'm learning so much from her.' Her voice became hesitant. 'It's just that . . .' She paused, put down her fork and wiped her mouth delicately with the napkin.

'Just that what?' Freddie was alert, like a shark that senses blood in the water.

Stella cleared her throat and blinked several times. 'Sometimes I feel my ideas are not getting through.'

'You mean she's stifling you creatively?'

'I don't want to be ungrateful.' Her spark had fizzled out. She looked at him with a doleful expression that made him think of the way the Afghan hound he'd once owned eyed him when she wanted to go for a run. Stella, however, looked more like a fragile bird of some sort, nervy and ready to take flight.

'I'll have a word with her.'

'Oh, no, please don't do that.' She placed her hand on his arm, as though to restrain him from swiping an unseen enemy with a cutlass. It would be a disaster if he told on her. 'We get along so well and I wouldn't want to spoil it. I'm not complaining. I can manage.' Her right eye started to twitch.

'You're sure?'

'Yes. Absolutely. I am quite sure.'

He patted her hand. 'Okay, but let me know if you have any more problems.'

She smiled. 'You are so understanding,' she said. 'No wonder everybody admires you.'

'They do?' Freddie was so astonished he couldn't help showing his delight in her words.

'Oh, yes. They worship you.'

Chapter 16

Desi found it hard to unwind from the pressures of her work at the end of the week. In truth, she didn't want to. Putting a team of talented people together and smoothing the way for them to make their best efforts made her feel she was doing something worthwhile. From Monday, Kelvin was to begin a stint with her to learn about television production, and that meant a new kind of challenge for her in the role of teacher. Even showing the reel of American commercials to Werner, Rod and Darryl, and discussing them afterwards, was something she knew she would enjoy. Sometimes she felt that the weekend was a waste of time, an enforced break from what she really wanted to do.

Tom sensed that her mind was elsewhere when he picked her up outside the office on Friday evening, so he entertained her by telling her disparaging stories about his mother's eccentric elder brother as they drove out of the city to spend the weekend with him. Since inheriting the family seat near Exeter, Uncle Charlie had become a gentleman of leisure. Tom neither liked nor approved of him; he'd wangled this invitation to amuse Desi and divert her attention from the job that obsessed her in a way he considered unhealthy for a woman.

'Charlie is fond of croquet,' said Tom, as the MG sped down the Hume Highway with the hood down. Desi, who'd tied a scarf around her head to keep her hair under control, had to lean towards him so as not to lose the thread of the narrative. 'He also loves *Alice in Wonderland*,' continued Tom, 'so his croquet mallets are shaped like pink flamingos and the balls are like green hedgehogs.' He glanced at her to make sure she was amused. She was. 'That's why he is known in certain circles as either the Red Queen, or the Queen of Tarts.'

'I can't wait to meet him,' she said, shielding her eyes from the glare of the sun hovering above the horizon. 'Tell me more.'

'Well. Don't be surprised if he puts on a floor show after dinner.'

'What sort of floor show?'

'He has been known to play dress-ups with the cook and do a couple of numbers from *No, No, Nanette* or *The Desert Song*.'

'Do we have to . . . participate?'

'No, thank goodness. All we have to do is pay attention and clap like mad.'

'That's easy. I can do that.'

As they began the gentle climb to the Highlands, the scorched plains and the monotonous grey-green eucalypts of the bush gave way to ranks of statuesque cypress pines and fluttery poplars laced together by dense foliage that marked the boundaries of private estates. There was no indication of what lay behind these walls of vegetation except for names at the gates—Kennerton

Green, Bridgewater Lodge, Yokefleet, Eastdene—that translated as England in the Antipodes.

Tom stopped the car at a pair of gates with no identification, hopped over his door to open them, swung the car into the gravel driveway and repeated his action in the reverse. They drove for a few minutes along a corridor of enormous trees that Desi imagined were oaks or elms before an imposing house came into view. Every room seemed to be lit up, showing to advantage the splendour of the late Victorian architecture.

'What a fabulous location!' she said.

'Yes, it is well sited,' said Tom, as the car slowed down.

'I mean for a commercial.'

'It's the weekend, Dizzy. Can't you switch off?' There was irritation in his voice.

The engine died and before she had a chance to reply a pack of barking dogs streamed out of the house like theatre patrons at the sound of a fire alarm. Desi was suddenly looking into the noble eyes of a Great Dane. It was too dark for her to be able to count how many dogs were scampering around the car but there must have been six, at least, of varying shapes and sizes. Down the front steps of the house at a more leisurely pace came a handsome elderly man of good bearing dressed in a caftan.

Tom leaped out of the car and came around to her side to open the door. As she stepped out and before Tom could introduce her, Uncle Charlie exclaimed, 'Oh, my dear, you *are* a tall girl.' The remark reduced her to feeling like the sixteen-year-old she had been when a boy she was keen on rescued her from being a wallflower, then abandoned her in the middle of the dance floor when he realised she towered over him.

'Uncle Charlie, may I present my fiancée, Desirée Whittleford.'

'Oh, I know who you are, darling,' said Charlie, taking her hand and continuing to hold it. 'I hope you don't think me rude. But I could have used a statuesque beauty like you on the catwalk in 1947. You're too young to remember Dior's New Look, but you'd have carried it off to perfection.' For once in her life she was speechless. She had never thought herself beautiful and was not used to extravagant flattery.

'Charlie was in the fashion business,' offered Tom, taking their overnight bags from the car.

'The rag trade,' corrected Charlie, as they walked towards the house with their raggle-taggle canine retinue. 'We copied everything that came from Paris and put our label on it. Stop that, Bandit!' Ahead of them a Cairn Terrier was nipping playfully at Tom's heels.

In the bright light of the entrance hall Desi noticed subtle traces of make-up on Charlie's eyelids and cheeks. His vanity made him seem vulnerable. He looked at her affectionately and said, 'I used to dress your mother, you know. How is the lovely Bo?'

Desi found her voice. 'I didn't know that. She is well, so energetic she puts the rest of us to shame.' She thought it odd that her mother hadn't mentioned even knowing him.

'I'm the black sheep of the family,' Charlie explained. 'They keep me hidden away here so that I can't embarrass anybody. Isn't that so, Tom?'

Tom looked uncomfortable. 'Nonsense,' he said. 'Mother sends her love.'

They were allocated separate bedrooms on the first floor, which indicated to Desi that they were expected to behave with propriety under Charlie's roof. Once inside her quarters, however, she realised how false that first impression had been.

Their rooms were connected by a door—and it was open. She and Tom faced each other on either side of the doorway and burst out laughing.

On the following night, by the time they were sipping cognac by the open fire after the other dinner guests had gone home, Desi was so at ease she felt she'd known Charlie all her life. They'd spent Saturday morning trudging to a farm with some of the dogs to buy eggs and hear about local goings-on: something feral had raided a chicken coop; old George had fallen off the twig; the rabbits were getting out of hand; it looked like being a good year for stone fruit.

After lunch, they played at bashing wooden hedgehogs with fake flamingos and forgot to keep score. Later in the afternoon Desi was given the privilege of seeing Charlie's collection of French and Italian haute couture that included a 1930s chiffon evening gown by Madeleine Vionnet, a 1950s brightly patterned jersey chemise by Emilio Pucci and a pair of baroque velvet shoes made by Roger Vivier for Christian Dior. The fashion show was a bit too camp for Tom, who preferred to listen to the races on the wireless in the library.

Dressing for dinner—simply, because an abundance of finery was not regarded as appropriate in the country—Dizzy wondered if Charlie had a lover. It was clear that the story about his cavorting with the cook was a fairytale. His cook, who worked for him part-time, was a middle-aged woman living in nearby Exeter with her husband and four children.

Dizzy fastened a single row of small, perfectly matched pearls around her neck as she walked into Tom's room. He was sitting on the bed knotting his shoelaces.

'Perhaps we should bring Darryl next time,' she said, with a cheeky grin. 'Although, now I come to think of it . . . I think he has a significant other. In that case, maybe Freddie.'

'Who's Darryl?' He didn't look up.

'The cutter at Rod Webb. I told you about him at the Christmas party, remember?'

'Another faggot.'

Desi froze. 'What did you say?'

He got up and grabbed her, pushing her bottom against him so that she felt a hard bump in the vicinity of her crotch. 'Why are you so interested in queers? What's wrong with a real man?'

At first she thought he was joking but the look on his face was unfamiliar to her. His eyes were as hard and metallic as ball bearings. She wondered if he'd been drinking, but there was no smell of alcohol on his breath. Vodka, maybe? This was not the tolerant and even-tempered Tom she knew. She pulled away and he let her go. Neither of them said another word but tension remained between them for the rest of the evening.

Two other guests had been invited to dinner, an artist of minor renown who'd converted a local abandoned church into a studio, and his house guest, the elderly English widow of an Australian winemaker who'd inherited his vineyard in the Lower Hunter Valley. On the strength of a generous amount of very good semillon the widow had brought with her, the talk was lively and the company convivial until the subject of Blues Point Tower arose.

'Brutal,' pronounced the artist. 'The desecration of a wonderful site. I don't mind the new AMP Building. It's appropriate to have an office block at the Quay. But the other one . . . You're an architect, Tom, what do you think of Harry Seidler?'

Tom finished a mouthful of tarragon chicken. 'Well, I'm a modernist, myself. He's Bauhaus-trained, you know. I think we're fortunate to have him.'

'But it doesn't suit our heritage,' insisted the artist. 'We're not Chicago. It sticks out like dogs' balls.'

As though to illustrate the point, a Basset hound named Blob rolled on his back on a hassock in the corner of the room with his legs in the air.

The widow was delightfully unfazed by the language or the dog. 'I haven't seen the building. What is the fuss about?'

Charlie needed an excuse to try to head off a possible altercation, so he seized the moment to take over the conversation and enlighten her. 'A gracious colonial stone house on McMahons Point was demolished to make way for the tallest apartment block in Sydney. It has polarised opinion. The romantics versus the modernists.'

'I remember that house,' said Desi. 'We often passed it in the boat. When I was young I dreamed of living there. Amazing aspect.' She thought about its panoramic views on three sides, the old stables and the row of terrace houses beside it. At least the Moreton Bay fig trees had been spared. Some, anyway.

Tom wanted to kick her ankle under the table or say something demeaning but he'd been brought up to be polite, at least in public. He counted to ten in his head before turning to her with a superior smile. 'My dear Dizzy, your pretty little head should not concern itself with anything more serious than a baby food commercial.'

Desi felt her face turning red and tried to hide it by studying her plate, as Tom addressed the others in a more serious tone. 'Sydney's population is growing and at some point we'll have to stop the suburban sprawl before it reaches the Blue Mountains. The only way to do that is to build up, not out.

'Australians will never live in high-rise flats,' said the artist. 'We're people of the land. We like a patch of dirt.' He took a great gulp of wine and Desi noticed the grime under his ragged fingernails. 'In any case, we have to stop tearing up our past. Next thing they'll be turning the whole foreshore into downtown Manhattan. On this magnificent harbour? In this climate?' He was starting to bluster. His ruddy face was getting redder as he continued. 'There's talk of tearing down our solid old buildings, the ones with load-bearing walls, and replacing them with skeletal structures with flimsy facades, all show and no substance.'

'We will soon have an opera house that will astonish the world,' said Tom.

'Soon? Never!' said the artist. 'It's too advanced for the petty officials in charge of it. It'll never be finished. A gigantic white elephant.'

Desi admired his passion and she felt sorry for him. He had sensibility and heart but they were no match for Tom's analytic mind, his powers of reasoning, his intimidating logic. 'I know what you mean,' she said. 'It would be a shame to lose our heritage. Lovely old sandstone houses with wide verandahs all round. Rain on a tin roof. The smell of gum leaves.' She'd had no real opinion about it before but she was beginning to have one now.

'More than a shame,' said the artist. 'A national disgrace.'

'Let us count our blessings for the space we have here,' intoned the widow, 'and let the city destroy itself, if it must.' She sighed and looked self-satisfied, like a little Pekingese after a good dinner.

'Do you have a hand in making this delicious wine yourself?' Desi asked the widow. They were now sipping sauternes with the apple crumble. Charlie could have kissed her for braving Tom's appalling put-down and shifting the attention from architecture.

'Oh, no, dear. We have winemakers to do that. I stay in the background.'

'But you run the company?'

'In a way. My accountant runs it for me.'

'Then you're a tycoon!'

'Desirée is a career woman, too,' announced Charlie. 'Television. She's a big-time producer.'

'No, no! I'm a small-time producer of television commercials.'

'Goodness, how advanced of you,' said the widow. She turned to Tom. 'You must be so proud of her.'

'Yes,' he said, avoiding Desi's eye.

It was almost three o'clock and the other guests had long gone by the time they said goodnight to Charlie and climbed the stairs. They'd eaten, drunk and said so much, all they wanted to do was sleep it off—in their separate bedrooms.

Tom must have joined her at some time in the early hours, Desi thought with relief, when she stirred and felt the body stretched out beside her. She turned over, put her arm around him and felt a hairy rib cage. It was the Great Dane. It lifted its head, let it fall back on the pillow and went back to sleep. A lump at the foot of the bed turned out to be a black-and-tan Welsh Terrier. It got up, wagged its tail and padded towards her over the bedclothes to give her face a whiskery lick.

Charlie, wearing jeans and a T-shirt—and no make-up—was in the kitchen when Desi went looking for coffee at about eleven.

'French toast is very restorative,' he said, dipping bread into a milky mixture and sizzling it on the griddle of the Aga. 'It's a bit early for a Bloody Mary.' He kissed her on the cheek and she sat on a tall stool at the bar to watch him.

They talked about the evening, recalling a few funny moments and sharing observations about the artist, the widow, the food and the wine. 'How's Tom this morning?' said Charlie, pouring the coffee.

'Still asleep. I think.' She knew she'd have to make amends with Tom as soon as he surfaced. She couldn't help feeling a bit hurt that he hadn't come into her bed. She was too proud—stubborn, more like it—to go to his. The old doubts were beginning to return.

'There's something I want you to think about,' said Charlie. She noticed that he was left-handed and there was a plain gold band on the third finger. 'I don't know what your wedding plans are, but if you'd like to have the reception here, I would be delighted.'

She was too surprised to say anything more than, 'Oh, Charlie, I . . .'

'Talk it over with Tom. I'd be happy to discuss it with Bo and your father, if you like the idea. There's a very pretty old Anglican church in Exeter. Perfect setting for photographs.'

A quiet wedding was what Desi really wanted but she knew that her wishes were secondary to those of her tribe; they were set on a big celebration. That being so, why not here? There was something charming and unpretentious about a country wedding and the old-established deciduous trees in the garden would be ablaze with colour in autumn.

'Ah, coffee.' Tom appeared, looking a bit rumpled, with three dogs in his wake. He gave Desi an obligatory kiss on the cheek and sat on a stool beside her. 'I have a confession to make. I have slept with someone else. More than one.'

'So have I,' she said. 'What breed were yours?'

He laughed. 'You're trying to upstage me. A Cairn Terrier. And two I couldn't identify.'

'That will be Mutt and Jeff,' said Charlie. 'Siblings of an indiscretion by Bandit.'

Alone with Desi in the rose garden afterwards, Tom put his arms around her. 'We mustn't quarrel,' he said. It was as close to an apology as he could manage. They were both hung-over and subdued, grateful not to have to engage in combat, except that he did feel the need to say, 'And I hope that next time there's a discussion about architecture, you'll be on my side of the argument.'

My role in his life is to agree with him, Desi thought. What if I don't? Although the idea made her uneasy, she didn't have the energy or the inclination to provoke him, so she let it pass. To keep the peace.

Motoring back to the city in the warmth of the afternoon, Desi dozed off. She was back in Charlie's house and he gave her the Vionnet dress to wear at her wedding. When she put it on, the dress was so tight she could barely breathe. It felt like a straightjacket, so she tried to wriggle out of it but she couldn't get it over her head and she started to suffocate. She tore at the dress, but it wouldn't come apart. Just as she was about to choke to death, she woke up with a start. After a few seconds to get her bearings, she looked around thankfully at the unremarkable landscape on the outskirts of Liverpool.

Chapter 17

Towards the end of November, the pace of work at the agency began to pick up. By the first week of December it had become frenzied. Most clients were anxious to finalise next year's campaigns before the holiday break that started at Christmas and lasted until the end of January. At odds with worthy industry was tradition, which dictated that this was a time for bonhomie and general revelry. The conflict made most people feel stressed, which in turn made them either hysterical or crotchety. The weather didn't help much, either. It was better suited to the beach than to work and Christmas shopping.

Freddie, deft politician that he was, removed himself from pressure by delegating. He was too busy hosting or accepting invitations to client lunches and dinners with Guy to be able to spend much time at what he termed 'the coalface', so the teams were left to manage as best they could.

Bea coped by getting to the office at eight o'clock, working late and avoiding the merrymakers. Stella followed suit, having been motivated by a win with her product names to rival Mr Sheen; three names from her list were to be tested in group discussion.

Desi managed to encourage production houses to meet stringent deadlines by rewarding them with praise and the promise of continued business next year. Kelvin turned out to be a willing gofer. He had begun to show an aptitude for filmmaking, so she encouraged him to spend time at Rod Webb, watching Werner on the set, going through takes with Darryl and learning a few tricks of the trade.

Everybody made lists. On Stella's were Helena Rubinstein's Apple Blossom perfume and a box of Darrell Lea Rocklea Road for her mother. The thought of buying anything for Roy made her feel sick but she knew there'd be ructions if she didn't, so she bought a tie, printed with an Aztec design, at a sale at Lowes. She'd never seen him wear one; maybe he'd take the hint.

She sought Desi's advice on whether she should give Bea a present. Desi thought that a little bunch of gardenias would be a charming gesture. Stella didn't seek her advice on a gift for Freddie, though; she knew it was not advisable but she wanted to do it anyway. Currying favour with the creative director would do her no harm. By now, she knew that Richard Hunt was the top place for menswear, so she bought a pure linen handkerchief with a hand-rolled edge. 'Perfect,' said the man behind the counter as he placed it carefully in a slender box lined with tissue paper, 'for the most fastidious gentleman.'

Since Stella was well aware of the power of packaging, she sought Jacques's advice on wrapping paper. His suggestion was ingenious and affordable without looking cheap: plain brown paper, shiny black string and red sealing wax. It was very Saul

Bass. Stella was ecstatic. He even gave her the paper and sent her to Penfold's for the rest. He regarded his generosity as an investment that might yield a favourable return.

As the days went by and each job was ticked off the schedule, the Christmas spirit began to spread through the agency like measles in a kindergarten. Serious partying got under way. The measure of a good one were the stories it generated next day and, sometimes, forever after. It turned out to be a vintage year.

The day Desi obediently joined her mother in hosting a ladies' lunch at the Queen's Club, Bea and Freddie were entertaining the Lustrée people at the Ozone, more a shack than a restaurant, run by a Frenchman at Watsons Bay. With their plates filled with bouillabaisse, their goblets never empty, their shoes kicked off and their feet in the sand, the little group felt they were in St Tropez, their inhibitions melting like ice cubes in the sun. The marketing manager, a prankster by the name of Ken, picked up Freddie's shoes and threw them into the water. Everyone found this screamingly funny, except Freddie, who became stony-faced. They were his best Oxfords, made to measure by Lobb's in London.

'We must get them back,' cried Bea, hauling the culprit along with her as she ran down the beach towards a cluster of rowing boats drawn up on the sand. Ken rolled up the legs of his trousers and manned the craft. Bea, hanging over the stern, retrieved the sodden footwear and held it up victoriously. Their triumph was short-lived. A very angry fisherman met their return and threatened to call the police until Bea, suddenly sober, talked him out of it by putting on an act of helpless femininity. Taxis were called and Freddie squelched home in a huff.

Werner was absent from Rod Webb's knees-up; he was on location shooting a commercial for a rival advertising agency.

Desi was irritated because she wanted to find out if he'd asked Bea for a date and, if not, what was stopping him. Instead of being the life of the party as usual Darryl, the editor, could barely hold back his tears. His boyfriend had moved out after almost six years of cohabitation, so Desi spent the evening consoling him and sympathising over his tale of duplicity and betrayal. Unstoppable matchmaker that she was, she was determined to find a way to introduce him to Freddie.

As office parties go, the agency's that year started by conforming to the norm. The board members—all of them men—acted in a gentlemanly way, pouring drinks for the 'ladies', who were all wearing new summer dresses except Bea; she told Desi and Stella that the white piqué sheath she coveted at DJs was far too expensive, so she was waiting to snap it up at the sale after Boxing Day. The party was subdued and orderly until the chairman and the managing director, each having made a blah-blah-rah-rah speech, left the building. That was the signal for excess.

Dan Barnes, having attempted to chat up Bea and been given the cold shoulder, grew belligerent, thrust out his chin and challenged Guy Garland to step outside and settle once and for all a longstanding dispute over his handling of the Emperor Motor Oil account.

Desi found Myra crying in the ladies' room after Kelvin had told her he'd been 'dying to cop a feel' and put his hand up her skirt. As his temporary boss, Desi felt obliged to take him into her office, close the door and give him a good talking to. Like a TV prosecutor in court, she towered over him, one hand on her hip while the other pointed its forefinger at him, her voice ominously hushed and controlled and awesomely posh. 'That kind of behaviour is unacceptable in this office,' she began. 'Not only here, but anywhere. What makes you think you have the right to molest a young girl just because she happens to be around when you feel like behaving like a hoon?' Kelvin knew he had to stand there and pretend to be contrite while he ridiculed her in his mind: crone, hag, battleaxe, bitch.

While the dressing-down of Kelvin took place, Gary vomited over the potted poinsettias on the windowsill of the boardroom and Stella left the party in disgust. It was only after everyone had gone and the place was locked that the scene turned truly ugly. For a reason that was never fully explained, Dan Barnes drove his Studley Series 21 sedan into the glass front door of the building and smashed it to smithereens. The alarm went off, the police arrived and there was hell to pay. The next day, Freddie was hauled upstairs to the managing director's office and told to pull his finger out and control his people. No charge was laid against Dan Barnes. Instead, psychiatric treatment and abstinence from alcohol were prescribed.

But the party nobody talked about was Bea's housewarming on Saturday the twenty-second. Because nothing unusual happened. Not that anyone wanted to share, anyway.

The first person to arrive that afternoon was Stella, on the dot of four o'clock, wearing her new padded push-up bra under a tight, shocking-pink sheath with a plunging neckline, the first store-bought dress she had ever owned. Shocking de Schiaparelli emanated from behind her ears. She carried a posy of gardenias.

Her eyes swivelled in every direction when she saw Bea's living room. This flat was the smartest she had ever entered. She noted every detail greedily, committing to memory the colour of the walls, the teak furniture, the bulbous lampshades, the crazy chair made of wire circles, the polished boards, the shag-pile carpet, the painting of a modern interior, hung against the burnt-orange wall. It was like walking into the cover of American *House & Garden*.

She followed Bea into the dining room, where fresh mint floated among slices of lemon in a glass jug of ice water next to chunky Orrefors tumblers on a hot pink-and-orange Marimekko tablecloth. She was introduced to Bea's sister, Audrey, who was lining up two rows of hollow-stem champagne coupes near ceramic platters holding vol-au-vents filled with chicken mornay, spears of asparagus wrapped in brown bread and halves of hard-boiled eggs cut-side down on a bed of unctuous mayonnaise. Arranged on a wooden board were smelly cheeses and Sao biscuits. There was a kind of garlicky meatloaf that Bea called a terrine and three truncheon-shaped loaves she said were baguettes. Several bottles of Great Western lolled among ice in a huge concave metal container with grapevines in relief around the rim.

'Oh, Bea,' said Stella, handing her the flowers, 'I love your place!' Her own dark flat seemed squalid in comparison. As she walked back into the sitting room with a glass of effervescent wine in her hand, she imagined herself living here, spending hours at the desk under the window, looking out at the harbour, writing invitations and thank-you notes on her own engraved stationery.

Suddenly the place seemed to fill with people, some unfamiliar to her, some she knew from the office. As soon as Freddie saw her, he came over and kissed her on the cheek. 'You naughty girl,' he said. 'You weren't supposed to give me a present.'

'Shhh . . . I wanted to,' she said softly. 'You've been so good to me.'

Jacques was studying the painting on the wall. 'It's beautiful, the Janet Dawson,' he said to Bea, who was circulating with a platter of food. 'How long have you had it?'

'Two weeks. It's my Christmas treat to myself.'

'My dear hostess,' said a voice behind Bea. 'Forgive me for crashing your party.'

She turned to find Werner smiling down at her. 'Oh, you're very welcome,' she said and felt her face flush. He had a way of looking people directly in the eye. She tried to divert his gaze by offering him the platter. He took a spear of asparagus.

'I'm Darryl and I'm a gatecrasher too,' said a young man she had never seen before. His face was gaunt and sorrowful. Horn-rimmed glasses gave him a bookish appearance.

'And I'm the culprit,' said Desi, delivering drinks to both men. 'I knew you wouldn't mind. Tom couldn't come so I made up for it by bringing two substitutes.' She kept silent about Tom's resentment of her work and his refusal to have anything to do with the friends she made there. In any case, she'd promised to be home by seven, at the latest.

'Where's Guy?' said Freddie as an excuse to join them and find out who the newcomer was. He knew Werner but not Darryl.

'On daddy duty,' said Bea. 'A kiddies' party at Balmoral Beach.' Nobody asked for a further explanation. Guy tried to be a good husband and father, but everybody knew he wasn't cut out for it. In Bea's unspoken opinion he'd married too young, before he had much experience of the world or any idea of what he was getting into. He was torn between loving his family and feeling trapped; he was stuck with it, mortgage and all.

Gary was on his best behaviour. Tagging along with him was his girlfriend, Shirley, suntanned and pretty, her hair done up in a high ponytail à la Brigitte Bardot. He poured water for both of them and picked at a bit of food. Clearly, he was there under sufferance. They stood self-consciously together pretending to be interested in the chatter of a middle-aged woman named Martha who knew intimate details about everyone who lived in the street.

Stella couldn't take her eyes off the harbour. For the first time in her life, she felt sophisticated, her image equal to the circumstances and the worldly people she held in awe. 'You sparkle today, Étoile,' said Jacques, using the chance to refill her glass as an excuse to study her newly burgeoned décolletage. It was smooth and flawless, like two little mounds in Bea's egg mayonnaise.

'Do you know the story behind the shape of this champagne glass?'

'No,' said Stella, innocently. 'Tell me.' She smiled at him sweetly.

'It is the shape of Marie Antoinette's breast.'

Now it was Stella's turn to blush. 'You're kidding me.'

'It's true. Ask anybody.' He knew that was unlikely because Stella would never bring herself to utter the word breast, even to herself. She looked delectable, he thought. Truly edible, like a ripe Mara des Bois strawberry.

By five o'clock, the level of talk had turned into a cacophony, stilled only momentarily when somebody dropped a glass and it shattered on the tiled floor of the kitchen. 'Ah,' said Jacques, pouring another drink for Stella, 'the party has begun.' He grinned at her, his moist lips drawn back over teeth stained with nicotine. She giggled.

Freddie stood by the window with Darryl. He was listening with folded arms instead of talking and gesticulating in his usual way. In the hall, Desi told Werner about Charlie's house and its potential as a location for an up-market product, maybe an expensive car, or a brand of cigarettes like Benson & Hedges, or a vodka like Smirnoff. He looked directly into her eyes and said, 'I'd love to see it. If you have time, we could do a survey after Christmas.'

'I'd like that,' she said and wondered how she could manage to arrange it without having to tell Tom. As they looked at each other it dawned on her that she and Werner were nearly the same height; she still had to slouch, but that came naturally to her in the company of men who were shorter—and there were plenty of those. For a horrible moment she wondered if he was wearing elevated shoes. She looked down at his feet and saw the same scuffed brogues he always wore. Then she looked at her own size nines. They were in ballet slippers instead of the courts she wore to the office. That's what had edged them towards being level.

By six o'clock almost everyone was dancing. The Isley Brothers' single 'Shout' was on the record player and Jacques was doing the twist with Bea. Stella felt neglected, so she went to the bathroom and sat for a while on the toilet wondering why the room was spinning.

Guy sped up the steps from the street and through the open front door, panting as though he'd just competed with John Landy to break the four-minute mile. He went into the kitchen, gulped a glass of Great Western, sighed, poured another one, then lit a cigarette and went looking for someone to talk to. Stella came out of the bathroom with unfocused eyes. 'I need something to eat,' she said to nobody in particular. Audrey took her into the kitchen, sat her down on a Bentwood chair and made her a substantial terrine baguette sandwich and some strong black coffee. Stella hadn't taken much notice of Audrey until now. She was an older, more timid version of Bea, an obedient copy rather than an original.

It was after seven when Desi checked her watch and realised she'd have to call it a day. Darryl had gone and so had Freddie—together, she hoped. 'I have to slip away now,' she whispered to Werner. 'You stay. Bea might need help to get rid of Guy.' He looked at Bea, waving her ivory cigarette holder and rocking back and forth to music only she could hear, as she sifted through LPs. 'I think she can cope,' he said. 'I've got a big day tomorrow. Do you mind a passenger?'

'Of course not. Let me see if Stella needs a lift.' Before she could make the offer, Stella had disappeared down the front steps with Jacques.

When the clock on the Welsh dresser struck nine, Audrey and Martha were helping Bea tidy up. 'Who is that thoughtful man who collected the empties and put them in the laundry?' asked Audrey at the sink.

'Darryl,' said Bea. 'He's not your type.'

While the women busied themselves, Guy sat at the kitchen table expressing his opinion about various subjects including one of the most-discussed topics of the time: last summer's bikini wars at Bondi, when girls were ordered off the beach for wearing two-piece swimsuits with lower halves an obscene five-plus inches below the navel. That reminded him of the tabloid photographs of Sabrina, the busty British showgirl—vital statistics 41 17 36—who had left Sydney in April vowing never to return.

It was clear to the women where his anxieties were, especially to Martha, her tea towel ready to take the next coupe from Audrey, whose rubber-gloved hands were shifting glasses from the suds in one sink to clear water in the other. Bea wiped the table, lifting Guy's glass and his pack of Kents. Why doesn't he go, was all she could think. She yawned. He didn't seem to notice. She made yet another pot of coffee while he inspected open bottles to find one or two that weren't empty.

By ten o'clock Audrey and Martha had gone home. Guy had grown maudlin, dwelling on his guilt at letting down his 'wonderful' wife who was too good for him and for not spending enough time with his 'beautiful' children, Troy and Charlotte. There was not a drop of consolation in any of the bottles or a cigarette left unsmoked, and that made it easier for Bea to take him to the corner and flag a taxi. 'You're a wonderful woman,' he slurred and she put her hand on his head, the way cops do with criminals, to prevent it from colliding with the doorway to the front seat.

The flat bore no signs that a party had been there, except for the smell of tobacco, a few records scattered about, some leftovers in the fridge and an impressive stack of empties in the laundry. Audrey was a good sister, totally reliable. Bless that Martha, too, thought Bea. A terrible gossip but good at heart. Every detail of what had gone on, though it was innocent enough, would be all over the building tomorrow.

She resisted an urge to put *Irma La Douce* on the turntable. A rough calculation fixed the time in London at about midday. That bastard. Who was buying his lunch today? She looked around for something to do. In a way, it was worse that the place was immaculate. She gathered the records, found their sleeves and put them away. Then she got into bed, unlocked the drawer of the bedside table, took out her vibrator and switched off the light.

Chapter 18

'Why didn't you stay?' Desi hadn't noticed until the words came out of her mouth that she was quite tipsy, otherwise she'd have kept them to herself. Having raised the subject, she felt she had to continue. It was apparent that he hadn't asked to see Bea again and she longed to know why. 'Bea is such an attractive woman,' she said. 'And trustworthy. That's rare.' She turned the Renault into city-bound traffic on Military Road in front of a cream Volkswagen. They heard the blast of a horn and Werner couldn't help bracing himself.

'Yes, she is,' he said when they shot forward and the danger was left behind.

'She is what?'

'Attractive.' He wondered why she felt compelled to throw her friend at him when it was clear that, although he liked and respected Bea, she did not fire him up.

'Why haven't you asked her out?' The words were there before she knew it.

As though timed to give him a chance to formulate a reply, the VW drew level with them on the right and the male passenger in the front seat yelled, 'Woman driver!' Desi turned her head, grinned and jerked two fingers at him before putting her foot down. The race that ensued was terrifying, at least for Werner.

'This is dangerous, Desi,' he said finally, as the two cars paced each other across the bridge, like two species of beetle competing for the same fodder.

'Prick!' she yelled, glaring at the other car as it eased ahead, triumphant arms waving and thumbs jerking out of the windows. 'I don't mean you,' she said, glancing in amusement at Werner. The blood had drained from his face.

She seemed to have forgotten the question, so he decided to do the same. He hated to think what she'd do behind the wheel of a Ferrari or something equally powerful. If they ever went to look at the location she'd talked about, it would be in his car, not hers.

They were turning from College Street into William when she said, 'You didn't answer my question.'

'What question?'

'Werner. You know the question.' She knew she was being cheeky but she felt skittish. What was there to lose?

'I am not in a position to ask anyone for a date.'

'What position is that?'

'It's a bit messy.'

When she didn't reply, he said, 'Ah, Desi, life is straightforward for you.'

Yes it is, she thought. Predictable. Tom would be furious by now. The idea made her feel defiant. Preparations for Christmas would be fun over the next few days but then there was the major production coming up in April. 'It's not so straightforward for me, either,' she said in a subdued voice, as they turned into Elizabeth Bay Road.

'This is your building?' If Desi had imagined the place where Werner lived, which she hadn't, it would not have been the bunker to their right when they pulled up in Ithaca Road. It was another Harry Seidler interpretation of worker housing for the informed and affluent, although it wasn't as bossy as his more recent edifice across the harbour.

'You seem surprised.'

'I wouldn't have picked you for a modernist.' She looked at him sideways, at the bushy brows, the shadows under his eyes and the blueish tinge of his jaw. His whole appearance indicated clutter. His dark hair was unruly, with a wild streak of grey sprouting from his forehead. He'd worn the crumpled tan suede jacket—far too heavy for the heat—so often it had taken on the shape of his body. The skivvies that went underneath it had been black before umpteen visits to the laundromat coloured them slate. In her mind's eye she saw him in a habitation of panelled walls, plaster cornices, waxed oak tables, French windows, stacks of books and a stringed instrument of some kind, maybe a cello. Steel and concrete were out of context.

He gave the parody of a sigh, as though tired of answering questions of this kind. 'I was in a hurry and it was available. It works for me right now.'

'I'm sorry. I didn't mean to pry.'

He gave her a forgiving smile. 'Would you like to see inside? It's not so bad.'

She hesitated. It was almost eight o'clock. 'I . . . I'd better not.' She thought of the weekend ahead. 'Oh, hell, why not? Just for a minute.'

In the back seat of the taxi, Jacques put his arm around Stella and let his hand fall in the vicinity of her armpit. 'The night is young,' he said. 'It's too early to go home.' She was sober and sleepy, so she rested her head on his shoulder. Despite finding her scent more nauseating than intoxicating, he rubbed his chin against her hair. It felt soft and silky. She made no effort to resist. If she'd been a cat she'd have purred, he thought, pleased with himself. The evening was going well.

Behind her compliant facade was a mind busily weighing up possibilities and consequences. Was he taking her to his place? If so, should she pretend to be reluctant and let him talk her into it? She expected him to make a pass and, if he did, how far was she prepared to go? He was by far the worldliest man she had ever had anything to do with, and she found him attractive, in an ugly kind of way. If she was going to lose her virginity, she could do worse than with an experienced Frenchman. She expected he'd know how not to get her pregnant.

He paid the taxi in Victoria Street and they went into a tiny restaurant that smelled faintly of vinegar and pork fat, and heavily of stale cigarette smoke. It was dark and crowded with people, mainly men. A couple of them nodded at Jacques, let their eyes roam over Stella and then went back to their plates of sausages and cabbage. A woman with orange hair and smudged eye make-up came from behind the till, called Jacques '*mon ami*' and led them to a table covered with a red-and-white checked cloth near the kitchen at the back.

Jacques excused himself and went towards a sign that said 'Toilettes'. Stella looked around. The noise level was low, a blur of voices, and nobody seemed to be speaking English. Everything had a tired and shabby look: the indistinct pattern of the wallpaper, the little parchment shades over the wall lights, the bottles holding candles that looked as though Vesuvius had erupted and spilled lava down their sides. Even the people looked damaged. In the candlelight their features were exaggerated, thrown into relief, heavy-lidded and weary. A woman wearing a black beret and dark glasses held a lit cigarette in one hand while a fork in the other fiddled with something on the plate in front of her. Stella had never seen morose faces or dark and dusty clothes like these at Miranda. She decided this must be what was meant by 'bohemian'.

The feeling of sophistication that Stella had experienced in Bea's flat came back to her. Conscious of her image, she lifted her chin to give Jacques a nonchalant smile when he returned. He lit a cigarette and she said, 'Can I have one too?'

'Of course.' He was surprised. 'I didn't know you smoked.'

She considered how Jeanne Moreau might respond before replying, 'There's a lot about me you don't know.' She'd never smoked in her life.

'You are a woman of mystery.' If he meant it ironically, she didn't notice. He took another cigarette from his pack of Gitanes, put it beside the one in his mouth, lit it, took it out again and placed it between Stella's lips, just like Paul Henreid did to Bette Davis in Now, Voyager.

'We are having choucroute,' he said, without looking at the menu.

'We are? What is it?' Without having inhaled, she took the

cigarette out of her mouth and held it awkwardly between her fingers.

'A speciality of Lorraine.'

Stella wondered who Lorraine was but she didn't ask. When the tip of the cigarette lost its glow, she stubbed it out in an ashtray that had Dubonnet printed on it.

The dish was disappointing, not to Jacques who attacked it heartily, but to Stella. Sauerkraut and frankfurts were not her idea of French cuisine. She did her best to reduce the navvy's portion on her plate but failed to make an impact on it. The plum tart that followed was much more to her taste and she demolished all of it.

'We must have a nightcap,' said Jacques, after he'd settled the bill and they were under the trees in Victoria Street again. He happened to live close by, he told her, and there happened to be a bottle of Moët et Chandon in the refrigerator. It's now or never, thought Stella, and before long she found herself in the top-floor flat of a converted nineteenth-century mansion in Challis Avenue.

'Sorry about the mess,' said Werner as he unlocked the door and led Desi into what at first sight seemed to be the lost-property office at Central Station. A chesterfield covered in cracked and faded green leather stood against one wall. Apart from that and a door resting on trestle legs and covered with an assortment of objects that included a portable typewriter, some sort of camera equipment, an anglepoise lamp, cans of film, several loose-leaf binders, a coffee pot and an untidy pile of broadsheet newspapers, the only furniture she could see were tea chests and suitcases. The room itself was as plain and colourless as a prison cell, with nothing on the walls, only a narrow strip of horizontal windows along one wall that was closer to the ceiling than to the floor. The place was so bleak she couldn't think of anything to say except for how ghastly, or how interesting, so she uttered neither.

He turned on the lamp, cleared some papers off the table and pulled out two unpainted upright chairs that were tucked under it. 'Tempe Tip,' he said. 'You never know what you'll find there.' When Desi sat down on one of them, the windows were too high for her to be able to see anything through them except the darkening sky.

'Don't feel you must compliment me on my skill as an interior decorator,' he said, reading her thoughts. 'For me it's a hotel room.' He disappeared into what seemed to be the kitchen and she got up and followed him, more by instinct than intent, reluctant to stay in what felt like solitary confinement. The kitchen was compact, functional and without character or warmth. He took two brandy balloons and a bottle of armagnac from one of the cupboards. 'I hope you ate something at the party, because I don't think . . .' He opened and closed a few doors and peered at the shelves, although he looked as though he knew there was nothing edible there.

'I couldn't eat another thing. In any case I must go soon.' Her frivolity had dissipated, leaving a fluttery feeling in her stomach and a sense of unease. She regretted not having gone straight home.

'How long have you lived here?' she said, trying to overcome the awkwardness she felt, as they went back into the main room with their glasses. She continued to stand and so did he.

'Let's see. I moved here in September. So, about three months.' A few moments of uncomfortable silence followed and he felt she expected some kind of explanation. 'I guess I should tell you that my wife and I are separated.'

Desi was pleased to have the question answered at last without her having to ask it. 'I'm sorry.' The brandy was warming her up and calming her down. Married but separated. So he was available. Sort of.

'Don't be. The marriage was beyond repair. She's American. It didn't work out for her here. She's gone back to Los Angeles. We keep in touch.'

'Still, breaking up is never easy.' She had no experience of such a situation but she didn't know what else to say and it seemed appropriate.

'It's funny,' he said, 'the tiniest thing finished us off.'

'Like what?'

'Well, she was happy to come with me to see if we could make a living here, and she made a big effort to adjust. Americans are spoiled by services you just don't get anywhere else in the world. And she put up with not being able to get things like Saran Wrap or Kentucky Fried Chicken or Sara Lee Fudge Brownies. But Pepperidge Farm Stuffing Mix pushed her right over the edge. It was kind of the last straw.' He gave a mirthless laugh. 'Ludicrous, huh?'

'That *is* quite funny.' Desi looked at him and they both burst out laughing.

'What did she want it for?' she gasped and put her glass down.

'For the turkey at Thanksgiving.'

That sent her into another bout of hilarity. Then she couldn't stop, rocking back and forth with her hands pressed over her nose and mouth to try to contain the cackling. It's not that funny, she thought, why am I hysterical? She sort of fell against him and before either of them knew it, they were in a clinch and her laughter was snuffed out like candles on a birthday cake.

They began to kiss. She was the one who started it, surprising herself with her audacity. As their ardour became more forceful they pushed against the table, dislodging the top of it so that it slid off the trestles. It fell to the hard floor with a terrible crash. Everything went flying, as though hit by a cyclone. Only then did they pause in the process of consuming each other.

They stood among the wreckage and gazed into each other's eyes.

'Werner,' she said.

'Desirée,' he said.

Just like Tristan and Isolde.

When they'd reached the top of the stairs and he unlocked the door, Stella was overcome with a sense of unreality, just as she had been at Bea's. Except that, instead of finding herself in a cover of *House & Garden*, she was now in a black-and-white French film—*Gervaise* or *Les Amants*. It was everything she imagined an atelier in Paris to be, skylight and all. There were posters on the walls and an easel with a paint-spattered sheet flung over it to hide whatever was underneath. After he'd uncorked the champagne, lit three candles, turned off the electric light, put a stack of records on the automatic player and Edith Piaf started singing 'La Vie en Rose', they curled themselves up on the wraparound sofa, shoes off but clothes on. Stella didn't want to give him the impression that she was easy.

While he told her an edited story of his life—most of it centred on his boyhood in Paris under Nazi occupation—his hands wandered over the undulations of her upper body and across her tightly encased rump. 'My father was in the resistance . . .' Stella was charmed that he pronounced it ray-zist-onz, 'and I was useful as a runner. I was small and skinny and I could climb through windows and steal things.' He was teasing her neck and shoulders with light little kisses as his hand reached the hollow at the back of her knee. 'Information. Documents. Sometimes food. But only from the Bosch. There was often nothing to eat but stale bread.' He took a nibble at the lobe of her ear.

'What about your mother?' Stella's mind was too engrossed in the story to notice that her body was responding encouragingly to whatever Jacques was doing to it.

'She worked on an underground newspaper. She was an artist, so she drew political cartoons, caricatures of Hitler and Goebbels and the rest of them.' He'd managed to slide her panty girdle down to her ankles without her ray-zist-onz. 'It was just as dangerous as my father in the railway, blowing up German supply trains.'

'What happened to them?' She feared the answer, as she kicked off something hanging around her feet.

'They survived. My mother died in 1953, my father two years later. Both of natural causes.' He kissed the bit of her neck under her right ear; a whiff of Shocking de Schiaparelli still clung there but it was too faint to be bothersome. 'So you see, not all were lost. They were among the lucky.' She smiled, like a contented child at the happy ending to a fairy story told at bedtime.

Her mind drifted into a dreamlike state. So much had happened, not just today but in the past few weeks, to change her life completely. She had a glamorous job, a fashionable new image, an interesting address, sophisticated friends and here she was being made love to by a French artist in his bohemian studio. In demographic terms, she reasoned that she had skipped through upper middle class altogether and landed in lower upper.

By the time the plaintive sounds of 'Non, Je Ne Regrette Rien' wafted from the record player she began to notice a pleasurable throbbing down below and she arched her back and let out a little moan. Her dress seemed to be bunched up around her waist, so she looked down. Jacques's head lay between her legs. For a moment the significance of what he was doing didn't register. Then it did.

'What are you doing?' she shrieked and tried to sit up. It wasn't the part of him that was supposed to be there.

He raised his head. 'I am preparing you, darling.'

'What for? Am I somebody's dinner?' For some reason, the sight of her Uncle Sid noisily sucking marrow out of veal bones entered her head, along with the revulsion she'd felt sitting opposite him at the dinner table when she was twelve.

'You filthy Frenchman!' She pushed his head away, gripped the sofa to raise herself and swung her legs over the side until her feet touched the floor. She knew about French kisses, but this licking her like an icecream was . . . perverted. When Stella thought of going All The Way, she'd imagined it to be like the climactic scene from *Les Amants* where their heads were together all the time. For most of it, anyway. Now she came to think of it, Jean-Marc Bory's head did disappear out of frame for a while . . . How was she to know where it went when Jeanne Moreau panted ecstatically?

Stella sat up, horrified. For a few moments she stared at nothing, holding her hand over her mouth, as though she'd just let out a string of expletives. Lovemaking was supposed to be tactile yes, slimy no. She remembered the awful fascination of sticking her finger into a sea anemone in a rockpool at Gunnamatta Bay and feeling its voluptuous mouth close around it. She stood up and looked around, as though searching for her lost innocence. 'What have you done with my pants?'

He responded as promptly as a soldier at the command of a superior officer, groping behind him on the sofa and then holding up the unglamorous elasticised chastity belt. She stood up and snatched the panty girdle from him, turned her back towards him and stepped into it awkwardly, wriggling as she pulled it up under her tight dress. Two of the candles had gone out, leaving only the stump of one burning, so she had to feel around in the darkness to find her shoes. She rushed into the bathroom to straighten her dress as best she could, fix her face and comb her hair. When she came out, he got up from the sofa.

'How could you do that to me?' she said, with as much composure as she could summon. The sight of his lips made her feel sick. 'I'm not a girl like that.'

'I am sorry, Étoile, I misunderstood,' he said, as his eyes skimmed over her figure-hugging dress and the cleavage caused by her plunge push-up bra. 'Your packaging does not represent the product.'

Chapter 19

At ten o'clock on Christmas morning, Audrey sat behind the wheel of her Morris Minor and drove to Pennant Hills to pick up Aunt Elva from the nursing home. By the time they got back to Kirribilli and Audrey had manoeuvred the wheelchair out of the back, eased her fragile and pallid relative into it again, wheeled her in and out of the lift and into her flat, she needed a drink. Bea was there; she needed one too. It was a day of good deeds, worthy and exhausting. Myrtle, the best friend of their late mother, was due at any minute, along with her retarded son, Vernon.

The ham was glazed and out of the oven, replaced by a stuffed chicken that was turning golden. Potatoes had been parboiled and were roasting to crispness with the pumpkin and sweet potato. Peas had been shelled and beans strung and sliced. The pudding Audrey had made in November and hung in a cloth in the doorway between the hall and the sitting room was now making a jolly gurgling sound in a covered pot on the stove.

'You've gone to such a lot of trouble,' said Aunt Elva, in a quavering voice. 'I'm deeply grateful.' She said it five times in the first twenty minutes until Myrtle arrived and she changed the subject to the state of her health. Both women found discussions about their doctors, ailments, symptoms and treatments engrossing and, as though a pact had been sealed between them, each was courteous enough to give the other a fair hearing. Their exchanges were not without competition, however, and when they discussed their stitches it had nothing to do with the needlework of gentlewomen. The number that had sewn up Elva after her hip replacement was moderate compared with the tally Myrtle had endured at her hysterectomy, a misfortune so traumatic, 'I've never been myself since.'

I wonder who she's been? thought Bea, passing within earshot. Then she chastised herself for such an uncharitable sentiment, especially at Christmas.

Vernon, his almond-shaped eyes vacant in his round face, sat silently staring across the harbour towards the Quay and the Harbour Bridge that gripped The Rocks and Kirribilli like a pincer. Bea smiled and said, 'Isn't it a marvellous view?' as she offered him a glass of lemonade. He took the drink, continued to direct his attention to the window and said nothing. She poured semi-sweet sherry generously into two glasses and took them to Elva and Myrtle, now in cosy collaboration, each with her good ear angled towards the mouth of the other, so as not to miss a word.

'Well, I never,' Myrtle was saying.

'I tell you no lie,' said Elva. 'By rights I should be dead by now. Wrong diagnosis.'

'Like the medication they gave me for the swelling. Made my legs worse. They blew up like balloons. I had to be rushed to emergency. I'm lucky to be alive.'

'Lunch is ready,' trilled the melodious voice of Audrey, who was a volunteer at the Mosman Musical Society. It wasn't quite the truth, but she knew it would take a good fifteen minutes to get Elva and Vernon to the table and that would give Bea time to make the gravy.

'Dizzy, what *are* you doing?' Bo watched as her daughter tipped a spoonful of salt into her cup of coffee. It was Christmas morning and they were both up early, breakfasting together on the terrace. 'Where is your head? You must still be asleep.'

'I'm sorry, I was miles away.' Desirée floated to earth again. She got up and flung the contents of the cup over the lawn. 'I didn't need that, anyway.' It was low tide. In the distance on the sand flats, she could see the figure of her brother with his pants rolled up flinging a stick into the water so Dotty and Spot could compete in its rescue. Each time, the loser let out a vocal protest that carried along the beach to drive the neighbours mad.

Bo smiled at her with satisfaction. 'You're in a dream world.' She hadn't been prepared for the relief she felt at finding her daughter so enraptured at the prospect of marrying Tom. At last, Desirée was showing all the symptoms of a woman in love. She'd lost her appetite, she was bright-eyed and so distracted Bo had to wave her hand in front of Desirée's eyes to catch her attention. She'd hardly been home during the last two days, tootling off in the Renault to celebrate with her friends. And then the long walk she took on Sunday evening by herself. She was so absentminded, she'd even forgotten to wear her ring. And it was wicked of that advertising agency to make her work yesterday when every other business in the country had closed down.

'We must start finalising plans for the wedding,' said Bo, adopting the authoritative voice she used at meetings of the Black & White committee, in the hope that the two of them could sit together long enough for some decisions to be made and some action undertaken. 'I've had a stab at a guest list and it's quite long already. You might want to add some of your friends from the office. Shall I go upstairs and get it?'

The last thing Desirée wanted to talk about was the wedding. She was in enough of a turmoil already. 'Oh . . . let's leave it until tomorrow. I must get myself together for the boat. What time are we boarding?'

'It's only just gone eight. Your father's sleeping in, so we might not get going until midday. All the food's ready. It's just a picnic on the harbour.'

'I promised to call a friend . . .'

'Isn't it a bit early? Dizzy, sit down for a minute. We have to talk.'

Clouds had moved away from the sun, like curtains parting at the theatre, so that it dazzled its audience like a benevolent diva. Desirée reached for her straw hat on the seat beside her and put it on. She slid down in her chair and tried to look interested.

Bo cleared her throat. 'I've been thinking about the wedding.'

'Yes. Me too.' The difference in the direction of their thoughts was not mentioned.

'There's so much to be done. I know you'll hate me for suggesting this, but we might have to delay it . . .'

Desirée stared at her with a startled expression. Then she put her face in her hands. When she took them away there were tears in her eyes.

'Oh, darling.' Bo took her daughter's hands in both of her own. 'Don't be disappointed. We all want the wedding to be wonderful, and that will take time and a lot of careful planning.'

'I know.' The catch in Desirée's voice made Bo feel a bit like a torturer applying thumbscrews, but she knew that everything about the wedding must be perfect and there was no way that could be achieved in three months.

'Why don't we postpone it until July?' Bo went on. 'The weather is often beautiful then and the bulbs will be out, hyacinths and tulips. What about white violets . . .'

The rest of what she said was lost on Desirée, who felt as elated as a large bird released from a small cage. She stretched her arms as though opening her wings.

'. . . it will give Madame du Val enough time to make the dresses. Invitations have to be engraved, and that takes ages. And of course there's Charlie's offer of the house at Exeter. I know that little church, it's beautiful. Blyth isn't too happy about the idea but I love it and I think you do too, so we'll have to talk him into it . . .'

'Yes. Of course, Mummy. You're quite right.'

'I am so glad you see it that way. I'll help you explain it to Tom when he gets here. He's coming with us today, isn't he?'

'Who?'

'Tom, darling. Your beloved.'

'Tom? Yes. He's coming. Now I really must ring my friend. I told her I'd drop in if there was time. She's alone today.'

'Would she like to join us?'

'Ah . . . I don't think so.'

'Go on, you sit next to Roy,' said Hazel.

'No, that's your place,' protested Stella.

They were standing outside the house at Miranda on Christmas morning about to climb into Roy's vehicle and ride three abreast in the cabin. Hazel, in her new daisy-patterned green shirtmaker dress with shiny buttons shaped like bumble bees planted down the front, her hair resembling a dandelion in bloom, carried a tray of mince pies that were still warm from the oven. Stella, with a grumpy look that squeezed the features of her face into a tight little knot, put her overnight bag in the back of the ute and folded her arms across her black T-shirt. To separate herself from the values and garbs of her relatives she'd decided to package herself as a beatnik, in skinny black pants, a black beret, heavy eye make-up and impenetrable sunglasses. There was no way she would sit next to Roy.

'Well, make up your minds, girls, or we'll be here all day,' said Roy affably from behind the wheel of the utility truck. He wore Stella's tie with a new brown suit. She thought it made no improvement to his unfortunate appearance.

'Aw, go on,' said Hazel, this time in the pleading voice of someone who knows her words are in vain. She prodded Stella with her elbow and looked at her determined little puckered mouth. 'Oh, all right then,' she continued, with a sigh. 'Hold these a tick.' She passed her the tray, stepped awkwardly into the cabin and settled herself beside Roy. Why that girl had to scowl like a thundercloud and dress like a widgie on the very day she wanted her to look her best in front of the family, Hazel was at a loss to understand. She had never actually seen a widgie but she knew Stella's get-up was exactly the kind of thing troublemakers wore.

'All right there, love?' Roy smiled at her. She returned it with a long-suffering one.

'Can't these go in the back?' Stella held the tray as though it might contaminate her fingernails, which were painted bile green.

'No, give them here. I didn't get up at four o'clock this morning to have my pies broken to bits in the back.'

Stella handed the tray to Hazel and climbed in beside her, grateful that nobody she knew would be likely to see her bouncing along the back roads of Sydney in a fawn ute.

'I've said it before and I'll say it again . . .' Hazel was telling Roy, as they crossed Tom Ugly's Bridge.

She will, too, thought Stella.

'. . . Beryl has always been very hospitable to me and mine. She has always welcomed us in her home, I'll say that for her. I know Sid is my brother but he can't be easy to live with.'

Roy patted her thigh. The gesture was not lost on Stella. She wished he'd just keep his hands on the wheel. Their intimacy reminded her of Jacques on Saturday night. The thought of what he did to her made her both shudder and throb a bit *down there,* and that was confusing. She could not forgive his lack of respect, even though he did follow her down the stairs when she left to see her into a taxi. She was glad she'd hung up on him when he rang on Sunday morning.

Stella gazed out of the window at houses that told her more about their inhabitants than she might have learned from meeting them in person. There were solid one-storey brick abodes warding off the world with niggardly windows and stingy verandahs, hung with baskets of dull and serviceable plants; a few two- or three-storey mansions with elaborate facades and pretensions to grandeur before their conversion into nursing homes, or residentials, their graceful balconies boxed in with plywood and glass louvres; fibro shanties with broken windows and weeds growing out of rickety front steps and the odd broken tricycle or busted tyre lying on dead grass in the yard.

A fair percentage of the houses they passed, though, were bungalows so immaculate they seemed better suited to robots than humans, their clipped growth brought into line by men who consoled themselves for lack of power at work by taking control at home. Inside these temples to virtue were women whose lack of power over men caused them to wield it over inanimate objects, banishing fingermarks from windowsills and light switches, relentlessly waxing floors, polishing silver, punishing carpets and upholstery to make them offer up their dust and stains like supplicants spilling out their sins in the confessional.

With few variations there was a uniformity about the streetscapes that made Stella feel claustrophobic. Pubs, with their tiled walls and Tooth's and Toohey's posters, all looked the same. So did the corner grocers, the delicatessens and the cake shops that usually displayed iced sponges and neenish tarts in the windows. Everything was closed for the holy day.

The houses were on blocks of land of the same cramped size, street after street of stifling conformity. The people who lived here knew their place and had no wish to change it. She felt instinctively that originality, imagination and any kind of quirkiness would not be tolerated. At least Rookwood Cemetery, looming on the right, had character, like it or not.

The farther north-west they travelled the higher the temperature rose and the more prevalent were unkerbed roads, pink crepe myrtle trees, oleander bushes and golden cypresses, until at last, after what seemed like hours, they reached Guildford and the home of Sid and Beryl Tinker.

* * *

It was the screeching of middle-aged females that sent the men into the laundry to gather around the keg, and drove the younger generation outside to look for some distraction, like a pet to torment, a magpie to throw stones at, or a ball to chuck around. Since the women hadn't seen each other since Wayne's birthday last June their instincts told them to fill the gap with noise, so they raised their voices, higher and higher, as though in a competition to out-squawk the sulphur-crested cockatoos.

'Everybody's talking, nobody's listening,' observed Roy.

'Hens in a barnyard,' said Sid, turning the tap of the bung and pouring frothy amber ale into glasses held at an angle to give them a good head.

'Poured like an expert,' said Roy. 'Ta, Sid.' He took a schooner with one hand, and undid the top button of his shirt and loosened his tie with the other.

'Put it down to experience,' said Sid. 'Bottoms up!'

'You had a pub, Haze tells me.'

'Used to. Out Blacktown way . . .'

The lounge room was crowded to its limits with a plastic Christmas tree as tall as Sid, red and green paper chains with gold bells twinkling across the airspace from one picture rail to another and a long dining table bedizened with festive kitsch. An assortment of mismatched chairs, stools and benches had been put in position for dining. Women hurried back and forth from the kitchen with further clutter for the table. Bing Crosby crooned of a white Christmas from the radiogram. The squeals of children and the clunk and thud of wheeled toys floated in from the street.

There was nothing for Stella to do but get in the way of serious activity, so she wandered down the back steps and into the yard where her cousin Rita, aged nine, straddled a yellow pushbike that was so shiny it must have been a Christmas present. After staring for several moments at the apparition she imagined must be a witch, Rita said, 'Watch me,' and pedalled off around the corner of the house, brushing an azalea bush as she went.

Stella sat down on the top step, flicked away a few persistent flies, lit a cigarette and surveyed Sid's realm. It was longer than it was wide, with what looked like a workshop and an old lavatory nudging the grey paling fence beyond the Hill's hoist at the back. It was not so much manicured as conquered, its few trees and shrubs surgically dismembered and hemmed in by cement paving. A little strip of dirt had been permitted along each of the side fences, and a few flowering plants—marigolds, petunias and black-eyed susans—allowed to grow there for as long as they made a good show. Its meanness of spirit was familiar and repellent to her.

A football whizzed through the air, hit the fence and bounced into a bed of red waxy flowers. A dog woofed savagely from the other side of the fence. 'Mind my begonias!' Beryl's voice rose from the kitchen window separating itself from the intermingling of over-excited chatter with the clatter of plates and saucepans. A teenage boy appeared from behind the outhouse, retrieved the ball from the ravaged blooms, and kicked it back to where it came from. He glanced at Stella, sniggered, then chased after the ball.

The screen door behind her creaked open, so Stella stood up to make way for her cousin Deirdre, who was smiling prettily and holding a plate. She wore a dress of red-and-white spotted voile with a full skirt and puffed sleeves. On the top of the alice band that held her brownish locks away from her freckled face was a white pussy bow. She smiled and wrinkled her nose, so that her pink nostrils quivered like a rabbit's. She was the image of her mother, although she still had a waist and her hair was the colour nature gave it. 'You're missing all the fun,' she declared. 'Why don't you come in?' Stella wondered what that fun might be. On the plate offered to her was what appeared to be a hedgehog in fancy dress: a halved grapefruit, cut-side down, forming a hillock into which were stuck toothpicks with red and green pickled onions threaded alternately with cubes of Kraft cheddar. 'No thanks,' said Stella.

She took off her sunglasses and held the screen door open before following Deirdre into the house. Stella felt as out of place as a weed among Beryl's begonias.

'Yes, they've been engaged since August.'

'October, Mum,' clucked Deirdre, pretending to be impatient. 'On his birthday.' She tittered, bit her lower lip, held up her left hand and wiggled her fingers to display her prize to the gathering around the table. The goofy look on the face of the gawky young man sitting next to her proclaimed him to be the culprit. Neither of them could have been more than nineteen.

'Isn't that lovely?' said Hazel, sawing at the turkey on her plate. Measly ring, Stella concluded, glancing at the small yellowish stone and returning her attention to her plate. Seated beside her, Rita watched every move of Stella's thrillingly gruesome fingernails.

'Lovely,' echoed Dawn, who lived next door. 'Pass the cranberry jelly, please, Wayne.' The boy who'd chased the football shoved the open jar towards her across a colourful depiction of Santa Claus, holly wreaths and jingle bells on the paper tablecloth.

'Very nice spread you've put on for us today, Beryl,' said Roy, tucking into his third baked potato. Hazel was proud of the deferential way he behaved towards her family. 'You're a lucky fella, Sid,' he added, just in case her husband chose to take the compliment the wrong way.

'Thank you, Roy,' said Beryl.

'If I have to have a ball and chain I could do worse,' said Sid from the head of the table. He was not known for bestowing lavish praise. His ruddy face and his hands were big but they were the only generous bits of him, apart from his paunch. His small, watery eyes were buried in pouches and his mouth was mean.

Beryl, at the foot of the table near the door to the kitchen, chose to ignore Sid's remark. Instead, she turned an eager face to her niece.

'Do you have a young man, Stella?'

The question silenced the group. Even the scraping of knives on plates ceased. The only sound came from two blowflies buzzing at the window. Although nobody had said anything, everyone had been curious about Stella in her funereal get-up. Hazel shifted in her chair, opened her mouth and closed it again. Stella felt everyone's eyes and ears straining towards her. She took her time in laying her knife and fork together on her plate. She tapped her lips lightly with a paper serviette that matched the tablecloth and folded it on her bread-and-butter plate.

'Yes, I do,' she said. 'He's French.' At that moment she wished he would materialise and carry her away.

Roy looked at Hazel but failed to capture her attention because she was staring at Stella, who was wearing her Jeanne Moreau face.

'Oh-la-la,' said Dawn, whose husband was away with the merchant navy, 'a Frenchman.'

'Where'd you pick him up?' leered Sid. His face was greasy from chewing on a turkey leg. He licked his fat fingers.

She turned her head away from him towards Beryl. 'We work together. He's an art director.'

'Oh, very nice,' said Beryl. 'A director . . .'

'Can I get down now?' said Rita.

'He's also an artist. His name is Jacques Boucher.' Stella knew they'd be even more impressed. Awestruck, too, because she pronounced it boo-shay in the French way.

'Yes, but don't go on the road,' said Beryl.

Beryl's mother, Mrs Doyle, whose grey hair had been dragged upward into a messy topknot as if to compensate for the descent of what used to be an hourglass figure, emerged from her habitual trance. 'I knew an artist once,' she said. 'He wanted to paint me without my clothes on. I told him where to go. Have we had pudding yet?'

'In a minute, dear,' said Beryl as she started to clear away the plates. All the women, except Stella and Mrs Doyle, stood up and made themselves useful.

The women repeated their screeching as the party broke up at around seven o'clock. The guests checked for their belongings in the bedrooms and behind the furniture in the lounge room. Beryl pressed packages of leftover turkey and pudding on them and they protested, but they didn't mean it.

At last they were bundled into their cars. Beryl waved and they moved off. Sid closed the front gate.

'What did you make of the de facto?' said Beryl.

'He's on a pretty good lurk,' said Sid, as they walked back to the house. He picked up a stone that had strayed on to the path, and pitched it over the fence into the street. 'She's always been as silly as a two-bob watch, that Hazel. No commonsense. Her kid'll come to no good, either, you mark my words.'

The moment they'd waved goodbye, even before the ute had turned the corner into Woodville Road, Hazel turned to Stella. 'What's this about a Frenchman?'

'What do you want to know?'

'Well, who is he?'

'Like I said in there, I work with him at the agency.'

'You never told me about him.'

'It's not that important.'

'Well, it was important enough for you to broadcast it to everyone else without telling your mother.' She rearranged the lumpy load on her lap. Instead of the mince pies, Hazel was now burdened with a Big Sister Christmas cake Beryl had insisted they take home along with the bag of leftovers.

'You have to keep an eye on those frogs,' offered Roy. 'You never know what they'll get up to with the ladies.'

'Jacques is very respectful,' said Stella. 'He calls me Étoile.'

'He ate what?' said Roy and swerved to avoid a pothole, causing the three of them to sway in unison and Hazel to clap a steady hand on the load in her lap. 'Sorry, ladies. No avoiding that.'

'Étoile! It's French for star. That's what he says I am, a star.'

'Oh gawd,' said Roy.

'Wonders'll never cease.' Hazel shook her head and stared up through the windshield, as though she'd just beheld a flying saucer.

'If you drop me at Bankstown Station I can get a train to Museum and take the bus.' Compared with what she'd been through today, Jacques seemed to be a knight in shining armour. Even if he was a pervert.

Chapter 20

The office was unusually quiet when Bea returned on the second of January. It was smart not to take an annual holiday this month when people with children did. In the absence of most account directors and clients, there was so little creative work to be done she could spend the time productively clearing files, transferring information into the new diary and generally putting her thoughts in order for the new year. If anyone sympathetic was around, a long lunch was on the cards and she could go home early without a qualm.

There was only one problem: Gary had time off but Stella did not. Bea was supposed to set a standard for her staff and she was irritated with Stella, however unfairly, because her presence curbed her own freedom. As she began to fit the 1963 pages of her new flip calendar into the metal holder on her desk, she put her mind to ways in which she could find something productive for Stella to do outside the office.

If she'd known that Desi would be going on a location survey she would have asked if Stella could join her. Too late now. Jacques had gone to Tahiti, otherwise he might have been persuaded to give her some sort of art appreciation course and a tour of the galleries.

Stella sensed Bea's disapproval and wondered if it was because she hadn't written to thank her for her party. Now she came to think of it, that was a bad oversight. She'd been distracted by what happened afterwards with Jacques. Where was he, anyway? His desk was completely clear. She tapped on Bea's door.

'Come in!' Bea was grateful for another presence, hoping it was someone dropping in to suggest lunch, until she saw that it was Stella. She tried not to be disgruntled. 'Happy New Year!'

'Same to you. I just wanted to say how much I enjoyed your party and what a gorgeous place you live in.' Stella was wearing a white piqué sheath that Bea recognised immediately. It was the one she'd tried on and coveted when she saw it at DJs before Christmas. Because she was a standard size twelve, it fitted her to perfection. The same could not be said for the way it hung on Stella's shape, clinging tightly across her bottom yet still loose above the waist, even though she must have stuffed cotton wool into her bra in an attempt to fill it out. It just didn't fit.

Bea tried not to give any sign that she recognised the sheath or felt irritation at Stella's underhand method of acquiring it. On the first morning of the sale, she must have been on the doorstep at 9.05 when the store opened because the dress was gone by the time Bea got there fifteen minutes later. Stella had an uncanny instinct for putting Bea at a loss for words, except for those that sounded petty and mean-spirited. All she could do was pretend it meant nothing.

'I'm so glad you enjoyed it. You got home all right?'

'Oh, yes. Jacques took me out to dinner.'

'Did he?' That was kind of him, thought Bea. Then she wondered if kind was the right word.

'I'm surprised he's not here.' Stella tried to make it sound unimportant.

'On holiday in Tahiti of the swaying palms. He thinks he's Gauguin. Which reminds me. I'm taking three weeks in February. You must let me know when you want to take your annual holiday, so we can make it official.'

'Okay, I'll let you know.' Stella hadn't thought about it because she couldn't afford to go anywhere as exciting as Tahiti. That left The Entrance, with Hazel and the de facto. She shuddered at the thought.

Before she left the room, Stella hesitated at the door. She turned to Bea and said, 'If you'd like someone to take care of your flat while you're away, you know who to ask. I just love your place.'

Tom was not pleased when Desirée told him she had to go back to work after New Year's Day. He eased himself off his deckchair, dived into the pool to cool off and swam a few laps before hauling himself up the ladder and padding a few paces towards her along the tiles beside the pool. She watched him carefully from behind her sunglasses. Werner's girth, not exactly pudgy but hardly washboard-flat, was no match for Tom's firm brown torso. She marvelled that being handsome had so little to do with sex appeal. That was a matter of taste, she supposed. Tom had such standard-issue good looks that he could have come off an assembly line that made talent for television commercials. She ought to cast him one day. She smiled to think how affronted he'd be by that suggestion.

'I don't know why you're amused.' He picked up a towel, rubbed his head with it and wiped the silvery beads of water from his face. 'There's nothing of any value going on in business at this time of year,' he said emphatically, towelling the rest of his body. 'I told you we've got the Bullmores' house at Merimbula for as long as we want it while they're away.'

'Your business might be slow but mine never lets up.' She knew she ought to be ashamed of herself for telling such a whopper but she wasn't. All she could think about was the prospect of going out of town for a few nights with Werner pretending to look for locations. 'Why don't you go and I'll join you at weekends?'

He sank into his deckchair. 'Oh, fun. Next thing you'll be sending your little brother to keep me company.'

'Now, there's a thought. Nicky would love it!'

By the end of the month, everyone was back at their desks. Guy said he had 'loved' being with his family at Kims Camp, up the coast at Toowoon Bay, but he didn't elaborate. Freddie was also reticent about his two weeks in San Francisco, although he raved about the spin-off trips to Las Vegas—where Frank Sinatra and the rest of the rat pack performed at The Sands—and to the Grand Canyon, where he claimed to have taken his life in his hands by descending it on a donkey. Jacques was far too worldly to talk about where he'd been unless someone asked, in which case he said that the Society Islands were 'beautiful'.

Discussing their planned journey to Lord Howe Island, Bea and Audrey made decisions about what to wear on the flying boat from Rose Bay and what to pack for a resort with a climate similar to Sydney's but with a population of no more than a couple of hundred permanent residents. They reminded each other of a dozen little details that had to be done before the day, such as drawing enough cash out of their bank accounts to pay the bill at Pinetrees, cancelling deliveries of milk and newspapers, having a spare set of keys cut and leaving them with someone trustworthy.

Throughout January, when a lot of people were away from their houses and flats, a spate of burglaries accompanied by vandalism had occurred in the affluent suburbs of the Upper and Lower North Shore and that made Bea feel nervous. She'd put a lot of effort, as well as whatever money she could afford, into making the flat comfortable for herself and the idea of having it defaced distressed her even more than the possible theft of a few possessions. Myrtle had offered to stay at Audrey's with Vernon. Having someone living in her own flat would give her peace of mind, thought Bea, as she sat at her desk making a list of things to be done before her departure. Her neighbour Martha could be relied upon to keep a watchful eye on the place but she was too nosy and such a gossip, Bea was wary of leaving keys with her. Then she remembered Stella's offer.

When Bea put the question to her, Stella beamed with delight. She needed a lift to her spirits. Since he'd been back Jacques had all but ignored her. The first time she saw him back at his desk she walked by with her head in the air expecting him to make a move in her direction. He paid no attention. The next time she passed his desk she said, 'good morning' but he was on the telephone smiling and speaking quietly in French. When she asked to borrow his magazines he just shrugged his shoulders and went on fiddling with transparencies on the light box. It was as though she didn't exist.

He had been so often in her thoughts during his absence, she began to think she was in love with him. Anything sordid in their last encounter began to fade, replaced by memories of his attentions at Bea's party, the moody atmosphere of the bohemian restaurant, the artiness of his studio. Sitting at her desk at lunchtime, she found herself playing the romantic tricks of the lovelorn: each twist of the stalk of an apple represents a letter of the alphabet, starting with a, and the letter reached when the stalk is detached represents the beloved's given name. It wasn't easy for the stalk to last until j so she cheated with tiny twists. Sometimes, when she carefully painted her nails, especially when she looked at the bare third finger of her left hand, she allowed herself to imagine the thrill of being Stella Boucher, Mrs Jacques Boucher, Madame Boucher. Goodnight Stella Bolt, good morning Étoile Boucher.

'Welcome to the Southern Cross, Mr and Mrs Dresner.' The receptionist shone a professional smile on the couple with only overnight bags for luggage as they faced him across the counter. He placed a registration card in front of Werner. 'If you wouldn't mind, sir . . .' While Werner filled in the details, Desi looked around at the sleek lines of the lobby, its modern fit-out so different from the stately old Windsor up the road, where the family often had Sunday lunch when they were in Melbourne. This place was a great slab of modernity and glamour, barely six months old, a towering presence in an otherwise low-rise cityscape.

'Great location,' she said with a wicked grin, as they crossed the lobby, Werner with his arm extended protectively at her back to shepherd her to the lifts.

* * *

'Where do they think you are?' He breathed against her neck where strands of her hair were damp and warm. She was more voluptuous than he'd imagined from the way she dressed. They were lying in a big soft bed like spoons in a drawer, both heads on the same expansive pillow.

'My family? Somewhere in the Southern Highlands with a team from the office. And the people at the office think I'm with a team from Rod Webb.' She turned her head to look at him but her body stayed within the arc of his. 'Where do they think you are?'

'Me? Nobody cares about my movements.'

'I do.' She rubbed her cheek against the stubble that had begun to appear on his chin. Even its abrasiveness was adorable to her. 'But I mean at Rod Webb.'

'They think I'm on a location survey.'

'Alone?'

'All alone.'

'Poor Werner.'

That nobody had any idea they were in Melbourne made their tryst all the more exciting. She turned over languidly to face him and the kissing started all over again. Later when they'd showered and put on towelling robes they decided to order steak sandwiches and fries from room service instead of grilled sole at Florentino, despite the luxury of being able to go out freely together without being recognised. Everybody she knew in Melbourne would be at Portsea at this time of year and Werner had been here too rarely to have made friends.

* * *

Sometime in the early hours of the morning she woke up and couldn't get back to sleep, plagued by thoughts of the decision she was going to have to make. She slipped out of bed quietly, put on a robe and sat beside the window, hoping she could see the spires of St Patrick's Cathedral, but she couldn't. It was too dark for anything outside to be discernible except the faintly lit footpath below, in front of the hotel's entrance.

There was no question in her mind about the need to break off her engagement with Tom and cancel the wedding. But she didn't want to alarm Werner with such a drastic move just yet. He'd feel responsible, obligated to her before he'd had a chance to declare what her father would have called his 'intentions'. If he had any. He'd said he loved her but he hadn't spoken of marriage. It was too soon. They hadn't been lovers for longer than a few weeks. She also suspected that if she moved too quickly he might reason that throwing one prospective bridegroom away without a qualm might mean she could do it just as easily again. Her hope for the outcome of these stolen days in Melbourne was that he would say he couldn't live without her. After that the rest would be easy.

When the telephone rang at Rod Webb the following afternoon, Rod was in a production meeting and Darryl was in a bad mood trying to cut a sixty-second commercial down to thirty seconds, so Kelvin, who was now spending as much time at the studio as he did at BARK, took the call.

'Hi, is Werner there?' said a lively female voice with an American accent. 'It's Libby, his wife. I'm calling from Santa Monica.'

'Oh. Hello Mrs Dresner. I'm Kelvin.'

'Hi Kelvin.'

'He's away for a few days, on a location survey.' Kelvin knew he was telling a lie. He happened to have seen two airline tickets for return flights to Melbourne among the mess on Werner's desk on the previous Friday afternoon. He only had to flip them open to find that one was for Werner and the other for Miss Desirée Whittleford. The locations they were supposed to be surveying were in the Southern Highlands, a couple of hours drive from Sydney, nowhere near Melbourne.

'Is there somewhere I can reach him? I just need his view on something.'

'Well, actually, he's in Melbourne.'

'Do you know the hotel?'

'No, but I know who he's with.'

'The team?'

'No, just one other person.'

'Rod, I guess?'

'No, my boss.'

'Rod is not your boss?'

'No, I'm from the agency. Desirée Whittleford is my boss. For now, anyhow.' To elevate his status, he added, 'I'm training for top management.'

'Just the two of them, huh?'

Libby had never met Desirée but she knew who she was, not only from Werner's having mentioned working with her, but from the social pages. You didn't have to live in Sydney long to know who the Whittlefords were.

Kelvin swallowed, then said, 'They've got the hots for each other.'

'They what?'

'Hey, forget I said that.' He gave a nervous laugh.

No reply came from Libby, so he felt obliged to fill the silence. 'Can I give him a message?'

'No. Thanks. You've been very helpful.' She hung up.

Feeling like an archer who's just scored a bullseye, Kelvin replaced the receiver.

Chapter 21

'We did it!' Freddie slapped Guy on the arm. Guy returned the gesture. They whooped like cowboys in a Hollywood western as they stepped out of the lift. It was incongruous behaviour for two briefcase-carrying executives in their best corporate garb. Mavis, earphones clamped to her head, fingers plugging and unplugging cords in the switchboard, glanced at them with alarm as they galloped past the reception desk.

'Youse blokes win the lottery or something?' Kelvin hovered around a stenographer as she collated sheets of paper at the Xerox machine. The rhythmic clanging of typewriters died down. Well-groomed heads looked up from their work.

'Better than that,' said Guy. 'We picked up the Phoebe Phipps business.'

'Cripes,' said Kelvin. 'Ladies' underdaks. My kind of account.'

Somebody giggled. The clatter of keys striking paper started up again.

'Get in line, junior,' said Guy, dousing his cigarette in the dregs of someone's coffee cup. 'Are those production quotes ready yet?'

'That's what I'm here for, boss.' Kelvin's hair had been cut so short that it stood straight up from his head, causing a wit from Dan Barnes's group to nickname him Dunny Brush.

'I'd be quicker if you stopped breathing down my neck,' grumbled the stenographer, whose name was Patsy. At 36-26-35 she was an eyeful for girl-watchers.

'We deserve a drink,' said Freddie. It was almost five on a Tuesday afternoon and they'd been performing for three hours in front of an abrasive manufacturer of corsetry in Surry Hills with nothing more to sustain or stimulate them than a cup of weak tea.

'Better go upstairs first and break the news to our superiors.'

'When's Bea due back?' asked Guy as they climbed the gloomy back stairs to bring good tidings to a higher authority.

'She's only just left. Gone for three weeks.'

'Bad timing.' Guy unlatched the steel door and held it open for Freddie.

'I'm not so sure about that.' Freddie liked and admired Bea, but she could be a threat to his position, so it was sensible to keep her in her place. They stepped on to soft carpet and breathed rarefied air. The atmosphere was rosy and hushed.

Freddie turned on his brightest smile as they approached Miss Leonie Braithwaite, keeper, protector and amanuensis of Felix B Bofinger, co-founder and chairman of BARK.

The brief was both exciting and challenging, Freddie told Stella in his office the next morning. He'd called her in five minutes before Guy was due to arrive at ten. 'This is your big opportunity, Stella,' he said, leaning towards her across his coffee table. 'There's no one standing in the way of your ideas this time.' He smiled collusively and offered her his pack of Marlboros. She accepted one and fitted it into a white cigarette holder she took from the pocket of the seersucker jacket she'd snapped up at Mark Foys' January sale. Her gestures reminded him of Bea's but her face was impassive. He assumed she was overwhelmed.

In fact, there was an unpleasant sensation in the pit of her stomach, a quivering nervousness. Bea wasn't there to hide behind. Stella felt exposed, as though she'd been asked to take her clothes off and dance for him. She shivered and tried to put the thought out of her mind, as Guy walked in with Kelvin.

'You cold?' Freddie looked concerned.

'No, it must be the air-conditioning.'

'I'll turn it down if you like.'

'No, I'm okay.' She forced a sweet smile but even he could tell it was fake. He was pleased to see that she realised the importance of the undertaking.

'This is right up your alley,' said Guy, handing her a thick document, spiral bound and labelled 'Confidential', while Kelvin placed a box on the coffee table. It was shiny white and much longer and wider than it was deep.

Guy began posturing, as he usually did when attention was focused on him, talking at length and elaborating unnecessarily, offering details that succeeded in complicating rather than clarifying the story, although the project was really quite simple: Phoebe Phipps & Co Pty Ltd's corselets, step-ins and brassieres were well-established in the market. The client now planned to branch out into lingerie. A new line of satin slips with matching scanties had been developed in racy colours—black and red—as well as traditional white and flesh-pink. The agency had been asked to invent a name for the line and to devise a television campaign that positioned it as both classy and sexy.

'Over to you, Stella,' Guy said finally, closing his copy of the document. 'Show her the samples, Kel.'

Kelvin opened the box, winked at Stella and let out a wolf whistle as he lifted slithery undies trimmed with lace from their tissue-paper wrapping and passed them to her for perusal. He licked his lips. Nobody suggested she should model the garments, but she didn't have to look at their eyes to know that's what they were thinking, although maybe Freddie thought he could carry off a fashion show better than she would.

'You can hang on to those for inspiration, but guard them with your life, okay?' said Guy, collecting his things before he stood up. 'How soon do you reckon we can see something?'

'First thoughts by Friday, Stella?' said Freddie. 'I know it's soon but let's not muck about.'

'Strike while the iron's hot,' said Guy.

And while the cat's away, thought Freddie.

People kept on intruding on Stella, disrupting her train of thought. The television department needed copies of the approved Cornicles scripts to go into production, so she had to rat around through various versions in Bea's filing cabinet, then take what she hoped were the finals to be verified by Guy who was in another meeting, which meant she had to hold on to them until he came out before she could take them to the photocopier. Assunta parked her trolley right in front of Stella's desk and wanted to know where Bea was, before she entertained everybody who came for a cup of tea with a description of her latest grandchild, born fortuitously on Australia Day. The accounts department rang to query a charge from a courier that seemed excessive for a delivery from York Street to Kippax Street in December. Patsy stopped by to ask for a contribution to a gift for Myra, who'd just become engaged. Bea's calls had been diverted to Stella's extension and, come lunchtime, Stella wondered if there was anyone left out there who did not know that Assunta's new grandchild was named Tito and that Bea was holidaying on Lord Howe Island and would be back at the beginning of March.

By mid-afternoon, she felt stupefied. Her mind was incapable of concentrating on the Phoebe Phipps brief. Not one relevant idea had entered her head.

She tapped on Freddie's half-open door and, when she poked her head around it, he looked up expectantly from a copy of *Advertising Age*.

'Cracked it already?'

'It's impossible out there,' she wailed. 'Nobody understands privacy. Could I work in Bea's office? I need to close the door and concentrate.'

'Sure, why not?' Then, as an afterthought. 'Don't get too cosy in there. She *is* coming back, you know.' She screwed up her nose at him.

Left to herself in the peace and quiet of Bea's domain, Stella re-read the brief and let her thoughts drift freely around the subject of undergarments, but they kept coming back to campaigns she'd seen before. Maidenform's 'I Dreamed I was A Tycoon' taunted her with its brilliance. She also remembered the slogan, 'Be exciting, be glamorous, be a Diomee girl' that had seduced Hazel into remaining forever loyal to spiral-stitched satin brassieres with cups shaped like missiles. By the end of the day Stella was bereft of a single original idea.

What was needed first, she said to herself as she boarded the ferry that evening at Circular Quay, was a name for the range. Phoebe's Fancies? Sounded like a packet of assorted biscuits. She plonked herself on the outside wooden bench facing east, where it was shaded from the searing orange sun. As they rocked past the construction site at Bennelong Point a breeze cooled her face. French Follies? Too sexy for nice girls. Princess Grace was a possibility, although that might be plagiarism, or something else Bea would consider unethical and illegal. Serene Princess was feasible if somewhat virginal, Stella decided, but she instantly felt better than she had done all day because the name was a possibility. The fresh air off the harbour clears the mind, she thought, as she stepped on to Cremorne Wharf.

As she walked up the hill to Bea's flat, another name occurred to her: Phoebe's Trousseau. With a line like, 'Lingerie so special you'll look and feel like a bride,' it could be a winner. The air over here is amazing, thought Stella, feeling exhilarated. She'd had two good ideas in half an hour and it was still only Wednesday.

After she'd eaten an egg salad and a slice of rockmelon with ice-cream, it seemed a sensible idea to write down the names she'd devised, along with the television ideas they'd conjured up, while they were still fresh in her mind. She went into the living room, sat at Bea's desk, took a few sheets of writing paper from the top drawer and started scribbling. When daylight began to fade and harbour lights started twinkling she switched on the reading lamp and kept on writing, occasionally scratching out lines or screwing up a page and throwing it in the waste basket.

It was almost ten o'clock by the time the work was finished to her satisfaction. She was tired but pleased with herself. All she needed now was a folder for her notes, so she pulled out the second drawer of the desk. When all it yielded was last year's diary, a thumbed address book, a rubber stamp with an ink pad, a dispenser with sticky tape, a box of paper clips and a pencil sharpener, she closed it and opened the bottom drawer. A manila folder labelled 'Ideas' was the only item there.

By the time the clock in the kitchen struck eleven, a piece of paper that looked as though it had been torn from a writing pad had been removed and the folder put back in the drawer, the rest of its random contents carefully placed in the order in which they'd been found. On the scrap of paper Stella had retained were the scrawled words 'Freudian Slip—for underwear!' She had a vague memory of Bea explaining the term to her some time ago. She hadn't grasped its meaning then and she still didn't understand it, but instinct told her it would make a useful third name to present to Freddie on Friday. Meanwhile, she would test her ideas on Desi first thing tomorrow. She went to bed and slept like an innocent.

'Have you got a minute?' Stella counted herself lucky to find Desi in her office at last. All morning she'd been out somewhere, at a studio, in a production meeting, or a casting session, or on location. On this sultry afternoon she sat staring out of her window with her hand on the telephone, as though about to pick up the receiver.

She smiled at Stella. 'Come in. Take my mind off the weather.' She waved her hand at the chair on the opposite side of her desk. 'Is it going to rain tomorrow? We're shooting the spaghetti commercial outdoors if the sun's out. It's supposed to be Italy.'

On Desi's desk was a little stack of cards and envelopes. Although the cards faced away from her, Stella could read what was printed on the top one: *Desirée Whittleford At Home*. It was set in elegant script at the top. She longed to know what had been hand-written underneath but she didn't dare let her eyes linger there, so she returned Desi's smile and put her folder on the desk and said, 'Um. Bea's away . . .'

'Yes I know. Lucky her.'

'. . . and I'm looking after her flat.'

'That is very kind, Stella. It will give her peace of mind.'

'Yes, but I wondered if I could try out some ideas on you.' Stella went on to explain the brief and to say how unsure she was because Bea was not around to guide her and assess her work before she took it to Freddie and Guy. To Desi she looked vulnerable, a day-old chick without the protection of a mother hen.

'Of course, if you think I can help.' Desi was touched and flattered. She listened attentively while Stella explained her thinking.

The commercial for Serene Princess would show a Grace Kelly type in her boudoir dressing for some kind of royal occasion. The words would go something like this: 'What makes a princess serene? Knowing she looks as beautiful in private as she does in public. Now you too can know that feeling with Serene Princess, new silky satin lingerie from Phoebe Phipps.' The final shot would be a tiara placed on a still life of a slip and scanties draped over the product package.

'That is feasible,' pronounced Desi, 'and very pretty.'

Stella screwed up her face in a nervous smile and blinked her eyes several times, then launched into a description of the Phoebe's Trousseau commercial, which would be much the same as the one for Serene Princess, except that the occasion would be a wedding and the final shot would be a bridal bouquet with the product. That, too, was given the nod.

'There's one more name but I haven't had time to develop a commercial for it.' No mention was made of its provenance or of her confusion over what the term meant. 'I wondered if you might help me make it work for television.' Her right eye began to twitch.

'Gladly.'

'It's called Froodian Slip.'

'Froodian? What is that?'

Stella felt her face flush. Slowly, she spelt the name. 'It's F-r-u-e-d-i-a-n.'

'Do you mean F-r-e-u-d-i-a-n?'

'I think so.'

'Freudian!' Desi opened her eyes and her mouth in unison. 'Stella! That is brilliant!' She'd had no idea the girl was so clever, so sophisticated, so witty. Her instinct was to leap to her feet but that would mean towering over Stella, so she remained seated while she improvised.

'It's *made* for television!' She tucked a lock of hair behind her ear, picked up a pencil, twirled it and put it down again. Stella watched her with concentration, then let her gaze fall again on the elegant card. A few moments went by before Desi continued, 'I can see it. A couple at a candlelit dinner. The man can't take his eyes off the lace top of a slip peeking out from the woman's low-cut blouse. It barely masks her cleavage. The male voice-over says, "Who's afraid of a Freudian Slip?" Pause for ten seconds of swelling, stringed music as we dwell on her peach-like bosom before the voice continues, "*He* is" as we cut to a close-up of the handsome man who is totally, helplessly, hopelessly in her thrall!

'Can you imagine it?' said Desi. In her mind the man was Werner. In Stella's he was Jacques.

'I can,' said Stella. 'It's powerful.'

'It might need a few words in the middle to explain the product but they should be kept short. Maybe something like, "Phoebe Phipps brings you a new line of satin lingerie so beautiful, so seductive, you might forget to hide it," . . . or, "it's a shame not to show it off." Something like that.'

'Yes, I can write that.' Stella was busy scribbling. When she'd finished, she looked up at Desi and felt a great surge of gratitude and relief, carrying with it more happiness than she could remember having experienced since she was nine and Hazel took her to a children's Christmas party at Anthony Hordern's where she was given a paper parasol with butterflies on it.

'I think we deserve a drink.' Desi bent down, unlocked a drawer in her desk and produced a bottle of Tio Pepe and two small stemmed glasses. Amazing what people keep in their bottom drawers, thought Stella, accepting a glass of dry sherry.

After the first glass, Stella plucked up the courage to say, 'I couldn't help noticing your beautiful stationery.'

'Oh,' said Desi, looking at the cards with a degree of unease. 'I'm supposed to be hosting a pre-wedding soirée. Girls only, to view my trousseau. It's not really my scene, but my mother seems to know best.'

'Mine too!' squeaked Stella. She sipped the sherry. 'Who does your printing?'

'Grenville & Sons, in Pitt Street. They're the best for engraving.'

They were on their third round and feeling chummy when Desi asked, 'Have you ever been in love?'

Stella barely hesitated before saying, 'Yes.' She was more forthcoming than usual; the sherry was adding openness to her exhilaration. She felt trusting and confident enough to say, 'But I don't think he likes me any more.'

'Why do you think that?'

'Well, he used to flirt with me. He was interested. You know, you can tell. But he takes no notice of me now. I might as well be invisible.'

'Do I know this person?'

Hesitation. A gulp for air. 'It's Jacques.'

'Ah.' I hope she knows he's a philanderer, Desi thought, but it would have been tactless and unkind to say so. 'Did something happen?'

'Aw. He did funny things.'

'You mean romantically?'

'Yeah.'

'Was he cruel, did he hurt you?'

'Oh no. Actually it felt . . . quite nice. But it wasn't right.' She squirmed and crossed her legs.

Desi reached for the bottle again and was astonished to find so little left in it. She shared the remains between both glasses.

'You know, Stella, when people are in love, they sometimes do things in the passion of the moment when they are alone—the sorts of things most people don't talk about.'

She was not the type to blush easily but she did marvel at some of the contortions she'd found herself in with Werner. 'As long as people are not hurting each other, or anyone else, there is nothing wrong with what they do in private to give and receive pleasure.' She took a sip of the drink and thought of Werner and their stolen nights in Melbourne. There was something about a hotel room that encouraged exploration; if you felt embarrassed afterwards at the thought of what'd you'd done, you just left it behind instead of being reminded by your own bed sheets or carpet or bathtub. Thinking along these lines brought on the painful awareness that he still hadn't said the crucial words.

Stella assumed she was thinking of Tom and wondered if he ever did to Desi what Jacques had done to her. If so, did she like it?

Chapter 22

It turned out to be a brilliant Friday morning. Swinging her basket woven from the leaves of kentia palms, Bea stepped barefoot along the sandy beach that skirted the placid lagoon. There was nothing on her mind except what to have for lunch after her swim—local garfish and honeydew melon?—and beyond that, a plan to take a siesta and then a bike ride with Audrey to Neds Beach at low tide to look at marine life through goggles.

Meanwhile, back at headquarters, Stella was trying to stop her hands from shaking as she finished her presentation to Freddie and Guy in the creative director's office and pretended to concentrate on putting her papers back into a neat pile.

The two listeners had remained noncommittal during her performance, but now Freddie said, 'I knew you could do it!' and started to applaud. Guy joined him. Then they stood up, still clapping.

Stella put her face in her hands and rocked back and forth in her chair. She had to make a big effort not to shed a tear. She swallowed and dabbed her nose with a handkerchief. 'You really think it's any good?'

'It's more than good, eh, Guy? I mean, they're all workable but Freudian Slip! That's inspired.'

'Ingenious,' said Guy. 'How did you think that one up?'

Stella gobbled up their praise as greedily as a half-starved urchin raiding a pastry shop. Her eyes glittered like little black sequins. 'The name just came to me in a flash. And after that, the commercial seemed to write itself.' Flushed with success, she began to feel very pleased with herself, impressed by her own cleverness. Her star had risen and it was dazzling them.

'I suppose we go to storyboard next.' She said it casually, not wanting to indicate how much she longed to see Jacques's face when he heard her ideas and to bask in the admiration they were sure to draw out of him.

'Not for this client,' said Guy. 'This guy's an entrepreneur. He doesn't need a storyboard. He'll either like the idea or he won't, eh, Freddie? He flies by the seat of his pants. Instinct, that's what he relies on. Jewish reffo, self-made smart cookie.'

A serious discussion began about the best way for the three of them to present the ideas to their smart-cookie client and to recommend the one they agreed was outstanding. Guy would arrange a meeting for the following Tuesday, by which time he'd have prepared an introductory document. Freddie would present the three ideas.

'What will I do?' asked Stella, feeling both relief and disappointment at not having a frontline role.

'All we want from you,' said Guy, 'is to hear your high heels clicking across the floor to take your seat beside Mr Wasserstein.'

'And if he asks any tricky questions,' added Freddie, 'give him your most charming smile and think up a really feminine answer.' Before she could ask precisely what he meant by that, he turned to Guy. 'I just had a thought. Why doesn't Stella dress like the lady in the commercial, you know, slip showing under the open blouse . . . ?'

'Mmm . . . Dunno. Might be overkill. Remember, Mrs Wasserstein is also in the business. She'll probably be there.'

'You're right. Just be your gorgeous self, darling.'

Stella felt put out at being given a cameo role—maybe not even that, just treated like a prop—while they shared the lead in what, after all, was her entire creation. She was *l'étoile* and they were upstaging her, snatching her ideas and running away with them. She wanted to protest but something made her decide not to. Client presentations were new to her. Wisely, and in the pattern of behaviour that had put her where she was today, she decided to observe the procedure and learn from it.

Settled on the sand at Blinky Beach, Bea smoothed lotion on her suntan, which was deepening satisfactorily to the shade of Cahill's caramel sauce, and pretended to discourage the attentions of a young off-duty waiter from the Swaying Palms Guest House. He squatted on his haunches beside her towel trying to guess the colour of her eyes behind the oversized sunglasses.

Audrey, sheltered under an umbrella beside them, finished writing wish-you-were-here postcards to everyone in her address book, and opened the leaflet she'd picked up from the general store, the island's only shop, on the day they arrived. 'Listen to this, Bea. The island is the home of the kentia palm and of teeming marine and bird life. It was uninhabited when a sea captain discovered it in 1788. But nobody settled here until 1833 . . .'

'Uh-huh,' said Bea. Why did her sister have to be so worthy?

'Full moon tonight,' said the waiter. 'We could go for a walk after work. My shift finishes a bit after ten.'

Audrey put the leaflet aside and looked up to admire the surfies riding in on crystalline breakers. 'You can't just come and live here if you want to,' she informed Bea. 'The man in the shop told me that. You have to be related to one of the old families.'

'Or be skilled at something they need that nobody else here can do,' said the waiter. He was looking at Bea's glistening thighs.

'I suppose that's why it's so beautiful and unspoiled,' said Bea, aware of the muscular shoulders under the waiter's white cotton shirt.

'No snakes or sand flies,' said Audrey. 'No roads either, just tracks. I saw a car yesterday.'

'Yeah,' said the waiter. 'There's only two on the whole island.'

Bea leaned back on her towel, closed her eyes and let the sun caress her body gently, like a warm hand. 'The lagoon must look wonderful by moonlight,' she said.

On Saturday morning, in a second-floor flat in Ithaca Gardens, Desi's capable legs were locked like a clip-on bracelet around Werner's loins as they both panted like a steam train grinding up the Razorback. They were making up for having been deprived of each other for almost a week, due to business demands and Tom's perfectly reasonable expectation of spending some time with his bride-to-be.

As midday approached, Stella whirled her way through Bea's flat with the vacuum cleaner and a feather duster while her mind grappled with the challenges presented by the upcoming meeting at Phoebe Phipps. Which persona to adopt? Since Mrs Wasserstein would be there, an impersonation of Jeanne Moreau would be unsuitable. Jean Shrimpton? She no longer found that role model exciting. Then she remembered Audrey Hepburn in *Breakfast at Tiffany's*. A little black dress, a fake pearl necklace and a long cigarette holder—although maybe not the cigarette holder—would turn her into an elegant gamine, an endearing innocent who posed no threat. She would certainly not wear the plunge push-up bra.

The only trouble was she didn't have a little black dress and the shops were about to close for the weekend. She turned off the vacuum cleaner and picked up the telephone.

'Hello, petal,' said Hazel. 'What a lovely surprise!'

As she worked all Saturday afternoon cutting, basting and tacking, and all day Sunday machining, pressing and hand-finishing, Hazel felt light-hearted. Stella had said she needed the dress for 'an important client meeting', but Hazel saw through that. She wasn't born yesterday. It was for the Frenchman. She remembered with satisfaction how impressed everybody at Guildford had been when Stella talked about him on Christmas Day. Maybe he was going to propose. Her imagination leaped ahead and she saw her daughter, radiant in a cloud of white tulle, walking down the aisle on the arm of someone who looked like a suave Charles Boyer, or a debonair Louis Jourdan.

'I get it, I get it.' Mr Wasserstein nodded his heavy head slowly and rhythmically and flapped his right hand at Freddie to indicate it was time for him to shut up. Freddie's voice faltered into silence.

'Whose idea is this?' Mr Wasserstein's head rolled sideways from Freddie to Guy to Stella, who'd been astute enough to seat herself not beside him, but next to his svelte wife. Having seen Mrs Wasserstein's quick and nimble movements when she entered the room, Stella at once decided to enrol herself in the June Dally-Watkins School of Deportment as soon as she could save up for a course. What Mrs Wasserstein lacked in flesh seemed to have been apportioned to Mr Wasserstein who, when he led the agency team into his office, trod heavily and squeakily on the brown linoleum as though the law of gravity had singled him out to test its pulling power.

'It was a group effort,' beamed Freddie.

'Yes, yes, but who thought of these words "Freudian Slip"?' Mr Wasserstein insisted in a heavily accented voice that indicated impatience with fools.

Reluctantly, Freddie was forced to relinquish the credit. 'Stella. It was her idea.'

Mr Wasserstein turned to the Holly Golightly lookalike. 'That is a very smart idea, little girl.' The lugubrious expression on his face made her think of a bloodhound.

She opened her eyes wide and gave him a sweet and modest smile, then turned to shine one on his wife. After that she looked down demurely at her hands in the lap of the sheath dress her mother had made from a length of black silk shantung, squirrelled in her sewing basket since 1957. Hazel had bought it to make a dress to wear to her mother's funeral but was too upset at the time to cope with it.

'I knew it would come in handy one day,' she'd said when Stella called on Saturday. 'Waste not, want not, that's my motto.' It wasn't in Stella's character to feel guilty about her mother spending most of the weekend at the sewing machine on her behalf. But she was grateful enough to pay for the raisin toast and coffee they had at Repin's when Hazel delivered her handiwork to the city by train on Monday.

Mrs Wasserstein, a dark-haired woman of middle age with heavy-lidded eyes and a lot of rings on her fingers, said, 'It is very clever. Very amusing.' She turned to Stella in a friendly way. 'We are from Vienna, you know, the city of Freud.' She looked at her husband. 'But I wonder if it is too sophisticated to be understood here. Might it go above the heads of most people?' Stella felt a jolt of recognition. She couldn't have agreed more but she didn't dare say so. She still wasn't sure she understood what it really meant, but since everybody else seemed to, she just kept quiet.

'I see your point,' said Guy, switching a smile on his face for Mrs Wasserstein, then shifting his gaze to her husband hoping for a clue.

'Ohh . . .' came a protest from Freddie. 'It will intrigue every viewer, male and female.'

Guy looked uncomfortable. 'That is of course the purpose of the exercise.'

What was that supposed to mean? Freddie had expected Guy's unqualified backing and here he was, weak-kneed and wavering.

'It is our belief that this brilliant idea will persuade every affluent woman, who has ever wanted a man's attention, to buy the product,' said Freddie. Stella was too terrified to say a word.

There was a pause while everyone waited for a pronouncement from the ultimate authority.

'I like it,' declared Mr Wasserstein. And that was that.

Nobody said a word when Freddie grappled with the sliding door of the cage lift and they descended slowly to the ground floor and walked around the corner, out of sight of the Phoebe

Phipps building. Then Freddie slapped Guy on the shoulder, Guy slapped him back and Stella did a little dance, like a toey whippet anxious for a sprint. Freddie's desire to throttle Guy for his disloyalty disappeared in the relief and excitement of triumph.

'Taxi!' yelled Guy at a Red Deluxe turning out of Foveaux Street. He opened the back door for Stella and Freddie before sliding into the front beside the driver.

'Where to?' asked the immigrant from Thessalonica.

'You know Beppi's?'

'Yurong and Stanley.'

'That's it.' Guy looked over his shoulder. 'Okay with you two?'

As they sped off along Elizabeth Street, Stella knew she would never in her entire life forget this day. If anything in the world could be as good as *Breakfast at Tiffany's* it had to be lunch at Beppi's.

It turned out to be memorable for another reason, too, something she'd sooner forget. With all the excitement, the copious glasses of Prosecco, the veal saltimbocca (which means 'jump into the mouth,' said Aldo) and the tiramisu, Stella's initiation into the inner circle finished with her reeling into the ladies' room and throwing up in the toilet bowl.

Chapter 23

As co-founder and chairman of Bofinger, Adams, Rawson and Keane, Felix Bofinger (known to all as FB and to some as Friggin Bore) did not often leave his cushioned enclave on the sixth floor to make his presence felt on the other two levels occupied by his advertising agency. So, when Stella happened to be back at her desk for a few minutes on Wednesday afternoon, the sight of his tall, praying-mantis frame bending over to speak to her caused a flutter of interest around the fifth floor.

Kelvin managed to ease himself near enough to hear the bigwig-from-above utter the following words: 'I believe you have done the agency proud, Miss Bolt, with your creative work for our new client. Well done.' When he'd moved on among his busy workers, hands clasped behind his back, looking this way and that like a schoolmaster supervising an examination, Kelvin replayed FB's words to Gary in the men's room, knowing they'd make him jealous, and to Jacques, who shrugged as if to say,

'What has that to do with me?' and went on laying down type on a Lustrée layout.

Desi, who'd just heard about the success from Freddie on the telephone, rewarded Kelvin with a suitably enthusiastic response and got up from her desk. Stella, sorting through her in-tray, saw her advance across the floor and felt a moment of alarm.

'Congratulations!' Desi enthused, standing over Stella in much the same way as FB had done. 'I hear they loved the Freudian Slip!'

'Yes they did.' Stella tried to seem modest, as she dropped a sheaf of papers into the waste basket.

'The commercial too?'

Stella nodded several times in quick succession and screwed up her face in a nervous little smile. 'Come in for a minute,' she said, indicating Bea's office. She was shaking with excitement. Desi followed and Stella closed the door behind them so that nobody else was within earshot. 'I just want to thank you so much for helping me with the commercial. They approved it without a change, not even a tiny one. The next step is a quote and we go into pre-production. Freddie said he'll handle all that with you.' Her arms reached up to Desi, like a child asking to be picked up by its parent.

Desi bent down and they hugged. She was touched almost to tears. 'The pleasure is entirely mine, Stella. I'm so pleased to have been useful. Freudian Slip is a great idea. All I did was give it a nudge along.'

Back in her office, Desi looked at the bowl of mauve roses on her desk—ah, Werner's romantic soul!—and thought how bittersweet it must be for Stella when her success in business was contrasted with her failure to entice the man she'd set her heart on. She got to her feet again, left her office and made her way purposefully through the typing pool in the direction of

Jacques. When she stopped at his desk, he stood up and gave her a lopsided grin; she had a presence that inspired respect in others, even someone as sceptical as Jacques. In fact, he regarded her as the only truly civilised person in the agency.

'You've heard the news about Stella?' Desi was as proud as a parent whose child has topped the class.

'Her campaign, you mean?'

'Yes! Even FB has been down here to congratulate her.'

'I noticed.'

'I know,' said Desi, as though the thought had just entered her head. 'Why don't we take her out for a drink somewhere? The Australia, maybe.'

'Now?'

'It's nearly going-home time.'

'I'm not sure she is interested in having a drink with me.'

'Oh, but she is. Believe me. Shall I ask her?'

He turned the palms of his hands and his shoulders upward in a gesture of compliance. 'If you wish.' She couldn't read the expression on his face but she thought she saw a faint spark of interest in his eyes.

'Stella,' said Desi, poking her head around the door to Bea's office. 'Put on your lippy. Jacques is taking us to The Australia for a drink.'

'There must be something we can do to give her a bit of privacy,' Freddie protested into the receiver. These money men understood nothing but balance sheets and bottom line. 'What about the small meeting room off reception?' . . . 'Yeah. The one near Guy.' They were so programmed to say no to everything, he was becoming exasperated and his voice went up a few decibels, making him sound hysterical. He looked at the Marlboro Man poster on his wall for moral support. 'Then let them book the one on the fourth floor, or get off their bums and meet at the client's.' He sat back, receiver to his ear, pulling faces at the ceiling. 'Well, why don't we have a look at it? What? Yeah, now. Right now. See you there.' He placed the receiver in its cradle and stood up. It was imperative to settle Stella into an office of her own, with her own accounts, before Bea was back standing in her way again.

Although it had no window and measured only eight feet by ten, the intimate space was fitted with niceties such as concealed lighting, slate-coloured carpet and apricot walls holding three framed prints of fashion illustrations by René Gruau that Freddie had bought for the company in Paris. This afternoon he used his considerable charisma and his licence as creative director to bedazzle Arthur Rawson, the overall-grey partner and company secretary who had a grip on the purse strings but none on imagination, into agreeing with him. While he was about it, Freddie managed to secure Stella a salary increase, what he termed 'a few extra bob'.

While Kelvin hovered, Gary brooded and Freddie fussed about in his role as interior decorator and mastermind, the boys from despatch removed the conference table and chairs on Thursday and replaced them on Friday with a desk, a standard lamp with a plain cylindrical shade, two chairs and a filing cabinet. Stella took possession on Monday morning, a week before Bea was due to return.

'Geez,' said Freddie. 'You look like Hedy Lamarr in *White Cargo.*'

Bea laughed. Mimicking the dusky seductress in the old 1940s film, she deepened her voice, looked over her shoulder and breathed, 'I am Tondelayo.' Of all the suntans that had appeared in the office that summer, hers was the smoothest, deepest and most covetable. She knew it. Just to be sure it made an impact before it began to fade, she wore a white linen suit on her first day back at the office.

'That good, was it?' he said as she positioned herself on his sofa and crossed her bare bronzed legs, swinging the top one rhythmically and tapping her toe on the floor. Through the crisscrossed white straps of her high-heeled sandals he saw that even her feet were brown and her toenails had been painted blood-red, to match her lipstick. He'd never seen her so relaxed.

'Pretty good,' she said with a languid smile. She thought about Joe, the waiter from the Swaying Palms. 'I don't know how I'll cope without my afternoon siesta.' She gave a theatrical yawn to show that she was joking. 'When I got home on Saturday my flat-sitter had left, the place was immaculate, supplies were in the fridge and a bunch of gardenias and a charming note of thanks were on the kitchen table. I have been spoiled.' She grinned and gave a great sigh of satisfaction. Then she tried to look businesslike, uncrossing her legs and putting her feet together. 'What have I missed?'

'Ah, same old stuff. You didn't miss a thing.' Freddie held out an open pack of Marlboros and she shook her head. He took one for himself.

'In that case I should have stayed another week.'

'Whoa! It's not *that* uneventful. Let's see.' He sat back in the armchair opposite her and blew smoke towards the corkboard behind his desk where a chart titled 'Critical Path' had been pinned; on it was a diagram coordinating all the elements of the Cornicles campaign and plotting its progress through the various stages of production. 'Bob Young is recording the Cornicles soundtrack on Thursday at Madrigal. You'd better liaise with the television department about that. Bonny Baby Food has just gone to air; it has a good showing at point-of-sale, but it's a bit soon to know if it's moving off the shelves. Lustrée is at finished art. Looks terrific. Jacques has done a great job.'

Bea nodded and smiled. Jacques could always be depended upon.

Freddie scowled. 'I wish I could say the same for the Taranto Spaghetti rushes. Nightmare. Total reshoot. But that's not one of yours, is it?'

'Maybe it should be,' she quipped.

'You've got enough on your plate.'

'Indeed I have.' She stood up and smoothed her skirt. 'I must go and find my group.'

'Oh, yeah. One more thing,' he said, lighting a new cigarette from the stub of the old one. 'We picked up a piece of new business.'

'We did?' She turned back to look at him with wide-open eyes. 'Great! Tell me it's not beer or house paint.'

'Phoebe Phipps. A new line of lingerie.'

'Bravo!' She clasped her hands together. 'When do we start?'

'We've already started.'

'Good.'

'In fact, we've finished. Stella came up with a fantastic campaign.'

'She did?' Bea couldn't quite believe what she was hearing. Stella had come good at last? What a relief.

'And the client loves it. She's named the range . . . you'll never guess what?'

'What?'

'Freudian Slip!'

'Freudian Slip?'

'Isn't that brilliant? She's at the client with Guy right now, being briefed on the trade presentation.'

Bea went back to her office, closed the door and sat at her desk. 'Freudian Slip—for underwear!' She remembered writing the words and tucking them away somewhere for future reference. But where? She got up and started flicking through the contents of her filing cabinet. The 'Futures' file held nothing but a news item about the possibility of a visit to Australia by a sensational new pop group called The Beatles. There was no file for 'Lingerie' or 'Underwear'. Then she remembered putting the scrap of paper with other bits and pieces of inspiration in a folder at home.

The buoyant spirits she'd brought to the office this morning slowly turned to lead. If someone else had come up with Freudian Slip as a name, Bea would have recognised it as a coincidence. Such things happened when creative minds applied themselves to the same brief. But given Stella's habit of borrowing ideas, she knew how unlikely it was that she had originated this one.

Her line of thinking made her feel uncomfortable, petty and selfish, as though she expected gratitude, or was envious and wanted to steal Stella's moment of glory. I should at least give her the benefit of the doubt, she thought, in the hope that Stella might be open about it and acknowledge her indebtedness when they were face to face. How likely was that? Clearly, she had led Freddie to believe it was all her own work.

On her desk was a package, wrapped in palm leaves, with a gift tag that read, 'For Stella, the best flat-sitter, with many thanks and love from Bea.' Inside was a cardboard box with three trophies she had collected from the beaches of Lord Howe Island and wrapped in cotton wool: a kauri shell, the fragile white skeleton of a heart urchin and a dried blue starfish. The island was so innocent of commercialism, there was simply nothing to buy there in the way of gifts, so Bea had become a beachcomber in order to find something to express her gratitude.

Since Stella was at a client meeting, Bea decided to leave the package on her desk.

'Stella doesn't sit there any more,' said Gary, looking up from his typewriter, a few desks away. 'She's got an office now, the meeting room near Guy. Freddie put her in there last week.' His face was noncommittal. She tried and failed to achieve the same effect with hers. She opened her mouth and froze.

That evening, the first thing Bea did after she'd let herself into the flat was to go to her desk and open the bottom drawer. She took out the folder marked 'Ideas' and sat down to go through it. There was no sign of a scrap of paper with the words she was searching for. It had vanished, like a mirage. Somebody had been prying.

Chapter 24

It was hard for Bea to shake off the feeling of being persecuted. It was just as difficult to decide on the most sensible way to deal with the two people she felt had betrayed her. She slept fitfully, stultified by the heat of a humid night and tormented by the poisonous nature of her thoughts. Stella had stolen her idea and pretended it was her own. Behind her back, Freddie had overridden her authority in elevating Stella's status by giving her an office, and probably a pay rise. She had no doubt they were in collusion. The dishonesty of their behaviour was what irked her most of all. She got up at dawn feeling as though she'd never been on holiday.

What should she say to Freddie? 'I see you've taken it upon yourself to give Stella an office of her own,' was too heavy with sarcasm. 'You have overridden my authority,' would make her sound pompous and insecure. 'Why wasn't I told?' was comic, like some old bat berating a neighbour over the back fence.

* * *

He was on the telephone and his door was half open, so she went in without knocking.

He waved her towards a seat but she continued to stand with her arms folded while he said, 'Gotta go. My meeting's arrived. Call you later,' and hung up. He looked at her with a smile that quickly faded. 'What can I do you for?'

'Freddie, I know that you have excellent timing. You never miss a beat. So giving Stella an office of her own while I was away cannot have been by chance. It was deliberate. Why did you do that?' She was surprised at the calmness of her voice and the clarity of her words.

He looked shocked, defenceless. He hadn't been prepared for a confrontation. The Bea he knew was a sideways-moving person, tactful, cooperative and patient.

'What do you mean?' he said, to give himself time for a more sensible answer.

'I don't think I can make it any clearer.'

'Ah, don't get your ti . . . knickers in a knot, Bea. It's only a box near the lift.' He raised his voice to make up for the feebleness of his words. 'She had a win with a client. You were away, otherwise of course you'd have been consulted. Business has to go on, even when people are on holiday.'

'I understand,' said Bea in a reasonable way. 'Waiting a week would have been intolerable.'

The coldness of her manner alarmed him. She was the agency's most valuable writer, with a reputation in the industry that would make her a prize for any important rival company to win. Freddie stood up, skirted his desk and put an arm around her shoulders. 'I'm sorry for not doing this by the book, but I assure you that I had no intention of undermining your authority. Trust me. I have the utmost respect for you as a person and as a professional.'

She looked at him with her big possum eyes. 'Okay. But don't try a stunt like that again.'

'Who me?' He put on his shucks-I'm-just-a-cowboy grin. 'I hope you're free for lunch. It's a gorgeous day for the Ozone.'

Stella looked at the words staring back at her from her typewriter and knew they didn't sound right: *Phoebe Phipps presents an exciting new development in ladies' intimate apparel.* The sentence was flat. Boring. What would Bea think of it? Bea would ask: Where is the promise? For the retailers Stella was targeting now, the answer would be money. Her forefinger pushed the return key and when the typewriter carriage clunked into position she typed the words, *Phoebe Phipps promises you profits beyond your wildest dreams from its exciting new lingerie line.* That sounded better. A bit far-fetched, but never mind.

Finding a few words that were adequate wasn't much of an accomplishment but it succeeded in helping to calm her nerves. They'd been on edge ever since she moved into this office. Even before then, when she presented the Freudian Slip idea to Freddie and Guy, she had felt tense; she kept on needing to go to the loo; her emotions seemed to seesaw between glee and apprehension. Self-analysis was not one of Stella's characteristics, so the less admirable aspects of her behaviour were buried and never dug up, therefore never examined. She had become prone to bouts of moodiness. On the surface, though, it was all too exciting. This pretty little cocoon was hers alone to work in. Her pay packet would be fatter this Friday. And Jacques was taking notice of her again.

She looked up with a start to find Bea standing in the doorway. She was smiling but her stillness sent an ominous signal. Stella bared her teeth in a smile that managed not to reach her eyes. 'Welcome back!'

'Thank you.' Bea had decided there was no point in mentioning the office. She simply placed the palm-leaf package on Stella's desk. 'A tiny token of thanks for looking after the flat so well.'

'Oh, don't thank me, I enjoyed it,' said Stella. She picked up the gift and read the tag. 'Can I open it now?'

'Of course.' Bea parked herself on the moulded plywood chair meant for guests. Freddie must have swiped it from reception. 'Don't expect the crown jewels,' she said with a smile. 'There is literally only one shop there and all it sells are groceries, suntan lotion and fishing tackle.'

The smile was still pasted on the bottom half of Stella's face as she delved into the contents of the box and retrieved the trophies with a little squeal of exaggerated delight. 'Gee, thanks,' she said. As she looked at the dead marine creatures, it was clear they meant nothing to her. They lacked a logo or a brand image by which she could measure their value.

Bea was grateful that she didn't have to ward off an attempted kiss. 'Freddie told me about your success with Phoebe Phipps,' she said, training her penetrating gaze on Stella. 'Congratulations. Freudian Slip! I'd love to know how that came about.'

'Bea, I long to go through it with you, but time's running out. Can we do it another day? I've got to write a script for the trade presentation. Guy wants to see it today and the client expects it tomorrow.' Stella felt her right eyelid beginning to twitch uncontrollably, so she covered it with her hand. 'I'm sorry, I think I got something in my eye.' She sniffed and stood up. 'I have to go to the ladies'.'

By the time she was back in her office, Bea had gone. Stella collected the scavenged items, put them back in their box and dropped it into her waste basket.

Their second bottle of chablis was brought to the table and uncorked. Bea looked out at the boats bobbing about in the bay as safely and uneventfully as rubber ducks in a bathtub. Beyond them, the bridge was a line drawing against the glowing western sky, every bit the image of its nickname of The Giant Coathanger. As the wine started to take effect and Freddie's voice gabbled on about an exhibition he'd been to at Macquarie Galleries her mood began to change. Indignation was replaced by resignation. Did it really matter if there was a misunderstanding about whose idea it really was? When an advertising campaign was successful you could get killed in the stampede of people claiming to own it. When it failed they ran a mile the other way.

Nevertheless, she wouldn't have been human if she weren't tempted to plant a doubt in Freddie's credulous mind. She re-positioned the sunglasses on her nose and peered at him. 'Did it occur to you that Freudian Slip might be a bit . . . sophisticated to be dreamed up by a girl like Stella?'

He shook his head slowly, not to indicate that the thought had never entered his head—although it hadn't—but because he felt saddened by her begrudging Stella her achievement. 'Let it go, Bea. You've been her teacher and mentor. You should be proud of what she's done.'

She looked across the water. A man in shorts emerged from the cabin of a small cruiser and tossed the contents of a garbage bin overboard.

'If you say so, Freddie.'

An air-conditioner stuck in one of the windows wheezed like an asthmatic, the ceiling fan creaked as though it had arthritis and there was a relentless roar, like the sound of an angry sea, from massed sewing machines on the other side of the closed door. Stella had to raise her nasal voice to cut through the interference and present her script for the trade presentation to Mr Wasserstein in his office at Phoebe Phipps. Nobody spoke until she had finished. Wheezes, creaks and roars filled the silence that followed.

'"Profits beyond your wildest dreams",' said Mr Wasserstein. He lifted his ponderous head and looked at Guy. 'How can we promise they will make this mountain of money? That is up to them.'

Guy pulled at the collar of his shirt, which had become too tight since he'd gained a few pounds. 'It's just . . . a figure of speech,' he said. 'Poetic licence.'

'Licence to be sued,' said Mr Wasserstein. He looked at Stella. 'Your other words are nice . . . very nice . . . but how do you say?' He turned to his wife.

'Polite,' said Mrs Wasserstein.

'Too polite,' said Mr Wasserstein emphatically. 'We need punch not polite.'

Stella cast a fearful glance at Mrs Wasserstein who seemed not to notice. There was no friendliness coming from that direction today. This time it was strictly business. Pleasing Mr Wasserstein was the only way to earn anybody's support.

'Punch we need,' declared Mr Wasserstein, punching his desk. '"From today, every one of your customers can have a more beautiful body with Freudian Slip!" *That* is a promise with punch!' He punched the desk again.

'I know what you mean,' said Guy.

'Do you?' Mr Wasserstein glared at him. 'Then bring me what you know what I mean.'

'Well, we'll certainly go back to the drawing board.'

As they left the building in defeat, Guy doubted that Stella was equal to a re-write. Her approach was too . . . airy-fairy. He'd have to call on help from Freddie. Better still, Bea.

In the end, it was Gary who was landed with the task of putting punch into the trade presentation for Freudian Slip. He'd done such a good job on the Bonny Baby Bloopers script, Freddie told Guy not to bother Bea with it because she had too much going on with Cornicles and other demanding clients to be able to spare the time. Stella was told to work with Desi and Lavinia on finding suitable actors for the commercial and to involve herself in all the other stages of pre-production.

The day after Gary's script for the trade presentation was approved, he walked into Bea's office and resigned. He'd been made an offer too good to refuse from George Patterson to work on the big-spending Colgate Palmolive account. 'And yeah,' he said, 'I get an office of my own.'

Chapter 25

The prospect of designing a tower block on the river in Brisbane took Tom Boyd and two of his colleagues north for a week and gave Desi the rarity of evenings without pre-marital obligations or the subterfuge of getting out of them. She was free to be with Werner in his bunker, which had become a place of beauty for her, not for its form but for its function. It was associated in her mind with more bliss than she had believed possible, in the era she defined as BW. Before Werner, she had been only half alive.

After a preliminary casting session that finished early on Wednesday afternoon she left the office—and her car parked in the company garage—and took a taxi to Kings Cross to buy leberkäse and sweet German mustard from Handler in Darlinghurst Road and a citron tart and four brioches from the Croissant d'Or in Macleay Street. By the time she was at the front door of the flat in Ithaca Gardens she'd also managed to acquire a bag of potatoes, a bunch of spinach, a loaf of bread and an armload of white camellias, so she had to dump her bags on the floor to fit her key in the lock.

Domesticity had never appealed to Desi before, but preparing potato salad, setting the table and uncorking a bottle of claret to let it breathe had become a luxury when she did it for Werner. A new album of Beethoven's Ninth Symphony recorded by the Berlin Philharmonic under Herbert von Karajan was waiting to be heard. Washing the spinach several times to get rid of any grit and skinning the boiled potatoes while they were still warm, she let her thoughts glide ahead. She was able to stay all night; as far as her parents knew, she was on a location survey again. Tonight she would try to manoeuvre the conversation around to the future and whether she and Werner had one together. It would be better still if he raised the subject, without being prompted. Ah, what an Ode to Joy that would be!

A vigorous knocking on the door startled her. Werner must have forgotten his key. She wiped her wet hands on a tea towel and hurried to let him in. The caller turned out to be a courier, so she signed for a foolscap envelope and saw that it came from J Walter Thompson. She put it on Werner's desk and went back to the kitchen to fossick for candles.

When Werner arrived with his briefcase at a little after six, he carried a bag of walnuts and a bottle of Krug. He took them straight into the kitchen before he turned to put his arms around her. They stood there for several seconds, each leaning against the other.

'This is the reward that makes a day worthwhile,' he said.

'Why don't we do this more often?' she said.

'That's the name of a song.'

'Is it? Sing it to me.'

'I have a tin ear and no voice.'

'Nonsense.' She was laughing now. They broke apart. She thought he looked tired. 'Let me do this,' she said and reached for the bottle of champagne. It was nicely chilled.

'Don't spoil me,' he countered, taking it from her. 'I might get used to it. Then you'd be sorry.'

'I like looking after you.' She was flirting, girlish, flushed.

'I like it too.' He took from the freezer the only two champagne glasses he possessed. They were wide and flat and their stems were hollow.

She flicked a fingernail at the rim of one and it rang like a bell. 'These are beautiful. Were they a wedding present?'

'I had to salvage something.' He said it with good humour and she took it in the same spirit.

It was too early to eat, so they sat on the Tempe Tip chairs sipping champagne and cracking the walnuts, a present from Rod Webb, whose brother-in-law grew them near Geelong.

Subjects that should have been forbidden—confidential inside information—were discussed, in the unspoken agreement that shoptalk was innocent as long as it was kept a secret between them. It was a way of letting off steam and of reaffirming intimacy. Desi talked about the disastrous Taranto Spaghetti shoot: they started late because of a set-to between the actress and a stroppy props assistant who'd chosen her wardrobe; the noise from a team of road workers and then a flock of crows interfered with the sound recording; a southerly buster brought a downpour just after the lunch break; it had to be a wrap with only a few takes in the can. 'There was a hex on that day! We'll have to pay for the re-shoot, and that makes me look bad,' said Desi.

'Well,' said Werner, 'I hope you loaded the original quote in case of an emergency of this kind.'

'I inflated it a bit, but I'm not sure it's enough to cover us.'

'The production house might be willing to carry some of the cost. They get plenty of work from you.'

'Bury it in future productions, you mean? I suppose so.'

'You're not the only one with problems,' he said, knowing it would console her to hear about his own difficulties. 'We have a running battle with the lab on a Kraft commercial for JWT. I'm sure there was nothing wrong with Rod's camera work. Something happened in the processing but they deny it. I'm expecting some correspondence on it.'

'An envelope arrived this afternoon. It's over there.'

'I'll look at it tomorrow. Did you say we have leberkäse?'

At the table Desi put a thick slice of the German meatloaf on each of their plates while he opened the jar of mustard. 'Is this comfort food for you?' she said.

'A happy childhood memory.' He helped them both to potato salad. 'From the old country, before we went to America, although sometimes we had it there too. It's almost as good as *kartoffelpuffer*, potato pancakes. My father used to make them. He was a good cook. It was relaxation for him at the end of the day.'

Desi thought of her own father, who'd never been in the kitchen except to ask May where she had put the corkscrew, or what was on for dinner. 'And your mother, did she cook?'

'She tried. She was an academic, a doctor of philosophy. She had never spent time in the kitchen. I'm afraid we teased her mercilessly. My father used to say to me, "How can your mother be Jewish when she can't even make chicken soup?" Then he'd laugh and she'd whack him with a book. They adored each other. She played the piano while he cooked.'

'Your father was Jewish too?'

'No. He was one of the *volk*, a German who came from what Hitler regarded as a pure line—whatever that might be. My father used to sneer at it. We were an impossible family under the Nazis so we got out in 1935, and moved to America.'

'And then what happened? I mean, I'm not trying to pry, but you know all about me. I don't know anything about you.'

'Well, I was thirteen, so I went to school. My father was a cutter, a film editor, so we settled in Los Angeles. He did very well in the business; they bought a pretty bungalow in West Hollywood. But he got into trouble politically.' Werner stood up and took their empty plates to the kitchen. When he came back he said, 'Are you sure you want to hear all this?'

'I do, I do!' said Desi and quickly regretted her choice of words, so nuptial they might put him off. 'Yes, I'm sure,' she added hurriedly and refilled their claret glasses. She put her elbows on the table, rested her chin on her clasped hands and looked at him, thinking how fine his features were and trying to guess which bits of him came from his father and which from his mother. His forehead was high, his eyes were pale and there were shadows underneath them. He had the hands of an artist, with long fingers and well-formed nails.

'I don't know whether you've heard about McCarthyism.'

'Vaguely. Something to do with anti-Communism.' Desi knew more about it than she let on; she loved the sound of his voice, and she wanted to hear his version. She started slicing the lemon tart.

'If you lived with the rise of Nazism, as we did in Germany, either you went along with it, or you were likely to turn to the left, to the ideals of Communism.' He took the plate she offered. 'Thank you. My father was not a member of the Communist Party—or of any political party—but he was a sympathiser.' He sliced a piece off the tart with his fork, put it in his mouth and swallowed. 'Mmm. That's good. After the war, paranoia about Communism started in America and a senator named Joe McCarthy stirred it up so that anyone accused of being a Communist in the film industry—not just in that industry, in others too—was black-listed. That means they couldn't get work. That's what happened to my father in 1952.'

'That's terrible, after everything your family had been through.' Desi was suddenly aware of how fortunate she had been. Her travels had always been thrilling luxuries. His had been prompted by grim necessity.

'He and my mother went back to Germany, to West Germany. What else could they do? He's retired now. They live at Tegernsee, on a lake near Munich.'

'That's when you came here?'

'Seven years ago. I wanted a clean start, and Libby went along with me on that. She tried her best, and it was okay at first. But the homesickness just got worse. She couldn't adjust. No hard feelings, though. We parted amicably.'

By now they'd cleared the table. In the kitchen Werner did the washing up while Desi dried. It was the marital nature of the evening, the comfortable way they behaved towards each other that pleased Desi as much as the anticipation of sharing his bed for the whole night.

Afterwards he put on the Beethoven recording. It was particularly moving, so much so that, curled up together on the chesterfield, they listened to all of it without exchanging a word. It was a luxury not to have to hurry. At least, not until they were in bed, when their need for each other became urgent and they let it take over. Desi forgot to be anxious about the future. The present was overwhelming.

They were both asleep, replete and breathing heavily, when there was a thunderous knock on the door, loud enough to wake the entire building.

'Christ!' said Werner, springing up like a jack-in-the-box when the catch on the lid is released. 'Who the hell can that be?' He reached for something to wrap around his nakedness and put his hand on Desi's fluffy lilac nightdress, lying on the chair beside the bed. He got up, tied the nightie roughly around his waist and muttered, 'Bloody couriers. What time is it?' not expecting an answer from Desi, who yawned and stretched, turned over and sank into the pillows again.

The next thing she knew, there was a scuffle and a flash, like lightning. Then another and another. Werner's shocked voice was saying, 'Who the hell are you?'

Another man's voice said, 'Are you Werner Dresner?'

'Get out of here,' shouted Werner. There was a thud and a kind of strangulated gurgle. Desi put a foot on the floor, hesitated as she tried to find her nightie, then retreated to the bed, covering herself up with the sheet when she saw two strange men crowding into the doorway of the bedroom. They both wore hats and looked like spivs in some third-rate gangster movie.

'Do you know that this is a married man?' demanded the one who thought he was Humphrey Bogart, while his weedier sidekick aimed a camera at her. Without even thinking she looked at the camera and smiled; it was automatic, sociable, simply what one does. Several bursts of light momentarily blinded her.

'Yes, I do,' she said brazenly and flung a pillow at them, knocking the hat off Bogart. While he looked startled and took half a step backwards to find his hat, she grabbed the other pillow and flung that with both hands, which caused the sheet to fall from her breasts. It was lights and camera once more before she could clutch the sheet to herself again.

The trespassers left as quickly as they had arrived. She heard the front door shut with a bang. She got out of bed, wrapped the sheet around herself and hobbled into the living room looking like a mummy. Werner stood there stunned, still ludicrously covering his manhood with Desi's baby-doll negligee, which had been loosened in the skirmish. They had been caught *in flagrante delicto*, a situation her father had mentioned in relation to low life in the courts of law. She'd also read about it, in greater detail, in lewd detective stories. The intruders were private eyes, no doubt sent by Werner's wife to look for evidence that would make her the innocent party and him the guilty one in a divorce on the grounds of adultery.

His eyes were wild. 'I had no idea . . . I'm so sorry. Are you all right?' He put an arm around her shoulders, the other clutching the bunched-up nightie modestly in front of him.

'How uncouth of them not to give me time for hair and make-up,' she joked, but he didn't smile.

He pulled one of the dining chairs out from the table and sat down heavily on it. 'I should have beaten the hell out of that first guy as soon as I opened the door, but it happened so quickly. There was a third one, a bloody bouncer lurking in the corridor. He grabbed me by the neck. I couldn't protect you . . .'

'They were thugs. There was nothing you could have done.'

'How could she do that to me? It was friendly, the way we finished.' He looked at the floor, his hair flopped forward and he pushed it back with both hands impatiently. The ball of chiffon sat in his lap like a fluffy domestic animal.

'She has to do that, to divorce you.' Happiness had begun to dawn on Desi but she tried to keep it out of her voice.

'Why didn't she warn me? I could have set it up, the way civilised people do. I mean, we've kept in touch. By phone once a month or so. I can't believe I've implicated you in this sordid business . . .'

'That doesn't bother me at all.' She was far happier at being named co-respondent in his divorce than having some lady-of-the-night hired as a stand-in. 'Your divorce will happen in California, anyway, won't it?'

'I guess so. That's where we were married.'

'Then you don't have to worry about my reputation.'

'She'll take me to the cleaners. I'll be a pauper.'

Desi fetched a towel from the bathroom and handed it to him. 'Here. You don't look your best in a baby-doll nightgown. I'll make some coffee.'

Chapter 26

When they came out of the Savoy theatre in Bligh Street on Friday night, the footpaths were slick and shiny. Rain was still falling from the blackened sky and, although it was not heavy, Jacques took off his jacket and put it around Stella's shoulders. They set off towards Hunter Street to look for a taxi.

Stella had been shocked by the climax to *Jules et Jim*. The film had been so much fun, she expected a happy ending instead of Jeanne Moreau driving herself and Jim into oblivion, leaving Jules bereft. The subtitles had been distracting so she wondered if she had missed something, some warning of disaster.

'Are you hungry?' Jacques asked as he hailed a taxi.

'No. Let's go home.'

'Paddington. Underwood Street.' They got into the back and the cab set off towards Macquarie Street. The tyres made a swishing sound on the road and the windows were so fogged up they couldn't see much more than a blur of lights whizzing past.

'She was immoral, wasn't she?' Stella pouted like a surly little girl as she watched the windscreen wipers sweep rhythmically back and forth making fan-shaped clearings, soon speckled again and glistening.

'Because she was in love with two men?'

'Well, you know, she strung them along.'

He smiled, took her hand and held it. He was being very careful not to offend her this time. He'd made a mistake after Bea's party in assuming Stella was more experienced than she was. With that knowledge he now saw her as a different sort of challenge; virgin ground to be broken. Stella's reluctance would keep him attracted to her for as long as it existed. He wondered if she sensed that and was playing a game.

A pot of coffee and a plate of buttered arrowroot biscuits were the innocent accompaniments to Jacques's tender overtures as they reclined on the divan. He was worldly enough to know that the seduction of Stella would take time and restraint. It was a matter of stimulating her desire but not fulfilling it until she found the frustration so unbearable that she took the initiative. He was prepared to wait.

So he sweet-talked her, murmuring endearments she only half understood such as '*Tu est magnifique*, Étoile, *amour de ma vie*', carefully avoiding anything as compromising as, '*Je t'aime*' or '*Je t'adore*', as he caressed her the way you might stroke a kitten or a puppy. Once her body—and his—began to respond, he gently detached himself, saying, 'It must be getting late. I have to go.' Then he kissed her with passion, though without the involvement of his tongue, and held her body as close to him as possible before wishing her a heartfelt '*Au revoir, cherie*', exiting the flat and closing the door softly behind him, leaving Stella throbbing in her nether region and wishing he hadn't been so respectful.

Over the bridge at Kirribilli, Audrey was handing around a cheese platter and glasses of red wine to her friends from the Mosman Musical Society after a performance of *The Mikado*. Bea had picked up photographs from their holiday that afternoon, so she brought them along but failed to interest anybody in giving them even cursory attention, except for Audrey, who started picking out the ones she'd like copied for herself. The rest of the group were so over-excited they seemed to have swallowed pep pills that wouldn't let them calm down. It was just the adrenalin, Audrey confided to Bea, who knew that already. It made her think of London and the evenings she'd spent in the theatres of the West End. Along with the lack of interest in her pictures and the appalling week she'd had at the office, the thought of Aidan and their wrecked marriage sent her deeply into the doldrums.

Desi left the Renault parked in Sussex Street, opened her umbrella and hurried around the corner into Hay Street and up a dark stairway to the first floor above a pub at the corner of Dixon Street. Through a fog of smoke she saw Werner in a booth beside one of the windows. He signalled and she wove her way through the crowded, noisy tables to reach him. So far, so good.

It seemed sensible for the time being, given the invasion two nights ago, to find a trysting place other than Werner's flat, and to go there independently of each other. The Tai Yuen restaurant, though popular, was unlikely to attract anyone Desi knew on a Friday night. At lunch maybe there'd be people of their acquaintance in business, but it was doubtful they'd be here at eight o'clock. And if they were, it shouldn't be too hard to play at being co-workers sharing a quick bite to eat before going their separate ways after a full day of filming.

Their ploy seemed to have worked. There was not a familiar face among the customers, many of them Asian, wielding chopsticks over bowls of fried rice, chop suey and chicken with almonds.

They sat opposite each other, their knees colliding deliberately under the table while their hands met above it. He lifted her fingers and kissed them. 'I haven't seen you for two days. Don't you know what deprivation does to me?'

'I hope it made you mad with passion,' she said, grinning at him and grasping one of his knees between both of hers.

'Isn't it a bit early for that kind of thing?' He returned the pressure under table with his own knees.

'Never.'

A waiter came with a notebook and the game of kneesies under the table ceased. 'Give us a few more minutes,' Werner told him. 'We haven't decided yet.'

'Any repercussions from the other night?' asked Desi.

'Someone complained about the noise, so the managing agent said. I told him that some unsavoury types had got the wrong address, the wrong building altogether.'

'Good thinking. That was all?'

He nodded. 'Now. What shall we eat?'

She was happy to see him so relaxed. 'Will you order for us?' she said. 'I'm not familiar enough with Chinese dishes. All I know is curried chicken and rice.' It wasn't quite true but she wanted him to take over. 'But no birds' nest soup.'

'I think we can do better than that.' He smiled and picked up the menu. He waved at the waiter and, while they discussed various dishes, Desi rehearsed in her mind the little speech she was going to make.

She waited until they were eating their first course before she said, 'Werner, I have something important to say to you.' His eyes flicked up at her, then down at the serving dish as he picked up a prawn cutlet with his fingers and bit into it. She cleared her throat and went on, trying to keep her voice even, 'Tom is due back from Brisbane tomorrow.'

Werner said nothing and kept on eating.

'When I pick him up from the airport . . . I'm going to break off our engagement.' She took a deep breath. 'I don't want you to feel that I'm putting pressure on you in any way. I just can't go through with it, that's all. I just wanted to let you know.'

He stopped eating, and looked at her in silence, trying to find the right words. A few moments passed before he said, 'Aren't you being a bit hasty, Desi?'

It wasn't what she wanted to hear from him. 'Hasty? No. I should have done it before but I didn't want you to misunderstand . . . to feel responsible or obligated.'

'I would certainly feel responsible if you did a thing like that. How could I help it? If it weren't for me you'd be . . .'

'Happy with him? No. I always had doubts. I have never felt about him the way I feel about you.'

'Desi, I can't compete with him.'

'What do you mean, you can't compete?'

He looked at her the way people look at a dimwit. 'I can't compete with someone who put the Koh-i-Noor diamond on your finger.'

'It's nothing like the Koh-i-Noor diamond!' It had been months since she'd worn the ring in his company. She'd assumed he'd forgotten it.

'It might as well be.'

'I don't care about that bloody ring. I'm giving it back to him tomorrow.'

'Well, *I* care about it. I hate the position I've put myself in. I have nothing to offer someone like you.'

A dish holding the bashed-up carapace of a large marine creature, all spikes and undulations, the colour of ox blood, was placed on the table. A black substance oozed out of it.

'Someone like me?' She could feel anger tingling at the roots of her hair. 'What is that supposed to mean?'

'You are out of my class.'

'Don't talk nonsense.'

'I don't mean socially or intellectually. It's something much more crude. It's money, vulgar money. You have money, I have none.'

'That doesn't matter a damn. I don't care about money.' Her voice had risen but the din around them swallowed it up so that nobody could have heard it but Werner and the waiter who busied himself plonking spoonfuls of rice into their bowls. His face was expressionless; she hoped he didn't understand English.

'Of course you don't. Because you have it. It's only important when you don't have it.' Werner managed to keep his tone calm and reasonable.

'I don't need money.'

'Yes you do. You've never been without it. You have no idea what that's like.'

'If you loved me, Werner, as you have said you do, you wouldn't be saying these terrible things to me. I am not a silly, frivolous woman. I can live without the trappings of money.'

'I do love you, Desi. And I don't want anything to change that. Let me tell you something.'

He picked up a crab claw and put it in her bowl, then helped himself to the other one. 'When I told you that my mother and father adored each other, that was only half the story.' He picked up the crab claw from his bowl, put it down again and leaned towards her to emphasise his words. 'After he was black-listed and couldn't work in Hollywood, they lost the house they loved. Their standard of living just fell away . . . It had to affect the way they felt towards each other. It was tragic to see my father withdraw because of his disillusion and guilt and my mother's bewilderment because he wouldn't share it with her. The strain, the tension, the unspoken humiliation. Their fall from grace was awful. I know what the lack of money does to people. I don't want that to happen to us.' He reached for her hand but she pulled it away.

'I have money of my own, family money.' She hadn't wanted to resort to mentioning her inheritance but it was the only argument left.

'I couldn't live like that. A kept man? You'd end up hating me.' He shook his head, picked up the crab claw and began wrestling with it.

'What do you want to happen, then? You want me to marry Tom and have a carry-on with you. Is that what you want?'

'I know it's not ideal but it might be a way of coping. I want what's best for you.' He managed to extract a juicy morsel of crab meat.

'Best for me would be to marry you.'

'I can't do that to you.'

'I can't believe you're saying this.' She grabbed the crab claw from her bowl and crushed it with the nutcracker. Black bean sauce spurted over the front of her cream silk blouse. Tears that did not usually come easily began to fill her eyes. 'It's ruined,' she said.

'Dry-cleaning will fix it,' said Werner, giving her his handkerchief.

'No it won't,' was all she could manage, as she dabbed ineffectually at the unsightly splodge and then wiped her eyes.

The seriousness of what had been said began belatedly to penetrate Werner's consciousness. He'd never seen her cry before.

'Let's go,' he said. 'We can't talk here.'

'There's nothing more to say.'

'Oh, yes, there is.'

He paid the bill and they walked in silence through fine rain to her car, Werner's arm holding her tightly around the shoulders. She let herself be kissed without responding. 'My car's in Campbell Street,' he said. 'Why don't we drive to the park at Rose Bay and talk this through properly?'

She nodded like an automaton.

'I love you, Desirée,' he said. 'Please remember that.'

From behind the wheel of the Renault she watched him through the rear-vision mirror as he walked up Sussex Street. She felt nothing, the numbness that happens after an accident, when the body goes into a state of shock. Then she turned on the ignition and headed eastward through the city and along New South Head Road, skimming past Lyne Park at Rose Bay without a glance, on her way home.

On Saturday morning, the Ansett flight was on time. Desi hoped her sunglasses were successful in masking the ravages that tears and lack of sleep had inflicted on her eyes. Tom's face lit up when he saw her and he urged his two colleagues to come with him to meet her. By the look on their faces she knew they'd won the contract. Success is an agent of transformation and it had conferred a kind of radiant invincibility on the threesome that hadn't been there when they'd boarded the plane to Brisbane on Monday.

'Congratulations!' said Desi, with a big effort at enthusiasm. She was considerate enough of Tom in his euphoric state to realise that this was not the time to deliver the bad news.

Chapter 27

As far as Bea was concerned, the meeting that Guy and Freddie had insisted she attend at Crop-O-Corn Foods at the Botany factory would be just another waste of a morning. The finished television and radio commercials for Cornicles, the magazine ads and supermarket posters, had been approved.

The agency's role this time was to present them and the thinking behind the campaign to a bunch of suited executives from administration and sales who hadn't been involved before. For the umpteenth time, the threesome from BARK would perform, as professionally as clowns at Wirth's Circus, their various roles in the entertainment, while Kelvin, everybody's dogsbody, tagged along to carry the exhibits, adjust the television monitor and ensure that no hitches occurred with its operation.

What they hadn't expected was the presence of William J Cabot II, vice president of marketing at Crop-O-Corn Foods

Inc, who'd flown in from Chicago the day before. He sat in the centre of the row of chairs between Russ Cowper and his boss, Gerry Batterham, managing director.

When the show was over and questions from the floor had been answered satisfactorily, the meeting broke up. The agency team were asked to stay behind for a private discussion. Guy told Kelvin to collect the exhibits and take them to the car and wait for him there.

With ice cubes tinkling in the glass in his hand, Gerry Batterham announced that William J Cabot II wanted to say a few words.

Mr Cabot, whose hair looked like the stubble left after a field of grain has been harvested and whose face was as smooth as a Jonathan apple, trained his sky-blue eyes on Bea and said, 'I have been mighty impressed with the work you guys are doing down here. Your thinking is similar to our thinking in Chicago. It has warmth and heart. It's Mom and apple pie. It's like a Norman Rockwell cover for *The Saturday Evening Post*. It's not sharp or cynical, like the stuff they turn out in New York.' He spoke in a measured way that gave every word conviction, letting his gaze wander over the group before fixing it again on Bea. 'Which is why, with the full support of my board of directors including the president, I am here today. I want to tell you in person that we have decided to take your campaign idea for Cornicles and run it in the United States.'

Guy's eyes switched from Freddie, whose eyebrows had shot up, to Bea, whose mouth had fallen open. Kelvin, having managed to take a lot of time in dismantling the presentation, was all ears.

'Well,' said Guy, rising to the occasion in a way that surprised even himself. 'I am not often at a loss for words, but I wonder if I can find an adequate response.' He cleared his throat and that seemed to solve the problem. 'I think this marks a great milestone in the relationship between Crop-O-Corn Foods and Bofinger, Adams, Rawson and Keane. More than that. It sets an industry precedent. For an Australian agency to export a campaign to the United States is unheard of. Ideas usually travel the other way.'

'Indeed,' said Mr Batterham, his chest puffed up like a pouter pigeon's.

'On behalf of my colleagues,' continued Guy, 'and particularly Freddie Hackett, the creative director, and Bea O'Connor, who dreamed up this campaign, all I can say is a humble thank you. We are deeply honoured.'

'Well said,' said Freddie.

'Let me also add,' said Guy, remembering to be a diplomat, 'that if it hadn't been for our enlightened client the campaign might never have seen the light of day.'

'Hear hear,' said Freddie.

'Shit,' said Kelvin, under his breath as he lumbered out bearing display boards and tapes, to sit drumming his fingers on the dashboard of Guy's Studley Series 21 sedan while the others got pissed on mutual admiration and whisky sours.

Before the day was finished, Felix Bofinger had approved a press release that was to be sent to trade publications, including *Advertising Age* in New York, proclaiming BARK's achievement—unprecedented in Australia, as far as anyone knew—in exporting a home-grown advertising campaign to the United States. Notably absent from the release was the name of the campaign's creator; FB was not interested in making Bea even more tempting to the competition than she was already. Miss Leonie Braithwaite had been in touch with FB's wife Allegra, with whom she was on first–name terms, to discuss arrangements for an intimate dinner in honour of Mr William J Cabot II at the Bofinger residence at Clifton Gardens in two days time.

When a black limousine, arranged by the company, delivered Bea and Freddie to the Bofingers' address on Friday evening, they thought they'd come to the wrong place. They stood staring at a great slab of concrete that, to Bea, looked like a giant version of the gun emplacements she'd seen left over from World War II on the English coast. Cold air drifted off the harbour. She shivered and huddled inside her mink stole and wished the invitation had called for black tie so she could have worn a long gown instead of a cocktail dress that let the wind whip around her calves and up her thighs to chill her bottom.

'Wait!' said Freddie, as the car was about to move off. He leaned down to the driver's window. 'Are you sure this is the right address?'

The driver nodded slowly several times at Freddie, then shook his head and said, 'Can you believe a bloke with his spondulicks could live in a cave like the Flintstones?'

By now, Bea had found what she thought was the front door, a carefully concealed inset in the concrete, like the entrance to the Great Pyramid of Cheops, or a rock that shifts when Ali Baba says Open Sesame in children's storybooks. She beckoned to Freddie and they both started giggling, Bea holding a gloved hand to her mouth, while Freddie fingered his spotted bow tie to make sure it hadn't gone askew and patted the colour-coordinated handkerchief in his breast pocket.

'Collect yourself, Mrs O'Connor. We are supposed to be serious executives.'

'Aye, aye, captain,' she said, taking his arm and pushing a forefinger against what she hoped was the doorbell.

Once inside—thanks to a lackey in a white jacket who took Bea's stole—the joking died on the lips of the two doubters. They found themselves in what looked like an arm of the Museum of Modern Art in New York. Before they'd even left the stark eggshell-white entrance hall, Freddie spotted a bronze sculpture that he recognised as a Giacometti and Bea's gaze took in the portrait of a woman by Modigliani that she could tell was not a print.

Another gallery, vast this time, opened up as they approached. A woman who could have been a stand-in for Claudia Cardinale detached herself from a clutch of people and made her way towards them, placing one foot after the other in a perfectly straight line, as though toeing a tightrope. She extended her cool, elongated hand, first to Bea, then to Freddie. The last time Bea had seen such mannered movements was at Sadler's Wells. 'I am Allegra. You must be Beatrice.' She pronounced it Bee-a-tree-chay. 'And you of course are Freddie.' Her accent was enchanting, her smile alluring, her dark hair so lush Bea wanted to cast her in a Lustrée commercial.

How does an old guy who looks like a praying mantis get a woman like that? Freddie wanted to ask Bea but was forced to defer the question to another time. Somewhere in the back of his mind was the hearsay that Allegra had come to Australia with a group of Italian models for a David Jones promotion in the 1950s and stayed on to marry FB.

After twenty minutes or so of drinks, introductions, chitchat that was mainly client/agency shoptalk, and furtive glances at the pictures that Klee, Kandinsky, Ernst and Morandi had contributed to the decoration, they were shepherded from that

space into another, this one softened by wax candles illumi-
nating the white tulips on a long table set with starched white
linen and plain white porcelain. The tumblers and wineglasses
with white streaks swirling around them had been hand-blown
in Venice. Sleek stainless-steel flatware was the handiwork of
Arne Jacobsen in Denmark. The whole setting was deeply,
desirably, uncompromisingly modernist. So much so, that Bea
felt the opal brooch she had pinned near the left shoulder of
her little black dress might be considered a lapse of taste.

Clearly, William J Cabot II ('Call me Bill'), who was seated
beside her, did not think so. Discussion about this piece of
jewellery, which Bea inherited from her mother, took up at least
fifteen minutes, as they were served risotto with mushrooms, and
Bea explained what she knew about opals, their source and the
superstitions about them. She and Bill were off to a good start
but she was obliged in the name of good manners to direct her
attention to the gentleman on her right, who turned out to be Russ
Cowper, not the most stimulating conversationalist unless you
were interested in the latest corporate gobbledegook. He told her it
was time to bite the bullet and implement organisational synergies
between their companies in order to go forward with concomitant
concepts conducive to ambient administrative innovation.

'I couldn't agree more,' said Bea, spying Guy's wife, Natalie,
seated on the other side of him. She leaned forward to engage
her attention in an effort to offset the claptrap Russ was going
on with. She succeeded, but fared no better, because Natalie
was interested in only two subjects: the difficulty of getting a
babysitter on a Friday night and the exceptional qualities of her
children, eight-year-old Troy and six-year-old Charlotte. Before
Natalie was moved to dig in her bag for pictures, Bea smilingly
shifted her attention slowly back to Bill and the fillet of snapper

with parsley sauce and rosemary potatoes that had been placed before her. Fortunately the self-discipline Allegra Bofinger applied to architecture and interior design did not extend to her kitchen. The food was luscious and abundant.

Sometime after the speeches—ah yes, the speeches—when the noise level had gone up to bounce on the ceiling and back down again, people had begun to slump a little or twist around on their chairs instead of sitting with Mondrian-straight backs. Bill lit a cigarette, turned to Bea and said, 'How would you feel about sightseeing with me tomorrow? It's my last day.'

Her eyes scanned the table briefly to see if anyone was listening, then she looked at him and said, 'I don't know that that's a good idea. Professionally, I mean.'

'Bea,' he said. 'I'm a happily married man. All I am asking you for is your company as an interesting and intelligent woman. You know this town. I've never been here before. Have pity on a guy.'

She pictured the weekend ahead: cleaning the flat, perhaps going to the pictures with Audrey or watching television, just like every other weekend since she'd been home, so she turned to him and smiled. 'I'd love to. What time shall I pick you up?'

'No, I'll pick you up. Say, ten o'clock?'

Isn't it amazing, thought Bea, how much more civilised a city becomes when you glide through it in the back of a chauffeur-driven limousine? Especially with a companion as attentive, charming and correct in his behaviour as Bill Cabot.

After the chauffeur, who said his name was Andy, dropped them at the top entrance to Taronga Park Zoo, they looked at kangaroos and koalas as they ambled down to board the ferry to Circular Quay, where Andy was waiting to take them to the art gallery in the Domain; there Bea treated Bill to the sight of her favourite nineteenth-century painting, *The Sons of Clovis II* by Evariste Luminais, a forlorn depiction of the near-death bodies of two handsome young men afloat on a barge. The hamburgers the sightseers ate afterwards in a milk bar at Bondi Beach made a suitable antidote and fortified them for a walk along the cliffs to Bronte, where Andy was waiting to drive Bill to the Hotel Australia and Bea home to Cremorne so that they could shower and change before they met again for a drink in the baroque Marble Bar at Tattersalls in the city. It had been a long time since Bea had packed as much activity as that into a Saturday.

Dinner and dancing at Romano's was the perfect finale. Although that wasn't quite the end of it. When Bill accompanied her home in the limo, Bea invited him in for a nightcap. He gave Andy a big tip and sent him home. Bea was glad she'd taken the precaution of changing the sheets and putting fresh towels and soap in the bathroom that morning.

Chapter 28

The tap on her front door was so gentle, Bea thought she imagined it as she spooned coffee grains into the Neapolitan pot and set it on the stove. But the sound was repeated, this time a little louder. When she answered the door, Martha, self-appointed guardian of the neighbourhood, stood there smiling with a newspaper under her arm. She was perfectly groomed at seven on a Sunday morning, while Bea looked exactly as she felt—a leftover from too much fun last night. It seemed only five minutes since Bill had left, but it must have been about two hours.

'I'm sorry. Did I wake you?'

'Oh, no. Come in. I've just put the coffee on.' It would be a mistake to appear grumpy, although Bea was feeling far from sociable.

Martha settled herself at the kitchen table, unfolded the newspaper and said, 'Isn't this your friend, dear, the one who came to your party?' She pushed the tabloid towards Bea, who took a few moments to comprehend what she saw on the front page. Martha gabbled on, 'I twigged there was something going on between them. He couldn't take his eyes off her. Oh, my goodness, she *is* in strife, isn't she?'

'I didn't know you read *Truth*.' Bea realised what a pathetic diversionary tactic that was but she was too stunned to think of anything else.

'It gives me a bit of excitement,' said Martha, in a jolly us-naughty-girls kind of way. 'My life hasn't always been as dreary as it is now.'

Across the harbour at Vaucluse, a boy on his bicycle chucked the newspapers over the front wall and sped off to the next house. Dotty and Spot pretended he was a burglar so they could run about making a satisfying noise, before fighting over which paper to pick up first and whose mouth should carry it to the front door.

Desirée, having been awake most of the night, groaned and turned over, covering her ears with bedclothes to muffle the barking. The past week had been a nightmare that left her feeling the hypocrite she was, as she witnessed Bo joyfully pressing ahead with plans for the wedding unaware that she had no intention of going through with it. It was like being in a car speeding down a hill when its brakes fail: a collision was inevitable. But she'd been unable to bring herself to tell Tom it was over. She was too stupefied to make the decision without knowing that Werner would be there for her.

* * *

Kelvin, up early at the newsagency at Kingsgrove to see the race results in the *Sunday Telegraph*, saw the *Truth* poster but wasn't prompted to buy the paper until he went inside and saw the front page.

'Cripes!' he said. 'Hey, I know her.'

'No kidding,' said the newsagent, straight-faced, attending to the next customer, an old-timer who winked as he took his paper. On his way out he nudged Kelvin and said, 'Pull the other one, sonny boy, it whistles.'

In Ithaca Road, Werner said, 'Good morning' to a neighbour, but she didn't seem to see him. At the corner shop he bought a bottle of milk and a pack of Senior Service from the owner, who must have got out of the wrong side of the bed, he was so unfriendly. As he left the shop, two girls giggled and looked him up and down. Was his fly open? He checked. Everything was in order. He went back home to make breakfast.

Having finished drinking milky coffee and eating a piece of toast with strawberry jam, Stella was still in her dressing-gown when she went into her tiny bathroom to practise her vowels in front of the mirror. She stood there watching herself mouth 'how now brown cow' when the telephone rang. It must be Jacques. Who else would ring her at this hour? She screwed up her face in happy anticipation and picked up the receiver.

'Hello.' She spoke softly, trying to concentrate her voice in the throat instead of the nose.

'Stella?' It was Roy.

'What's up?' Her vowels lapsed. No need to make an effort with him.

'Have you seen *Truth* today?'

'*Truth*? No. I don't read that crummy paper.'

'Well, you might want to read this one. Your socialite friend's in a bit of hot water.'

'What socialite friend?'

'The nob from Vaucluse.'

'Desi?'

'That's her.'

'What's she done?'

'Got off with a married man.'

'*What?*'

When the conversation was over and Roy returned to the breakfast table, Hazel, in her padded floral nylon housecoat, was dishing up sausages, eggs, baked beans, fried bread and bubble-and-squeak. She had attached little bows of pink ribbon to the hairnet over her head, to make herself more feminine to Roy at breakfast.

'What'd she say?' She sat down and poured tea over the milk in her cup. The striped tea cosy over the pot had a scorch mark and she made a mental note to rummage in her knitting bag later for the wool to make a new one.

'Didn't have a clue. She's gone out to buy the paper.' He sloshed Worcestershire sauce over the sausages on his plate.

'I never had a good feeling about Stella mixing with those people. They're all hoity-toity on the surface, but look what really goes on.' She waved her hand dismissively at the tabloid, open at page three, lying on the table. 'Look at the man that hussy's got herself involved with, look at him! He's depraved. It's disgusting.'

'Too right,' said Roy, noncommitally. He knew enough not to say anything she might interpret as critical of Stella or her associates. Hazel was the only one allowed to do that. If he said anything there'd be hell to pay. He'd only made that mistake once.

'I worry about Stella getting above herself. She looks down her nose at us living together, but look at her so-called friends! It's not right. She doesn't confide in me like Deirdre does with her mother. Even Dolores down the road—her mother knows every move she makes.' She picked up her cup and held it in both hands to warm them. 'What's happened to the French boyfriend, I'd like to know? Don't ask *me*. I'm only her mother. I'm the last to know.' She sighed. 'Nobody knows what I've been through.'

'Never mind, love.' Roy was dying to finish his breakfast and take the paper into the lavatory to read the salacious bits properly.

'I do mind, Roy. She's my flesh and blood,' she said, poking a forefinger at her chest. 'Not that she takes after me. I wouldn't be seen dead with that fast crowd if you paid me. She's just like her father. Inflated ideas about herself. That was his downfall. Too big for his boots. Living above his station. Well, look where that got him.'

'Where's he now?'

'How would I know? And good riddance to bad rubbish.'

Roy belched, pushed back his chair and picked up the newspaper. 'I'll just retire to the thunderbox,' he said, shuffling towards the door in his slippers.

Stella was in an agitated state. She couldn't believe her eyes as she stood outside the newsagency in Oxford Street staring at the screaming words on the front page of *Truth*:

Socialite's Illicit Love Nest

and, in slightly smaller bold type underneath,

**Prominent Vaucluse family shamed
by daughter's sordid indiscretion.**

There was an alarming photograph of Desi, seemingly naked, with a fiendish look on her face, her left hand clutching a sheet to her bosom and her right arm flung up in the air. In the top left-hand corner of the picture was a white blur.

The caption read, 'Tempestuous Dizzy throws a tizzy with a pillow when her night of love is disrupted.'

The moment Stella was back in her flat, she turned on the light, put the newspaper on the table, pulled up a chair and read the rest of the words on page one:

> Desirée Whittleford, daughter of one of Sydney's most prominent barristers, and known to intimates as Dizzy, was found in a compromising position with Werner Dresner, a married man, in his flat at Elizabeth Bay in the early hours of the morning last Thursday week. Private detectives, hired by the adulterer's estranged wife, said they had been investigating the pair for some time.
>
> Miss Whittleford is understood to be engaged to be married to the brilliant architect, Tom Boyd, who presented her with a 5.2-carat diamond engagement ring last year.
>
> Photographs taken of Miss Whittleford at the scene have left no doubt as to culpability. Some are too explicit to be published in *Truth*. Mr Dresner was clad only in a ruffled

feminine tutu, raising the possibility of unsavoury practices. Photo gallery, page 3. Profile, page 34.

Stella turned the page, to find the following on page three, under the headline:

Sprung!

Dizzy Whittleford's parents gave their daughter every chance in life, only to see her fall from grace in an adulterous liaison with a married man. They must ask themselves: What Have We Done Wrong?

The rest of the page was filled with photographs with captions underneath that read:

Dizzy Whittleford's dazzling smile from the adulterer's bed.
Werner Dresner, Don Juan in frills, in the early hours of that fateful Thursday.
The unlikely love bunker in Ithaca Road, Elizabeth Bay.
Dizzy dances with her fiance, Tom Boyd, in happier times at the glamorous Point Piper wedding of her cousin last year.
Her father, Mr Blyth Whittleford, QC, pillar of the establishment, seen in his robes of office in Macquarie Street this week.
Her mother, Mrs Blyth Whittleford, at a fundraising luncheon at Prince's in aid of the Royal Blind Society of NSW earlier this year.

Stella's trembling hand flicked through the paper to page thirty-four and she began to read:

Dizzy Whittleford,
darling of Sydney society

She is the heiress with everything—looks, brains, social standing—but for one night of love, the 24-year-old statuesque 5 ft. 11 in. blue-eyed blonde has risked it all in her passionate pursuit of a married man.

The only daughter of Mr Blyth Whittleford, QC, and his wife, the former Miss Boadicea Ostler of Echidna Bottoms in Tasmania, Dizzy grew up with her two brothers in a harbour-front mansion in the privileged environs of Sydney's Eastern Suburbs.

After her schooling at SCEGGS in Darlinghurst, where she excelled academically and athletically, she spent a year at the finishing school Institut Villa Pierrefeu near Montreux in Switzerland before 'coming out' in London in 1956. She was presented to Her Majesty, Queen Elizabeth, at court during the London Season, which lasted for six months. By all accounts, Dizzy was a dazzling debutante, squired by the most eligible of the younger generation of aristocrats and plutocrats to lavish dinners, dances and cocktail parties in the elegant town houses of Mayfair and Belgravia, and in stately homes and royal palaces across the land.

However, Miss Whittleford proved to have interests beyond those of the typical deb. She extended her sojourn in London to study filmmaking at the London School of Film Technique at Brixton before returning to Sydney in 1959 to secure a career in the production of television commercials for the advertising agency Bofinger, Adams, Rawson and Keane.

According to those who know her well, she is as charming and gracious as she is strong-willed and independently minded. Given the initiative she has shown in business and her devotion to her job, some insiders have expressed doubts as to her ability to adapt to the secondary role of wife and mother, a position that may not be the fait accompli it seemed before the fateful night she spent in the arms of her forbidden lover.

Stella was so shocked she sat still for several minutes before re-reading the entire text. How could Desi, who seemed so lady-like, so superior, so level-headed have such loose morals? Would her family throw her out? Her fiancé must feel like murdering her and Werner Dresner. She'd have to give the ring back. BARK would probably sack her; being named in *Truth* would be bad for their image. Then what would happen to Stella's commercial that Desi was supposed to produce?

As she began to think through the implications of the scandal on her own image, she was led to an even more disquieting thought. She had aligned herself with the wrong party, alienating Bea and associating with someone who would not do her personal life or her career any good whatsoever. She'd made a bad mistake and she was too confused to work out what to do about it.

As usual on a Sunday, the Whittlefords were still in bed when May set the table at around nine o'clock and put orange juice and cereal on the sideboard in the breakfast room. While she waited to hear someone stir, so she could start scrambling eggs and making toast and coffee, she started to unroll the newspapers she'd brought in from the doorstep, slipping off their rubber bands, flattening them out and piling them on the sideboard. She knew that Mr Whittleford liked to read all the newspapers, including the disreputable tabloids, because their reports often had a bearing on his work.

When she unrolled *Truth*, she stifled a little scream, put her hand on her heart, then rushed into the kitchen with the newspaper clutched to her chest, as if to hide its hideousness, even from the dogs lapping at their bowls. She sat down on a stool at the kitchen bench. The front page of the paper was like an assault with a deadly weapon. As she looked at the cruel photograph and read the ugly words, tears rolled down her cheeks. 'Oh, God no,' she kept repeating, as she turned to page three and then to page thirty-four.

Desirée was so deeply buried under her patchwork eiderdown, May wasn't sure which bit of her she was patting—she hoped it was her shoulder—in an effort to wake her. The body stirred. 'I've only just got to sleep,' pleaded the muffled voice. 'What time is it?'

'Wake up, Dizzy,' said May quietly. 'There's something you'll want to see.'

Something or someone? Had Werner broken all the rules and come to the house for her? She separated herself from the cocoon of her bedclothes and smiled sleepily at the reassuring old face she'd known all her life.

'There's something about you in the newspaper.'

Desirée hadn't been to any event recently that was worthy of coverage in the social pages. Maybe it had something to do with publicising the agency in the business pages. Neither possibility was worth waking her up for, so she moaned, 'Oh, May, that's not important.'

'Yes, it is, darling. You're on the front page of *Truth*. It's about your indiscretion.'

Chapter 29

Like most families, the Whittlefords had had their share of catastrophes. Blyth's parents were bankrupted in the Great Depression and his father took his life with a gun in his mouth in 1932. Blyth worked at a series of menial jobs to help support his mother and put himself through university. His cousin Jock got into a bit of strife with the taxation department and the family clubbed together to help him out. Some said that Bo's father had got up to a few tricks in acquiring land holdings in Tasmania, but all his dealings proved to be above board, at least officially, and when the gossip persisted it was dismissed as envy. Bo's first pregnancy ended in a miscarriage at three months. Peter, their eldest boy, contracted meningitis as an infant but mercifully made a full recovery. Nicholas was expelled from Sydney Grammar for his involvement in a prank that led to the destruction of two valuable musical instruments. But, never in the known history of either branch of the family, had there been a scandal involving lust and adultery—until Desirée was photographed in Werner Dresner's bed.

Thanks to May, who'd returned to the kitchen to make coffee for her, Desirée was alerted before the news spread like a crippling disease through the house. Sitting up in bed with the front page glaring back at her, she was struck by the blatancy of the type and the crudity of the picture. Flashbulbs on a camera make no allowance for nuance or subtlety, so the image was coarse and stark; there were no shades of grey. The technique alone made her look like a criminal. She turned the page and felt that she'd been bludgeoned when she saw the humiliating photograph of Werner and read the caption. They'd turned him into a clown. At first, she'd been ashamed. Then horrified. Now she was angry. She reached for the telephone.

'Werner, it's me.'

'Desi! My love. I've missed you so much.'

'Have you seen *Truth*?'

'*Truth*?'

'The Sunday rag.'

'No, I don't buy it.'

'Werner.' She tried to keep her mind clear and her voice steady. 'They've got hold of the photographs of us from the other night and put them all over the newspaper. I'm on the front page.'

'You are *what*?'

'You'd better get a copy. Mummy and Daddy haven't seen it yet. And Tom. Oh, God, Tom.'

'I'll come straight over.'

'Will you?'

'I can't let you face them alone.'

'Hurry, Werner. I can't keep it quiet for much longer.'

* * *

As fate would have it, while Werner waited at the oak front door for his knock to be answered, Tom in his tennis gear arrived at the gate, saw him and ran up the path. The moment May opened the door, Dotty and Spot sprang out barking and Tom shouted, 'You bastard!' and swung a punch at Werner, who reeled back into a potted bay tree. Spot, confused and enraged, threw himself at Tom, digging his fangs into his right forearm. Tom let out a yelp, flailed about trying to get the dog off, lost his balance and fell down the front steps. May screamed. Blyth's voice boomed from the hallway, 'What in God's name is going on here?'

Pretty soon Nicholas in his football jersey, Bo in her dressing-gown and Desirée wearing blue Capri pants and a jumper were on the front verandah watching in dismay as Tom staggered to his feet, leapt up the steps towards Werner and attempted a kick, since a punch would have been painful. This time Werner retaliated, with a carefully aimed blow that struck him just under the ribs, winding him, so he crumpled over in pain, holding his stomach and trying to catch his breath.

Only then, as she restrained Spot by his collar, did Desirée look towards the street and notice a photographer standing just outside the front wall with his camera poised. 'Inside, everyone!' she said in a panicky voice. 'Quickly.' Blyth had his arm around Tom, Desirée took Werner's hand and May shepherded everyone inside and closed the door.

'Will someone explain to me what is going on?' commanded Blyth, in the voice he usually reserved for the courts of law, as they all shuffled into the sitting room. Desirée hastily closed the heavy curtains on the windows facing the street, which cast the room into shadow, so she turned on the celadon porcelain table lamps. The illuminated faces showed a range of expressions: bewilderment, anxiety, disbelief, embarrassment and anger.

Looking at Werner, who stood awkwardly in front of an eighteenth-century Coromandel screen dabbing his bloody nose with a handkerchief, Blyth continued, 'I believe, sir, we have not met. My name is Blyth Whittleford.' He held out his hand.

Werner kept his left hand floating around his nose while he offered his right. 'I'm Werner Dresner. A friend of Desirée.'

'Friend!' gasped Tom. 'Bloody adulterer!'

'Daddy,' said Desirée, 'there's something I have to explain.' She stopped, not knowing where to start.

'Mr Whittleford,' said Werner, who assumed—incorrectly— that by now Blyth had seen a copy of *Truth*, 'I am in love with your daughter and I must take full responsibility for implicating her in the sordid matter of my divorce proceedings. It was not meant to happen that way and I apologise for it.' He turned to Bo. 'I am so sorry, Mrs Whittleford.'

Bo let out a little cry and sank, with her hand held like an awning over her eyes, on to an overstuffed sofa covered with a Josef Frank fanciful tree-and-vegetable print. The dogs had exhausted themselves—both felt guilty without knowing why—and lay still but watchful on a rug in front of the marble fireplace. Nicholas hovered in the doorway with his eyes and mouth wide open. May stood as a self-appointed guard beside Tom, who sat nursing his arm on a lacquered upright chair and was still trying to catch his breath.

'I don't understand. What are you saying?' Blyth was losing patience and beginning to feel fear.

Desirée decided to try again, this time with the bald facts. 'Werner and I have been in love for some time.' She glanced at her wounded fiancé and said, 'I'm sorry, Tom,' before continuing.

'Private detectives photographed us together in Werner's flat. They sold the pictures to *Truth*. They are in today's edition. I'll go upstairs and get it.'

It was Blyth's turn to sit down. He plonked himself on the yellow Fornasetti sun chair that had always been the talking-point of the room—illustrated on its back was half a human face above the horizon with spikes radiating from its head—an absurdity as surreal as the situation going on around it.

'May,' said Bo, regaining her equilibrium. 'I wonder if we could trouble you to make some fresh coffee?'

On that Sunday, anybody who had ever known the Whittlefords, along with the masses who hadn't, drooled over the cover story that boosted the edition's sales to a record high, as people who wouldn't be seen dead with that particular Sunday paper found various ways of getting their noses into it.

Stella rang Jacques. Jacques rang Bea. Bea rang Freddie. Freddie rang Guy. Guy rang Felix Bofinger. FB rang his fellow board members. Each board member rang one or more of the agency's clients. Several inhabitants of Ithaca Gardens met to compose a letter to the building's managing agent to demand the expulsion of Werner Dresner from the premises.

Back at Vaucluse, Bo rang the doctor. Tom rang his parents. Nicholas was told to watch for paparazzi, a task to which he applied himself with aptitude, spying from behind the oleanders with binoculars and the cunning of James Bond. When the coast was clear, Tom's father arrived to take him home, but they went by the back route, along the beach and through the gardens of their neighbours, just in case a prying lens was still about.

Finally, Desirée rang Freddie. The voice that answered was not his. It sounded familiar but she couldn't quite place it.

'It's Darryl, Desi.'

'Darryl! I'm sorry, I must have dialled the wrong number.'

'No. It's the right number. I'll get Freddie.'

While she waited, her mind was distracted from her own quandary by the significance of Darryl, the film editor at Rod Webb, being in Freddie's flat on a Sunday morning. How long had that been going on? Maybe since Bea's pre-Christmas party.

'Thank God somebody else in this life is not perfect,' were Freddie's first words. 'How are you bearing up, darling?'

'Oh, Freddie. I don't even know.'

'Listen. I'll call you when I'm in the office tomorrow and we can talk about the work and what needs to be done. Don't worry about it now. You might need to take a few days off. We'll sort it out tomorrow.'

'Thank you for understanding.' She meant it. However maddening Freddie was at times, he was good in a crisis.

'Hang on a sec. Darryl wants to say something.'

'Desi. Anything we can do?'

'No, Darryl, but thank you.'

'Well if there is, let us know. And tell Werner he'd better look after you, or else.'

'Wait a minute,' she said. 'There is one thing you could do. Are you anywhere near Elizabeth Bay?'

'We're in Greenknowe Avenue, just up the hill.'

'Would you mind driving past Ithaca Gardens to see if the press are hanging around? Werner's here. He has to get home some time.'

* * *

After Stella and Jacques had discussed the scandal and were settled on his wraparound sofa with glasses of champagne on Sunday afternoon, a disturbing thought occurred to her. If a crass invasion of privacy could happen to someone as well connected as Desirée Whittleford, how vulnerable was Stella herself?

'Jacques?' she whispered in his ear.

'Yes, Étoile?' He nuzzled her neck.

'Are you married?'

If she'd accused him of being a murderer he could not have been more startled. 'Married? Me? No, no, no!'

'I was only asking,' she said. 'I'm glad.' She wriggled and pressed herself against him. She had arrived a virgin, but she didn't want to go home one.

Her body language was explicit and he understood it perfectly. It was a form of communication in which he was fluent.

A bit of heavy breathing followed, but before it went too far, it was Jacques's turn to ask a question. 'Are you on the peel?'

'The peel, what peel?'

'The no-baby peel.'

'No. You have to be married to get that pill.'

How naive she was. What a shame he'd have to take precautions. He reached over her and switched off the light.

Chapter 30

The exposé of Desi was the talk of the office on Monday morning, but mainly in hushed and respectful tones as everyone took her side—at least they said they did—and awaited the appearance of the colleague who'd suddenly become a notorious scarlet woman.

Their disappointment at her no-show gave way to titillation when Kelvin rushed in just before lunchtime with a gleeful look on his face and an early edition of the evening tabloid, the *Daily Mirror*, under his arm. He went first to the typing pool where everyone gathered around Patsy's desk to read page three:

Dogfight over Dizzy

Fiancé mauled by adulterer's vicious Alsatian in brawl over blonde heiress

Following *Truth*'s revelations on Sunday of socialite Dizzy Whittleford's part in an adulterous relationship, a skirmish took place on the front verandah of the Whittleford mansion at Vaucluse yesterday morning.

Dizzy's fiancé, the brilliant architect Tom Boyd, and the adulterer, German-born Werner Dresner, came to blows over the 24-year-old blonde heiress. It is understood that during the donnybrook in which punches and kicks were exchanged, a vicious Alsatian, rumoured to belong to Dresner, attacked Boyd, necessitating urgent medical treatment. As yet, there has been no demand for the offending animal to be put down.

Although no charges have been laid, according to observers the saga has just begun. It is understood that Dizzy will be cited as co-respondent in Dresner's divorce.

Under the subhead 'Violence at Vaucluse' four pictures were positioned around the page. Their captions read:

The horror-struck Whittlefords witness the unseemly scuffle between their daughter's fiancé and her outlawed lover.
Werner the warrior wipes his bloodied nose.
Tom Boyd felled by the savage Alsatian.
Dizzy in distress herds the family indoors.

A line at the bottom of the page directed readers to pages thirty-two and fifty-seven.

When everyone had read every word and let out little gasps and shrill cries as they went, Kelvin turned to page thirty-two, where they read the leading item in Thalia's column:

Engagement on the rocks

They say that diamonds are forever, but the adage is not likely to apply to socialite Desirée (Dizzy) Whittleford after certain unbecoming events were revealed at the weekend. The 5.2-carat Eternal cut diamond ring that Tom Boyd placed on her engagement finger last year has no doubt been returned. The knuckleduster was fashioned by Garrard of London, jeweller to the Royal Family. On whose lucky finger are we likely to see it next?

Among the sports reports on page fifty-seven, an anonymous writer made this comment:

All bets are off

Judging by the standard of fisticuffs by sparring swains at Vaucluse on Sunday morning, neither combatant is ready to put on the gloves for a round in the ring with Sugar Ray Robinson. A good catch like Dizzy Whittleford could do a lot better.

The squeals from the typing pool brought Freddie and Guy from their offices and caught the attention of Bea and Stella. Soon everybody on the floor was craning a neck to see the story.

'Shocking,' said Guy as he finished reading page three.

'*Merde alors!*' said Jacques, puffing a Gitane.

'Don't believe a word of it,' said Bea, waving smoke away from her face. Since Lord Howe Island, she hadn't touched a cigarette.

'I don't mean the punch-up. I mean the riffraff reporting it,' said Guy, shifting his viewpoint to suit the occasion. He patted his pockets and realised he'd left the Kents in his office.

'Mamma mia!' said Assunta, peering at the pictures and crossing herself.

'Poor Desi. They'll never let up on her now,' said Freddie, offering Guy an open pack of Marlboros.

'The peasants victimise her because she is rich and discriminating,' said Lavinia, before turning to undulate her way back to her office.

'Will she really have to give the ring back?' said Stella.

'Yes, Stella,' said Bea. 'She will. And I bet she does it happily.'

'What will happen to her image?' said Stella.

'Her image?' At first, Bea thought she must mean a portrait. Then she understood. 'Do you mean something as ridiculous as her image as a *brand*?'

'Well, yeah, her image.'

Having nursed a grudge that was looking for an excuse to express itself, Bea turned on Stella and spoke slowly, clearly and loudly: 'Desi doesn't need to cultivate an image. She has substance. Strength of character. Integrity. That's why what you call her image can never be damaged. But I don't expect you to understand that, Stella. You're all show and no content.'

Bea knew she had gone too far, but she was in no mood for regrets. Everyone was silent except Assunta, who raised her eyebrows at Bea and muttered, 'I am agree wit you,' as she pushed her trolley towards the lift. Feeling shamelessly satisfied, Bea turned and walked back to her office, leaving the group to disperse and Kelvin to gather up the pages of his newspaper to take upstairs to show Miss Leonie Braithwaite.

'What's with Bea?' said Guy when they reached Freddie's door.

Freddie raised his shoulders and his open hands as if to say 'Search me', but all he uttered was, 'Women!'

It was the kind of benign autumn morning when May would have laid the table for breakfast under the pergola on the terrace overlooking the harbour, if it had not been for the possibility of lurking paparazzi. These parasites, as Blyth referred to them, might be training their zoom lenses on the house from any one of the craft anchored offshore or cruising past. So on this Monday morning the Whittlefords had to tap the tops of their soft-boiled eggs and spread Dundee marmalade on their toast in the gloom of the dining room because even the sunny breakfast room was not removed enough from intrusion.

Desirée was uncharacteristically meek. Instead of her father putting on a tirade, which would have stirred an equally spirited response from her, he had taken yesterday's news with a strange calm. Maybe he was in shock? When the furore had died down and the doctor had left, everybody showered and changed and pulled themselves together. In fact, they were all so frightfully civilised that Werner was invited to stay overnight, since Freddie and Darryl had reported that photographers were encamped outside Ithaca Gardens. Fortunately, Peter was still at Oxford and spared this messy business, so Werner was offered his room.

The only person permitted to answer telephone calls—and there were plenty of them—was Blyth, whose autocratic manner and courtroom voice made him excel at intimidating members of the press and other busybodies.

So, here among them at the breakfast table on Monday was Werner, grateful to be able to hide his embarrassment by engaging in small talk with Bo, who was expert at finding out about people without seeming to probe, as she passed the butter and offered more coffee. Desirée listened with a mixture of resentment and admiration as her mother winkled out of Werner tidbits about his life that she herself had not known: his father worked as an assistant editor on the Billy Wilder film *Sunset Boulevard*, although his role wasn't important enough to merit a credit on the titles; the playwright Lillian Hellman was a close friend of his mother; each July he went back to Germany to see his parents in Bavaria; his mother's arthritis made it difficult for her to play the piano these days, so he sent her LPs of music he thought she'd like whenever he came across them.

A telephone call took Blyth away from the table for a few minutes, and when he returned he said that someone in his chambers was sending a messenger with a copy of the *Daily Mirror*, which contained what was described as 'another salacious story'.

'Daddy, we'll have to sue them!' Desirée tried to hold back tears that were evidence of the frustration she felt at being besieged and not having the means to retaliate.

Blyth glowered, so that his eyebrows stood out from the ruddy landscape of his face like spinifex. He sat down and picked up his napkin. 'One does not sue,' said the man who made a lucrative living out of litigation. In his view, washing one's dirty linen in public was the prerogative of charlatans, exhibitionists and members of the lower classes. 'We have other means,' he said, helping himself to the fruit compote.

The knowledge that she had to rely on her father's powerbroking instead of being able to resolve the situation herself added to Desirée's distress. She looked at Werner, but his eyes were on Bo; they were now talking about Comalco mining bauxite on Cape York Peninsula and what it might do to shares. How could he bring himself to think of anything but the mess they were in? She got up from the table and left without a word.

When she reached the hall table at the bottom of the staircase, she stopped and looked at the white phalaenopsis orchid that Bo had placed there long ago when it had two blooms and three buds. In six months, one bloom had dropped and one bud had opened. She surveyed it with distaste. It was so serene and elegant, so passive and pure, so full of itself. 'For Christ's sake,' she hissed at it, '*do* something.' She lifted her hand to smack it off its perch when a door opened and May came out carrying a pile of pressed linen.

'Are you all right, Dizzy?' said May.

For the first time in Desirée's life, her nickname made her shudder.

After breakfast, Blyth invited Werner into his study, and the two remained there until lunchtime having what Desirée imagined to be a man-to-man talk of which she was the subject. Being excluded made her seethe quietly to herself. How dare they?

It annoyed Bo to find Desirée sitting moodily in the drawing room twiddling her thumbs. Despite her superficial acquiescence, Bo felt that her daughter needed to be made aware of all the trouble and pain and damage she had caused—was still causing—and be quietly punished for it. Desirée was familiar with the judgmental stance her mother sometimes took and had thought of it as 'Boadicea in her war chariot' ever since she'd learned the term in primary school.

The warrior woman sat down with her daughter in the drawing room and, instead of listening sympathetically to her side of the story, as a mother might have done, she went through all the tightly knit threads of the wedding plans that now had to be unravelled.

Under pressure from Blyth, they'd said no in the most tactful way to Charlie's offer of Exeter as the venue and decided instead on a ceremony at St Mark's Darling Point and a marquee in the garden at home for the reception. Bo would now have to visit the vicar and Desirée would be required to go with her to explain and offer a donation to the church for the inconvenience. Madame du Val had designed the wedding finery and her needlewomen had begun to work on it, so that would have to be stopped. The embossed invitations, place cards and order of service would finish up as expensive trash in the incinerator. The caterer and florist would have to be cancelled and compensated financially. Desirée sank into the cushions on the patterned sofa feeling like a ten-year-old caught wagging school to go to the pictures, smoke filched cigarettes and pinch lollies from a corner shop.

Bandit struggled and yelped, setting up a hullabaloo among the other dogs, as Charlie tried to keep a grip on him while he fumbled for his reading glasses. He succeeded in manoeuvring the Cairn Terrier on to his lap in order to peer at his feet. He crooned soothingly as he reached for the tweezers. Just as he deftly extracted a thorn from Bandit's back left paw the telephone on the wall rang. The dog wriggled free and fled out of the kitchen into the garden.

'Uncle Charlie?'

'*C'est moi.*'

'It's Desirée Whittleford.'

'Darling! I didn't recognise your voice. What a lovely surprise.' He dragged a chair towards him and sat down in anticipation of a long chat.

'I guess you know why I'm calling.'

Charlie took a moment to speculate. 'You've persuaded Blyth to let you have the wedding here.'

'There isn't going to be a wedding.'

'It's off?'

'Haven't you seen the papers, I mean the Sydney tabloids?'

'Oh, we don't bother with that rubbish up here. We're on a higher plane, darling.' Out of the corner of his eye he saw Blob the Basset trying to mount Mutt, a leggy mongrel far too tall for him. Charlie took off his monogrammed velvet slipper and threw it at them but they carried on as before.

'There's been a terrible scandal. Remember when you told me you were the black sheep? Well, that's me now.'

'What on earth happened?'

'It's too complicated to explain on the telephone. Could we come and stay with you for a few days? We need to hide.'

'You and Tom? Of course. Stay as long as you like.'

'Not Tom. Someone else. You'll like him.'

Ah, I hope so, thought Charlie. 'When can I expect you?'

'I guess about dawn tomorrow.'

'Oh, my dear. I'll be dead to the world.' He paused again. 'Why don't I leave the front door unlocked? I'll keep the dogs with me so they don't think you're burglars. You know where the bedrooms are.'

Had the paparazzi been doing their job properly, they'd never have let two shadowy figures escape undetected from Vaucluse in a navy blue Ford Falcon, with a dent in the left front mudguard, at three o'clock on Tuesday morning.

Over sherry in front of a log fire in the drawing room that evening, Desirée brought out the *Truth* clippings. When Charlie read them he was both sympathetic and amused. 'My boy,' he said to Werner, 'what were you doing in that tutu?' Werner tried to make light of what had happened, but the more he explained how and why he'd wrapped himself in the discarded frippery, the less convincing he sounded.

Finally, Charlie joked, 'I'd better keep you away from my frock collection.' He approved of Werner, although he felt compelled to say to Desi the following afternoon when they were dead-heading roses, 'He'll have to get rid of that frightful suede jacket.'

On Thursday night a fierce wind rushed through the tops of trees, like heaven's housekeeper on an obsessive cleaning spree, whipping the branches of the poplars until their leaves went flying. Clouds scuttled across the sky as though fleeing a malevolent deity. Werner sat up in bed and lit a cigarette in the dark. It was not the unfamiliar sound outside or the quaking windows that had awakened him, but the confusion in his troubled mind. His life was suddenly out of his control, a plane in a nosedive with someone else in the cockpit while he was strapped to his seat.

Although he could barely see her beside him in the unlit room, he knew that Desi was lying on her back with one arm flung around her head, the other buried in the bedclothes. He envied her ability to sleep deeply and peacefully. That she trusted him should have made him happy. Instead, it made his guilt even more burdensome. She was young, sixteen years his junior. He should never have let himself fall in love with her. She was too exotic for his world, an orchid in a bed of dandelions. Due to him, she had been tainted with the stench of his sordid divorce. Her father hadn't put it in those exact words during their lengthy talk in his study last Monday, but his message was clear: Werner was unsuitable as a son-in-law, the family would never accept him. He'd known that all along. She was a luxury he couldn't afford.

They went for a walk on Friday morning, through a forest at the back of the property and out on to a dirt track that wound into a valley. The Great Dane, whose name was Ophelia, loped along behind them, occasionally sticking her nose into a bush or a burrow, like some dowager duchess on an official visit to the commoners. The clouds of last night had been blown to safety or oblivion, leaving the sky a colour Desi described as Greek blue. They stopped for a rest on the hillside where they were protected from the worst of the wind. Beyond the treetops in front of them, the sun turned the sloping grassland a streaky yellow. The distant hills were a hazy blue. There wasn't a house in sight.

Desi sat with her arms around her knees looking down at a trail of ants weaving their way through the jungle of grass.

'I can't believe the malice,' said Werner, staring at the horizon. 'Our split-up was by consent, hers as well as mine.'

'She couldn't have known the pictures would be sold to the press.'

'I guess not.'

'Perhaps she wasn't as convinced as you were that it was over.'

'She's the one who suggested it in the first place.'

'She might have wanted you to persuade her to change her mind. Or to pack up and go with her.' Her eyes followed the progress of one ant, as it struggled to carry a load almost as big as itself.

'But she was so reasonable. What happened to her? She must hate me to have sent that scum . . .'

Desi pushed her hair back impatiently. 'Why can't you just let it go? Let her divorce you. Cut your losses. You can start again from scratch. We can make money together.'

He said nothing.

'Unless you think it's over between us.'

'Of course it's not! I'm not abandoning you after what's happened.'

'Ah! You're sticking with me out of duty?'

'Don't be foolish, woman!' He lunged forward to grab her but Ophelia, not wishing to be excluded, stepped between them and began licking Werner's face. 'It's impossible to talk here.' He stood up. 'Let's go back.'

By the time the newspapers appeared on Sunday, Desi and Werner were still trying to agree on what to do next. She had decided it was time to move out of the family house and find a flat of her own. He was determined to find out who or what had influenced his wife to become antagonistic and destructive towards him when she'd always been so civilised. He also had to find a way to make some real money.

Fortunately, in the convivial company of Uncle Charlie and his six dogs, they were spared *Truth*'s glaring front-page story:

DIZZY DUZZA BUNK

Has she eloped with her German lover, or fled from his arms?

That was the question being asked in the elite clubs of the city and the drawing rooms of the Eastern Suburbs where speculation has been rife since the sudden disappearance this week of blonde heiress Dizzy Whittleford after her scandalous affair with Werner Dresner, a married man, was revealed by this newspaper a week ago. Mr Blyth Whittleford, QC, father of the missing socialite, did not respond to *Truth*'s request for comment.

The truth of the saying, 'today's news is tomorrow's fish-and-chips paper' was borne out in relation to the two escapees. After Sunday's disrespectful front page, *Truth* and the *Daily Mirror* dropped the case, focusing instead on their next circulation-booster, the gunning down of a petty criminal outside a house of ill-fame in Surry Hills and the underworld investigation that followed. Whether or not Blyth had had a private word with a powerbroker was not discussed.

But while the press were silent, the public were not so forgetful. The carrying-on of a glamorous socialite named Dizzy with a married man stayed in the mind of just about anybody who'd read about it. It was as unforgettable as the titillating scandals from Britain: juicy details aired in the divorce of the Duchess of Argyll; the high jinks known as the Profumo Affair involving call girl Christine Keeler and an important politician in the Conservative government. The memory sat there, curled up like a snake, waiting for a goad to loosen its venomous tongue.

To the disappointment of curious thrill-seekers, from Kelvin to Roy to Bea's neighbour Martha, the press made no further mention of the disreputable pair. No sighting of the lovebirds in some expensive restaurant. No speculation on where they might be hiding. No progress reports on the divorce in which Desirée Whittleford was to be cited as co-respondent. Having served their purpose, they'd been dumped in the garbage bin, like the pages that made them notorious. Hazel might have said—and probably did—good riddance to bad rubbish.

Meanwhile, the girls in the typing pool at BARK looked up from the clack and rattle of their Underwoods every time the door from reception opened, each hoping to be first to witness the return of the dissolute Desi.

'What if she's up the duff?' said Kelvin, helping himself to the Monte Carlo on Patsy's saucer. Although he had smartened up his appearance since his recent elevation to account manager for Go-Go Tyres, his behaviour had yet to show improvement. He bit into the biscuit, put it back, sniggered and walked away.

'Ugh! You are so obnoxious,' Patsy said, pulling a face. Fastidiously, she picked up the biscuit's remains and dropped them into a waste basket. She watched him disappear into Guy's office.

'Maybe she *is*,' she said thoughtfully, spooning sugar into her cup of coffee and stirring it. Myra giggled.

'Do not say such things.' Assunta sniffed and let hot water from the urn splash over a teabag. 'God will punish you.' Her trolley was parked outside Desi's empty office.

'Bad girls don't get pregnant,' sniffed Noreen, Arthur Rawson's thin-lipped secretary, taking the cup of tea from Assunta and turning on her heel with her nose in the air.

'What does she mean?' said Myra.

Patsy rolled her eyes. 'Did you come down in the last shower? Bad girls have *ways*.'

'What do good girls have, then?'

'The ring on the finger,' said Assunta, poking at the substantial plain gold band on the third finger of her left hand. With a look of disgust tempered with satisfaction, she shoved her trolley in the direction of Bea's office.

Just after Patsy had gone back to her typewriter and Myra to her desk outside Guy's office, the door from reception opened and there was Desi, in her navy flannel suit from last winter and her Ballantyne cream cashmere rollneck jumper.

The clatter of typewriters continued, more frantically than ever, as though the fingers flying over them had suddenly been infected with St Vitus Dance. Although not a single pair of eyes were upon her as she wove her way through the desks to her office, Desi had never felt as conspicuous in her life.

Once her door was closed, the mechanical frenzy eased. The typists exchanged glances. They felt let down in some way, although nobody knew why and nobody said anything until 'She looks the same,' said one.

'What did you expect?' Patsy masked her disappointment with a try at nonchalance.

'I thought she'd look different.'

'Like what? Scarlett O'Hara in that red dress when she's been seen throwing herself at Ashley Wilkes . . . ?'

What none of them could have known is that, on the advice of Bea, Desi had bought a relentlessly of-the-moment outfit at Mark Foys to wear on her first day back at the office. 'You have to be bold and rise above it all,' Bea had said. 'You have to make a statement.' Desi allowed herself to be persuaded, but when she put on the Nina Ricci red silk dress with a black sable collar this morning she felt ridiculous, so it went back into the wardrobe. It didn't feel right. It wasn't her style to be blatant.

The first thing she did when she got to her desk was to ring Miss Leonie Braithwaite to make an appointment with Felix Bofinger so that she could apologise for having discredited the agency. It was only then that she noticed the bowl of violets on the windowsill. Inside the sealed envelope propped up in front of it was a handwritten card that read, 'We'll get through this, darling. I love you, Werner.' She felt a surge of optimism and with it came a burst of energy and a renewal of her self-confidence. She opened her door and went in search of Assunta for a cup of coffee. Then she marched into Freddie's office and said, 'What's doing? For heaven's sake, put me to work!'

Chapter 31

'Well, which day *would* suit you?' persisted Hazel. She was not surprised to hear Stella's sigh at the other end of the line. It was further confirmation that she'd got above herself, thinking a telephone call once a week was enough to keep in touch with her mother. Well, Hazel was not going to take that lying down. 'Just tell me what day and we can meet once a fortnight.'

'I don't know,' wailed Stella. 'My job isn't like that now.'

'You have a lunch hour, don't you?'

'Yes, but . . .'

'No ifs and no buts. Why don't we say Mondays. Every second Monday I'll meet you at Repin's in Market Street at one o'clock and you can get back to work by two.'

Stella was trapped. 'Oh, all right then.'

'That's better, darl, I'll see you there tomorrow.'

Roy looked up from his newspaper when Hazel opened the screen door to the patio and came outside with a colander and a basket of peas in their pods. He'd gained a little weight and the side of the love seat where he usually sat had sunk, so the whole contraption listed, like a disabled ship. Hazel sat on a wicker chair opposite him, all the better to command his attention.

'I pinned her down at last,' she said, spreading her knees under her skirt so the colander could rest between her thighs. She started to shell the peas, splitting each pod with her thumbnail, dropping the contents into the colander and the pods back into the basket. 'Tomorrow and every second Monday I'll meet her in town.'

'Good,' said Roy, licking his thumb and turning a page.

'I worry that she's got herself into the wrong company.'

'I know, love.'

'I want to see for myself what sort of people they are.'

Roy shook the paper and turned it over to read the back page.

'Are you listening to me?'

'I am, love.' He folded the paper and put it down beside him. 'Would you like a cuppa tea?'

'That would be nice.' Hazel was grateful for small courtesies.

'I'll get it, Haze.'

'It's getting a bit chilly again. I might come inside too.'

On Monday morning, after she'd seen Roy off to work, Hazel sprinkled 4711 eau de cologne into her bath water and dressed carefully in the outfit she'd sewn just for this occasion: a suit in bottle-green wool bouclé and a pillbox hat she'd made herself from the same material. The buttons on her jacket were shaped like four-leafed clovers. She pinned an oval porcelain brooch with a pink rose on it to the lapel. Her best donkey-brown calfskin bag and shoes had been polished at the weekend, after she'd finished knitting a pair of gloves to match her jacket. Surveying herself in the mottled mirror on the door of her wardrobe, she was pleased. She was no longer a size twelve, but she still had a waist, sort of, the seams of her stockings were nice and straight and her ankles were not bad. Stella had nothing to be ashamed of in her mother.

Hazel took a train that arrived at Town Hall station almost an hour before she was due at Repin's. Her early arrival was deliberate. She had no intention of going straight to the coffee shop, having planned instead to surprise Stella by meeting her at the agency. That way, she could get a good look at the people who worked there and size them up.

After Mavis—the receptionist with earphones hooked over her head—invited Hazel to take a seat, the next person to speak to her was a gawky youth who thought she must be there for a casting session, she looked so out of place. When she told him she was Stella's mother, he said, 'I'll go and get her, if you like,' quick to recognise the chance to be close to Stella and maybe cop a feel.

'No, I'm early,' said Hazel. 'I'll just sit here and wait until she comes out.'

Kelvin was looking for an excuse to delay having to get a signature on the finished art of a Go-Go Tyres advertisement from Dan Barnes—he was even more unpleasant now that he was on the wagon than he had been as a drunkard—so he sat down beside her on the leather sofa.

'Good afternoon, Bofinger, Adams, Rawson and Keane,' said Mavis. 'One moment, please.'

'Off to lunch, are you?' Kelvin wondered where she'd managed to find the pancake she wore on her head.

'Yes, we meet every fortnight.' It gave Hazel a thrill to be able to say so.

A door beside the reception desk opened and two men came out. One was lanky with a face that managed to look both rugged and seedy. The other was a good six inches shorter and he seemed to bounce rather than walk. They were both dressed in well-pressed suits. Spilling from their breast pockets were handkerchiefs that matched their spiffy ties.

Mug lairs, thought Hazel. She watched them walk to the lift, before asking Kelvin who they were.

'Good afternoon, Bofinger, Adams, Rawson and Keane,' said Mavis.

'The tall one's Freddie Hackett, the creative director. The runt's name is Guy Garland. He's an account director.'

'Married men, are they?'

'Guy is. But Freddie's . . . um . . .' He turned his head towards her and whispered, 'A pansy.' They exchanged meaningful looks. Hazel shook her head and adjusted her hat.

'Good afternoon, Bofinger, Adams, Rawson and Keane,' said Mavis. 'One moment, please.'

The next person to emerge was a fleshy woman, with an air of superiority. As she passed Mavis she said, in a posh voice with a slight foreign accent to it, 'I'll be at International Casting, if anybody asks.' She glanced at the prim housewife perched on the edge of the sofa next to Kelvin with her feet together and her handbag on her lap and thought she looked familiar.

'Is that Bea?' asked Hazel.

'No, it's Lavinia. She's in the television department.'

There was no mistaking the lofty blonde who emerged from the lift just before Lavinia stepped into it. She crossed the lobby in three long strides, smiled at Mavis and said, 'Any messages for me?'

'Just these,' said Mavis, handing her two little slips of paper. 'Good afternoon, Bofinger, Adams, Rawson and Keane.'

When Desi had disappeared through the door, Hazel looked at Kelvin, shook her head again and said, 'No shame.'

He grinned back at her, slyly. He still found it comical to imagine Desi as a nymphomaniac in the cot with a bloke in a skirt.

By the time Lavinia landed on the ground floor, she'd realised that the woman in reception must be Stella's mother. The resemblance was striking.

Hazel thought she'd never seen a man as sinister-looking as the one who turned up next carrying a large flat board. His eyes were heavy-lidded, he was dressed in black—no tie, just a rollneck jumper—and his face had an unhealthy pallor.

'Hi, Jacques,' said Kelvin. Hazel jumped, as though somebody had exploded a puffed-up brown paper bag next to her ear.

Jacques just waved and gave a nod to Hazel before he went up the stairs.

'He's the Frenchman?'

'Yeah. He's an art director.'

Hazel was shocked into silence for several seconds before she said, 'Well, he's no oil painting, is he?'

'He gets the girls, but,' said Kelvin. There was envy in his voice.

'Good afternoon, Bofinger, Adams, Rawson and Keane,' said Mavis. 'Just putting you through.'

At last, the door opened again and there was Stella, in her guise as a businesswoman: dusty pink worsted suit with off-white revers made from *lapin*. She froze at the sight of her mother sitting there next to Kelvin, both of them showing their teeth like mischievous chimpanzees. 'What are you doing here, Mum?' she said.

'I thought I'd surprise you, darl,' said Hazel with a nervous chuckle, getting to her feet with the help of Kelvin. 'This nice young man has been keeping me company.'

'Let's go,' said Stella, advancing towards the lift closely trailed by Kelvin and then Hazel. 'I've got to be back by two o'clock.'

Kelvin's hand, on its way back from pressing the lift button, managed to brush Stella's backside and linger there for a moment. She ignored his touch, pretending he didn't exist, although she took a step away from him.

'See ya,' he said, as the two women entered the lift and the doors closed.

Repin's was crowded, so they had to wait ten minutes before a booth was free. Once they were seated and their orders had been taken, Hazel looked at her watch and said, 'I don't want you to be late back to work.'

'It doesn't matter,' said Stella. 'I don't have a meeting until three.'

'Why didn't you tell me that before?'

'I forgot,' Stella lied.

'What a nice boy that Kelvin is,' said Hazel when her raisin toast arrived.

'Ugh,' said Stella.

Hazel took a dainty nibble of her toast. 'I saw your Frenchman, too.'

Stella looked at the baked beans on toast being placed before her, picked up her knife and fork and said, 'And?'

'Not much to look at, is he?' Hazel ventured.

'That's a matter of taste,' said Stella. She took a mouthful, swallowed and then said, 'Jacques is an artist,' as though his calling overcame any insufficiency in his looks or character.

When they'd finished eating, Stella wiped her fingers on the paper serviette and twisted the gilt clasp on her handbag to open it. A whiff of Shocking de Schiaparelli drifted out of it.

'I've got something to show you,' she said, taking out an envelope and carefully opening the flap. Hazel expected a photograph of her daughter, possibly with the boyfriend. Stella extracted a cream card, about the size of a postcard, and handed it to her mother.

Hazel found her glasses and peered through them at the words, engraved in silver and positioned towards the top:

étoile at home

'What's this supposed to be?' Hazel was genuinely puzzled. She turned the card over to see if there might be a clue to the meaning of it on the back.

'It's my personal invitation card. For when I ask people over to my place socially.'

'But there's no address,' said Hazel, turning the card over and back again as though the movement would bring hidden words to light, like ironing does to invisible ink.

'Oh,' said Stella, with a lift to her chin and a little shake of her head. 'I can write the address on the bottom. I'm not staying in Paddington much longer. I'm looking for a flat in Double Bay.'

'What about your name?' Hazel handed the card back.

'Étoile, that's my name,' said Stella, taking the card and pointing to the type. 'You see how avant-garde it is to have the initial in lower-case, instead of a capital? That's to emphasise the accent.'

'What's wrong with your real name, the name I gave you?'

'It is my real name. Étoile is Stella in French.'

'Is that so?'

'Well, sort of.'

I'll never understand what I've done wrong, Hazel said to herself, over and over again, on the way home in the train. I've worked my fingers to the bone to give that girl a good home and what thanks do I get? Nothing's good enough for her. Nothing. Not her name or me or our home or anything else. She looks down on Roy and me for living together and there she is gaga over that socialite and her German adulterer. And that Frenchman, as ugly as a cartload of monkeys. What's wrong with an Australian, I'd like to know? Her father, for all his faults, was not a bad looker. As for Roy, what if he *was* behind the door when the good looks were given out? He's been a godsend, a kind man with a good heart.

Hazel repeated her worries out loud to Roy when he got home from work and she'd changed her clothes to get tea ready.

'Never mind, love,' said Roy opening a bottle of Reschs DA.

'But I do mind, Roy,' said Hazel, dipping floured lamb cutlets into beaten egg and then breadcrumbs. 'She's my flesh and blood.'

'I know, love.' Roy had become subdued since they'd been living together. It happened so gradually Hazel didn't seem to notice the change in his personality, and he didn't seem to be aware of it himself. Sometimes, when her whingeing got on his nerves, he told himself it wasn't important enough to complain about and risk unpleasantness. Worthy woman though Hazel was, she had a way of wearing a man down. It was easier to give in. He went into the lounge room and turned on the television.

Chapter 32

Freddie, Desi, Stella and Lavinia were lined up behind a long table at Rod Webb's studio when the freelance director who'd been appointed to handle the Freudian Slip commercial arrived punctually at ten. By unspoken agreement, it had been decided that giving Werner Dresner the job would not be a good idea, even though it had been three weeks since the scandal known on the quiet as The Dizzaster had taken place. The newcomer was an Englishman named Stanley Cooke-Ridley, who'd made a name for himself with the British new wave film *Goodbye Fred, Hello Freda*. It had been nominated for best British film in the Society of Film and Television Awards of 1961, but it lost out to *A Taste of Honey*.

Stanley, a stringy chap of indeterminate age with receding fair hair and a red cravat tucked into a white shirt under a navy blazer, joined them at the table. Lavinia passed along copies of the list of women they were about to assess for the role of enchantress in the commercial. She nodded to a production assistant, whose job was to open the door to admit each contender and to close it after her.

A woman with startling red hair and a gushing manner stalked into the room and stood, one pointy foot in front of the other, one hand on her hip, baring her teeth at what she thought looked like a row of starlings preening themselves on a clothesline.

'Thank you, dear,' said Stanley, whose accent was more Bow Bells than Belgravia. 'Your agent will get back to you.'

She left without a word. Stella was shocked that he hadn't bothered to ask a single question, if only out of courtesy. It was so brutal.

'If she's twenty-six, I'm sixteen,' said Freddie.

'Next,' said Lavinia.

A pert little thing with cropped black hair and a bubbly personality skipped in and said, 'Hello, I'm Chantelle.' She wrinkled her nose and wriggled her hips.

'Thank you, dear,' said Stanley.

'Your agent will get back to you,' said Lavinia. She was beginning to enjoy herself. No mucking about with this director.

'She was cute,' ventured Stella.

'Too cute,' said Freddie.

'Next,' said Lavinia.

A well-groomed young woman, whom everyone except Stanley recognised from her appearances in commercials selling dishwashing liquid, insect repellent, baby food and toothpaste, presented herself.

Stanley asked her about her professional experience and she reeled off all the brands her face had helped to flog.

'Thank you, dear,' he said.

'Your agent will get back to you,' said Lavinia.

'She was quite attractive,' said Stella.

'Typecast and over-exposed,' said Freddie.

And so the parade went on. Sometimes, Stanley or Freddie or Desi would ask a question, but each hopeful was sent away knowing in her heart that it was unlikely she'd hear from her agent and if she did it would be bad news. To the covey of inquisitors, each applicant was too aloof, too common or too demure, too sexy or not sexy enough, too old, too young, too flat-chested or too bosomy. She had bad skin, crooked teeth, pop eyes or jug ears.

Until, like a miracle, towards the end of the day a vision came through the door. She was tall but not too tall, beautifully proportioned at 34-22-34, with a creamy complexion, expressive green eyes, long eyelashes and a lot of dark shiny hair. Her name was Violet Valesco, twenty-two years old and nineteenth on the list.

'Tell us about yourself,' said Stanley, coming to life for the first time that day.

'What would you like to know?' she asked him with a winning smile, which she then bestowed on the others.

'Your professional experience. What have you done?'

'I'm a mannequin for various fashion houses, including Mark Foys and Farmers. I've also been photographed for fashion by Laurence Le Guay and Bruce Minnett. But I have never been in a television commercial and I'd like to do that very much. I've only just signed up with International Casting.' Her confidence matched her looks.

'Violet,' said Stanley, as he stood up. 'May I ask you to wait outside for one moment?' He walked around the table to escort her to the door. 'I'd like to confer with my colleagues.' He ambled back and stood in front of the table. 'Well, for my money, she's it. What do you think?'

'All we need is a bloke who can measure up to her,' said Freddie. 'Let's have a drink.'

Full production of Freudian Slip was soon under way and Stella, never tiring of being introduced as the writer, did not miss a meeting. She spent two tedious days casting the male role and was disappointed when her choice was overridden by everyone else; they agreed on an actor named Bobby Tanner they said looked like Charlton Heston, but she couldn't see any similarity. She preferred a slick one who looked like Tony Curtis, but the others said he was too oily.

She went with Desi to supervise the set being built; to inspect the wardrobe; to engage the make-up artist, hairdresser and caterer; to cast the male voice-over; to brief the composer on the soundtrack and to discuss the font for the titles with Jacques. By chance, because she was in Desi's office when Freddie came in to discuss the budget, she witnessed the quotes from competitive production houses and noted the generous percentages added by the agency to cover its own costs and to shield it from financial loss in the event of something going wrong. Guy insisted on taking her to meetings with Mr Wasserstein a couple of times a week to explain the progress and secure his approval of the decisions being made. Fortunately, both Wassersteins were happy with the screen tests of Violet Valesco and the male actor chosen to play opposite her.

It was a busy time for Stella and she hoarded every detail of her experiences, going over them with the relish of a miser counting his gold. At the end of each day she was usually too tired to want to go out anywhere, and that was just as well because she had dropped her old friends without having made new ones, except Jacques who'd become distant again, ever since they'd gone All The Way. 'Keep yourself nice or he won't respect you,' had been about the only advice her mother had offered on the subject of sex before marriage, and Stella began to have the uncomfortable feeling that Hazel might have been right. The deflowering had not been the transcendental experience she'd expected. She didn't have time to worry about it during the day, but at home alone in the evening, grilling a chop or handwashing her smalls, she recalled the disappointment and tried to work out what had gone wrong.

'Did you come?' Jacques had said, as he lifted himself off her.

She lay on her back in the crumpled sheets wondering if that was all there was to it. 'I think so,' she said.

'You'd know for sure if you did.' He settled down beside her and pretended to go to sleep. He found her inability to reach orgasm a slur on his manliness.

A little later, he'd gathered the strength to try again. This time she knew what was coming and her body started to resist, although she didn't want it to. She realised that she didn't like being penetrated. It was an invasion of her most private self. Cuddles and petting, yes. Messy poking around, no. I suppose that's something women just have to put up with, she thought.

As far as Jacques was concerned after that, Stella was yesterday's conquest and today's has-been, the kind of female he'd once heard described in an American bar as a lousy lay. All she did was to lie back in submission, making the missionary position the only one she found acceptable. She was probably frigid.

Chapter 33

B ea glanced at the handwriting and turned away, as though some obscenity was scrawled there instead of her name, care of Audrey's address. She put the envelope in her pocket.

'Aren't you going to read it? It's from London.' Audrey was mistress of the obvious.

'Yes, I can see that.'

At the sharp edge in Bea's voice Audrey decided to change the subject. She pointed at the street directory open in front of them on the coffee table. 'If we went via Pennant Hills, we could call in to see Aunt Elva at the nursing home.'

'We could.' Bea hoped her voice contained some enthusiasm, although she'd suddenly gone cold on the idea of a trip in Audrey's Morris Minor to a pub at Windsor for lunch. The sun was out but the westerly wind was even more vicious this year than it normally was in August. 'Audrey, I've got a better idea.'

Audrey closed the directory, prepared to accept the inevitability of her plan being superseded by one of Bea's, as usual. She looked at her younger sister compliantly, without resentment.

'Why don't we visit Aunt Elva and come back here for lunch? I could light the fire and warm up the pea soup I made last night.'

'If you like.'

'Save you driving all the way to Windsor and back in this foul weather.' Like many people, Bea was skilled at dressing her self-interest in the guise of thoughtfulness for the wellbeing of others.

As they approached Elva's room along a shiny corridor with bare walls painted mist-grey and a floor of something squeaky and fawn, they passed a man in a white coat with a frown on his face and a stethoscope around his neck. A nurse with a mitred damask napkin on her head, a watch pinned upside down on her chest and a clipboard in one arm smiled and stepped aside for them. Before they reached their aunt's room her quavery voice drifted towards them through the smell of ether, floor polish and disinfectant.

'Have I seen you before?' Aunt Elva was saying.

'Oh, yes, many times,' they heard a younger woman reply. 'I'm the one who plucked some hairs out of your chinny chin chin.'

Audrey looked at Bea, who pressed her forefinger vertically to her lips as a caution not to give in to mirth. But it wasn't easy, so they stood outside the open door for several moments to control themselves. When the potted cyclamen Audrey was holding stopped shaking they entered the room.

Aunt Elva lay on her back under a cotton blanket with her feet sticking out; they were bony and pallid, like chicken claws. Attending to them at the end of the bed was a plump young woman wielding an emery board. 'Oh, look,' she said, 'you've got visitors.'

'Lucky me,' said Elva, wriggling her toes. 'Yippee-yi-yo-ki-yay!'

After the pedicurist had packed up her kit and Elva's extremities had been tucked under the blanket, the conversation went like this:

'I thought you might like these, Aunt,' said Audrey.

'Oh, poppies. My favourite.'

'No, they're . . .'

'Yes, aren't they lovely?' said Bea.

'We used to grow them, you know. Put them there, where I can see them.'

'You water it from the bottom,' said Audrey, placing the potted cyclamen on the windowsill, as instructed.

'Sit here, Gladys,' Elva said to Bea. 'How are the girls doing at school?'

'She's not . . .' said Audrey.

'Audrey and Bea have left school now, Elva,' said Bea, insinuating her bottom on to the edge of the bed.

'Time flies. I was only saying that to Henry this morning.'

'Uncle Henry?' said Audrey. He'd been dead since she was fourteen, twenty years ago.

'He was here a minute ago. He might still be out there.' She waved a flimsy hand at the doorway. 'He'd love to see you.'

At midday the rattling of plates and cutlery in the corridor indicated that lunch was on the way, so their stay came to an end with kisses and the reassurance of a return visit soon. As soon as they were out of earshot, retracing their steps along the corridor, Audrey said dolefully, 'Hasn't she gone downhill since Christmas?'

'She might just be having a bad day,' said Bea, knowing it wasn't true.

On the way home and as she lit the fire later Bea didn't have much to say. Audrey took the knitting out of her bag to work on the sleeve of a raspberry-red jumper in blackberry stitch. She filled the silence by talking about her work as a bookkeeper at the insurance company and the doings of the Mosman Musical Society. Most of what she said was lost on Bea, who was distracted not by the preparation of lunch—that was simple enough—but by the vision of a future in which she and Audrey, two old maids in a nursing home, were in each other's company for twenty-four hours every day.

By the time Audrey left and Bea was alone in the late afternoon, orange and black coals had settled like a scorched piecrust in the fireplace. The mellow after-effects of red wine soothed her mind. She went into her bedroom, opened the wardrobe door and felt for the envelope in the pocket of her tweed jacket.

Back in the sitting room, she studied the sweeping diagonal curves of the words 'Mrs Beatrice O'Connor' for several minutes and was tempted to toss the letter unopened into the fire. It was two years since they'd been in touch. Repeatedly, she had told herself she wanted nothing more to do with Aidan O'Connor, but she didn't seem able to bring herself to dismiss him altogether. As she ran her finger under the flap of the envelope to loosen it, her stomach felt queasy.

She refilled her glass and unfolded the pages. Although the only identification on the impressive writing paper was a watermark, she knew it had been filched from some benefactor. It had a fusty smell, as though it had rested in old lavender-scented underwear. With a sniff of distaste, she opened a window and waved the pages in the breeze off the harbour in an effort to freshen them, then closed it, sat down and began to read.

My dear Beatrice,

The other day, I opened a book of poetry. As it happened, it contained a few works by one of your favourites, Keats, and a curious thing happened. As I read, 'A thing of beauty is a joy for ever: Its loveliness increases; it will never Pass into nothingness . . .' a snapshot fell out from between the pages. It was a picture of you under the Laburnum Arch at Bodnant in Wales. A thing of beauty indeed. We were on our honeymoon. Do you remember? If I could bear to part with it, I would have included it with this letter. But I cannot.

Madeleine and I have decided to go our separate ways. It could never have been a lasting thing. I should have known that from the start. There has only ever been one woman for me and I have paid dearly for the loss of her. You know whom I mean, Beatrice, don't you?

It is time for me to start a new life. A chap in the Salisbury the other evening told me about an immigration scheme that might put me on the shores of your country for ten pounds, if someone would agree to be my sponsor. It is my deepest wish that you might consider it.

Yours always, Aidan

The bloody cheek of him. Her hands shook as she took a cigarette from the box on the coffee table and looked around for her lighter.

Chapter 34

Edgecliff Road made a curved ascent from Ocean Street, so Bea took it slowly. On her right, houses and apartment buildings set back from the street rose up from their well-kept gardens in a commanding way, as though their maturity gave them authority over everything else in view. On the left, the land fell away so all she could see were the tops of trees and roofs that gave little indication of the structures they sheltered. The gate with the number she was looking for opened to a small wooden bridge over a drop of about eighteen feet and led to a darkened porch and a door with stained-glass insets. The brass knocker, polished to a fine glow, was shaped like a hand. Trust Desi to find a place both mysterious and refined.

'It hasn't taken you long to settle in here,' said Bea as she sank into submissive cushions on a sage-green velvet sofa. The room, its walls a faded colour that was halfway between peach and apricot, was large and well proportioned, with egg-and-dart moulding on the cornices and French windows opening to a balcony fenced with fancy cast iron. Beyond it were the tops of trees and roofs of properties in the street below. In the distance twinkled the harbour.

'Rejects from the family home,' said Desi. 'At least, from my mother's family seat in Tassie.' She emphasised 'family seat' in a disparaging way, to distance herself from its pretension.

As Bea looked around, she realised that the room wasn't really decorated. Things came together because every item was valuable, worn and classic, hand-me-downs of the most desirable kind. It was as good an example as she'd ever seen of English upper-class style: lived-in, comfortable, uncontrived and slightly shabby.

Bea had brought a bottle of Mateus Rosé unaware, until the moment Desi poured some of it into two stemmed glasses, that the colour of the wine matched the walls. Somehow that made it seem kitsch. Maybe Desi thought so too because she straightened up and looked at the walls. 'I'm not sure if I can live with that colour. I'd like to paint the whole thing white and get Shaker furniture.'

It takes more than a coat of paint to whitewash the past, thought Bea, but she held her tongue. Thinking about colour suddenly made her aware of her red jacket standing out garishly against the subtlety of her surroundings. Everything else, including Desi's oatmeal jumper and pants, the cream floor-length curtains, the faded carpet, the ceramic lamps, the bowl of pink carnations, was soft and seasoned. Nothing looked new. Bea felt as conspicuous as a post box. She slipped the jacket off and folded it so that its nondescript lining faced outward and was less intrusive. Her light-grey woollen tube dress having agreed with the room, she felt more comfortable. I'm becoming a fusspot like Freddie, she thought. An image of Aunt Elva also came to mind.

'I hope you'll stay to dinner,' Desi said. 'Werner should be here soon and it will do him good to see a friend.' She looked at her feet encased in cream kidskin flats. 'This wretched business has been a disaster for him.'

'Not to mention you,' said Bea. Lately she'd noticed that Desi had lost some of her buoyancy and tended to be moody. She had always stooped a little because of her height but now she seemed hunched over.

'How are your family taking it?' Bea continued.

'They're fine. Fully supportive, at least of me. Our friends are, too. They've closed ranks against the enemy. Werner has no such luck. I still have my job but he's freelance. His work has just evaporated.'

'The agency needs you. You're good at your job.'

'So is he! But he has no one to stand up for him.'

'What about Rod Webb?'

'He's been trying. But everybody backs off at the mention of his name. Clients don't want him associated with their products, so their agencies have just dropped him. Werner didn't tell me that. Darryl did.'

'As if the general public would know who the hell directs the commercials!'

'I know that, but they're playing it safe. Industry gossip tends to get out. It's terribly unfair.' Desi was becoming agitated. She stood up and started moving about restlessly, turning on the table lamps and re-positioning objects around them. 'Daddy spoke to FB. They've known each other since Sydney Grammar. I'm okay because my father belongs to the old boys' club. Werner doesn't. Besides, he's half Jewish. That's the final offence. No, the absolutely final offence is that he's half German.' Bea had never heard Desi sound bitter before.

'You know what?' She turned and looked at Bea as though she was about to deliver an oration of global significance. 'This is the first time in my life that I've seen my family's position as a setback instead of a privilege. It's standing in the way of everything I want in life. Ironic, eh?' She pressed her lips together into a thin line and her nostrils lifted, as though a bad smell had drifted under them.

Bea didn't know what to say. Her own problem, which she'd hoped to talk about with Desi, seemed paltry in comparison.

'He doesn't live here with me, you know. He doesn't want to sully my reputation any further.' Her laugh was so false it could have come from Stella. 'He's got a crummy bed-sitter at the Cross. They threw him out of Ithaca Gardens.'

'I'm so sorry,' was all Bea could think to say.

A rat-tat-tat from the direction of the front door was followed by the sound of a key turning in a lock. Desi stood up and Bea noticed the changed expression on her face. Her features lifted and life was back in her eyes. She disappeared into the hall. After the front door closed there was silence. Bea imagined them holding each other. Not a voyeur, she was embarrassed so she got up and went to the French windows, pretending to be absorbed in the flight of seagulls swooping over Double Bay.

How stupid, she thought, that his pride gets in the way of their being together. It could be so straightforward. Yet the moment the thought entered her head she knew how false it was. Nothing was simple, unless you accepted that whichever choice you made was no-win. Look at her own dilemma: grow feeble and senile with Audrey, relying meanwhile on the odd one-night stand for excitement, or accept the awful reality of a charming husband she'd have to carry like a child for the rest of their lives or until he found a more lucrative sponsor.

To his credit, Werner began by making a big effort to be sociable and Bea responded by pretending not to notice the subtext of their three-way conversation. In the absence of shoptalk—it would have been unforgivably tactless to talk about business, given what she now knew—Bea found herself gabbling on about Margaret Smith winning the women's singles at Wimbledon and the phenomenal success of Bob Dylan's subversive new song, 'Blowin' in the Wind'.

With those two subjects exhausted, she wanted to know the correct proportion of gin to vermouth for the perfect martini, knowledge that resided only with Americans, she said. 'The Poms can't do it because they don't understand ice, and Australians aren't picky enough to bother.' She knew she was chattering like a dumb cluck, making it up as she went along, but Werner indulged her by joking that all you needed to do was to take an eye-dropper to the bottle of dry vermouth and extract precisely one drop for a cocktail glass of chilled gin.

At last Bea found a subject that stirred up some real interest. The Great Train Robbery was a daring and carefully planned escapade undertaken just that month in England in which a gang raided a train running between Glasgow and Euston Station in London and got away with more than two-and-a-half million pounds.

Desi was dishing up a Greek stew called stifado—recipe courtesy of Elizabeth David—when Werner said, 'I'd sell my soul to the devil to be a member of that gang.'

'They'll go to prison,' said Desi. She put the lid on the cast-iron casserole dish and sat down.

'If they get caught,' said Werner.

'Of course they'll be caught. It was registered mail from the post office. A lot of those notes would have been recorded so they're traceable.'

'I still think it would be worth the risk. What do you think, Bea?' He picked up the bottle of claret and refilled her glass.

'I'm too chicken to be a good crook. I'd be scared out of my wits.'

Desi refused Bea's offer of help as she began to clear the plates from the table. As her footsteps receded down the long passage to the kitchen, Bea experienced a moment of panic at having to push the conversation along again in a jolly way.

When she took out a cigarette, Werner lit it for her. Then he lapsed into silence, lost in some reverie that was probably sparked by the idea of robbing a train and getting away with it. At the distant whirring of an egg-beater, Bea thought of her friend in the kitchen, fixing up some pretty pudding to try to please him, while he sat here brooding, doing nothing but feel sorry for himself.

Her anger came suddenly, as sometimes happens when people who are usually patient are roused. Unintended words began to spill out of her mouth in a voice that was no longer sweet. 'I don't know why you are being so obstructive, Werner. You love her, don't you?'

At least she had his attention now, although he was too surprised to say anything.

'If I had someone as dotty about me as Desi is about you, I wouldn't let anything stand in my way,' she said.

'I don't think you understand.'

'Understand what?'

'My position.'

'Your position is with her.'

'That's impossible. She's an heiress. I'm a pauper.'

'What's wrong with you men? I thought you were a man with a brain, Werner. She told me that's what she first loved about you. You don't conform. You think for yourself. What happened to your famous powers of reasoning? She loves you. You love her. That's the position. What's the problem?'

Footsteps were approaching. Werner was saved from the need to defend and explain himself to this pop-eyed woman who had no right to stick her nose into his affairs. His life was complicated enough without a self-appointed judge pointing out his inadequacies. He knew enough about them already.

'Voila!' said Desi, bearing a tray with three parfait glasses, filled with something creamy and pale pink. 'Zabaglione. I got it right this time!'

Chapter 35

In September, Werner was approached by a hotshot production house in Melbourne to direct a series of television commercials and a two-minute cinema film for Carlton United Breweries. For Desi, the commission was like a stay of execution and she brightened up at the prospect of his career righting itself again once clients were reminded of how brilliant his work could be. The commercials involved Australian Football League players so they had to be shot in Victoria after the grand final at the end of September, and that was welcome, too. He'd have to spend the next few months in Melbourne. She could join him at weekends.

On the Friday before he left to go south, Bea noticed him in the queue behind her at the bank at lunchtime. After she'd collected her money from the teller she waited for him at the door. He must have seen her when he paused at the counter to stuff notes into his wallet because he moved to one of the side tables and pretended to be interested in the brochures stacked there.

Although it was obvious that he was trying to avoid her, she waited. When it became clear to him that she was not about to leave, he faced the inevitable and came towards her without returning her smile.

'I owe you an apology,' she said.

He held the door open for her to go out ahead of him. 'What for?'

'For the things I said a while ago at Desi's.' She waited outside while he continued to hold the door for the woman behind them. When he joined her on the footpath she squinted in the sun and said, 'It was wrong of me to meddle in something that's none of my business.'

'Forget it,' he said. 'I have.' It was not true but he managed a conciliatory grin and a pat on the shoulder that made her think her words had not been hurtful. In fact, he'd been stung by what she said. His good humour today had to do with the prospect of challenging work in a city removed from interference by Desi's well-meaning friends.

That afternoon, Stella sat with Freddie, Desi, Guy, Stanley Cooke-Ridley and Rod Webb in the theatrette at Rod's studio as Darryl threaded up the reels to screen the first double head of the Freudian Slip commercial. As Stella now knew, the term double head was used to describe the hooking up of image and sound in sync, to produce an approximation of the final result, give or take a few technical tweaks. They'd all seen and heard the various parts piecemeal but it was only when these elements came together that they knew whether they had a cohesive piece of communication and persuasion, or what Rod had been heard to describe as a two-headed monster, and Darryl would have called a marital mismatch.

This marriage turned out to have been made in heaven. Encores were called for, as much for the pleasure of looking at Violet Valesco's veiled cleavage and its effect on Bobby Tanner, as to assess the level of music to voice, and to consider the positioning of the graphic on the closing pack shot.

Over drinks afterwards, while Freddie and Guy paid extravagant compliments to Stanley, Stella and Rod, Desi was tempted to voice a tiny little worry but decided not to; she was honest enough to wonder whether her reaction might be affected by the knowledge that, but for the scandal, Werner instead of Stanley would have been receiving the praise.

Yet her doubts persisted. Now that the commercial was there in reality, it seemed a little too, well, blatant. Although nobody else but Stella knew it—and she wasn't about to tell anyone—the idea behind it had been Desi's and she now felt a certain responsibility for it, questioning her wisdom in having tossed it off so lightly, without reflection or consideration of the consequences.

'Why so serious?' said Freddie, giving her a nudge. 'This is one of the best commercials the agency has produced; one for the show reel.'

'Yes, it is.' She tried to sound enthusiastic. 'It will certainly be noticed.'

'What more could we ask?' said Guy. 'Well done, Desi.'

The Freudian Slip commercial went to air in Sydney and Melbourne on Channels Seven and Nine in October. It was not permitted to appear before 9 pm due to what The Australian Broadcasting Control Board deemed to be 'explicit sexual references'.

It took only a day before objections started arriving in letters to the editors of newspapers and in telephone calls to the Board. Two members of parliament also received complaints from constituents outraged at commercial television's contribution to declining moral standards in the community. A small item in Column 8 on the front page of *The Sydney Morning Herald* drew attention to a fight between two customers in Farmers' lingerie department over the last remaining size eighteen Freudian Slip in black.

A week later, Mr Wasserstein was forced to extend work hours at the Phoebe Phipps factory in order to produce enough Freudian Slips to meet the demand from Myer in Melbourne, Mark Foys in Sydney and a dozen or so specialty salons whose stocks had been depleted. The manufacturers of competitive brands, such as Berlei and Hickory, were rumoured to be reassessing their advertising agencies.

Within two weeks, BARK had been invited to pitch for the Elizabeth Arden Cosmetics account and to come up with an idea for a new deluxe cigarette from Pederson Morley targeting upwardly mobile women, aged eighteen to twenty-four. A promising designer of swimwear, seated beside FB's wife Allegra at a David Jones fashion parade, asked if her husband's company would be interested in handling her label's image and advertising. Suddenly the agency found itself in the world of fashion.

The more stories of this kind reached Stella's eager ears, the more her starry eyes glittered and the more accolades she felt were her due. But her elation was counterbalanced by a creeping terror at the knowledge of what Freddie and the rest of the agency now expected of her. She could still count on Desi as an ally—Stella was pleased yet puzzled that she still had her job, given her public disgrace—but Bea was unlikely to be persuaded to trust her again, much less offer the creative guidance she needed.

Bea remained courteous but distant, full of her own importance at exporting an idea to America. She thinks she's Joan Sutherland, thought Stella, Possum turned into La Stupenda, with everyone saying how brilliant she was. For the life of her, Stella couldn't fathom why it was okay to swipe a song from *Oklahoma!*—more than okay, it was heroic—and a capital offence to borrow an idea from Clairol or Maidenform. Bea had also talked Freddie into letting her hire a junior writer to replace Gary and this one, a couple of years older than Stella and trained in the advertising department of Farmers, was a bright girl named Isabel, who could draw as well as write. Stella didn't like that at all.

Professionally and personally, Isabel was a threat. The way Jacques pronounced her name—Eesa-bella—slowly, with his fleshy mouth closing around the word as if it were a crème caramel, made Stella feel empty inside, hungry for something less definable than food or sex. Without him having said anything, she knew he'd lost interest in her.

These were not her only worries. Given her liking for clothes, shoes, cosmetics and pricey hairdos from Digby Darling, Stella had trouble making ends meet. After she'd paid for the essentials of rent and food, there was not much left for the things she really wanted: pretty tableware, significant books and pictures, fresh flowers, writing paper—engraved with a more impressive address than the one she had now—and envelopes lined in tissue paper. A salary increase was necessary, but that could happen only if she had another brilliant idea, so there she was, back at the core problem.

To mask her fears, Stella had developed a frenzied manner to hide behind, a kind of gushing insincerity that warded off intimacy and even passed for happiness in the eyes of people who did not know her well. She was given to letting out little squeals to indicate a delight that she did not feel.

The morning Freddie called a meeting in the boardroom for the team to be briefed by Guy on the new Pederson Morley cigarette, Stella fought a desire to offer an excuse to stay away. But she knew that not turning up would be self-destructive, much worse than wagging school because she'd never catch up. Nobody would share the experience with her. They'd be too anxious to stand out themselves, to clutch their own feeble ideas in secrecy before revealing them to a meeting of the group so that everyone knew who'd dreamed them up.

Stella dithered around in her office, collecting her notebook and cigarettes, and looking for the Parker pen that had been a mascot since her fifteenth birthday. As she skirted the typing pool, she saw Jacques trailing Isabel into the boardroom and every instinct told her to run in the opposite direction.

Once inside, her only choice of a chair was one between Kelvin and Humphrey, the media planner, at the wrong end of the table, or next to La Stupenda Possum. She managed a taut little smile and an uncontrollable twitch of the eyelid as she took the chair beside Bea, whose amused attention was on Guy as he fiddled ineffectively, as usual, with the slide projector. Seated side-by-side opposite them were Jacques and Isabel, who radiated enthusiasm and confidence that Stella found offensive.

Without being asked, Kelvin got up and adjusted the projector dexterously. The presentation began. It consisted mainly of charts showing market shares, demographic profiles and consumer spending patterns that Stella found irrelevant to the project. An analysis of the elements that contributed to the success of the Marlboro brand was also of little use to her.

Although she kept her eyes on the screen, her attention was on the twosome sitting across the table, mocking her with their playfulness, which amounted to flirtation. Anybody could see that. She wondered why nobody raised an objection, called them into line, told them to stop . . . doing what? Their hands were on their notebooks, their attention was on the screen, but their desire for each other was palpable.

Finally, Guy got around to talking about the new cigarette. It would be small and slender, about the size of an exotic Sobranie, but in plain white with a gold ring near the filter tip.

'The agency's task,' said Guy with the pomposity he reserved for important briefing sessions, 'is to a, name the product; b, design the packaging; and c, devise a personality and an advertising campaign for the brand.'

Stella felt sick.

Chapter 36

'Athink tank, that's what we need,' said Freddie. He walked back to Bea's office with her and stood in the doorway, leaning against the frame with his eyes on the blank wall where the Smirnoff poster used to be. 'Hey, what have you done with Sean Connery?'

'Spring-cleaning. Do you want it?' She opened a cupboard and began shifting folders and boxes. 'Here.' She hauled out a roll of stiff paper with a rubber band around it. 'I'm replacing him with that gorgeous Russian who defected.'

'Rudolf Nureyev? Show me!'

'It's at the framer's.' She handed over the Smirnoff poster and fixed on him the sort of look a mother gives a child who wants more lollies than his share. 'Don't tell me you want Nureyev too.' The Royal Ballet poster of him with Margot Fonteyn had arrived from London three days before with a note, in Aidan's flowing hand, that read, 'The seat beside me for *Giselle* was meant for you.' She should have been uncomfortable at the blatancy of Aidan's ingratiating behaviour but she wasn't. Instead, her senses were alert; she was skittish, nervous at being in touch with him again.

Freddie laughed. 'After you, madame, when you're tired of him. I'll make do with Sean for the present.' He put the poster under his arm. 'As I was saying before you distracted me . . .'

'Sean Connery distracted you.'

'Yes, well. Rather than all of us sitting down by ourselves, thinking about this cigarette and waiting for divine inspiration, why don't we have a think tank?'

'Good idea.'

'Out of the office, where nobody can get to us.'

'A hotel?'

He pulled a face. 'I don't think FB would agree to pay for it. With room service for this lot, it would cost. It's the agency's money, remember. This is just a pitch. No big budget until we get the business.'

'We need someone's flat.'

'Mine's a shoebox,' said Freddie. 'We'd need room to move around.'

'I'd be happy to do it at my place but Cremorne's a bit out of the way, isn't it?' She thought of Martha, snooping around, finding excuses to intrude and broadcasting their doings to the neighbourhood.

'I suppose we could have it here at the office,' he said, 'but I don't see how we can stop the interruptions. And it should be somewhere a bit more stimulating than a workplace.'

'What about Desi?' said Bea. 'Her flat would be ideal.'

* * *

When Stella read Freddie's memo inviting her to an all-day think tank at Desi's flat in Edgecliff Road on Friday, she experienced the kind of relief that happens when a tooth stops aching or menstrual pain goes away. That night she slept better than she had done in weeks.

A think tank, which she rightly assumed to be a grandiose term for a brainstorm, was where the individual was submerged in the collective so that, at the end, nobody remembered precisely who had contributed what to the outcome. Responsibility for the finished result was shared equally, regardless of how much or how little each person had brought to solving the problem. However, Stella did not permit herself to think along these lines for long. All she knew was that she was happy. Her only concern was what to wear on the day.

Peonies were in season and Desi's flat was filled with the pale voluptuous blooms. Their slightly decadent scent hung on the warm air in the sitting room where the group had gathered. Coffee had been consumed by the time any serious discussion was under way.

'The gold ring could be a clue,' said Freddie. He sat on the carpet with bent knees, one leg lying flat and the other propped up for him to lean on. He had a blue cashmere jumper slung around his shoulders, like an Italian. 'Has anybody smoked one of these things yet?' He tossed a cigarette to Bea, sitting opposite him on the green velvet sofa.

'I didn't dare,' said Bea. She wore narrow black pants and an oversized white cotton shirt with the collar turned up. 'Aren't they just dummies?' She twirled the cigarette between her fingers.

'It doesn't matter how they taste, as long as they look good,' said Stella, with her recently acquired wisdom. Her own packaging today was inspired by a magazine photograph of Jacqueline Kennedy wearing a sleeveless floral print dress with a full skirt on holiday with her husband at Hyannis Port, the Kennedy Compound on Cape Cod.

'It's pretty obvious that gold should be in the name.' Bea slipped her shoes off and tucked her feet under her on the sofa.

'Maybe,' said Isabel, 'but if we want it to be exotic, like Sobranies, we could give it a Russian name, like Tatiana or Natasha.' Her dress was a fashion statement, acquired in London, where she worked for two years: a white cotton jersey tube that clung to her firm round bottom and barely covered her knees. Its neckline was a V-slit in navy blue. Several bangles clanked along her right arm.

'Or an artistic name,' put in Stella, not to be outdone. 'Ballerina, or something.' She sat on a spindly upright chair near the French windows. Her legs were crossed and she let the balmy easterly breeze ripple her skirt so that it crept up above her knees. Jacques took notice, then looked away.

'Odette, the good swan in Swan Lake,' said Desi.

'Diva,' said Freddie. He stretched out both his legs. 'Except they wouldn't get it. They'd make it rhyme with diver.'

'Are you sure you're comfortable there?' said Bea. She tossed two cushions in his direction.

'Thank you, darling,' said Freddie, stuffing one between his back and the wall.

'Not everyone wants to be Russian or a ballerina,' said Desi, who wore her blue Capri pants with a jumper to match. She was sitting on the floor barefoot with her back against the sofa. Her long legs seemed to stretch halfway across the room.

'Pederson Morley,' said Bea. 'Can we do something with the initials PM?'

'Post meridiem, after midday,' said Freddie. 'Don't we want them to smoke all day, not just after lunch?'

'Prime minister,' said Desi. 'Too male and stuffy.'

'Paree Metro,' said Jacques, who was seated at Desi's desk doodling.

'That's where I'd like to be,' said Desi. 'In gay Paree.'

'Post mortem,' said Isabel, and shrieked with laughter as Freddie threw a cushion at her.

How childish, thought Stella, resentful of the way Freddie was grinning at Isabel. She wasn't even pretty. She had a snub nose and her legs were too short and she was a bit on the plump side. But she was striking in a completely one-off way. And she did have beautiful white skin, removed from any history of having laid out a beach towel at Cronulla. When they were eating pumpkin scones in the kitchen earlier, Jacques had told everyone how chic Isabel was. He called her dress *Le Sac*, a look that he said had just been invented by Balenciaga. 'It's an el cheapo copy from C&A Modes in Oxford Street!' announced Isabel merrily, waggling her bosom and her bum. To Stella, it just looked like an ill-fitting tennis jumper. If *she'd* been in London, she'd have found something far prettier than that.

'Perry Mason. Isn't he every girl's dream?' said Freddie.

'Not this girl's,' said Desi.

'We all know about you and your dreamboat,' said Freddie.

'Careful,' said Desi.

'Product manager,' said Stella and they all groaned.

'What about PM Gold?' said Bea.

Nobody spoke for a few moments while they evaluated the potential of the name.

'I like it,' said Jacques. The pack design was taking shape in his mind: a gold bar with the name looking as though it had been engraved on it, like a hallmark.

'It says rich and glamorous,' said Desi.

'Live rich! That could be our slogan,' said Bea.

'Now we're cooking with gas,' said Freddie. 'Aspiration, wish-fulfilment.'

'Success. Striking gold,' said Isabel.

'Winning,' said Stella.

'It needs music, a big sound,' said Bea. 'It can only succeed on emotion, not reason. Smoking's not exactly good for anyone. Let's go for a song.'

'Okay,' said Freddie. 'Let's write a song.'

Bea stood up, cleared her throat and began to sing:

> I want to live rich, yes I want the best
> I want to be number one among the best dressed
> I want to eat breakfast off a big silver tray
> And I'll smoke PM Gold every day!

Desi started to applaud and the rest of them took her cue. Bea gave an exaggerated bow, blew kisses and sat down. It was apparent to everyone that the words were too polished to have been invented right there, off the cuff, in a few seconds. Just as Freddie had hoped, she must have been working on ideas at home in preparation for today; maybe the extra effort was prompted by competition from Stella and Isabel. It was a terrific start to the think tank.

'First-rate idea, Bea. Keep it going. It needs a couple more stanzas,' said Freddie.

'I have more stanzas!' she crowed. She was on her feet again, bellowing in a passable imitation of Ethel Merman:

And when I dine at the Lodge I'll have the best seat
I'll be that cel-ebri-ty everyone wants to meet
When I say that I want to live rich I mean all the way
I'll smoke PM Gold every day!

'Hurrah!' shouted Isabel.
'Bravo!' yelled Freddie.
'Encore!' said Desi.
Rats, thought Stella, but she didn't say so.
Bea took a breath and continued:

As for the Opera House, well, just on the quiet
If the price is right, I think I might buy it
Oh yes I know how to work and I know how to play
I'll smoke PM Gold every day!

It was difficult for the rest of them not to feel intimidated by Bea's seeming ease at finding solutions to difficult creative challenges. While she sat on the sofa faking nonchalance, Freddie lit a Marlboro, Jacques lit a Gitane, Desi got up and secured a curtain that had been loosened by the wind, Isabel scribbled something in her notebook, chewed the end of her pen, scratched out what she had written and wrote down something else and Stella re-read Guy's brief.

'Now, team, any other ideas?' Freddie said when his cigarette had become a bumper. 'Guy expects two or three viable concepts before we choose one to develop for the client pitch.' He picked up one of the new cigarettes and looked at it. 'Can't we do something with the gold ring?'

'Marriage,' said Stella. An image of the whopping diamond Desi used to wear came to mind. How could she have given that back?

'Is that a good idea?' said Freddie.

'It's what every girl wants,' said Desi, of the ringless hands.

'Smoke this and he'll marry you? That's some promise,' said Bea, catching Desi's eye and winking.

'I see what you mean. We might be sued for breach of promise,' said Desi.

'To tame a bull, put a ring in his nose,' said Jacques.

'Something tells me it's time for a break,' said Freddie.

'The gold ring gives it status,' said Isabel, lifting her head from her notebook and staying put while the others started getting to their feet and stretching. 'The gold ring shows other people that it's expensive, that you have refined taste, like the cigarette has refined taste. But it doesn't have to be in the name. We could call it anything that associates it with refinement. Paris or Ritz or Savoy.'

'Those names might be taken already,' said Bea, 'but go on. We can think of others.'

'We could associate the cigarette with other refined things,' said Isabel. 'Beautiful clothes. A Chanel suit. A Dior dress. Exquisite gloves. French perfume.' At the look of encouragement on Bea's face, Isabel continued, her voice rising and becoming more excited, 'Boucheron jewellery. A Cartier watch. The cigarettes coming out of a superb handbag, like an Hermès Kelly or a Louis Vuitton make-up case.'

Show-off, thought Stella.

'Did you hear that, Freddie?' said Bea as he was about to step on to the balcony.

'Tell me.' He turned and came back into the middle of the room. Isabel repeated what she'd just said to Bea.

'Good thinking,' said Freddie. 'Why don't you work that up?'

It was one o'clock and the caterer had been and gone. Desi steered everyone into the kitchen where plates of sandwiches and cakes, bowls of fruit and bottles of wine were laid out on the table. Freddie reached for the corkscrew and did the honours.

'After you,' said Isabel when she and Stella almost collided over the plate of chicken sandwiches. Stella took two triangles and a sprig of parsley and bestowed on Isabel the screwed-up expression that passed for a smile.

'I think your Freudian Slip commercial is great,' said Isabel, helping herself to a less ladylike quantity of food.

Stella was caught off guard. 'Oh, thanks,' she squealed. 'The product's walking off the shelves.'

'I'm not surprised. It's such a clever idea.'

After her second glass of riesling, Stella suddenly said, 'Jacquie.' She was sitting at the kitchen table staring at a pot of geraniums on the windowsill.

Freddie turned his head to look in the same direction, as if he expected a stranger to be peering through the window. 'Jackie. Who's Jackie?'

'Jacquie Kennedy. Everybody wants to be Jacquie Kennedy.'

'Not bad, Stella,' said Bea, taking the cigarette holder out of her mouth, then putting it back in again.

'Work on it, Stella,' said Freddie. 'That could be our third possibility. It needs to be handled carefully, though. We can't imply that it's endorsed by the First Lady of the United States of America.'

By five o'clock their minds had grown fuzzy with wine and empty of thoughts other than what each of them planned to do with the evening and the weekend. Freddie said it was time to call it a day and leave Desi in peace. He thanked her on behalf of the agency and the team and presented her with a small package in which she, with a gasp of surprise, found a bottle of Guerlain's Vol de Nuit, a scent, he said, that should be worn only by 'a very brave woman'.

'Why is that?' said Isabel, who was bold as well as inquisitive.

'Because that's its character,' said Freddie. 'Home, wench,' he added and smacked her on the bottom. 'Come on, everybody.'

Chapter 37

'Do you mind if I stay for a while?' said Bea. 'I'll go if you'd rather be on your own.'

'No, no. I'd love you to stay.' Tiredness had lengthened Desi's face. Now that the others had gone she looked morose. Bea realised that her welcoming manner and her cheerfulness all day had been an act.

They were in the kitchen. Desi filled the kettle, put it on the stove and lit the gas underneath. 'You know the story behind that bottle of scent Freddie gave me?'

'No.'

'It's based on a novel about a woman who waits all night while the man she loves crashes his plane in a storm somewhere in South America and dies!'

'I wouldn't take that seriously,' said Bea, in her best school-marm voice, as she put teacups on a tray.

'Depressing, though. He could have chosen something more positive. Jicky or even L'Heure Bleue.'

Bea picked up the tray. She had to find a way to change the subject. 'I thought you might be off to Melbourne.'

Desi uttered a sound that was more a grunt than a sigh. 'Not this weekend. Werner's shooting again. I wouldn't see him.'

They sat on the balcony with the pot of tea and the remains of a sponge cake with passionfruit icing left over from lunch. The wine had made them hungry for something filling and sweet. At seven the sun was turning the view into an impressionist painting.

'Look at us,' said Bea. 'It's Friday evening and here we are. No man, no date, no hope. Two single ladies drinking tea.'

Desi laughed and she sounded genuinely amused. 'If we were men we'd be up at the Cross picking up talent.'

'Would you be game?' Bea's eyes looked more like a possum's than ever.

'Would you?'

'It's not what I want.'

'Nor I.'

'Anyway, there's always next weekend for you in Melbourne.'

'I wish that were true.' Desi looked at her half-empty cup and felt as twee and precious as the fine bone china, with a fluted edge and forget-me-nots sprinkled all over it.

'What are we doing, falling into this genteel colonial habit?' All of a sudden she had regained some of her old spirit. 'Freddie put a bottle of Taittinger in the fridge.'

'What are we waiting for?'

Bea cleared away the remnants of tea while Desi attended to the serious matter of dispensing champagne. Lights were winking on the harbour and marking the boundaries of New South Head Road. An orange dot glowed at the tip of Bea's cigarette. The semi darkness was protective, an encouragement for confidences that might not be aired in the glare of daylight.

'It doesn't work, going to Melbourne, because we're not doing the commercials together. I'm from a rival agency, so I feel like an enemy when I'm there.'

Bea made no reply. She didn't know what to say.

Desi's voice continued in the darkness. 'He's taken a serviced flat in Lonsdale Street. The telephone never stops ringing. They're females, usually, wanting his ear about schedules, appointments, dramas and all the rest of what goes on when you're making big-budget commercials. I'm superfluous. Worse than that, I'm in the way.'

'Even at the weekend?'

'It's the team thing. They'll all go off to dinner together, consolidating. I know about that. It's quite sexy, the proximity, the feeling of oneness, the sense of purpose.'

'It's only for a short time, remember,' said Bea. 'He'll be back in a few weeks.'

'I'm becoming a jealous shrew. I think he's trying to shake me off.'

'That can't be right. He loves you.'

'Maybe, but he can't get past this obstacle of my money and his lack of it. He can't see that it doesn't matter. Daddy, for all his bluster, would stand by me no matter whom I married. Werner's the problem. It's his ego.'

'We need to eat something,' said Bea. 'Did you say there were more leftovers in the fridge? Stay there. I'll get them.'

She returned with her handbag and a plate of sandwiches, which they devoured as though they hadn't eaten all day.

'You know,' said Bea, brushing crumbs from her fingertips, 'you and I have fallen in love with the wrong people. We should do a swap. Werner would feel quite unthreatened by my modest assets, and Aidan would have no trouble marrying an heiress. In fact, that's his dearest wish.' She opened her bag and took out the letter. 'You think *you* have problems. What am I to do about this?'

It didn't matter that the letter was illegible in the dark. Bea knew it by heart.

'I'm home!' called Freddie as he opened the front door and stepped on to the polished oak parquetry floor. The velvet voice of Nat King Cole singing 'Nature Boy' soothed the air. Bea would have been surprised to see how spacious was the 'shoebox' he'd told her he lived in. In fact, apart from the vast sitting room with its lofty view of the harbour, the flat contained three bedrooms—one converted into a study—and two bathrooms. The building dated from 1912, so the layout of the flat and the proportions of the rooms were splendid. Few outsiders had ever crossed the threshold since Freddie had taken possession. He was strict about keeping his living arrangements private, particularly from anyone at the office.

Darryl, wrapped in a terry bathrobe, came out of the bathroom towelling his hair. They kissed. 'I'll fix a martini in a minute,' he said and disappeared into the dressing room to change.

'How was your day out with the other girls, Floss?' Darryl handed Freddie a drink and sat on the sofa facing the view.

'Not as bad as it could have been. We actually got some work done.' Freddie arranged himself elegantly in a high-backed leather chair.

'Did the randy art director get lucky?'

'I doubt it. He's after Isabel now, but she's got a life-drawing class tonight at East Sydney Tech. I think she's wise to him.'

'Not like Stella?'

'Poor little Stella. She's suffering a bit. She was quite subdued today. I'll have to find a way to cheer her up.'

'More money.'

'Ha.'

The record finished with a click and Darryl replaced it with Judy Garland singing 'The Man That Got Away'. It was his favourite.

'What's the flat like?'

'Desi's? It's lovely. Not flash. Comfortable. They know how to do it, that old-moneyed lot. And how was your day, Darlene?'

'Boring. I had to go through endless takes, over and over again, with a client who couldn't make up his mind and then in the end we went back to the shots I'd used in the first place.'

He got up and took Freddie's empty glass along with his own. 'Anyway, it's Friday!' He did a little hop and clicked his heels in mid-air before sashaying into the kitchen for seconds. 'What are we doing tonight?' he yelled.

La Veneziana in Stanley Street was crowded and noisy with diners squashed together at the tables, just the sort of excitement most people were looking for at the end of a working week. Freddie's charm, his height and the way he dressed always seemed to work magic in Italian restaurants, so they didn't have to wait for a table. They ordered chicken livers and a bottle of chianti and waved to a couple of men they recognised from Bar Coluzzi in William Street. Later, they walked home to let the hood down on the Studley and cruise around looking at the action in Darlinghurst and the Cross.

It was after eleven, too early for bed, so Darryl suggested they drop in at the Mauve Artichoke, a camp nightspot in Kensington. 'There's a new show on, so Tony said. He should know, he styles their hair.'

'Whose hair?'

'The drag queens. Tinkerbell and Peter Pansy. And another one. I can't think of her name . . . Gladioli or something.'

Few of the Mauve Artichoke's patrons would have given the place a second look during the day, but late at night, tanked up and ready for fun, they felt they were in Christopher Isherwood's Berlin. It was dark and seedy and stuck in a place that was halfway to nowhere. What went on there was raunchy and rebellious.

The show started with the entrance of Tinkerbell, her hair styled à la Brigitte Bardot, a gold sequined leotard defining her curves. Three spangled ostrich feathers sprouted from her tail. She minced on to the stage ringing a little gold bell and asking for attention while she warmed up the audience with a few off-colour jokes. Peter Pansy, a roly-poly boy with spiky ginger hair, fake freckles, back-buttoned short pants and a school cap, joined her for a bit of slap and tickle.

They were followed by a succession of solo acts by female impersonators miming to the playback of popular recordings, notably Mel Tormé singing 'Blue Moon' and Billy Daniels with 'I Get a Kick Out of You'. When Shirley Bassey let loose her current hit, 'I Who Have Nothing', Freddie took Darryl's hand, squeezed it and held it for the length of the song. A twosome with tarantulas for eyes, skimpy white fur coats and black fishnet stockings aped Pearl Bailey and Hot Lips Page singing 'Baby,

It's Cold Outside', before the red plush curtains swept to a close across the stage and the whole place was blacked out.

After several seconds of darkness, during which whistles and catcalls were flung at the stage by the audience, a spotlight hit the curtains and, when they parted, engulfed a tacky set loosely based on Mae West's boudoir in *She Done Him Wrong*. Tumultuous applause greeted the entrance of Gorgeous Glorianna, a voluptuous platinum blonde bedizened with enough sparkle for spectators to need sunglasses. Her hourglass figure was poured into a size twenty red satin Freudian Slip trimmed with black lace. Behind her danced four men wearing top hats, white tie and tails and red satin toe shoes.

To the accompaniment of slow and sensuous belly-dancer music which Bea, had she been there, would have recognised as the Bacchanale from Saint-Saëns's *Samson and Delilah*, Glorianna began to half-sing, half-recite a song she told them she'd composed, all on her own. Her male chorus line performed graphic actions standing on tiptoes to illustrate the words:

> When I went out to dine
> With some boyfriends of mine
> Their hands took a grip
> On my Freudian Slip

Darryl hooted, bounced back and forth and nudged Freddie's arm with his elbow: 'Did you get that?' Freddie sat frozen in his seat.

> Keep your mitts of my knockers
> You miserable shockers!
> Don't you dare put a rip
> In my Freudian Slip!

Freddie opened his mouth for air, like a snapper flapping in the bottom of a fishing boat.

> Rock Hudson came by
> With a gleam in his eye.

'Wooooo . . . hoo . . .' yelled the crowd.

> He asked me to strip
> To my Freudian Slip.

'Give it to him!' someone shouted.

> Little Lady he said
> Come hither to bed.

'Go, Rocky!' came from the back row.

> And let's take a trip
> Up your Freudian Slip.

With that, Glorianna's chorus line lifted her above their heads, dumped her on the bed and fell in a heap on top of her. As her Freudian Slip flew across the stage and into the eager grasp of a grey-haired man in the front row, the curtains slowly closed and the crowd stamped their feet and roared, 'More! Encore!'

There were two replays before the spectacle was over. Each time, Glorianna wore a new Freudian Slip, which ended up in the anxious paws of someone in the audience. When the lights went up, Darryl was still clapping. 'That's the best show I've seen here. Wasn't it fabulous?' His face was boyish with the sheer fun of it all. He turned to look at Freddie and his smile vanished.

'What's wrong? Are you feeling okay?'

The blood had drained from Freddie's face, leaving it as white as Gorgeous Glorianna's powdered pompadour.

Chapter 38

Dipping the cloth into a bucket of hot water laced with methylated spirits, then swishing it over the window-pane, Bea thought for the umpteenth time about her conversation with Desi the night before about Aidan's letter.

Her friend had advised her to reply, in a noncommittal but friendly way, asking for precise details of what he expected her to do. It was a way of finding out how serious he was about emigrating and of giving herself time to think it through.

'Think of your own interests first,' said Desi. 'What's best for you?'

The advice was sensible, but the look in Desi's eyes was more eloquent than her words. What Bea read there was: You're in love with him, he wants to be with you, what are you waiting for? Smoothing away the moisture on the pane with a dry cloth, Bea couldn't help herself thinking: Is Aidan all there is?

When her windows showed her the world with admirable clarity, she sat at her desk and penned the following on a cream card engraved with her name and address:

> Dear Aidan,
> Your letter came as a surprise. Perhaps you could let me have details of what would be expected of me if I became your sponsor.
> Yours sincerely, Bea
> P.S. Thank you for the Nureyev poster.

She put it in an envelope, wrote his address on the front and attached a postage stamp to the top right-hand corner and a 'par avion' sticker to the top left-hand corner. She hesitated at the front door, tempted to keep it overnight to ponder the wisdom of sending it. Oh, what the hell, she thought, what have I got to lose? She walked to the post box at the end of her street and slid the letter into its open mouth.

On weekends, after they'd slept late, Freddie and Darryl were in the habit of skipping breakfast in favour of something special for brunch. But on this particular Saturday, after a disturbed night, Freddie had little appetite for the eggs Benedict that Darryl made so well, although he had no trouble putting away several glasses of Buck's Fizz.

That absurd piece of burlesque, mocking the agency's most recent stroke of brilliance, had done a bump-and-grind through his brain all night, becoming even more lurid and grotesque than what he'd seen onstage. As the creative director of BARK he was duty-bound to discuss what he had witnessed with his fellow executives, but how could he do that without revealing himself as a homosexual? Of course, not everyone who went to the Mauve Artichoke was queer, but there could be few doubts about the orientation of a man nearing forty and still a bachelor. It was one of those delicate matters that had always been left unsaid. He knew that many of his colleagues must have known his sexual preference but nobody talked about it because the practice of homosexuality was a criminal offence—and a terrible embarrassment to most people who were straight.

Darryl's patience was running out by the time they sat at the card table in the sunlit study with Freddie nibbling a piece of toast and Darryl faced with two helpings of poached eggs and leg ham smothered in Hollandaise sauce.

'When I was upset about Desi, didn't you tell me that all publicity is good publicity?' He stuck his fork into an egg and its yolk ran into the Hollandaise and over the ham and toast.

Although he was seated at the other side of the table, Freddie seemed to have been snatched away by aliens. He looked at Darryl and his eyes refocused.

'Well, I was wrong.'

'I don't get it. Aren't these things selling? Does it matter who's buying them?'

'Does it matter? The client would have a heart attack if he knew that his undies were the latest fashion for fags. He thinks he's selling them to the ABs.'

'Who?'

'The top demographic. High-end women with rich husbands. Ladies of the Eastern Suburbs and the North Shore who want to be sexy again, to attract their husband's attention. Or arouse the interest of somebody else's. It's a status thing. That was our brief.'

'Listen, you don't have to worry. Your client, Mr Whatsisname, would never have seen a drag show in his life, much less turn up at the Mauve Artichoke. He wouldn't know it exists.'

'I hope you're right. Give us a bit of that egg, lover.'

Chapter 39

It was late on a Thursday evening by the time Mr Wasserstein switched off the lights in his office, trudged heavily and squeakily over the linoleum, grappled with the metal doors of the cage lift and locked the building after him. He sat wearily for a while behind the wheel of his Mercedes-Benz without starting it and thought about the problems the success of the new line had inflicted on the production capability of Phoebe Phipps. The philosopher in him experienced a wry satisfaction in the paradox of this situation.

Normally, activity started to taper off in early December, after Christmas stocks had been delivered to the stores, but this year demand for Freudian Slips had accelerated at an alarming rate. The content of re-orders was atypical, too. The most popular colours were red and black in the largest sizes. Were society women getting fatter? He made a mental note to consult government statistics on whether Australian women's shapes and sizes were changing, because any variation had a direct bearing on the garments he produced.

He turned the key in the ignition, eased the car into Elizabeth Street and set off towards home at Bellevue Hill. Conscious of how tired he was, he drove carefully. Emanuel Wasserstein was a cautious and law-abiding man who did not wish to bring trouble upon himself or his family. His achievements as an Australian citizen and businessman were acknowledged by his peers, and the support of various charitable organisations had earned him and his wife Alma the respect of the wider public. He felt himself to be a pillar of the community.

Halfway along William Street, he slowed to a stop as the traffic light ahead turned to amber. Waiting for it to change, he shot a vaguely interested glance at two girls standing on the corner smoking cigarettes. Their lips were very red, their skirts very short and their heels very high. The one with orange hair and a purple feather boa caught his eye and winked. She dropped her cigarette, crushed it under her purple pointy shoe and swung her hips towards him. She said something he couldn't hear, so she indicated by a few spins of the wrist that he should wind down the window on the passenger side. The traffic light was still red, so he found it amusing to do as he was bidden.

She thrust her head through the open window and he registered simultaneously the bluish shadow around her chin and the muscular shoulders straining out of a red satin slip. When she put a large be-ringed hand on top of the car, a tuft of dark underarm hair was level with his face.

'How about a Freudian Slip, big boy?' said a baritone voice from between the lewd lips.

The light turned green but Emanuel Wasserstein sat as inert as an Easter Island monument. He was shocked to life only when the creature opened the car door and tried to get into the front seat beside him.

'Out!' said Mr Wasserstein, warding her off with his left arm. 'Get out or I am calling the police!'

'That's no way to treat a lady,' she said, gathering her boa around her and looking sulky as she slammed the door and stalked away. Then she turned around and, in a voice as shrill as a power tool cutting through metal, screeched, 'Fuck off, Grandpa! You probably can't get it up anyway!'

By then, the Mercedes had jumped forward, almost running down a man in a military greatcoat with a bottle-shaped brown paper bag who staggered sideways and shook his fist, but by then the car had almost reached the top of William Street at Kings Cross. Emanuel was so agitated he hadn't noticed the speed at which he was driving, so he slowed down along Bayswater Road and tried to calm himself. His heart was thumping against his ribs and he found it difficult to breathe but his mind was numb, unable to make any sense of what had just happened.

Guy was in his office discussing the Elizabeth Arden presentation with Freddie when his telephone rang. He picked up the receiver, said, 'Guy Garland' and switched on his smile. 'Mr Wasserstein, good morning!'

During the pause that followed he picked a pencil out of the ceramic pot. 'Sure, what time?' He scribbled something in his diary and looked at the Omega strapped to his wrist. 'See you then. Goodbye.'

'One happy client?' asked Freddie, trying to keep his voice light and confident.

'I hope so. He wants to see me right now, on the double.'
He shrugged on his jacket. 'Let's finish this over lunch, if I'm
back in time.'

'Beppi's?'

'Why not? It's Friday.'

Freddie's usual table beside the window was taken, so he had to sit
at one in the back room where bottles of wine lined the walls and
nonentities were accommodated. He didn't mind today, though.
The darkness was restful and at least it was quiet. As he sipped
a gin and tonic and drew on a Marlboro, he considered possible
reasons why Mr Wasserstein would need an urgent meeting with
the agency when the campaign was all wrapped up for the year.
Perhaps he wanted to roll out the commercial in other states?
On the other hand, it had been such a success he might want to
give it a rest for a while so that production could catch up with
demand. Maybe he wanted to give Guy and the agency a pat on
the back by arranging a celebration party. In any case, there was
no way he could know what was going on nightly at the Mauve
Artichoke, so there was nothing to worry about.

Guy arrived in disturbing haste, plonked himself in the chair
opposite Freddie and loosened his tie. His face was red and there
were beads of sweat on his forehead.

'Phew, it's a scorcher out there. I'll have a gimlet,' he said
to the waiter who was tossing a starched napkin across his lap.
'With vodka.'

He sighed, looked at Freddie and rested his elbows on the
table. 'Clients! Spare me.'

'What happened?'

'He wants a research study into who's buying Freudian Slips. At this stage!'

'And this time of year,' said Freddie. 'It's only three weeks till Christmas. Everybody's winding down, not gearing up.'

'I told him that. He doesn't listen. He's got a fixation.' He took an appreciative gulp of his gimlet. 'It seems some transvestite accosted him in William Street last night and propositioned him by using Freudian Slip as a . . . well, euphemism I guess you'd call it, for an obscene act.'

Freddie buried his attention in the menu. The roots of his hair had begun to tingle. 'What are you going to do?' he said to the list of antipasto.

'I'll have to do as he asks, persuade some research outfit to cancel their parties and go into the stores and quiz shoppers during the Christmas rush. Or interrogate the salesgirls, who are frazzled enough already. Or whatever they have to do to get results for Mr Wasserstein. I'll have another one of those,' he said to the waiter.

He looked at Freddie and grinned. He was used to hiding his homophobia, but he couldn't resist sneaking in a little dig. 'Hey, wouldn't it be a hoot if . . . ?'

'Don't even think about it!' Freddie waved his hand to ward off the words Guy was about to say, as though he believed that, once spoken, they would prove to be true. 'I'm having the scaloppini, how about you?'

Begley and Hecht was a newly formed partnership of two former employees of a large market-research company. They were keen for new business so they accepted Guy's offer to help solve the mystery of who was buying Freudian Slips. During the time left before Christmas, they would plant scouts—female, of course—in the lingerie departments of Mark Foys, David Jones and Farmers to observe and question buyers of the product and the staff who served them. The information they gathered would be collated and analysed so that conclusions could be reached and delivered by the middle of January.

The fear of what Begley and Hecht might dig up took the shine off pre-Christmas festivities for Freddie. He'd be at a client lunch, on his third glass of Great Western, when suddenly he'd think about those scouts, snooping around mannequins clad in brassieres and step-ins and quizzing anyone who wandered near the fixtures where Freudian Slips were displayed, and he'd dread whatever they were scribbling in their notebooks at that moment.

A terrible compulsion drew him again to the Mauve Artichoke with Darryl in the unspoken hope that the satirical sketch had been replaced. But there it was, as bawdy as ever, stirring the audience to greater bursts of enthusiasm than last time. Darryl laughed himself stupid and Freddie felt like clocking him one. A few days later when he asked him what he wanted for Christmas, Darryl put a forefinger to the dimple in his chin, pretending to be engrossed in an imponderable question, and finally came up with 'A Freudian Slip, honey.' Very funny.

It was some consolation that the agency scored the Elizabeth Arden account, a valuable acquisition since it looked immensely impressive on the client list yet it made virtually no demands creatively. All it required was the adaptation of overseas material to the local market, an easy if tedious job for a copywriter and an art director. Freddie appointed Stella and Jacques to the task.

Guy would run the account with Kelvin doing the legwork and Humphrey the media planning.

'Does this mean a salary increase?' Stella wrinkled her nose and let gratitude shine out of her eyes.

'Not this time, darling.' Freddie was becoming a little bit wiser.

Chapter 40

Graham Begley welcomed the reports that came in from the field on Christmas Eve because they gave him a valid reason to be back in his office the day after Boxing Day. It was a Friday and considerate companies let their staff take it off, to give them a five-day break, so there was nobody else in the building.

Being with Angela and their four-year-old twins for forty-eight hours might have been bearable if it hadn't been for the further obligation of receiving and visiting an absurd number of parents, step-parents, grandparents, godparents, aunts, uncles, cousins, second cousins and family friends with whom he had little in common. The relief he felt at escaping from Chatswood should have made him feel guilty but it didn't. His solitude and his immersion in figures were as therapeutic as a dip into mineral springs.

In the silence of his small office, Graham sorted through the papers and collated them into neat piles. As well as information gathered from customers and sales people, he had addresses to which stocks of the product had been delivered from the three stores surveyed. In studying these locations, he began to see a pattern.

'Good God,' he said to the empty room. 'That's bizarre.'

Guy was first to hear the news when he was back at work in early January. At a meeting with Graham Begley and his partner, Bob Hecht, he tried to influence them to re-phrase some of the findings to make them less sensational, but there was no way of hiding the facts.

'What does it say?' said Freddie as Guy opened his briefcase on the coffee table and slapped a bound document on Freddie's desk.

'We're done,' said Guy and took a chair opposite him.

'Shit!' Freddie blurted out and reached for a Marlboro.

'You won't believe who's buying them.'

'I think I might, but tell me.' He closed his eyes and put his head in his hands. His unlit cigarette stuck out from between his fingers.

Guy flipped the pages of the report and started to read randomly.

'While buyers were scattered across Sydney, from Wahroonga in the north, to Lilli Pilli in the south, from Dover Heights in the east, to Parramatta in the west, the biggest and most frequent orders by far went to what could be termed questionable neighbourhoods. These included Chippendale, Redfern, Surry Hills, Darlinghurst, East Sydney and Woolloomooloo . . .

'The largest single order came from an address in Kensington. Footnote: It seems odd to these researchers that someone who wanted sixty Freudian Slips would purchase them from a retailer instead of approaching the manufacturer in an effort to secure them at a wholesale rate . . .

'Many, but by no means all, of the women who presented themselves at the counter looked, in the words of several respondents, "tarty" or "common". When glimpsed as they changed in the fitting rooms, a number of them seemed quite masculine. "Their calves were as sturdy as upside-down ninepins," said one respondent. "Their feet were enormous," said another. Few were the stores' account customers . . .

'In conclusion, it is apparent that the main buyers of the product are people who do not belong to the A B demographic.'

Guy closed the document, averted his gaze from Freddie and said, 'In other words, hookers and transvestites.'

Before he set up a time for Begley and Hecht to present their findings to Mr Wasserstein, Guy ducked into Freddie's office. 'Shouldn't we alert FB? In case of repercussions?'

'He's skiing. In the Dolomites, or somewhere.'

'I know. We could send a telex.'

'What would that do, except make him anxious? Or cranky at being disturbed.'

'Yeah, I suppose so. He'll be back soon enough. You coming to the presentation?'

'I guess I have to,' said Freddie wearily. 'When is it?'

The meeting occurred at 10 am on Wednesday 15 January, in Mr Wasserstein's office. Within half an hour it was over. Mr Wasserstein made no comment. He took his copy of the study, stood up and said, 'Thank you, gentlemen,' and showed them out.

'That was easy,' said Bob Hecht affably, as the lift descended.

'Easy for you,' said Guy. 'There'll be hell to pay for us.'

At eleven o'clock on the following Monday, Miss Leonie Braithwaite telephoned Guy and asked him to bring Freddie to FB's office at once.

'You're looking fit. How was the holiday?' said Guy with gusto he didn't feel as FB, his face as burnished and smooth as toffee, motioned them to sit down.

'We have lost the Phoebe Phipps business,' he announced without preamble.

There were several seconds of silence.

'I'm sorry to hear that,' said Guy. His forefinger ran around inside the collar of his shirt. 'Any particular reason?'

'I'm surprised you have to ask.' FB glared at him.

Freddie cleared his throat. 'He approved that campaign, so surely he must share some of the responsibility.'

'He approved it because he trusted the agency's judgment.'

'I'm sorry, FB, it's my fault,' said Guy.

'No, I'm the one in the hot seat,' said Freddie. 'Clearly, the campaign was totally off target.'

'But I'm to blame for letting the excesses of the creative people get out of hand.'

Freddie restrained himself from overreacting to Guy's attempt to position himself as the leader and win points for integrity. 'Ultimately, the creative product is my responsibility.'

'There is no need for anybody to fall on his sword. Neither of you could have anticipated this outcome. Of course.' FB rubbed the bridge of his bronzed nose. 'But you could have exercised more caution in selling the client such a . . .'

'Controversial . . . ?' said Guy.

'Racy . . . ?' offered Freddie.

'. . . questionable idea.' He stood up. 'You'd better get back downstairs and start massaging your other clients. We can't afford any more defections. And don't let this get out of the agency until we've put together an official explanation.'

'Due to a possible conflict of interest . . . ?' said Guy.

'Something like that,' said FB.

A great wave of relief washed over Freddie as he and Guy left swiftly and smiled obsequiously at Miss Braithwaite, positioned at her desk outside the door like a stone dragon guarding an imperial temple. It was done. He could have kissed FB if it hadn't been inappropriate—and open to misinterpretation.

They were on the back stairs before Freddie thought to say, 'I guess we'd better tell the team.'

Chapter 41

It was late in the afternoon by the time everybody could be brought together in the boardroom. Stella had spent most of the day in a product and marketing familiarisation meeting at Elizabeth Arden. Desi was at Madrigal briefing Bob Young on an experimental track for PM Gold. Although Bea had nothing to do with the Freudian Slip fiasco, Freddie invited her out of respect for her seniority and to please her; he needed her allegiance more than ever now that Stella was turning out not to be the asset he had hoped.

Guy had been delegated to break the bad news. He stood at the head of the table and, in an attempt to behave like a statesman, pressed together the fingertips of both hands and began his oration.

'In business, as in life, there are good times and there are times that are not so good.' He turned and took a step to his left and then turned to front the attentive faces. 'What I am about to tell you must remain within these walls until further notice.' If Bea, Stella, Desi, Jacques, Humphrey and Kelvin had been in church they could not have been more hushed and respectful.

'As you know, we have just acquired a valuable and lucrative piece of business in the Elizabeth Arden account. We have also been asked to engage in top-secret projects for two other clients. So, when I tell you that we have lost the Phoebe Phipps account, I don't want you to feel that we have failed.'

A little squeak came from the direction of Stella. She covered her open mouth with her hand and stared incredulously at Guy.

Freddie then rose and said, 'Nobody is to blame. It's just one of those things.'

'We have to roll with the punches,' said Guy.

Stella's eyes glistened as tears filled them and trickled down her cheeks.

'Why? What happened?' said Desi, who was seated beside her. She looked as shocked as everybody else except Bea, who hid an unworthy feeling of triumph behind an impassive expression. Justice had been done.

Freddie and Guy exchanged glances. 'After you,' said Freddie.

'Well,' said Guy, loosening his tie. 'It's true that the name and the commercial succeeded in selling the product in unexpectedly large numbers . . . but to the wrong people.'

'What?' snuffled Stella.

It was Freddie's turn to choose his words carefully. 'You see, before the introduction of the Freudian Slip, Phoebe Phipps had been making basic middle-of-the-road garments. This new product was Mr Wasserstein's first venture into the top end of the luxury goods market. He had great ambitions for it. What Christian Dior and Pierre Balmain are to fashion, Phoebe Phipps could be to lingerie. That was his thinking.'

'But it travelled the wrong way,' said Guy. 'It went down market instead of up. To tell you the truth,' his eyes darkened and Bea thought he looked like a vicar warning about damnation, 'it is being bought by an undesirable element in the community.'

'It's not my fault!' Stella's voice rose to a scream.

'Of course it's not,' said Freddie.

'We're all in this together,' said Guy.

'No, it's my fault,' said Desi, who knew what nobody else did, except for Stella. Hadn't she outlined the commercial to Stella and had misgivings when she saw the result? The whole disaster was her responsibility. 'I'm the one who gave—'

Before she could finish the sentence, Stella let out a primitive howl and her eye started blinking like a malfunctioning traffic light. She pummelled Desi with her fists and screamed 'No, no, no, no, no!' She was blubbering now, holding a handkerchief to her face as she stumbled to her feet and made for the door, leaving the others too stunned to utter a word for several moments.

'You were saying?' Guy looked at Desi.

'Oh, nothing important.' She rubbed her upper arm where it stung from Stella's blows.

'I need a drink,' said Freddie.

'What was all that about?' muttered Guy as he took a tray of ice from the fridge. Freddie shrugged and reached for the bottle of Beefeater.

Stella was nowhere to be seen when Desi went searching for her. In the washroom, she ran into Bea, repairing her lipstick at the mirror.

'Do you have time for a drink on the way home?' Desi asked. 'We could go to the Metropole. It's not far from your ferry.'

By the time they were sitting in countrified gentility in the lounge of the grand old 1890 hotel sipping martinis, Bea had begun to regret having felt pleasure in watching Stella receive her comeuppance. Bea knew that she would have been in Stella's shoes if she hadn't been on holiday when the agency was given the assignment. She was honest enough to concede, if only to herself, that she wouldn't have been able to resist presenting the name as her recommendation; it was clever and witty and memorable. Stella had been too naive to know that the cookie she'd stolen was poisoned.

'There's something I have to tell you,' said Desi, shifting uncomfortably in her armchair and placing her glass carefully on a coaster on the little table between them. She tucked a lock of hair behind her ear, looked into the distance, then back at Bea. 'I wouldn't be a bit surprised if you didn't believe me, but . . . I gave Stella the idea for that commercial.'

Bea studied her face for a long moment. 'I believe you. And I wonder if you'll believe me when I tell you that Stella stole that name from my file when I was on holiday and she stayed in my flat.'

They stared at each other. Dimples appeared in Desi's cheeks. An impish light danced in Bea's wide eyes. They both burst into laughter and kept it up as the full extent of Stella's deception became clear to them. At the next table, a woman wearing a fuzzy pink hat shaped like a flowerpot turned to look at them.

'We shouldn't laugh,' said Desi finally, wiping her eyes. 'It's too cruel.'

'She's been a silly girl,' said Bea. 'She's brought this calamity on herself. Imagine her dilemma. If she tells the truth, everyone will know she's a thief and a liar. If she doesn't, she's responsible for a bomb. Either way, she can't win.'

'And we get off scot-free. Poor Stella. The punishment is too severe for the crime.'

Although Bea was not sure she agreed, she did say, 'I don't think it's our business to tell anyone, do you?'

'No, that's up to Stella.'

Bea chuckled. 'She'll never do it. Telling the truth is beyond her.'

'You're right. It takes courage.'

'She doesn't know what that means.'

'Even so,' said Desi. 'It doesn't make me feel any better. Chin-chin.'

Stella fled the building and flagged down the first taxi she saw. When she left it in Underwood Street, she was so distressed she dropped her keyring and almost lost it through a grille in the gutter. Once inside, she flopped on the divan and let torrential tears swamp her, spilling out of her eyes, nose and mouth like heavy rain overflowing an inadequate drainage system. She went into the bathroom for a box of tissues and looked at herself in the mirror. Her misery did not paint a beautiful picture. All those tearful women depicted in loveliness in the movies were a lie. Her face was flushed and puffy and her eyes were bloodshot. Even her hair looked depressed, limp and exhausted. The sight of her ravaged face brought on another bout of uncontrollable weeping. Although the air was stifling, Stella swathed herself in a black shawl with a fringe that drooped as forlornly as her hair and gave her body up to the language of defeat.

Her powers of rational thought seemed to have drowned in the flood. She felt victimised. Freudian Slip was Bea's idea, not hers. The sexy commercial wasn't her idea, either. It was Desi's. Why was their failure her responsibility? She felt cheated without being able to work out why.

Chapter 42

During the following weeks a mood of seriousness settled over the agency. Everyone kept their heads down, as though they felt that industry might make up for the loss of the account that had created so much excitement before it disappeared out of the door in shame.

Nobody in or outside the agency believed that BARK had relinquished the account because of the 'possible conflict of interest' that FB's press release claimed. Somehow, word went around that Freudian Slips had got in with the wrong crowd. That is, if you could find them any more. The line had been withdrawn from the market, turning up only now and again in second-hand clothing stores and flea markets. Eventually they became collectors' items.

Although Stella had pulled herself together, she was downcast, concentrating on re-jigging Elizabeth Arden copy for press adver-tisements in various sizes that would leave space at the bottom for a retailer's logo. When she tried to discuss the layouts with Jacques, he seemed to listen with half his attention, shrugging in a surly way and looking bored. But he did them correctly, so although he and Stella were far from comfortable with each other and the work was dull, at least they were productive.

With Werner now back in Sydney and living with her at last, Desi felt that her life had regained its balance. The commercials he made in Melbourne had been received with enthusiasm by Carlton United and were scheduled to go to air in March, when footy fever would start to catch on again. Better still, he'd been approached by Rod Webb to direct a series of Palmolive commercials for George Patterson. His career was picking up again.

Instead of two halves trying to find a way to get together, they'd become something singular, and although there were sometimes glances of shocked or derisive recognition when they were out together—shopping in Knox Street, or having coffee at the Cosmopolitan—they were impervious to them.

Blyth and Bo put up no resistance to Werner, aware that if they didn't go along with Desirée in the way she wanted to live they might lose her altogether. Now that everyone seemed at ease about it, she and Werner often spent Sundays on Blyth's cruiser and had supper afterwards with the family at Vaucluse, with May smiling and the dogs competing for attention. Werner had a particular fondness for Spot, who'd infamously felled his enemy in such a distinctive way.

After they'd left and Bo was slipping out of her step-ins while Blyth drifted into boozy oblivion in bed, she said a silent prayer that her daughter's infatuation with this charming but totally unsuitable foreigner would soon begin to fade.

Perhaps it was her sense of repleteness and the knowledge of how fortunate she was that made Desi think often of Stella, especially when she passed her open door and noticed the frown and the tightly shut lips as she thumped the keys of the typewriter; or saw her standing with her arms folded talking to the indifferent shoulderblades of Jacques.

One afternoon when Desi was in Freddie's office, seeking his signature on invoices before they went to Accounts to be paid, she decided to have a word with him about what was on her mind.

Easing himself back in his chair with his hands behind his head, he listened to her plea for Stella to be given something more interesting to do than adapting overseas material. When she finished, he sighed. 'Stella hasn't got it, it's as simple as that.' He yawned. 'She's a dud.'

'You're not going to sack her over Freudian Slip?'

'Of course not. She's not going to be fired. But she's useless here, the stuffing's gone out of her. Isabel runs rings around her. Don't lose any sleep over Stella, Desi.' He patted her hand. 'We're working on the case.'

Bea was intrigued when Desi dropped into her office with the news. 'Did he say what they have in mind?'

'No. He just said not to worry because they were working on it.'

'But not sacking her.'

'That's what he said.'

'Hmm,' said Bea. 'Curiouser and curiouser.' Maybe she'd be demoted to secretary. She was much better at that than she was at writing copy. Bea felt expansive in a way she hadn't for a long time, as though a burden had been lifted, making her light-hearted and frivolous.

'Can I give you a lift to Rod Webb?' said Desi. 'They're having drinks after work for Darryl's birthday.'

Bea was full of the milk of human kindness, as well as quite a lot of Bollinger, when she arrived home after the party that evening and found a letter in her mailbox. The writing on the envelope was unmistakable. She eased the flap open as soon as she reached the flat without even taking off her jacket, took out the page it held and read:

> My dear Beatrice,
> At one time I regarded myself as a poet, but I must not be a very good one because I cannot find words to express what I felt when I saw your handwriting again and read the words you penned.
> If only my visit to Australia House had filled me with as much joy! It seems that since I was born in Dublin and am therefore a citizen of Eire, I may not be eligible for the ten quid scheme. As you know, Ireland was neutral during the War, so I imagine there are other people more needful of assistance than I, although my circumstances at the moment are not at their best.
> I trust we may continue to keep in touch and send you my blessings and my love.
> As always, Aidan

A struggle between relief and disappointment sent Bea's emotions into turmoil and tears of frustration followed. Damn, was all she could think. Damn, damn, damn!

Chapter 43

'Four whole days!' said Desi, rousing herself from sleep to stretch her bare arms above her head. She lay on her back and looked at the way the early-morning light coaxed into view the rosette in the middle of the ceiling. She turned over on her side and her left hand climbed around the hillock that was Werner—breathing heavily with his back to her—and felt its way to his groin. He stirred.

'We could spend the whole of Easter in bed,' she murmured, punctuating the space between each word with a moist little kiss on his bare shoulders.

'It's Good Friday,' he muttered.

'Meaning?'

He turned over and pushed himself against her. 'Are we sure this isn't forbidden?'

'Not in my religion.' She spread her legs and rolled on top of him.

'You're insatiable.'

'Guilty, your honour.' She arched her back so that her breast grazed his mouth. 'Just one more time.'

Later, when they'd toasted hot cross buns and finished the pot of coffee, she noticed how quiet everything was, as though the population had been wiped out overnight. As usual on Good Friday, there were no newspapers. Nothing moved outside the French windows except trembling leaves. Even the birds must have been told to pipe down for the holy day. The absence of noise or signs of activity was strangely unnerving. It became a prompt, urging them to act in some way to assert themselves, to break the unnatural silence.

'We could go out on Daddy's boat. His brother's down from Scone for the Show.'

'I'm not feeling sociable.'

'You old grump.'

'Enough of the old.'

'Well, let's go to the Show and lose ourselves in the crowd.'

Over at the Showground at Moore Park there was no chance of silence. The smell of manure and other animal emissions mingled with the sickly sweetness of fairy floss as creatures great and small made their presence felt at the annual Royal Agricultural Show. They chattered, cried, shouted, oinked, whinnied, mooed, barked, miaowed, cawed, crowed, flapped their wings and stamped their feet, raising dust to induce hay fever in those prone to it.

You could pick the bushies by their slow gait, wide-brimmed hats and the weathered backs of their necks. Desi and Werner joined them in the grandstand to admire upright figures on obedient horses in dressage. Elsewhere, as a serious judge in a white coat draped a blue ribbon over a Brahman bull and another inspected the bearing of a standard poodle, spruikers inveigled the sauntering crowds into Jimmy Sharman's tent to cheer at boxing matches and take up the challenge, if anyone dared, of shaping up to a pro. Behind a tacky curtain the bearded lady waited like a hairy spider to shock the innocent. Adolescent boys tried their luck at the shooting gallery while adolescent girls went in twos to have their fortunes told by a gypsy with a crystal ball.

In the Hordern Pavilion, Guy was over-burdened with his children's sample bags while Charlotte whined for a doll on a Bo Peep crook and Troy needed to go to the gents' urgently. Natalie complained of sore feet and the absence of anywhere to sit in the shade. Guy cursed himself for bringing them on the one day of the long weekend when no liquor was permitted there.

Stella and Stanley Cooke-Ridley, his arm around her waist, glided sedately up and down on the ferris wheel. Since he'd never been to the Show before, Stella seized the opportunity to accompany him there, to foster a friendship that might be useful some day. More than willing to cooperate, he took her on an exhilarating ride on the dodgems and then the octopus, hoping to get her into an over-excited state that might be rewarding for him.

Freddie and Darryl watched the sheepdog trials and canine relay races and went afterwards to talk to the breeders. Waiting for the wood-chopping to start, they had a fight over the cruelty (Darryl) or otherwise (Freddie) of raising a puppy belonging to a working-dog breed in a flat in the city. A compromise was reached when they agreed to visit the RSPCA after Easter and make a decision there.

'A cat would be better, anyway,' said Darryl.

'Maybe we should rethink the whole thing,' said Freddie. 'Wouldn't you prefer a trip to San Francisco?'

Roy would rather have been at the wood-chopping than trailing behind Hazel as she admired awesome displays of farm produce, the oversized pumpkins and marrows, the pyramids of apples and oranges, the sheaves of wheat. If she told him once she told him ten times that her mother used to preserve chokos and onions and bottle them to look just as decorative as the jars of peaches and apricots displayed before them.

Bea was nowhere to be seen at the Show. Audrey didn't often take the lead with her but, when it came to Good Friday, she insisted on observing tradition, just as their parents had done. In the morning they attended a devotional service in St Peter's Presbyterian Church at North Sydney and drove back to Audrey's flat to lunch on boiled potatoes and smoked haddock poached in milk.

In the afternoon they visited Aunt Elva at the nursing home. After their tin of Quality Street chocolates had been placed on the bedside table and they'd chatted for ten minutes or so, during which Elva again mistook Bea for her mother, she suddenly became agitated.

'Don't think I didn't know you set your cap at Henry,' she said. 'But he wasn't interested in *you*, Gladys! That didn't stop you, though, did it?' Her expression was ugly. There was panic in her eyes and the knuckles of her clenched fist protruded like a ridge of bleached rocks.

'We don't want to tire you, Aunt,' said Audrey. 'You'll probably want a little nap.'

'I never sleep in the afternoon, Sister, as you know.' Having mistaken Audrey for someone in authority, she began to calm down. 'There are some goodies, I think. Where are they?'

Audrey took the lid off the tin. 'Oh,' said Elva, 'the purple one's my favourite.' She picked out one wrapped in shiny orange paper. Bea kept a smile on her face until it started to hurt. By then Elva had eaten the orange crème and her eyelids were beginning to droop.

'Well, we won't keep you any longer,' said Audrey and they tiptoed out.

'Do you think our mother did that—flirted with Uncle Henry?' said Audrey as they crossed the manicured garden to reach her car.

Bea shrugged. The clipped orderliness of the grounds reminded her of Rookwood Crematorium, where their parents' ashes were filed away behind brass plaques in a brick wall. 'Who knows? Maybe he was my father. Or yours.'

'That's a terrible thing to say!' If Bea had delivered a string of four-letter words, Audrey would not have been more shocked. 'She was just rambling. You've become such a cynic, Bea, I worry about you. Where's your respect?'

Bea had always been grateful for the stability of her background—her father an accountant and a good provider, her mother family-centred and artistic in the home—but the numbing respectability of the way she'd been brought up had caused a restlessness in her, a need to flee the limitations of the North Shore middle class. What if there had been some lapse by the symbol of virtue her mother had always seemed to be? She tried to remember what Uncle Henry looked like. She and Audrey were so different.

'No way of knowing now,' she said.

After some persuasion, Werner agreed to join Desi for lunch with Blyth's extended family at Vaucluse on Easter Sunday because it would have been churlish and anti-social to resist.

'They want to meet you,' she said.

'I bet they do. Do you think they'll recognise me without my tutu?' he laughed. She joined him in it, pleased that he could feel relaxed enough to joke about it.

Back at their flat afterwards, Desi was encouraged by the success of the day to broach an idea that had been forming in her mind for some time: the possibility of their starting a production company of their own, not with her money but with backing from some of her father's friends who had dull jobs, heaps of money and would be thrilled to be associated with an enterprise as exciting as the making of television commercials and possibly even feature films. For the backers, she said, 'It's a bit like surgeons buying vineyards to counterbalance the grim reality of what they do.'

Werner could see how seductive the idea was and, although he dared not become too enthusiastic, he let himself dream along with her for the rest of the evening.

Monday was cloudy and storms were forecast for the afternoon.

'Let's make the most of it,' said Desi. 'Back to the salt mines tomorrow.'

'*The Leopard* might be on somewhere. You know, the Visconti film they've been raving about?' Werner flipped through the *Herald* to the classifieds.

'If it's on we could go to the five o'clock. I wouldn't mind some exercise now, though.' She stood up from the breakfast table and stretched her arms to touch her toes several times.

He closed the paper. 'We could drive to Mona Vale and walk on the beach.'

'You like that beach, don't you?'

'It's beautiful and empty. They bypass it on the way to Palm Beach. It's unfashionable.'

'You're a reverse snob.'

'Let's just say I'm not one of the herd.'

'You don't have to tell me that.'

The beach at Mona Vale was indeed beautiful, a lengthy arc of yellow sand giving the Pacific breakers a wide embrace. The day was too cold and overcast to attract surfers, so the only other person there was a distant figure with two leggy dogs gambolling around him.

They left the car, crossed the grassy hummock, took off their sandshoes and socks, rolled up their pants and walked along the tide line with their arms around each other. A blustery wind from the south made a mess of Werner's hair and sent Desi's extra-long scarf flapping around her like a flag.

At the end of a spit of sand, Werner stopped. 'I have something to tell you, darling.'

Desi realised that her feet were cold.

He turned to look at her. 'I'm going back to the States on Friday.'

She hadn't seen it coming.

Chapter 44

'Good afternoon, Bofinger, Adams, Rawson, and Keane. One moment, please,' said Mavis and waved at Desi as she came out of the lift. 'Bea wants to see you straightaway.'

Desi attempted a smile and gave up. It was futile.

Bea's hands were exercising themselves on the keys of her typewriter when Desi sank into the chair opposite her.

'Everything okay?' The clatter stopped and Bea studied her friend's face. Even without a black shroud she was clearly in mourning.

Desi seemed to have difficulty finding her voice. 'Well, the flight got off on time.' She couldn't swallow; the lump in her throat was too stubborn to be dislodged.

Bea ripped the paper out of her typewriter, screwed it up and flung it into her waste basket. 'My brain is not working today.

What's the time? Nearly half-past twelve.' Suddenly she looked up towards the half-open door and yelled, 'Freddie!'

'You called, madame?'

'It's Friday and my muse is having the day off. And we're hungry, aren't we, Desi?'

Desi was incapable of speech.

'Where to?'

'Look at the day!'

'Okay, the Ozone.'

They called it an Indian summer, settled days of brightness and unseasonal warmth for April, when it would have been a sin to stay indoors. The three of them sat at a table outside on the little promenade in front of the Ozone at Watsons Bay drinking chablis and wondering whether to have the bouillabaisse, the moules marinière or the coquilles St Jacques. Desi's stomach was too unsettled to cope with anything rich, so Bea suggested a piece of plain grilled snapper with spinach.

'He'll be back, darling,' said Freddie.

'No doubt about that, at all,' said Bea.

'I might follow him there.'

'That is not a good idea unless you want to lose him,' said Freddie.

The arrival of their dishes diverted attention from the need to cheer Desi up, but it wasn't long before the conversation drifted back to the demons tormenting her.

'I should have got pregnant. Then he couldn't get away.'

'I know you don't mean that,' said Bea.

Desi smiled in agreement. The wine was beginning to help. 'But I do hope to have children one day.'

'Well, it's never going to be on the cards for me,' said Freddie. 'How about you, Bea?'

'I had one but I threw him away.'

Speechless with shock, the two of them stopped eating and stared at her.

'My ex husband, Aidan.' By demeaning him, Bea was making a big effort to diminish his importance, to have him recede, the way a city does when a plane takes off from an airport and keeps on climbing until it's above the clouds.

Freddie laughed nervously. Desi gave her a wry grin.

'Very funny,' said Freddie, relieved that they weren't about to hear a horror story involving Bea's innards and a backyard abortion.

'I wonder where Werner is now,' said Desi, looking at the sky as though she might be able to see his plane.

'Close to New Zealand I should think. Next stop Fiji,' said Freddie.

'I think I'd better go after him,' said Desi.

'Restrain this woman,' Freddie said to nobody in particular. He signalled for another bottle.

'Didn't he say it was only for a little while, to settle the divorce?' said Bea.

'And to try to get work in the industry and make some money,' said Desi. 'Who knows how long that could take?'

Bea looked at her affectionately, knowing that even if Werner didn't come back Desi would be more than able to run a film production company on her own—and probably make a fortune out of it.

When she got home, Bea was surprised to find herself unnerved by what was happening to Desi. Her resolve to get rid of Aidan had weakened, so she poured herself a brandy and sorted through her LPs for something calming to play. Elvis Presley singing 'Are You Lonesome Tonight?' depressed her so effectively she sank quickly into the self-pity to which she was prone. By her second glass, her thinking went like this: Why don't I just send him the airfare? Why am I waiting, sitting here getting drunk alone, mooning over a man I know is never going to change? And my feelings for him are never going to change, either. Why deprive myself of the one and only person I've ever been in love with, imperfect though he is? By her third glass, she'd made up her mind.

On the following Thursday, Guy broke the news that their pitch to Pederson Morley had failed to win the business. As a name, PM Gold was unacceptable for two main reasons: the company did not wish its initials to be incorporated into a brand name; the initials also stood for prime minister and that would not go down well in Canberra. The recommended commercial was equally unacceptable in that it urged people to smoke 'every day', when the whole subject of smoking had become a sensitive one, health-wise. The pesky medical profession was becoming vocal about the evils of tobacco.

Although Bea felt put out by the uncomfortable reminder that her work was not infallible, she was surprised at how little she cared about the failure of her cigarette campaign. Gliding home on the ferry at the end of the day, she had something more important to look forward to. Tonight she would write to Aidan, enclosing the bank draft in pounds sterling she'd picked up from the Bank of New South Wales that afternoon. It would cover his airline ticket to Sydney and incidental expenses.

At four o'clock the following morning, Bea was wide awake. She'd been fighting off disturbing thoughts for most of the night but, at this hour, they intruded and she couldn't rid her mind of them. What was to stop Aidan taking the money and disappearing with it? She might never see him again. She couldn't bring herself to trust him, and that was no basis for a lasting relationship. What kind of an idiot was she to have fallen for his sweet-talk all over again? Fortunately, the letter and its enclosure were still sitting on her desk.

On Saturday morning, just as Bea left the flat to buy the *Herald* and a loaf of bread, she heard her telephone ring. She stood for a moment outside her front door wondering whether the summons was worth the trouble of unlocking it and going back in. Her sense of duty made the choice for her.

She lifted the receiver to hear a lot of crackling on the line; she assumed it meant an international call and steeled herself to hear Aidan's voice. Instead the accent was American.

'Bea? It's Bill Cabot.'

'Bill!' She lowered herself into the chair at her desk. 'This is a surprise.'

'A pleasant one, I hope.'

'Yes, very. How are you? *Where* are you?'

'At home. In Chicago.'

How disappointing. She thought he might be on a return visit. Before she could think of something to say, he went on, 'And I'm missing you.'

What did he expect her to reply? She hadn't allowed herself to think about him, much less hope to hear from him again. There was no future in pining after somebody else's husband.

'We did have a great time, didn't we?' It was as diplomatic a response as she could manage.

'We did. I thought we might try it again.'

'Oh?'

'I've got some business in Hawaii later in the month. I wondered if you'd like to join me there. It's halfway between your place and mine.'

She laughed at the your-place-or-mine inference.

'Think about it,' he said. 'I'd love to be with you again.'

'You know what?' said Bea, who suddenly felt light in spirit, as though she could fly to Hawaii on her own wings. 'I don't need to think about it. I'd love to be with you again, too!'

'You would?'

'I would.'

'Bea, you have made me a very happy man. I'll get the ticket and all the details sent over by courier. Give me your address again?'

After she'd hung up, Bea stayed seated at her desk, staring at the view without taking it in. How quickly her outlook had changed with just that one telephone call. There was no promise in it, beyond a few days of fun with an exciting man in a foreign place, yet it affirmed for her that she had a future and Aidan had no part in it. Whether there was a place in it for Bill remained to be seen. He was sending her the ticket and it would be first class all the way. A kept woman. She'd never been one in her life! There's a first time for everything.

She looked at the letter containing the bank draft on her desk and felt blessed that doubt had prevented her from posting it. The telephone call had given her a surge of belief in herself. Alone or in tandem, she had enough substance to make the most of her life, to give it purpose, to survive whatever came along. She felt alive, animated by the kind of vigour she hadn't felt since she was a wide-eyed novice on her first trip abroad.

The telephone rang again. It was Audrey, telling her about a revival of the old Judy Garland movie *Easter Parade* and suggesting they go to a matinee.

'I would have loved that,' said Bea, with joy in her voice, 'but I have too many things to do before next week.'

Chapter 45

'I wonder, Miss Bolt, if you might be available for a posting overseas?' God was speaking on the telephone—FB from on high—and it wasn't a dream because she was sitting here in her pokey little office checking copy for an Elizabeth Arden Blue Grass gift set for Mother's Day. Stella was momentarily speechless. 'Think it over. Discuss it with your family, if you need to, but let me know as soon as possible because I need to finalise a few staff changes when the board convenes tomorrow afternoon.'

Stella found her voice. 'Yes,' she squealed, 'I am available!'

Staring at the sure black lines of a fashion figure drawn by René Gruau hanging on the wall in front of her, she felt as exhilarated as the woman depicted there. A posting overseas, FB had said. London, here I come! Or was it New York, advertising's ultimate brand name? No, it would be London for sure. She had a desperate need to talk to Freddie, but when she sprinted to his office it was empty. She realised it was after five, so it was unlikely he'd be back. There was no sign of Bea or Desi, not that she felt inclined to take them into her confidence—unless they had useful information in return, but that was unlikely. Stella had to keep her excitement to herself.

All the way home on the bus and for the rest of the evening, images of London came unsummoned into Stella's mind. Most of them were from storybooks she'd read as a child: red double-decker buses, guards with bearskin hats at Buckingham Palace, Christopher Robin saying his prayers, Peter Pan and Wendy.

'Mr Hackett is with a client today,' Mavis told her the next morning, 'at a car dealers' convention at the Showground. Mr Garland is too. They'll be there all weekend.'

'Well,' said Stella, huffily. 'I suppose I'll have to wait till Monday.'

'He's got Monday off. To compensate for working at the weekend.'

How irritating. At least she'd be able to break the news to Hazel when they met for lunch at Repin's on Monday.

As it turned out, Stella didn't have to wait as long as that to parade her good fortune. When she went to the washroom to powder her nose at the end of the day, Isabel was perched on the edge of what the girls termed 'the menstrual couch' glaring at a ladder that had begun to run up her stocking from the heel. 'Cussed thing!' she said, her body twisted around awkwardly so that she could glower at the defect. 'These were new this morning.'

Stella was pleased to see her discomfited. 'Oh, poor you. Were they seconds or something?'

'No, I paid full price! I can't go out looking like this.'

'Dab a bit of nail polish on it. That'll stop the run.'

'It's too late. Look!' Isabel stood up, turned around and raised her skirt. Both girls looked with gleeful horror as the ladder sped straight up Isabel's leg.

Stella realised how useful Isabel could be in providing contacts in London. 'I've got a spare pair in my drawer. 'You can have them if you like.'

'Could I?' The look on Isabel's face as it turned towards her reminded Stella of Jennifer Jones blissfully gazing heavenward in *The Song of Bernadette*. 'That is so generous. I'll replace them on Monday.'

When Stella the saviour returned with the stockings she sat down on the couch to witness Isabel detaching the offending stocking from her suspender belt, rolling it down her leg and slipping it off.

'Can you keep a secret?' she said slyly.

Isabel paused before easing her foot into the new stocking. 'You can trust me,' she said. 'I'm a clam when it comes to secrets.'

As Isabel anchored the new stockings to her suspenders and smoothed the seams so that they were straight, Stella told her she was being sent to London to work at BARK's associate agency.

Roy sensed there was something wrong when he was taking off his boots at the back door. The wireless wasn't on. When he padded into the kitchen there was no sign of Hazel or food preparation. He went into the lounge room and called, 'Haze!' After no response he went into the hall and called her name again.

'I'm in here,' came a whine from the direction of the bedroom.

She was lying on her back fully dressed except for her shoes. Her eyes were closed and she held a damp flannel to her forehead. An artificial camellia sprouted from her chest as if it were growing there. The eau de nil chenille bedspread had been folded back neatly on itself at the end of the bed and the venetians behind the cretonne curtains were closed.

He approached the bed cautiously. 'What's up, love?'

A sigh came from somewhere very deep. 'I've got a headache.'

'Have you taken a Bex?'

'Yes, but it doesn't work on a migraine.'

'Want me to get the doctor?'

'Don't be silly.' She stirred. 'I'll get up in a minute and make the tea.'

'No, you stay there. I can cook, you know.'

'I'll get up in a minute.'

Roy washed his face and hands in the bathroom and went into the kitchen to fossick for something to fill his empty stomach. He was sitting at the table crunching his third Sao-and-Kraft-cheddar sandwich when Hazel, now dressed in her floral housecoat and slippers, dragged herself in. She looked small and white, like a ghost of herself, and there were shadows under her eyes.

'Sure you won't let me . . . ?'

'No, you sit there. I'm feeling a bit better.' She took a slab of rump steak from the Crosley Shelvador and started fetching things out of drawers and cupboards.

Roy put his newspaper aside and said, 'How was your lunch?'

'Oh,' she groaned, 'don't speak to me about it.'

Her reply did not bode well. He was sorry he'd raised the subject but it would all come out eventually, so he might as well plunge on. 'Stella all right then?'

'All right?' Hazel dug the eyes out of the potatoes with vigour. 'She thinks she's Lady Muck. They're sending her to London.' She put down the knife, covered her face with her hand and started sobbing.

'You wouldn't read about it. Some girl in there filling her head with more big ideas. She's got to stay away from Earls Court because it's common. She's got to live somewhere la-di-da, like Anna Neagle in *Maytime in Mayfair*. What next? Buckingham Palace? After all I've done for her!' Suffering was strangling her voice.

'I know, love.' He put his arms around her and patted her back.

'I knew those people were a bad influence. Didn't I say that to you?' She pulled away and he released her gently.

'You did, love.'

She blew her nose, put the hankie back in her pocket and started cutting up the vegetables again. 'And you know who's behind it?'

'Who?'

'Those women. The socialite and the other one. Filling her head with ideas.' Hazel had a murderous look on her face as she twisted the stems of a bunch of frilly parsley until they snapped. 'I swear to you, Roy, I could wring their bloody necks.'

On Tuesday morning, Freddie called the creative people into his office at ten for what he said was a meeting they would not want to miss.

They shuffled in carrying coffee mugs and spare chairs and managed to seat themselves in an orderly if higgledy-piggledy way due to there not being a lot of elbow room. Their proximity to each other forced intimacy that some, under normal conditions, would not necessarily have welcomed. Not so Jacques in relation to Isabel; he took a seat directly behind her so that his eyes were fixed on the spot where her dark hair finished and her pale neck began. The others were forced to exchange a few civilities and convey a semblance of camaraderie.

'Well, team,' said Freddie standing up behind his desk, a lit cigarette between his long fingers, 'we all know how important it is to have our creativity invigorated and stimulated, from time to time. The way to do that is to embrace change and run with it. Who knows where it might lead?'

He cleared his throat, advanced from behind his desk and perched on the corner of it at the front. 'So it gives me great pleasure to tell you about some of the moves that are coming up over the next few weeks and months to strengthen even further the power of the creative product coming out of BARK.' Not a sound issued from anyone else. All eyes were on him and he loved it.

'First of all, and effective immediately, Bea O'Connor has been appointed deputy creative director. That means if you want to see me and I'm not around, you go to her. Congratulations, Bea!'

Everyone turned to smile at Bea. If there was resentment nobody showed it. Not even Stella. She sat cockily, waiting for the big announcement that would surprise everyone and turn them green with envy. Isabel had given her an address at Beaufort Gardens in Knightsbridge that she said had affordable rooms to let. The area was posh, she said. Harrods was there. So was Scotch House, the place to shop for cashmere twinsets.

'As well as continuing her role as a writer, Isabel Jacobs has expressed an interest in film production. So she will also become an assistant producer under Desi Whittleford learning the tricks of the trade and applying her artistic ability to the medium. Good luck, Isabel.' Jacques blew air at the back of Isabel's neck and she flicked it away, as she would a blowfly.

'After serving this agency well for six years, Dan Barnes is being transferred to the office of our associate in Tokyo to share with them his expert knowledge of the motoring industry. If anyone can get through to the Nips, you can, Dan.' A smattering of laughter was all the group could manage, apart from a bit of shifting of bottoms on seats.

'Since it's the policy of this company to promote from within, whenever possible,' Freddie went on, 'Dan's chief copywriter, Owen Griffith, will take over as group head of Dan's accounts. Well done, mate.'

'And finally, we come to Stella Bolt.' Freddie looked at her in a friendly way, but the expression on his face was missing the benevolence that had been there in earlier times. 'Stella is being posted to New Zealand, to take up the role of copywriter and personal assistant to the manager of our branch office in Auckland.'

When Bea looked sideways at her, Stella's face had turned to stone.

That Stella was disappointed, nobody would ever be allowed to know. She couldn't afford to lose face, so she pretended to be elated at the prospect of her new job. She kept up her pretence, eventually persuading even herself that the move was a positive one. Auckland might not be the most stimulating city in the world but at least she was going somewhere and being paid for it, away from the malevolence that was stifling her here. To make a show of being thrilled and to radiate success, she decided to blow a hole in her budget and give a party.

Chapter 46

As part of her plan to improve her image, Stella had developed a finely formed if rather flowery style of handwriting, and she found this skill thrilling to put into practice when she sat in her courtyard one Saturday afternoon penning invitations on her *étoile at home* cards. Also on the round table, which she'd washed and dried thoroughly that morning and had now covered with a cotton cloth, was a list of the recipients and their home addresses.

She took the first card and wrote *Freddie* at the top left corner of it. Underneath *étoile at home* she began to copy the words she'd roughed out at work on a piece of copy paper:

5 pm on Saturday, 9th May,
to celebrate her posting overseas.
310 Underwood Street, Paddington.
RSVP

She didn't mention that the party happened to be on the weekend before her birthday, which fell that year on Wednesday. No need to complicate the invitation or seem to be expecting any further presents. They might think that was venal.

Over the next few days, those who received the invitations had mixed reactions—benevolence, amusement, indifference—but all of them, except for Jacques, were momentarily confused about the identity of étoile. Then they were embarrassed when they realised that Stella had taken a flippant nickname seriously enough to have it engraved on a card.

A tribute was paid to Stella by whichever celestial being governs the weather because, on the afternoon and evening of her soirée, the sky was cloudless. The air was still, retaining some of the warmth of summer tempered with the freshness of autumn. It was the kind of weather Sydney pretends it turns on all the time.

Stella had been counting on it. The trestle table had been taken apart and reassembled in the courtyard where stumpy candles had been planted here and there around the perimeter to provide romantic lighting as the evening progressed. Two hurricane lamps stood on the table, which had been covered by a white double bed sheet—all on loan from Anita upstairs. Onion dip, devilled eggs and stuffed tomatoes were ready before the first guests were due. Swedish meatballs and cocktail frankfurts were standing by to be re-heated. A dozen bottles of sparkling Barossa Pearl sat among ice in a large tub—on loan from Hugh upstairs—under the trestle table.

Stella, in her spotted taffeta top and navy culottes, was grateful to sit down for five minutes, after she'd remembered to hide the pink chenille toilet-seat cover and the matching mat in the bottom of the wardrobe. Giving a party was not all swanning about with a drink in your hand.

Everybody arrived at once, so she was rushed into a panic as they thrust bottles into her hands, wanted to know where to put their bags and jackets, made insincere remarks about the 'charm' of her flat and generally created such a crowd, she became too stupefied to act on anything. Freddie and Guy noticed and they were soon opening bottles and handing around glasses.

She came to life when she realised Desi was apologising for sneaking in another guest—Darryl—who made himself useful by picking up the onion dip and handing it round with the basket of water biscuits. Guy was apologising for the absence of Natalie, who hadn't been able to find a babysitter; he didn't mention that she could never trust one again since their evening at the Bofingers' when the sitter smuggled in her boyfriend and did unspeakable things with him in front of the children, leaving Charlotte to tell on her and Troy to display an unhealthy preoccupation with his external male organ. Hugh was deep in conversation with Bea about someone they both knew in London. Jacques was talking to Anita and appraising her tribal necklaces and waist-length black hair while he managed, at the same time, to keep an eye on Isabel, who'd been cornered by Stanley Cooke-Ridley. From the front, Isabel was a model of decorum in a black sheath, until she turned around and revealed her bare and curvaceous back, all the way down to her waist. Freddie brought Stella a glass of wine and told her how soignée she looked. She began to relax. The party had taken off of its own accord.

When the light began to fade, Darryl lit the lamps and somebody else took a match to the candles. Stella went into the kitchen to heat up the meatballs and franks. Isabel must have been looking for an excuse to detach herself from Stanley because she followed and offered to help.

They were sticking toothpicks into the meatballs when Stella felt someone's hands steal around her waist from behind. 'Little Étoile,' breathed a French accent. 'How grown-up you have become.' The hands were moving up very gently to skim the undersides of her plunge push-up bra. She turned her head to him as he pressed her stomach and rubbed his chin against her hair, but Jacques wasn't looking at her. His eyes were on Isabel. In a flash Stella knew that she was bait.

Without a word, Isabel picked up the plate of meatballs and the rest of the toothpicks and took them outside, treating Jacques to an enticing picture of her flawless back as she went.

At that moment, there was a knock on the front door, loud enough to make itself heard above the din in the courtyard.

'I'll get it, Stella,' shouted Darryl.

Stella had pulled away from Jacques and turned around to face him to deliver scathing words she hadn't yet formulated, when a familiar, crow-like voice reached her.

'Is Stella there?'

'Yes,' Darryl said slowly and cautiously.

'I'm her mother. And this is my husband, Mr Paine.'

'Come in. I'm Darryl,' he said pleasantly. 'Stella! Your mother and father are here!'

'I hope we haven't come at an awkward time,' said Hazel, taking in the scene. She wore a new maroon worsted dress in the button-through style she favoured; the buttons were in the shape of ladybirds, hand-painted red with black spots. Roy followed carrying a package wrapped in cellophane with a large pink bow.

Released from Jacques, who evaporated as soon as he heard the identities of the new arrivals—or was it when Isabel disappeared?—Stella stood in the doorway to the kitchen with a scrunched-up smile on her face and a sinking sensation in her stomach.

'Mum!' was all she said.

'Happy birthday, love,' said Roy handing her the package. There was no ignoring the hubbub in the courtyard. 'We didn't know you were having a party.'

'It's only a few friends from work,' said Stella, weakly. She put the package on the divan.

'Don't open it until Wednesday,' said Hazel, giving her a peck on the cheek.

Guy appeared, with a hospitable look on his face and a tray of drinks in his hands. 'Hello, I'm Guy. No need to ask who you are, Mrs Bolt. For a minute I thought you were Stella's sister.'

'Thank you,' said Hazel. She was pleased, although she felt it her duty to correct a misunderstanding. 'The name is Mrs Paine. This is my husband, Roy Paine.'

Mrs Paine? It was news to Stella.

'Oh, sorry,' said Guy, extending his hand to Roy. 'How are you, Roy?'

'Very pleased to make your acquaintance,' said Roy.

'Come and meet everyone,' said Guy. 'I didn't know your parents were coming, Stella.'

'Me neither,' she said under her breath.

'If I'd known you were having a party I'd have made sausage rolls and a rainbow cake,' said Hazel, unable to withhold the reprimand.

Roy tapped Hazel on the arm and whispered, 'If we're going to stay, I'll duck up the road and get some beer. Be back in a tick.'

Stella felt tension in the back of her neck as Guy took Hazel around introducing her to everyone but, to her surprise, nobody gave any sign that they thought she was out of place.

After meeting Jacques, Hazel moved away as quickly as she would from someone with a contagious disease. Desi spoke to her warmly but Hazel had difficulty understanding her rounded vowels and throaty resonance; in any case, she'd already made up her mind that Desi was a trollop and could think of nothing nice to say to her. She was more comfortable with Stanley's Cockney chirpiness, and he went out of his way to keep her glass from being empty and to entertain her with backstage stories. She was shocked but titillated to hear that Rex Harrison was unpopular with his fellow actors; that Vivien Leigh was more than partial to a romp in the hay; that when Cary Grant married the millionairess Barbara Hutton, they were nicknamed 'Cash & Cary'; and that Peter O'Toole took to drinking as naturally as he did to acting.

Back from the pub with four bottles of Reschs Pilsener, Roy was at first a bit overwhelmed by the company, but when Bea found out he was a brickie, she expressed wide-eyed interest in the dry stone walls she'd seen in Wales and he gained confidence by being able to explain the technique that kept them together.

A change of mood took over the gathering after Anita vanished upstairs and returned with her guitar. By then Jacques had left and so had Isabel, whether together or not Stella hadn't noticed; she'd been busy moving in on Stanley. Hugh brought a chair out into the courtyard and Anita arranged herself on it, fiddling with the instrument and tossing her head when her hair fell across her soulful face. She lifted her chin and her dangly earrings, juicy and red like chewy jujubes, flashed in the candlelight. She closed her eyes and began to sing 'When I was a bachelor I lived all alone, I worked at the weaver's trade . . .' Everyone listened in respectful silence until 'Foggy Foggy Dew' was over and they gave it a wholehearted response.

'A bit spicy, eh?' Roy said to Bea, his new friend. She laughed, prompting Hazel to peer in their direction. 'Blowin' in the Wind' came next.

'She's great,' Freddie told Hugh and wondered which account on the agency's client list might benefit from the seeming artlessness of a sexy sandal-wearing folk singer. All he could imagine was a wholegrain breakfast cereal for crank vegetarians but the market was too small.

A few ballads later, Anita looked up and in her soft voice announced, 'This last one is for Stella, who'll be leaving us soon, to take her first big journey into the outside world. We're all going to miss her. Stella, where are you?'

'Go and stand beside your mother,' whispered Stanley. Stella took a step out of the shadows. Hazel linked an arm with hers and looked at Roy, willing him by ESP to join them, but whatever senses his mind had were not endowed with extra perceptiveness.

'The song is called "Babe I'm Gonna Leave You",' said Anita. There was a little intake of breath from Hazel and a click as she opened the clasp on the handbag hooked over her arm, and fished inside it for a handkerchief.

Anita's rendition was surprisingly powerful and charged with enough emotion for most of her audience to feel a lump in the throat, or moisture in the eye, but when it came to her drawn-out cry about rambling on, a long mournful wail like that of a prairie wolf came out of Hazel and she bent over as though she had a stomach-ache. To steady her from toppling forward and cracking her head on the cement, Roy held up one side of her and Guy propped up the other. By now, she was sobbing and clutching her midriff.

True artist that she was, Anita finished the song. By then Hazel had been led inside, leaving Stella in a huff at her mother's hijacking the spotlight that was supposed to be trained on her, so she lingered in the courtyard embracing Anita and letting herself be kissed by Hugh and cuddled by Stanley while others fussed over her mother inside the flat.

As Hazel started to calm down and everybody except Bea, Desi and Roy went outside again, her sentimentality turned to anger at having been put in a position where she couldn't help making a fool of herself in front of Stella's so-called friends at a party she'd known nothing about until she turned up on the doorstep, purely out of the goodness of her heart, to bring her daughter a lovely twinset she'd knitted as a birthday present to keep her warm in New Zealand. She knew that, as far as Stella was concerned, she and Roy were outsiders, not smart enough for the fast crowd who thought they were above everybody else.

'I think we'd better be making tracks now, Haze, if you're feeling a bit better,' said Roy, who was sitting beside her on the divan with his arm around her shoulders. He helped her to her feet while the other two smiled and murmured kind and consoling words.

'Of course, you'll miss Stella, but how proud you must feel about her being given an overseas posting,' said Bea.

'To Auckland, a lovely little city,' said Desi.

The superior way they looked at her, together with what they said, had the curious effect on Hazel's mouth of opening it to let spill all the words that had been locked inside her head.

'You career women,' she spluttered. 'You've alienated my daughter's affections from me . . .'

'We'd better be making tracks, love.'

'Let go of me, Roy, I haven't finished . . . And don't think I didn't see you fawning all over *her*.' She nodded at Bea, who stood beside Desi. Both were speechless.

'You and your false values,' Hazel continued, glaring at one woman and then the other, her voice gaining momentum. 'You've lured my daughter away from her family and the decent people she grew up with. Stella used to be such a sweet girl. Innocent and loving. Well, thanks to you she's got above herself. All she can think of now is leaving us behind. I'm her mother! She's my only child! She's not getting rid of me, much as you might like her to.'

'No, no,' said Desi. 'That's not the way it is, at all. Stella knows exactly what she wants . . .'

'And how to go about getting it,' put in Bea, not without irony.

'Let's go,' said Roy.

'Well, I've said my piece,' said Hazel. 'I just want you career women to know that you're not as good as you think you are and I'll thank you to mind your own business and not meddle in my family's affairs. Come on, Roy, we're leaving.' She left the room briskly and marched down the corridor to the front door with Roy bringing up the rear.

Bea looked at Desi. 'What have we done?' she said.

'Now we know where Stella got her spunk,' said Desi with a lift of her eyebrows.

'Pity she didn't inherit her honesty,' replied Bea.

On the day of Stella's departure, the only creatures awake when she got up after a restless night were the birds, noisily staking out their territory. By the time Freddie's cab pulled up outside, she'd been ready for two hours, wavering between the anticipation of challenging new experiences and the terror of the unknown. She'd checked the contents of her handbag several times to make sure she hadn't forgotten her passport, Qantas Empire Airways ticket, travellers' cheques, *étoile at home* cards and address book, and studied herself in the mirror, adjusting her pillbox hat, checking the seams of her stockings and fussing with the pearl buttons at the wrists of her elbow-length gloves. If you didn't dress properly they wouldn't let you on the plane.

On their way to the airport at Mascot, it was difficult for Freddie to get a word out of Stella. She just stared out of the window. Her hands, fiddling with the handbag in her lap, were trembling. By the time they'd checked in her bags and she'd received her boarding pass, Desi and Bea were in the upstairs bar waiting for them with a bottle of Great Western. The tradition of seeing people off that began when ocean liners sailed from Sydney Harbour, amid playing bands and flying streamers, was continued, in a subdued way, with airline departures. On this particular morning, everyone was full of self-conscious jollity.

'That's your plane I think, Stella,' said Freddie, pointing through the window at the tarmac where a sleek airliner was parked. He was pleased at being able to identify it. 'It's an Electra L188C made by Lockheed in California.' Mobile stairs with Qantas branded on the sides led to the aircraft's front and back entrances.

'Which stairs do I go up?'

'The back ones.'

When Stella visited the ladies' room for the second time, Freddie said, 'She looks a bit scared. Sort of vulnerable. I hope she can cope over there.'

'She'll cope,' said Bea.

A few moments after Stella returned, they heard a squawky, 'There she is!' and Hazel, wearing her bottle-green bouclé suit with four-leafed clover buttons, bore down on them. Roy followed.

Stella's right arm made an involuntary movement of protection, as though to ward off an attacker. 'You said you wouldn't be coming,' she said.

'Yes, I know,' said Hazel, with surprising cheerfulness. 'I hate farewells, but I had to come. Roy's quite right, New Zealand's not far away, and we can always get over there to see you.'

Freddie stood up to give her his seat and she thanked him as she took it. Everybody smiled determinedly while they searched about for something to say. Freddie charmed the people at the next table into letting him take two of their chairs.

'Quite chilly this morning,' said Roy, keeping his eyes away from Bea so as not to raise Hazel's ire. He needn't have worried; Stella had her full attention. As he drifted towards the window Hazel confided, 'Roy's got the morning off, just to see you off, darl.'

'Big bird that one, eh?' said Roy as Freddie joined him to gaze through the glass at the awesome contemporary manifestation of mankind thumbing its nose at gravity.

'Sixteen passengers in first class, forty-seven up the back,' said Freddie, full of knowledge newly acquired from the brochure that had accompanied Stella's ticket from the travel agent.

'Struth!' said Roy. 'See that, Haze? That's her plane.'

Hazel's eyes skimmed him as she said, 'I don't want to look at it,' then turned back to Stella. 'Will you be warm enough in that suit?' She studied the dusty pink worsted suit with the rabbit revers; she knew it was wool but it looked a bit lightweight.

'Where's your mackintosh? It never stops raining over there, you know.'

'That's the south island, Mum.' Stella had done some homework.

'Yes, well, you never know. Got your ticket?'

'Yes, Mum.'

'Show us your passport picture.'

'Oh,' said Stella, impatiently fishing the document out of her bag and handing it to her mother.'

'Very nice. Look, Roy.'

He took the open passport dutifully and studied it. He longed to tease her about the picture looking like a police mug shot but decided it was not worth the risk. 'Yes, very nice,' he said as he handed it back.

'I think that was your boarding call,' said Freddie. 'Where the hell is Guy?' Stella jumped in her seat and started gathering her belongings together. 'I'd better be going, then.'

'Here they come,' said Bea, waving at two figures hurrying into the lounge.

Stella smiled when she saw Guy coming towards her, but her expression changed when she recognised the young man with him. It was Kelvin.

'Oh,' said Hazel. 'That nice young man is here. I told you about him, Roy, the day I went to Stella's office.'

'What's he doing here?' Stella muttered to Freddie.

'Hello, Mrs Bolt,' said Kelvin, tipping his fedora. His shoes were as shiny as only a new pair can be. He was quite the impressive executive in a dark single-breasted suit, although he still looked underfed, hungry around the eyes, in contrast to the glossy wellbeing of Guy.

'Actually, it's Mrs Paine.'

'Gee, sorry,' said Kelvin with a confident smile. Witnessing his newfound aplomb, Desi wondered who'd been schooling him in deportment and courtesy. He'd even remembered to take off his hat.

'Hey, Guy, I thought you told her,' said Freddie.

'Look, I've been flat out. Haven't had a minute.' Guy turned to beam at Stella. 'Kelvin's been appointed manager of BARK New Zealand. He's your new boss.'

By now they were all on their feet and Hazel was saying, 'Isn't that lovely? You'll have someone you know over there.'

'Too right,' said Roy. 'You'll look after her, won't you, son?'

'I'll give it a go.' Kelvin offered his arm but Stella pretended not to notice.

They were last seen disappearing into a crowd as thick as a mob of sheep. It carried them towards the boundary beyond which only departing passengers were allowed to go. The sightseers were left to crane their necks, raise their voices, wave their hands, wipe their eyes and get in each other's way.

'Don't forget to send us a postcard!' screeched Hazel.

Acknowledgments

My first thanks must go to those loyal friends who put up with my self-absorption and propped me up with their goodwill: Anke Beining, Peter Bracken, Lesley Brydon, Lana Dopper, Philip Engelberts, Ken Groves, April Huxley, Yun-sik Jang, June McCallum, Kay Russell, Patrick Russell, Nell Schofield and David Tilley.

Others were invaluable in a more direct way. Shelley Gare encouraged me to start writing and to keep going with it. As the word count grew, Barbara Horton, Des Sullivan, my brother Bill Aylward, the State Library of New South Wales, and Elizabeth Masters from the National Archives of Australia provided specialised information. Robin Huxley and Norma Watson filled some gaps in my memory.

But the heroine of this tale has been Marion Hume, with her positive attitude, her ability to get things moving and her introduction to Adam Worling. Their observations and comprehensive notes on what I had believed to be the final draft made all the difference to the shape and cohesiveness of the finished story. I cannot thank either of them enough for their time, their generosity and their expertise.

An introduction to The Cameron Cresswell Agency by Richard Beck led to Sophie Hamley representing me. Thanks to her enthusiasm and her professionalism it wasn't long before I was signing my name on a contract with Hachette and setting to work with a group of stimulating and talented women, including Claire de Medici, who edited the manuscript, and Kate Ballard.

Two exceptional people have made the process of publishing this book an absolute pleasure for me: the savvy Louise Sherwin-Stark and my outstanding and infinitely patient publisher, Vanessa Radnidge. My gratitude to both of them is boundless.